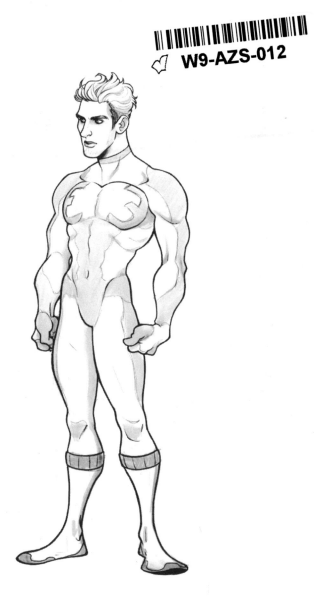

GHOSTED

A SECOND CHANCE ROMANCE

J.M. DARHOWER

This book is dedicated to everyone who has ever loved a story so much they could quote it.

There's nothing in the world quite like being a part of a fandom. Never let anyone shame you for it. Read those books. Watch those movies. Binge those TV shows. Love those characters. Admire those celebrities. Write that fan-fiction. Draw that fan art. Go to those conventions. Sing that (on-hiatus, totally-not-broken-up) boy band at the top of your lungs.

Do what makes you happy.

PROLOGUE

ONE YEAR AGO

Drip. Drip. Drip.

Rain fell from the overcast sky in sporadic bursts, quick manic showers followed by moments of nothingness. The weatherman on channel six had predicted a calm day that morning, but the woman knew better. A tumultuous storm was rolling in. There was no way to avoid it.

Thump. Thump. Thump.

Her heart beat frantically, blood surging through her veins, mixing with enough adrenaline to make her stomach churn. She might've been worried about getting sick if there had been anything left inside of her to give, but no... she was empty. Burying her mother had taken everything out of her. This, on top of that, was too much for her to bear.

Boom. Boom. Boom.

Kennedy Garfield stood on the front porch of the two-story white house, staring out into the yard as thunder clapped in the distance. Lightning illuminated the darkened afternoon sky, giving her a better view of *him*. Her uninvited visitor stood a mere ten feet away, dressed in a designer suit that cost more than she made in a year, but yet he still somehow managed to look thrown away. His black tie hung loosely around his neck, his button down soaked and clinging to his ashen skin.

"Why are you here?" she asked, unable to handle his silence or his sudden presence. As quickly as this storm rolled in, she needed it to go back away.

"You know why I'm here," he said quietly. Despite his passive tone, he must have worked up a lot of nerve for him to show his face. Even from a distance, she could tell he'd been drinking, his eyes bloodshot and glassy.

"You shouldn't be here," she said. "Not now. Not like this."

He said nothing for a long moment, running his fingers through his thick blond hair, the ends curling from being wet. He was drenched, although the rain had since slowed to a steady trickle. She wondered how long he'd been standing outside before she noticed him. Before she sensed him.

She imagined it had been quite awhile with the condition he was in.

Beep. Beep. Beep.

The yellow cab parked along the curb blew its horn, the middle-aged driver growing impatient. Kennedy nearly laughed at the sight of it. She figured taking a cab would've been beneath him those days. Limos and town cars, with chauffeurs and security, were more his level.

Or so she'd heard, anyway.

He glanced back at it, his face flickering with a hidden aggression, before he turned back around to face her. His expression softened when their eyes met.

"I'm sorry," he said. "I heard about your mom and I just... I wanted to be here."

Crack. Crack. Crack.

It was the sound of her heart being torn apart once again.

"You shouldn't have come," she said. An assault of tears burned her eyes, but she refused to shed a single one. Not while he was there. Not while he was looking at her. So many years later and he still got under her skin. "You know that. You're just making this all so much harder."

"I know, but..." He paused, his blue eyes imploring. "I was hoping I could... I mean, I wondered if it would be okay if..."

"No," she said, knowing right away what he was asking, but there was no way it would happen—not then, and certainly not with the condition he was in. He knew better than to even *ask*.

"But—"

"I said *no*."

He sighed as the driver laid on the horn for the second time. Eyeing her warily, he took a step back, and then another, before turning to leave without saying 'goodbye'.

They'd already said enough goodbyes to last them a lifetime.

Stomp. Stomp. Stomp.

Kennedy stiffened as footsteps stomped through the house behind her, on a mission as they hurried her direction. The front door flung open, a tiny human tornado appearing at her side, wearing a fluffy black dress with her brunette hair in pigtails. Despite all the darkness surrounding the little girl, she was all bows and sunshine, innocence and happiness, and Kennedy would do everything in her power to keep her that way. She didn't need to know more devastation. She was too young to endure that kind of pain.

Too young to have her heart broken by Jonathan Cunningham.

"Who was that, Mommy?" the little girl asked, watching the cab as it disappeared into the storm. "Did they come for Grandpa? Were they Nana's friend?"

"It was no one you need to worry about, sweetheart," Kennedy said, gazing down at a pair of twinkling blue eyes—something her sweet little girl had inherited from *him*. "The man was just a little lost, but I sent him back on his way."

ONE

KENNEDY

The beeping of the checkout scanner is monotonous, a dull drone I barely hear anymore, as it melds with Wilson Philips's *Hold On* playing on the station over the loudspeaker radio. The same songs, day in and day out. Same constant beeping. Same everything.

Same customers in and out of the store, buying the same things they've bought before.

My life has become a predictable loop, a real-life version of *Groundhog Day* that I have no intention of trying to change. I'm the personification of an alternate ending where Phil accepts that he's stuck listening to Sonny & Cher every morning until the end of time.

If you'd have asked me years ago if this would be my future, I would've laughed in your face. Me? Kennedy Reagan Garfield? I was destined for greatness.

I'd been named after a pair of iconic presidents. My mother, the idealistic liberal, and my father, a strict conservative, never saw eye-to-eye on much... except for me. They never agreed on healthcare or taxes, but they were both convinced their little *oops* baby would be somebody.

And here I am—somebody, all right. Assistant Manager Somebody at Piggly Q Grocery in a 'blink and miss it' kind of town in upstate New York. Thirteen dollars an hour, forty-plus hours a week, with a full benefits package including (unpaid) vacation days.

Not that I'm ungrateful. I'm doing better than a lot of people. My rent is paid every month. My electricity hasn't been cut off. I've even got overpriced cable! But deep inside, I know this isn't the kind of greatness my parents envisioned for me.

"Assistance needed on three!"

The high-pitched voice squeals over the loudspeaker, drowning out the music. My gaze scans the register area, waiting for someone else to respond, but nobody does. It always falls to me. Shaking my head, I stroll over to lane three, to the young blonde girl running the ancient register, ringing up an older woman's groceries.

The cashier, Bethany, looks at me, dramatically pouting as she wiggles a can of chicken noodle soup in my face. "It's coming up a buck and a quarter but Mrs. McKleski says there's a ninety-nine cent sign back there."

It's $1.25. I know it is. Even Mrs. McKleski probably knows and wants to make a fuss about something. I smile, though, and override the register, giving it to the woman at the discount.

I step away to let Bethany finish ringing up the groceries as Mrs. McKleski asks, "How's your father doing?"

I don't have to look to know she's talking to me. I start straightening up the candy rack near the register. "He's hanging in there."

"Thought about baking him a pie," she says. "Does he have a favorite? Apple? Cherry? Thought about pumpkin, or maybe pecan."

"I'm sure he'll appreciate whatever you make," I say, "but he's more of a chocolate cream pie guy."

"Chocolate," she mutters. "Should've known."

The radio moves on to Lisa Loeb's *Stay*, and that's about when I decide I'm done with this day. I stroll to the front corner of the store, to where Marcus, the manager, hangs out in an office tucked behind Customer Service. Marcus is tall and slim, with brown skin and black hair that's starting to show signs of impending gray.

"I'm going home," I tell him.

"Now?" He glances at his watch. "It's a little early."

"I'll make up for it tomorrow," I say, clocking out.

Marcus doesn't argue. He knows I'm good for it, which is why

14

he gives me leniency.

"Actually, I know how you can make up for it," he says. "I need an extra shift worked, if you're willing to pull a double on Friday. Bethany asked for the day off but there's no one to cover."

I want to say no, because I hate running registers, but I'm too nice for that. We both know it.

"Do me a favor," he says. "Stop by on your way out and tell Bethany I'm approving her request."

"Will do," I say, walking out before he can ask me for anything else. I stroll down the cereal aisle on my way through, snatching a box of Lucky Charms off the shelf. Bethany stands at her register, skimming through a magazine she grabbed from the rack beside her.

I glance at it, rolling my eyes.

Hollywood Chronicles.

The epitome of trashy tabloids.

I set my cereal down on the conveyer belt and pull out a few dollars. Bethany closes the magazine and tosses it down in the bagging area before ringing me up.

"Marcus approved your day off," I tell her.

She squeals. "Really?"

"He told me to tell you."

"Oh my God!" She shoves my cereal in a white plastic bag. "I didn't think there was anyone to cover my shift."

"Yeah, well, I could always use the overtime."

Bethany squeals again, reaching across the lane to grab ahold of me, squeezing me in a hug. "You're the best, Kennedy!"

"Special day?" I guess when I pull away, holding the money out to her before she can even tell me my total, hoping she'll take it instead of hugging me again. Alanis Morissette's *Ironic* is coming on, and if I don't get out of here soon, I'm going to lose my sanity.

"Yeah... I mean... sort of." She blushes as she shoots me a look. "It's kind of stupid, really. There's a film that's supposed to be shooting in the city. My friends and I are hoping to go down and maybe, you know... see what we can see."

I smile softly. "There's nothing stupid about that."

"You don't think so?"

"Of course not," I say. "I went to a movie set once."

Her eyes widen. "Really? *You?*"

The way she says that makes me laugh, although I probably should be offended by her incredulous tone. It's not like I'm some uptight old lady. I'm not Mrs. McKleski. I'm only a few years older than her. "Yes, really."

"What movie?"

"It was just one of those teen comedies. The titles all kind of sound the same."

"Who was in it? Anyone I might know?"

She wants to hear all about it. I can tell by the curious gleam in her eyes, but I have no desire to get into that story tonight. "It was so long ago that I really can't even say."

Bethany counts out my change, and my eyes drift to the magazine she's been reading as I grab my bag. All at once, my insides freeze, ice running through my veins, the cold striking me straight to the bone. Plastered on the cover is a face I know. Even wearing a black hat and dark sunglasses, ducking his head, he's easily recognizable.

My gut burns, twisting and coiling and *ugh ugh ugh…*

He's standing beside a woman with platinum blonde hair. While he shies away from the camera, she's wide-open, looking right at it, her green eyes vivid in the photo. Black leather covers her supermodel frame, while red lipstick accentuates a set of pouty lips. Her skin is a deep tan, like the woman lives on a beach somewhere.

Ugh, it makes me sick.

Even I have to admit she's beautiful.

Below the photograph of the pair is a massive caption, written in bold:

JOHNNY AND SERENA'S SECRET WEDDING

My eyes linger on those words.

I think I'm going to throw up.

"Do you believe it?" Bethany asks.

My gaze lifts to meet hers. "Believe what?"

"That Johnny Cunning and Serena Markson eloped."

I don't know what to say. I don't know what to believe. I don't know why it even matters to me. Don't know why my chest feels tight at the mere insinuation that a wedding might've happened somewhere, at some point, a wedding where he was the groom but I wasn't present. I feel like an obsessed, lovesick fangirl, convinced the heartthrob was supposed to be mine, but he wasn't.

"I think, where Johnny Cunning is concerned, anything's possible."

"Yeah, you're right," Bethany says, picking the tabloid back up as I head for the exit. "Really hoping to run into them this weekend."

My footsteps falter. "Them?"

"Yeah, the movie that's filming? It's the new Breezeo one."

Something happens inside of me when Bethany says that, something that knocks the wind out of my sails. *Whoa.* It's a crushing, soul-sucking sensation that starts deep in my chest, right where I used to keep my heart. It's gone now, locked away in a steel-reinforced safe, padlocked and hidden where no one can get to it without my blessing, the spot where it used to beat now nothing more than a black hole that desperately pulls at the rest of me, trying to swallow me up at the sound of that word.

Breezeo.

"They're still making those?" I ask, trying to keep my voice steady, but even I can hear the change in my tone. *Pathetic.*

"Of course!" Bethany laughs. "How do you not know? I thought everyone knew."

"I haven't really been paying attention."

More like I've actively avoided, but that's another long story.

"You've seen them, though, right?" Bethany narrows her eyes. "Please, tell me you've at least watched the others."

"I've caught bits and pieces," I admit.

She throws her hands up dramatically, like my answer is absurd. "That's just… insane. Oh my god, you need to watch them!

The stories are amazing… so funny and just… I don't even have words! And Johnny Cunning, that man is serious eye-candy. You're totally missing out. I'm dead serious, you need to watch them!"

"I'll keep that in mind."

"Good," she says, smiling like she won something. "The first one is called *Transparent* and the second one is *Shadow Dancer*."

"And the one they're filming now?"

"*Ghosted*."

I look away from her when she says that.

"Well, good luck this weekend," I mumble. "Hope it works out for you."

Bethany says something else but I don't stick around to hear it, carrying my Lucky Charms as I jet out to the parking lot. Puddles cover the asphalt, since it rained most of the morning. It always seems to rain at times like these. I dodge the water, making my way to my car.

It's only a few blocks from the grocery store to my father's house. In this tiny town, it's only a few blocks to get anywhere. I pull my old Toyota into his driveway and park as brakes screech in the street, a big yellow school bus coming to a stop in front of the house. *Perfect timing.* Lights flash and the door opens, a bundle of energy bursting off of the bus and rushing toward me. "Mommy!"

I smile as I gaze at her, her hair wild even though I put it in a tight braid this morning. "Hey, little one."

Three-and-a-half feet tall, just shy of forty pounds—average, for a five-year-old, but that's the only thing *average* about Maddie. Smart, compassionate, creative. She insists on dressing herself, which means nothing ever matches, but the girl somehow makes it work.

Everything I do is all about her—anything to keep the smile on her face, because that smile is what keeps me going. It's the reason I get out of bed in the morning. That smile tells me I'm doing okay.

In a world filled with so much wrong, it's nice to know I'm doing something right.

She wraps her arms around my waist in a hug as the bus pulls away. I hear the screen door bang and watch as my father strolls out onto the porch.

"Grandpa!" Maddie says excitedly, running to him. "I made you something!"

She yanks her backpack off, dropping it to the old wood, and digs through it for a piece of paper—a drawing. She shoves it at him, and he takes it, a serious look on his face. Rubbing his scruffy chin, he squints his eyes as he studies it. "Hmmm…"

Maddie stands in front of him on the porch, eyes wide. I stifle a laugh. How many times have I seen this play out? His house is wallpapered with her art. Same routine, every single time. She eagerly waits for his assessment, nervous, and without fail, he always says it's the best whatever-she-drew he's ever seen in his life.

"This," he says, nodding, "is the greatest puppy I've ever laid my eyes on."

Maddie laughs. "It's not a puppy!"

"It's not?"

"It's a seal," she says, yanking the top of the paper down to look at it. "See? It's all gray and it's got a ball!"

"Oh, that's what I meant! A baby seal is called a puppy, too."

"Nuh-uh."

"Yep."

Maddie looks to me to be referee. "Mommy?"

"They're called pups," I tell her.

She turns back to him, grinning. "It's a good puppy?"

"The best," he confirms.

She hugs him before grabbing the drawing and running inside the house to hang it up.

I join my father on the porch. "Nice save."

"Tell me about it," he says, eyes studying me for a moment. "You're off work early today."

"Yeah, well… it's been one of those days," I say—one of those days where the past comes rushing back. "Besides, I have to work a double tomorrow, so I've earned it."

"A double." He looks confused. "Don't you have plans

tomorrow night?"

"Yep." I pause before correcting myself. "Well, I mean, I did."

I so rarely have time for a social life that I haven't even considered that.

"But I could use the money, and I've already got a babysitter on tap," I say, slapping my father on the back. "Can't say no to that."

Shaking his head, he sits down on an old rocking chair on the porch. It's starting to drizzle again, the sky darkening. I lean against the railing, staring out at it as Maddie comes back outside, leaping off the porch.

The girl loves storms.

I can't remember the last time I played in the rain.

That's what I think as I watch her running through the small front yard, splashing in the puddles and stomping in the mud.

Did I ever have that much fun?

Was my life ever that carefree?

I can't remember.

I wish I could.

"Something's bothering you," my father says. "It's *him*, isn't it?"

Turning around, I lean back against the wooden banister, crossing my arms over my chest as I regard him. He rocks back and forth, an identical chair beside him glaringly vacant. My mother used to sit there with him every morning, drinking coffee before he set off to work.

We buried her a year ago.

Twelve long months have passed, but the wound still feels raw, the memories of that day gnawing away at me. It was the last time I saw *him*, too, as I stood right here on this porch. If the headline I caught earlier is any indication, he's had quite an interesting year.

"What makes you think it has anything to do with him?" I ask, forcing myself not to react, like it doesn't matter, but I'm not an actress.

"You have that look again," my father says. "That vacant, lost stare. I've seen it a few times, and it's always him."

"That's ridiculous."

"Is it?"

"Of course. I'm fine."

"I didn't say you weren't fine. I said you *looked* lost, not that you didn't know your way."

He's eyeing me warily. I'm not sure if there's even a point to lying about it when the truth is written all over my face.

And the truth is, I do feel lost.

"Caught a story in a tabloid," I say. "It said he'd gotten married."

"And you believe it?"

I shrug. "I don't know. It doesn't really matter, does it? It's his life. He'll do whatever he wants."

"But?"

"But they're filming in the city again."

"And you're worried he'll show up? Worried he'll try to see her again?"

My father motions past me, at where Maddie is still running around in the rain. I smile softly, as she twirls, oblivious that she's the topic of conversation.

"Or are you worried he won't?" he continues. "Worried he gave up and moved on?"

Maybe, I think, but I don't say it. I don't know which possibility worries me more. I'm terrified he'll force his way into her life and break her heart with his brokenness like he once broke mine. But at the same time, the thought that he might've given up scares me just as much, because that'll hurt her someday, too.

The rain starts falling harder as I mull over those thoughts. Maddie is running circles around the puddles, soaked. Water streaks her face like falling tears, but she's smiling, so happy, ignorant to my fears.

"I should get going," I say. "Before the storm gets any worse."

"Go on, then," my father says, "but don't think I haven't noticed you didn't answer my question."

"Yeah, well, you know how it is," I mumble, leaning down to

kiss my father's cheek before grabbing the backpack from the porch. "Maddie, time to go home, sweetheart!"

Maddie runs for the car, yelling, "Bye, Grandpa!"

"Bye, kiddo," he calls out. "See you tomorrow."

Waving goodbye to my father, I follow her. She's already buckled up when I get in the car.

My eyes seek her out in the rearview mirror. Tendrils of her dark hair fall into her face. She tries to blow them away, her blue eyes watching me. She has a way of looking at you like she's looking through you, like she can see how you're feeling on the inside, those things you try not to let show. It's unnerving sometimes. For being so young, she's quite intuitive.

Which is why I plaster a smile on my face, but I can tell she doesn't buy it.

Home is a small two-bedroom apartment a few blocks away. It's not much, but it's enough for us, and it's what I can afford, so you'll hear no complaints from me. As soon as I open the front door, Maddie takes off through the apartment.

"Straight into the bathtub!" I shout, locking up behind me. I flick on the hallway light as I make my way to the bathroom, passing Maddie's bedroom as I go, seeing she's rooting through her dresser, looking for the perfect pair of pajamas.

She's fiercely independent.

Something she got from her father.

"I'm ready, I'm ready, I'm ready!" she says as she runs into the bathroom when I get the water started. Shoving between the bathtub and me, she grabs the pink bottle of bubbles and squeezes some under the faucet, giggling, as always, when they start to form. "I got this, Mommy."

I take a step back. "You got this?"

"Uh-huh," she says, not looking at me, fixated on the filling bathtub. She sets the bottle of bubbles down on the floor near her feet before turning the knobs, shutting off the water. "I got this."

Like I said… independent.

"Well, go on then. Do your thing."

I don't close the door, but I give her some leeway, keeping an eye on her from outside the bathroom. I can hear her splashing, playing in even more water, like the rain hadn't quite been enough for her. I use the time to gather up laundry, trying to distract myself, but it's pointless.

My mind keeps going back to him.

I sort two weeks worth of dirty clothes into piles on my bedroom floor. Every time I pause, my eyes flicker to my closet, drawn to the old ratty box on the top shelf. I can't see it from here, but I know it's there.

I haven't thought about it in a while. I haven't had a reason. Life has a way of burying memories.

In my case, they're buried under a mountain of other junk in the closet.

I fight it, for a moment, but the pull is too much. Abandoning the laundry, I step straight for the closet, digging out the box.

The cardboard rips when I yank it down, falling apart in my hands. Things scatter around the floor. A picture lands by my feet.

I carefully pick it up.

It's *him*.

He's wearing his school uniform… or as much of it as he ever wore. No sweater, no jacket, and no dress shoes, of course. His white button down is unbuttoned, the tie draped around his neck. Beneath it, he's wearing a plain black t-shirt. His hands are in his pockets, his head cocked to the side. He almost looks like a model, like the picture belongs in a magazine.

A knot forms in my chest. It's suffocating. I can feel the anger and sadness bitterly brewing inside of me, growing stronger as the years go on. My eyes burn with tears, and I don't want to cry, but the sight of him takes me back.

"All done!"

My gaze darts to the doorway as the small cheery voice echoes through the bedroom. I grip the picture tightly, holding it behind my back. She's dressed in a pair of red pajamas, her hair drenched on the ends, a few bubbles around her ears. Mud still streaks her right cheek.

"All done?" I ask, raising my eyebrows. "Did you even wash your hair?"

"Nope."

Of course she didn't. She can't.

"And what about your face?" I ask. "I'm starting to think you only played in the bubbles."

"So? I'm gonna get more dirty later!"

"So?" I gasp, acting horrified. "You can't stay dirty. You have school tomorrow!"

She looks about as thrilled about school as I was as a child. Rolling her eyes, she shrugs, as if to say, 'why does *that* matter?'

Before I can say anything else, her attention shifts to the mess scattered along the floor, her eyes widening as she gasps. "Breezeo!"

She dodges forward, snatching up the old comic book encased in a plastic protective sleeve. I freeze. I wouldn't call it vintage, nor is it worth more than a few bucks, but I couldn't ever bring myself to part with that comic.

To me, it meant too much.

"Mommy, it's Breezeo," she says, her face lit up with excitement. "Look!"

"I see," I say when she holds it up to show me.

"Can we read it? Please?"

"Uh, sure," I say, moving one hand from behind my back to take the comic book from her. "But first, back into the bathtub."

She groans, making a face.

"Go on." I nod my head toward the doorway. "I'll be there in a minute to wash your hair."

Turning, she trudges back to the bathroom. I wait until she's gone to set the comic book down and pull the picture out from behind my back. I stare at it for a second, letting myself feel those things once again, before crumbling it up into a ball and discarding it on the floor with all of the other memories.

Pulling out my cell phone, I scroll through it, dialing a number as I stroll down the hall, hearing it ring a few times before voicemail clicks on.

'It's Andrew. Can't make it to the phone. Leave a message and I'll give you a call.'

Beep.

"Hey, Drew. It's, uh… Kennedy. Look, I'm going to have to take a rain check on tomorrow night. Something came up, and well, you know how it is."

TWO

JONATHAN

The limo slows as it nears Eighth Avenue, the traffic thick at seven o'clock in the morning, just south of sunrise as the world heads to work. Friday. I'm sure the detours don't help people get where they're going, but it's New York—they ought to be used to it. Never a day goes by that something isn't going on here. They're some of the most adaptable people on the planet—New Yorkers— but they're also some of the most no-nonsense. They don't have time for bullshit.

And this morning, it feels like we're all knee-deep in it.

People line the streets as we near the metal barricades. Out-of-towners, I'm assuming, because locals aren't usually the type to give a shit when filming happens in their territory. We're more of a nuisance than anything, blocking off streets and shutting down neighborhoods, disrupting lives. I have nothing to do with any of that—I don't pick the place, I just show up when they tell me to— but more than once I've had the blame thrown my way. Smug bastard, who does he think he is, shutting down part of Midtown during rush hour?

"Word must've leaked," the flippant voice says from the seat in front of me, unfazed as usual. Clifford Caldwell, powerhouse talent manager. Nothing ever seems to bother him. Believe me, I've tested his limits, so I know. *No PR is bad PR*. He's typing away on his beloved Blackberry, attention glued to the screen, but I know he's talking about the crowd packing the streets.

"You think?" I mutter, glancing out the window as we crawl

past at a snail's pace. Despite the fact that the tinting is pitch black, making it impossible for anyone to see inside, I keep my head lowered, an old black ball cap pulled down low, the battered brim shielding my eyes.

Production is running under a fake name to keep people away, so prying eyes won't spoil things they might see on the set, but somebody must've already leaked that information for so many people to show up here this morning.

"I'll talk to them about tightening security around you," Cliff says. "See if we can work with the location department to shake up your schedule."

"Don't bother," I say. "They'll always be a few steps ahead."

Cliff laughs under his breath. "Your optimism is astounding."

"Tell me about it," a lithe voice chimes in from the seat beside me. "Something about this movie turns him into a moody prick."

I cut my eyes at Serena as she musses her freshly dyed hair—deep brown now, instead of her usual blonde. Gotta get in character. I can sense her gaze, even though she's wearing sunglasses. It's a damn harsh glare. She isn't happy with me this morning. Or *any* morning.

Not a morning person.

Across from her sits her long-time assistant, Amanda, ignoring us all as she busies herself filtering Serena's email, like every morning, weeding out anything that might trigger a tantrum.

"That true, Johnny?" Cliff asks. "Because as your manager, I want you to be happy, and as her manager, it's my job to make sure her co-stars aren't being moody pricks."

"I'm fine," I say. "It's just been a long week."

The metal barrier is moved out of the way as the limo approaches it, and we drive into the quartered off area, past a wall of security. There's a slight commotion outside, a few fans screaming, as the limo slips past into a small alley and comes to a stop just out of view. Cliff helps Serena out, taking her hand, while I let Amanda go before stepping out of the limo.

Serena doesn't hesitate, waltzing out of the alley and straight to the crowd, a smile suddenly plastered to her face. There are a few more screams, some shrieks as the fans freak out.

No hiding now.

I leave her to it. She loves that part and eats it right up. The limelight does her wonders—the adoring fans, the camera. Serena was always destined to be a star.

Me? I wanted to be an actor.

I head straight for the row of trailers set up along the backside of the alley, fanning out into the lot of a massive warehouse. Mostly interior shots today, with some filming in the street as they coordinated a mock explosion, according to the call sheet that Cliff shoves at me before disappearing... *somewhere.*

Sets are always chaos.

I'm greeted with a genuine smile as soon as I step into the first trailer. *Hair & Makeup.* Jazz, with her warm brown skin and bright red lips, is a welcoming sight. It's not always easy finding a friendly face at this hour, everyone so focused on business. This trailer is the busiest, one of the biggest, half a dozen makeup artists scattered around at brightly lit stations, but I go straight to Jazz.

"Hey, superstar," she says, patting the seat of a chair in front of a big mirror, motioning for me to sit down. "Looks like I've got my work cut out for me."

"You always do," I say, dropping down in the chair and taking my hat off, setting it aside before running my hands through my thick hair. It's Jazz's job to make me look good, and that isn't always easy—especially when I've been sleeping like shit for over a week, dark bags under my bloodshot eyes.

She gets to work, doing what she does, babbling away about something. I'm vaguely listening, my mind drifting to some damn dangerous thoughts I keep having. Thoughts of a life I could've had but threw away like a fucking idiot. It always happens when I find myself back in New York, a magnetic pull that's hard to ignore, but I do whatever I can to resist it.

It's even harder this time, though.

I'm dragged back to reality when Jazz says, "So, I read

something scandalous the other day."

"One of those kinky whips and chains books?"

She laughs. "Not this time. No, I picked up a copy of *Hollywood Chronicles*…"

I groan, closing my eyes and leaning my head back, covering my face with my hands when she says that. I'm fucking up whatever progress she's made in making me look human again, but I'd rather rip my own balls off and juggle them like a trained monkey than even acknowledge that piece of shit tabloid exists. They've been the bane of my existence for far too long, insisting on putting *my* face on the cover all the time.

"Why do you hate me, Jazz?" I mutter. "Please tell me you didn't give those assholes your money."

"What? Pfft, of course not," she says with a laugh, snatching my hands away from my face to get back to work. "I said I picked it up, not that I bought it. I was in the checkout line at the store."

"Yeah, well, whatever it said, I don't want to know…"

"It said you and Miss Markson got married."

I groan again. "I just said I didn't want to know."

"Well, I told you anyway," she says. "So, what do you think about that?"

"I think you shouldn't waste your brain cells on trashy tabloids. You're better off sticking to the kinky books."

She shoots me a look but drops the subject. I know what she's asking. She's hinting around, trying to get me to spill what's been happening in my life since we filmed the last movie. She wants to know if there's any truth to that story, but I'm not in the mood to get into it.

Once the makeup is done, I switch over to hair, before I bid Jazz goodbye and head to the wardrobe trailer to get my costume on. My stunt-double is there, already rocking the slick light blue and white suit.

I slip mine on—or well, I get shoved into it like they're stuffing fucking sausage into its casing, the material showing every goddamn ripple, so they poke and prod and tape down and tuck.

Mesh, and chrome, and layers of foam, covered in tweaked flexible material made to look like simple spandex without, you know, being *spandex*.

It's as uncomfortable as you're imagining.

"Congratulations, buddy," my stunt-double says, slapping me on the back. "Heard you got hitched! Lucky man."

I cringe. "Who told you that?"

"Jasmine."

Jazz.

I'm going to strangle that woman.

It takes damn near thirty minutes to get me situated in the suit, to get my junk looking right and my muscles padded up, since I'm nowhere near superhero strong. I walk out when I'm done, running right into Serena with her assistant at her heels.

"Well, well, well," Serena says, grinning, as she looks me over. "It's good to see you back in that suit."

I glance down at myself, stretching to try to loosen up the material. "I look ridiculous."

She laughs. "You do not. You should wear it all the time. I'm talking all day, every day—even at night."

"Keep dreaming, Ser."

"Oh, I will."

She slips past me, biting down on her bottom lip as she ogles me from the backside. It's fucking embarrassing. I damn near blush, as ridiculous as it is, watching as her assistant steers her to wardrobe so we're not late to start today.

"Hey," I call out. "You should know that Jazz is telling everyone—"

"That we're married? I know." Serena rolls her eyes and laughs it off. "Apparently, we made the cover of Chronicles again."

"Yeah, apparently," I say as she goes inside the trailer, heading onto set once she's gone.

It's a long day. Take after take after take. I'm sweaty from running and tired from standing, my head pounding from the loud bangs and booms, the pyrotechnics rocking the neighborhood.

There's a breech of security around mid-afternoon, a woman slipping past the barrier after the shots move to the exterior, but they catch her.

I try to not think about it. Try to not think about any of them. I try to not think about *her* when I feel eyes watching me, but it's hard pushing her from my mind. We're filming a sequence where Maryanne, the love of Breezeo's life, had been kidnapped. Serena's tied up with a bomb about to go off, and it's my job to save her from imminent death.

I do it, and I do it well, pouring my soul into every moment. It's nearing the end of the story, even though we're still at the beginning of filming. It takes everything out of me, because endings are hard. Endings are fucking impossible... especially endings that remind me of a girl I'm trying damn hard not to think about.

I breathe a sigh of relief when we wrap for the day, my shoulders slumping as I run a hand through my hair. I try to walk away when Serena throws herself at me. The sun is setting, darkness creeping in, but the shuttering flash of cameras lights up the area as she jumps into my arms.

"That was amazing!" she says. "Like... wow. You acted your ass off, Johnny! You made me believe every word!"

She kisses me before I can respond, more camera flashes going off. It's just a peck, but I imagine some paparazzo will be making a pretty penny on those pictures tonight. I can see it now. Caption: *Johnny fucks Serena in front of everyone!*

She pulls away when Cliff approaches.

"Great job, you two," he says, his voice devoid of excitement, his gaze fixed on his Blackberry as usual. "They're going to stick to the current schedule, so you'll be back here in the morning, Johnny."

"You, too, Serena," her assistant says.

"Sounds great to me." Serena grins as she backs away, her gaze lingering on me. "Get changed, Johnny. We're celebrating!"

"Don't stay out too late," Cliff calls out. "Car will pick you both up tomorrow at six sharp!"

Serena makes a face at him but doesn't argue, heading for the lingering crowd to greet everyone again.

"You did good, moody prick," Cliff jokes, smacking me on the back. "Go get out of the suit. I know it has to be uncomfortable."

I do just that, changing into my jeans and plain white t-shirt, putting my hat on. With filming done for the night, security has gone lax, the crowd moving closer onto set... close enough that some of them surround me when I step out of the trailer. *Shit*.

Cameras flash, a barrage of questions pelting me. "Johnny, can I have a picture?" "An autograph, Johnny?" "Can I have a hug?" Those I don't mind, and I would do it all damn day long if it weren't for the others. The *vultures*.

"How long have you and Serena been together?" "Is it true you two got married?" "What's your father up to these days?" "Have you forgiven him?" "Have you seen him?" "When was the last time you even went home to visit?"

I hate the personal questions and never answer them. I hate the prying. I hate the rumors. I hate it all and for good reason— there are too many skeletons in my closet, too many secrets I've been concealing. Too many things I can't let them taint in a world so pure that I'm no longer welcome in it.

Serena appears at my side, ready to go. She smiles, playing it up for the cameras, charming everyone as she answering what she can, answering what I *won't*.

✤ ✤ ✤

We have dinner at some exclusive private club in the upper eastside. Serena, having started her career modeling here in Manhattan, always seems to know everybody everywhere she goes. Some of her friends are hanging out, laughing and chatting, socialites and trust-fund assholes, sharing bottles of vintage wine and doing a few lines.

Cocaine.

As soon as the white powder surfaces, I'm making my excuse to go. These people used to be my people, too. Friends. But Serena's the only one who seems to be concerned about my hasty exit. She grabs my hand, trying to stop me when I stand, her green eyes eerily dark. "Please? Stay! Celebrate! We never get to hang out anymore like this."

"I would... you know I would... if I could," I say, nudging her chin as she stares up at me. "Don't party too hard, okay?"

I leave before she can try to stop me again, keeping my head down, avoiding eye contact. Instead of taking the awaiting limo and heading straight back to the hotel, I stroll a few blocks, slipping into a small bar. It's quiet, not very busy despite it being Friday night. I find an empty stool along the edge of the bar and as the bartender approaches.

It doesn't take long, just a few seconds, before recognition happens, his eyes widening, but he doesn't announce my presence.

"What can I get for you?" he asks, not calling me by name.

"Whatever's on tap."

He pours me a beer. I don't ask what it is. I sit in silence after he slides it in front of me, wrapping my hands around the cold glass. I can smell it. It's cheap. Not the cheapest shit, but still... *cheap*. My mouth waters, and I can damn near taste the golden liquid, my tongue tingling from anticipation as I stare at it.

"Something wrong?" the bartender asks after a few minutes, motioning to the beer I'm not drinking. "Would you like something different instead?"

"No, it's fine. I just... I haven't had a drink in a while."

"How long?"

"Twelve months."

It's been a long year—longer since I touched anything harder. I'm stuck between steps eight and nine of AA, between admitting I've wronged people and making up for what I've done. You see, there's a catch to those steps, one nobody mentions until you get there. It isn't so cut and dry. There's a bit of fine print to making amends that says 'except when doing so would cause further harm'.

"So, I know it's none of my business," the bartender says, "but twelve months is one hell of a streak. You sure you want to ruin that?"

"No," I admit. "Not sure about much these days."

He doesn't wait for me to say anything else. The beer in my hand is snatched away and replaced with Coke.

The *soda*. Not the drug.

"Been a while since I've had one of these, too," I tell him, but I don't hesitate to sip this drink. It's heaven in a plastic pint glass. Soda does hell on the body, though, with the empty calories, the bloating. Or well, at least that's what the nutritionist says that the studio hired to make sure I stay in shape.

"You wanna talk about it?" the bartender asks.

"About what?"

"About whatever has you almost breaking a twelve-month streak of sobriety tonight."

I shake my head. I would if I could. It's been eating me up inside. But what's bothering me isn't something I can talk about, because unlike most of what *Hollywood Chronicles* peddles, this is a real scandal.

"I appreciate it," I say, taking another sip of the soda before standing up. I toss a few dollars down out of gratitude and turn to leave before I'm tempted to spill my guts and tell the guy a story that could earn him retirement-level money.

Using my phone, I order a car and step out of the bar as it connects me with a driver. *Three minutes away.* The second the warm night air greets me, something else does, too—a small crowd. A couple girls, just teenagers. Nobody ever gives teenage girls enough credit. They're smart. They probably aren't even old enough to hang out a bar, but they knew how to track me down. No paparazzi yet, but they won't be far. They never are.

The requests fly at me. Autographs. Pictures. Hugs. This time I stop for them. I've got three minutes to spare. The least I can do is give back to a few of the fans that have probably been looking for me all day. Hell, I'd be nothing without them. I scribble my name in sharpie on whatever they shove my way—pictures, t-shirts, even an arm—and take a few photos, putting on a smile that would make Cliff proud.

"Can you sign this? Please?" a blonde girl asks, shoving a DVD of the first Breezeo movie at me. "And make it out to Bethany?"

"Bethany," I mumble, jotting down her name, earning a squeal when I say it out loud. "How you doing tonight?"

"Amazing," she says, sounding like she means it. "My friends and I drove the whole way down here to see you when we found out you were filming."

"Yeah? How'd you find out?"

"It was all over the gossip blogs," she says. "There was even a video of Serena talking about it."

Serena. No matter how many times she's warned, she always slips up and says shit she shouldn't. "So you drove down here? From where?"

"Bennett Landing," she says.

My stomach sinks. "You're from Bennett Landing?"

"Yep."

"Nice place," I lie—or maybe I'm not lying, but as everything gets fuzzy, it sure as hell feels that way. "I've been through there a few times."

"I know!" she says. "Or well, I mean, I've heard stories."

"Stories, huh? What kind of stories?"

"I heard you got arrested once for running around naked in Landing Park."

She blushes as she spits out those words, while I laugh—genuinely laughing. I haven't done that in a while. "Damn, didn't think anybody knew about that."

"They do. They talk about it all the time. They say you got drunk and went streaking."

"Not quite," I say. "I wasn't streaking. I was with a girl."

Her eyes light up. "Really?"

36

"Really," I say. "She was hiding when the police showed up. The charges were dropped the next morning, but it's nice to know my moment of indecent exposure lives on in infamy."

She laughs. I laugh. It's a nice moment. I almost forget myself because of it, letting my thoughts slip back to that time, letting myself think about that world again. Guilt eats me up inside. I take a photo with Bethany and sign a few more autographs before my car shows up to whisk me away. Six o'clock will come early, without a doubt, and I have a feeling I won't be getting much sleep tonight.

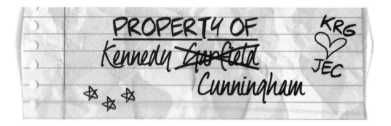

A few minutes outside the Albany city limits sits an elite private high school.

Fulton Edge Academy.

Fulton Edge has the distinction of having taught more government officials than any other school in the nation, an honor they carry with pride, evident in the fact that it's displayed everywhere. Seriously. *Everywhere.* There's even an unsightly banner hanging in the main corridor. College preparatory, with an emphasize on political science, it's the perfect place for a high-profile congressman to send his rebellious teenage son—a fact you know well, considering that's how *you* ended up here, drowning in a cesspool of blue and white uniforms for your fourth year in a row.

Classes have already started, first day of your last year, but you're wandering around, in no hurry to get where you're going—*American Politics.* Not to be confused with *Comparative Politics*, of course, which you'll have later in the afternoon, bookending the oh-so-exciting subjects of Literature (*Political Literature Between the World Wars*) and Math (*Mathematical Methods in Political Science*). The only thing in your schedule unscathed is P.E., likely because they haven't figured out how to incorporate the government.

Fifteen minutes late, you open the classroom door and walk in, disrupting the teacher already invested in a lecture. Your footsteps stall for a fraction of a second, like your feet can't bear to go on, before you shut the door and commit to being here. You're a walking, talking dress code violation, with your tie hanging loose, your white button-down not tucked in, a bit of chaos in the midst of manufactured perfection, throwing off the whole *political prep school* aesthetic.

"Mr. Cunningham," the teacher says, casting you a narrowed look. "Nice of you to grace us with your presence this morning."

"Pleasure's all mine," you say, your voice dripping with sarcasm as you head to the back of the classroom, to the lone empty desk. "Would've shown up sooner, but well... I didn't really care to be here."

There's an awkward stirring, a throat clearing, a long pause of nobody talking, as you settle into your seat. You don't just throw off the aesthetic—you alter their whole image. It makes them uncomfortable.

"As I was saying," the teacher says. "The Founding Fathers..."

The man talks. He talks *a lot*. You rock your chair on its hind legs. Your gaze scans the classroom, surveying your classmates, faces you know well but not ones you care to look at, until you glance to your right, to the desk beside you, and see *her*.

A face you've never seen before.

She's just a girl, nothing special about her. Brown hair falls halfway down her back, hanging loose. Her skin isn't sun-kissed like the other girls here. There are only three of them in the entire twelfth grade—three out of a class of thirty. A mere *tenth* of the senior population is female.

Maybe that's why you stare, why you can't seem to tear your eyes away. Girls are like unicorns in this place, even the most common ones. They can't all be royalty.

Or maybe there's another reason.

Maybe it's something else that sets her apart.

Your gaze, it's not easy to ignore, although the girl tries. Her

40

skin prickles as if you're touching her. A shiver flows down her spine. She's fidgeting, toying with a cheap black ink pen on top of a notebook that she hasn't yet written in.

Nervous, she lets go of the pen and balls her hands into fists as she shoves them beneath the desk. Your gaze lifts, blue eyes meeting hers for a moment before she looks away, acting as if she's paying close attention to the lesson, but nobody cares *that* much about the formation of the first cabinet.

The class drags on for forever and a day. The teacher starts asking questions, and nearly everyone raises their hands. She keeps hers hidden beneath the desk, while you continue to rock your chair without a care.

Despite not volunteering, the teacher calls on you. Over and over. *Cunningham.* You rattle off answers, rather bored with it all. The others stumble, but you don't even have to pause. You know your stuff. It feels a bit like a circus act, like a lion jumping through hoops.

If they poke you too much, making you perform, might you start ripping heads off? *Hmm...*

When class is over, everyone packs up their things. You drop your chair down, making a loud screech, as you shove to your feet. You didn't bring anything with you. No books. No paper. Not even a pencil. You stall between the desks, leaning closer to the new girl.

"I like your nail polish," you say, your voice playful, as she picks up her yet untouched notebook.

She looks up, meeting your eyes. You're amused, the first hint of anything beyond boredom. Her gaze shifts to her nails then, to the chipped blue glittery polish coating them.

You walk away.

"Be on time tomorrow, Cunningham," the teacher calls out.

You don't even look at him when you say, "No promises."

The day drags on and on and on. You sleep through most of Literature and don't do a single Math problem. Comparative Politics is repetitious as you again spew out answers to questions. The girl sits near you in every class, close enough that your attention drifts to her whenever there's a lull. You watch her as she fidgets. You watch her as she struggles. You watch her fumble her way through wrong answers. Others watch, too, whispering to each other, like they're trying to figure out how a commoner weaseled her way onto their court, but you watch her like she's the least boring thing you've encountered.

When P.E. arrives at the end of the day, you're more interested. It's mindless, running lap after lap, and you're *fast*—so fast it annoys the others. They don't like you being better than them. On top of ruining their image, you're putting a dent in their self-confidence.

When class is over, everyone heads to the locker rooms. You're soaked with sweat but don't bother to change, standing right outside when the girl exits, but she barely makes it a step before an administrator's voice calls out. "Garfield."

She stalls, turning to look at the man as he lurks in the hallway. "Sir?"

"I know you're new to the school," he says. "Have you had the opportunity to read the handbook?"

"Yes, sir," she says.

"Then you know you're in violation of school policy," he says. "Nails are to be natural, which means no polish. Rectify that by tomorrow."

He walks away.

She looks at her nails.

You laugh.

You, who have been in violation of that policy all day long without anybody saying a word about it.

There's a small parking lot beside the school for the students who drive, but you head around to the front, to a circular driveway for pick-up. She goes that way, too, lingering in the back of the crowd, sitting down on the ground and leaning against the building, pulling out her notebook.

Opening it, she starts writing.

Black sedan after black sedan swings through, the crowd whittling down. After a half hour, only a handful of kids remain.

After forty-five minutes, it's just you and her.

You're pacing around, your gaze flickering to her. "Guess I'm not the only one stranded."

"My dad works until four," she says, pausing her writing to look up. "He should be here soon."

"Yeah, well, my father's an asshole," you say. "He enjoys making me suffer."

"Why don't you drive?"

"I could ask you the same thing."

"I don't have a car."

"I do," you say, "but my father's an asshole. He thinks if I have my car, I'll skip my classes."

"Would you?"

"Yes."

She laughs, and you give her a smile, as a black car approaches the school—*a limo*.

"So, Garfield, huh?" you say. "Like the cat?"

"More like the former president."

"You got a first name to go with it?"

"Kennedy."

43

You give her the strangest look. "You're kidding."

"My middle name's Reagan, you know, to bring it all full circle."

"Ah, man, that's fucking *rough*. Here I thought I had it bad being a Cunningham."

"Like the current Speaker of the House?"

"Also known as the asshole who took my car keys," you say. "You can call me Jonathan."

"Jonathan."

You smile when she says your name.

The limo pulls up, and you look at it, hesitating, like maybe some part of you doesn't want to leave her alone there.

Or maybe your reluctance has more to do with who awaits you.

Speaker Grant Cunningham.

The back window rolls down, and there the man is, his attention on something in his hands as he says, "Get in the car, John. I have things to do."

His voice carries not an ounce of warmth. He doesn't even look at you.

You glance back at the girl before getting in the limo, while she turns back to her notebook.

And you don't know this, but that girl? The one left outside of that school alone? She's sitting there writing about you. You have all the makings of a modern-day tragic hero, and she's never felt so compelled to explore somebody's story before... even if that's kind of creepy, *ugh.*

44

THREE

KENNEDY

"Kennedy, oh my god, you won't believe the night I had!"

Those are the first words Bethany says when she strolls in the store twenty minutes late Saturday morning, as I scan somebody's groceries on her register, doing her job instead of my own. I stopped by on my day off to finish up some paperwork for Marcus and want nothing more than to get the heck back out, but no such luck.

"What happened?" I ask. "Did you sneak on set?"

"No," she says. "Got close to it, though. Real close. I even got to see him in the suit!"

"That's nice," I mumble, although it doesn't feel nice to me. No, it's making my stomach gurgle, my insides clenching and doing horrible things.

"It was… wow." Bethany lets out a squeal as I finish ringing up Mrs. McKleski's groceries and take her money. The woman shops here every single day. Today's purchase? Chocolate cream pie ingredients. "We stood around all day but it was so worth it! Serena came out to see us. She was so nice, oh my god… I expected her to be super bitchy, you know, because people talk, but she took pictures and was joking around!"

"That's nice," I say again—and once more, it doesn't feel that way. I'm feeling a bit sick in the stomach about it all, as absurd as that is. "I'm glad she made your trip worthwhile."

"Oh, it wasn't her—it was totally him," she says. "We found Johnny Cunning coming out of some bar later. He actually talked to us. Oh my god, he was nicer than I expected him to be, and talk about dreamy!"

Bethany shoves her phone in my face, forcing me to look at the screen, at a picture she took of the two of them, a cheap hole-in-the-wall bar visible in the background. I can tell he'd been trying to go unnoticed, but he smiles for the camera. It doesn't look like he's drunk, but well… he's at a bar.

"He asked where I was from," she says, "and he laughed when I told him they tell stories about him here. He wanted to know what people say, so I told him about the naked one, you know, at the park? You know that story, right?"

"Vaguely," I mumble.

"Well, get this! Not only is it true, he really got arrested, but he said he'd been there with a girl! Can you believe that?"

I give Mrs. McKleski her change and offer her a smile when I see the knowing look in her eyes. She says nothing—*thank god*—as she leaves. There are a few people in town to which these aren't just stories… they're memories. It was only a few years ago, but life moves on. Bethany would've been just a kid when these things happened, not old enough to know anything about the troubled son of a politician. She only knows the actor he came to be, the one who has nothing to do with his family.

"That's nice," I say for the third time, and this time I know, without a doubt, I don't mean it. There's nothing nice about how I'm feeling. "You're already thirty minutes late, so I need you to clock in."

Flustered, she rambles out an apology, but I jet away without listening to it. I find a quiet place to hide in the stockroom in the back, sitting down on a box and lowering my head, taking deep breaths to ease the turmoil brewing inside of me.

Too close for comfort.

I do a few things, not much, before telling Marcus I'm leaving. He laughs, waving me off. "Good, you're not even supposed to be here."

I head to the front of the store, where Bethany is finally

working her register.

"I'm glad you had a good trip," I tell her, genuinely meaning that. "I'm glad he didn't disappoint you."

With that, I leave.

I drive to my father's house, parking my car in his driveway. He's on the couch in front of the television, snuggling up with my half-asleep daughter, and I groan when I realize what they're watching.

Breezeo: Transparent

"Seriously? What happened to Saturday morning cartoons?"

"That hasn't been a thing in a while," my father says. "But this was on, and she wanted to watch it."

It's the first movie. I've seen it before. It's impossible to have not seen it, since cable plays it on regular rotation these days. It's where he learns to adapt, an illness triggering something in his DNA that makes him fade away. *Invisibility.* He becomes the wind. He earns his name because he's like a soft breeze. You know he's around, you can feel him ghosting across your skin, but unless he shows himself to you, you can't see him, looking right through him like he's not even there. I know, it sounds like some crazy sci-fi nonsense, but it's more of a coming of age story, more of a love story. It's about selflessness, about sacrificing your own happiness for others, about being there for them even when they don't know you're around.

"You've got mail on the kitchen table," my father says before I start spiraling. "Don't forget to grab it."

Strolling into the kitchen, I snatch up the small stack of mail, mostly junk leftover from me never changing my address after I moved out ages ago. I sort through it, throwing the junk away, and stall when I reach the last envelope. It's not unusual. I've seen dozens like it. But every time one shows up, it makes me hesitate, my gaze flickering along the return address, to the name.

Cunningham c/o Caldwell Talents

I don't open the envelope, although I used to out of curiosity. Every single time a check would be inside, the amounts steadily increasing.

"You going to cash that one?" my father asks, stepping into the kitchen behind me.

I cut my eyes at him, tossing it straight into the trashcan. "I don't need his money."

"I know, but what you should do is save the checks and cash them *all* at once. Wipe out his account. Then go riding off into the sunset in your brand new Ferrari."

"I don't want a Ferrari."

"*I* do," he says. "You could buy me one."

"Nice try, but no. Although, I might be able to squeeze enough out of my next check to buy you the Hot Wheels version. Hey, I've gotten enough overtime this week you might get *two*."

"Well, you know, if you wouldn't throw away that check, you wouldn't need to work overtime."

"I'm not interested in taking a payoff."

"That's not what it is."

"That's sure what it feels like," I say. "He can't even be bothered to send the checks himself, you know. His manager does it all. It's hush-money."

"Oh, cut him some slack."

"Cut him some slack?" I look at my father with disbelief. "You've never even liked him."

"But he's Madison's father."

I roll my eyes. It's probably childish, but if there's ever a reason to roll my eyes, this moment is it. "Yeah, well, somebody ought to tell him that."

"He knows. Hell, you've got the check right there to prove it. And I know, I know, before you say *but his manager sends those*, I'll point out that he's shown up here a few times to see her."

"Drunk," I say. "He was drunk every single time. Half the time he was so high that I doubt he remembers coming. I'm sorry, but I don't hand out participation trophies to addicts who don't make an effort to get clean. I'll cut him some slack when he gives me a reason."

He lets out a long, dramatic sigh and says nothing for a moment, like he's figuring out how to reframe his argument.

"You can cash it, if you want," I say, pulling the check back out of the trashcan and setting it on the table. "I mean, we still owe you from that one time."

"It's not about the money. Not even about him."

"Then what is it?"

"Madison's growing up, and you…"

"What about me?"

"You're giving up," he says. "And if you're losing hope, well, we're screwed, because we can't *both* hate the guy. Someone's gotta care for her sake."

"I don't hate him," I say, my stomach doing that twisting and turning again. "I'm just… tired. She'll be six soon. And I have to wonder, at what point am I just making it worse? Because six years is a long time for her to not know about him."

"This is why we still need your mother around," he says. "She was always the optimistic once."

"Yeah, well, what would Mom say?"

He motions toward the living room, where the movie still plays on the television. "She'd say if *that's* the only way Madison will ever have the chance to know the guy, so be it."

I don't argue with that. I've never been sure how to handle it all. Maddie hasn't asked many questions, so up until now it's been swept under the rug, but I know that won't fly when she gets older. I just have no idea how to explain any of it.

"We should go," I say, dropping the subject. "I promised I'd take her to the library today."

We head back to the living room, where Maddie is now wide-awake, captivated by the movie as Breezeo makes his big move and saves the day. I sit down on the arm of the couch beside her, watching. It's still so strange, after all these years, seeing that familiar face on the screen.

Jonathan Cunningham.

Johnny Cunning.

✿ ✿ ✿

Six books. That's how many Maddie picks up at the library to bring home. But yet as soon as we walk in the door, before we even settle in, she pops up in front of me clutching the comic book wrapped in plastic that she swiped from my bedroom.

"Can we read Breezeo now, Mommy? Please?"

"Sure," I say, taking it from her, "but it's not the whole story, sweetheart. It's just the very end."

The last volume in the *Ghosted* storyline.

"That's okay," she says, climbing up into my lap on the couch. "I like the ends the best."

Sighing, I pull the comic from its protective sleeve and open it. I start to read, filling in the blanks, narrating the pictures. It picks up with the big warehouse explosion, as Breezeo saves his lover, Maryanne, from death.

'Who are you?' she asks afterward, standing in the street as the warehouse burns, unable to see him, but she can feel him. She doesn't know who Breezeo is. She doesn't know it's the man she gave her heart to so long ago—Elliot Embers. She thinks he died in *Shadow Dancer* from the illness that has been turning him into nothing, so he's spent *Ghosted* in isolation. 'Please, show yourself. Tell me. I need to know.'

He considers it, standing right in front of her. It would be so easy. He could use what energy he had left to show himself, but doing so would change everything. It would change her perception of reality. Would change her memories of him. It would alter their story in irreparable ways, and knowing the truth might put her life in further danger. He couldn't do that to her. He couldn't destroy the life that she'd built for a single moment of acknowledgment only to have to disappear again.

It would be too cruel, appearing only to leave her once more, when she'd finally had the courage to say goodbye.

So he leans closer, softly kissing her mouth. It's barely a breath

50

against her lips. She feels a tingle, followed by a breeze that rustles her dark hair, and then nothing.

He leaves.

He leaves and never looks back, giving her a life of freedom, a life where she can live a quiet existence and be happy without him. He's destined to do bigger things, and staying would be selfish, so as much as he wishes he could be with her forever, he has to let her go, because that's what love means.

It's loving someone enough to set them free.

Tears sting my eyes. *Ugh*, this freaking story. Maddie glares at the comic. I think she expected a happy ending.

"Does he come back, Mommy?" she asks.

"Well, I guess it's possible," I say. "There's really no such thing as 'the end' in comics. People come back all the time."

"Okay, then," she says, accepting it just like that as she hops off of my lap to snatch up one of the library books. "This one now!"

FOUR

JONATHAN

"Let's take a break!" the first AD—assistant director—yells, his voice edged with annoyance. "Everyone back in twenty minutes. Markson, please, pull yourself together!"

"I'm trying," Serena mutters, squeezing her eyes shut and clutching the sides of her head. "I'm just a little under the weather."

Under the weather, my ass.

She got maybe two hours of sleep, rolling into the hotel close to four o'clock in the morning. I know, because she insisted on waking me up by trying to crawl into bed with me, but I wasn't interested. She's probably still somewhat drunk, probably having one hell of a comedown off of coke. I used to show up on set like that every morning and barely survived filming. I was killing myself. The moment *Shadow Dancer* wrapped, Cliff sent me straight to rehab, putting me in a program.

It wasn't my first stint in rehab, not by a long shot, but it was the first time I stayed the full ninety days. Every other time, I walked out within a month and relapsed before Cliff even realized I'd given up. But sobriety gripped ahold of me last year and I worked the program as reality sunk in.

And reality, it turns out, is a bitch to an addict.

"Here, drink some water," I tell Serena, handing her a bottle. "It'll help you feel better."

"What will help is a *pick me up*," she mutters, chugging some water before looking at me. "You don't have anything, do you?"

"You know I don't."

She scowls, chugging more water before stomping away. The crowd around set seems bigger now. If people didn't know we were out here yesterday, they do today.

"The missus seems a little testy," Jazz says, strolling over to blot the sweat from my forehead. "Honeymoon over, superstar?"

I stare at her. She thinks she's slick, but it couldn't be more obvious what she's doing. "If you're referring to Serena, she's just not feeling well."

"Uh-huh," she says, not convinced, as I take a sip from a bottle of water, not wanting to get into Serena's business. "She's not knocked up, is she? You'd make a good daddy."

I choke. I seriously choke. The water pours down my windpipe and I start fucking heaving, losing my breath, turning colors. People rush to intervene, smacking my back and forcing my hands up, trying to get air in my lungs as I violently cough.

Inhaling sharply, my chest on fire, I wave everyone away and glare at Jazz. "Don't even fucking *say* that."

"What?" she asks, acting innocent as she presses her hands to her chest. "It was just a question."

"She isn't pregnant," I say. "It's not possible."

Jazz brushes it off with a laugh, but now she's got me frazzled. *You'd make a good daddy.* My chest is tight, burning from the inside, the knot barely loosening by the time we're due back on set. Serena returns a lot more chipper, her pupils like fucking saucers. It's obvious she's high, but nobody says a word. I notice Cliff is watching her, though.

Serena's on point now, wide-awake and feeling beautiful, while I keep fucking up, take after take after take. It's a mess. The movie's going to be a goddamn disaster if we can't get our shit together.

"Cunning, your timing is off," the AD says. "What did you two do, switch places?"

"I'm getting it together," I say, stretching. "I just need to clear my head."

Serena steps closer, whispering, "I got more if you want it."

Do I want it? Fucking right I do. I want it all day, every day.

But I don't need it, and I sure as hell shouldn't have it, so I shake my head. "I can't do that anymore, Ser. You know that. And you shouldn't be doing it, either."

"Whatever." She rolls her eyes. "You're not the boss of me, you know."

"I know, but I am—"

"Quiet on set!" a voice shouts, cutting off our conversation. "Let's try this again! Give us a good one this time!"

We do. We give them a good one. Hell, we give them a few. But after nightfall shit starts deteriorating again. Serena runs out of coke while I run out of patience for her attitude.

"Ugh, this sucks," she growls, messing up her hair as she clutches her head. "I feel like *shit.*"

"You're more cocaine than woman at this point," I say, frustrated that we're not through yet. "I'm surprised you can feel *anything* anymore."

"You're such a prick," she snaps, shoving me.

"Oh, whoa, whoa!" Cliff gets between us as she clenches a fist like she's about to swing at me. "This is not happening. You're frustrated? Fine. Get a room and screw each other's brains out. But this? Oh, no, no, no... *not* going down."

"What needs to go down is some *detox,*" I say. "Some counseling."

"Shove your judgment up your ass, Johnny," Serena says. "Just because you went full-blown junkie doesn't mean the rest of us will, too. I'm *fine.* So why don't you worry about how much of a fuck-up you are and leave me alone!"

She storms off set, crying, and the shoot is postponed— officially, because Serena Markson is *under the weather.*

Unofficially? Turns out, I'm an unsympathetic asshole.

I run my hands down my face. "Could this day get any worse?"

"Never say that," Cliff says. "Because as soon as you say that, it'll get worse."

"I don't think that's possible."

"Look, give her time to calm down," he says. "Give her time to *come* down. We'll come back tomorrow with a clear head."

I go to wardrobe, getting out of the suit, grateful to be back in jeans and a t-shirt. I don't wait around after I'm changed, because I'm damn sure not riding in the limo back to the hotel with Serena, so I order a car and skirt past the lingering crowd to meet it on the corner, not wanting to wait for it to pass through security. A few folks catch up to me. I sign a few autographs but turn down requests for photos, enough cameras flashing in my face.

I hate the fucking paparazzi.

I'm standing on the corner, waiting. The car's a minute away. They're pelting me with personal questions that I do my best to ignore—although, I want to sucker punch one of them when he asks about my father.

"Fuck him," I mutter under my breath.

"What did you say?" the paparazzo asks.

"I said *fuck him*."

Ah, that's going to be one hell of a sound bite.

Before I can say anything else, there's screeching nearby, a group of fans rushing toward me. *Shit.* People are pushing, shoving, as the crowd closes in around me, fans trying to get past the assholes with cameras who keep drowning them out with their inconsiderate questions. Nobody's watching what they're doing, and I'm losing my cool. *Fast.* I can't even meet my damn car on the street without this chaos. I sign some more stuff that's shoved in my face, and I try to calm myself down, but these assholes do everything imaginable to antagonize me.

Footage is worth more when I lose my temper.

The same guy who asked about my father tries to get closer, to get a better angle, mowing a young girl over. She stumbles and I catch her, grabbing her by the arm. She can't be more than thirteen or fourteen. It pisses me off.

"Back the fuck off before you get someone hurt," I say, shoving the guy away, just to get some goddamn *space*, but it seems to trigger panic in the crowd. Some try to disperse, and that young girl dodges forward, out into the street, because there's nowhere else she can go. *Shit.* She doesn't even look. Headlights swallow her up. A horn blares. I can see the horror in her eyes.

The girl fucking freezes.

No.

It's instinctual. I don't even think. She freezes and my feet move. I dart out into the street and grab the girl again, shoving her back to the sidewalk. She knocks into the crowd, losing her footing, but I have no chance to make sure she doesn't get trampled. I turn, and the car is *right there*, tires squealing, brakes screeching—

BAM.

Everything feels like it's in slow motion. My brain doesn't register it right away. Flashes surround me as I fly backwards and then—holy fuck—*pain.* It's like a shock, every nerve ending in my body screaming as I slam into the asphalt.

Blackness. I'm blinking, but I can't make out much. People are yelling all around me. My head is pounding. Their words are vibrating inside my skull and I want them all to shut the fuck up. Police lights and sirens, paparazzi cameras flashing, panicked screams from someone. I try to sit up but something warm runs down my face, soaking my white shirt.

I look down at it. Blood.

The sight makes me woozy. *Whoa.* My vision goes black and then Cliff is there. I hear him before I see him, hear his warbled voice before his face greets me. "Take it easy, Johnny. Don't move. We've got help coming."

He looks worried.

I wasn't worried.

I wasn't… until I looked at him.

"Is she okay?" I ask, my chest aching.

"Who?" he asks.

"The girl," I say. "She was in the street. There was a car coming. I don't know. Is she…?"

"Everyone's fine," he says, glancing around before turning back to me. "They're freaked out, but nobody else is bleeding.

What were you thinking?"

"That she was gonna get hit by a car."

"So you took her place? Jesus, Johnny, you're taking this superhero business *way* too personal."

I laugh at that. It hurts.

I close my eyes and grit my teeth.

Where is that goddamn help?

❀ ❀ ❀

You're lucky.

That's what the doctor said to me.

It's your lucky day.

But as I lay in the stark white hospital bed in the dim private room, surrounded by people I don't care to look at, with security posted at every corner as phones ring and ring and fucking *ring*, I don't feel very lucky. This day has become unimaginably worse.

Severe concussion. Laceration to the temple. Broken right wrist. Bruised ribs. Besides an array of cuts and scrapes, swelling in places that aren't happy about this shit, that's all that seems to be wrong with me.

So maybe I am lucky, but the voices all around me right now don't think so.

My manager, a studio exec, the movie director, and a shitload of PR cram into the room, hashing out details of how to handle this nightmare. My lawyer is here somewhere. I remember seeing him earlier. They're worried about lawsuits and insurance quotes and how this is going to impact the production, but I'm more worried about this sensation flowing through my veins at the moment. *Fuck.* It's the middle of the night, and my head is swimming, my stomach queasy. I'm uneasy. My legs keep tingling and I feel like I'm starting to float outside of my body.

Whatever drug they're pumping into my IV is strong.

Too strong. I'm going numb.

It's been a long time since I've felt nothing.

I press the call button, over and over until the nurse bursts in, shoving her way past the crowd of suits to reach the bed. Cliff slips away from the others, approaching.

"Whatever this is," I say, motioning to the IV bags, "I need taken off of it."

"The morphine?" the nurse asks with confusion, setting her hand on my shoulder. "Honey, you're going to want that. You'll be hurting without it."

"I can handle the pain," I say. "Not so sure about the drugs."

She looks even more confused now, so Cliff chimes in. "Mr. Cunning is in recovery, so anything *feel-good* is problematic, if you get my drift."

"Oh, well, I'll speak to the doctor," she says. "We'll see what we can do."

I close my eyes as she rushes away. Regret hits me, gripping tight, a voice in my mind saying tell her you've made a mistake, but that's the addict in me screaming out, the pathetic son of a bitch that gets off on the numbness. That gets off on forgetting. But *goddamn*, the sensation feels good.

Maybe I'll enjoy it for just a little while.

I open my eyes again when Cliff nudges me, holding his Blackberry out, and I glance at the screen, reading the headline of a news article.

WHEN FICTION MEETS REALITY

Superhero-Actor Saves Girl

I don't read any further.

"You'll be down for awhile," Cliff says. "They'll rearrange the shoots, do what they can do without you there. Production hopes to pick back up with you sometime before summer."

Summer. It's barely Spring right now. "What am I supposed to do until then?"

"Go easy on this superhero nonsense, for starters. Take a vacation. Go sit on a beach somewhere surrounded by beautiful women. The point is to rest. Relax. *Recover.* When's the last time you even had any fun?"

"Fun." I consider that. "Does jumping in front of a car count?"

There isn't much fun to be found at Fulton Edge—unless your idea of fun is politics. But once a week, on Friday afternoons, they have club meetings, which suck slightly less than sitting in classes.

Drama club. That's where you always go. They gather in the school auditorium, a mere two-dozen people in a room meant for hundreds.

The meeting has already started today when you stroll in. Not that it matters, since they're doing nothing but arguing. You stall in the aisle, staring at them scattered along the stage. The debate is what production to put on this year—Macbeth or Julius Caesar.

You turn away from them, about to leave, when you catch sight of someone lurking in the back of the auditorium. It's her. The new girl. She's not paying attention to the meeting. Instead, she's reading.

You're a few weeks into the school year, but this is the first time she's appeared in the auditorium. Curious, you stroll over, sliding into a nearby seat, leaving the one between you empty. She's reading a comic book. That takes you by surprise. Around Fulton Edge, you sort of expect to see copies of Atlas Shrugged.

"Haven't seen you in here before," you say. "Hastings recruit you so he has enough people for his annual Shakespearean wank?"

She laughs, looking at you. You can probably count on your fingers the number of times you've seen the girl smile. Laughter has been even more rare. She shows up every day, keeps her head down, and she does whatever is necessary, always the first one here and the last one gone. But you can tell she's not happy, maybe even unhappier than you are, when you hate being here so much that if there's a chance for you *not* to be here, you take it and run.

You've already missed six days of school in a little over a month. They fine your father for your truancy, but otherwise, they let you slide.

"I've tried all the others," she says. "I suck at chess. Debate team was a disaster, book club was reading something written by a fascist, and it turns out 'writing club' is writing letters to Congress, so..."

"So here you are."

"Here I am," she says, holding up her comic. "Making my own club."

"Ah, the good old *'fuck your clubs'* club," you say. "I'm tempted to start that one every year when these idiots start bickering."

"You're welcome to join me," she says. "Might not be much fun, but it can't really be any worse, can it?"

"No, it can't," you say, motioning to the stage. "If this whole acting thing doesn't work out, I might take you up on that. Always need a fallback plan."

The Drama Club settles on *Julius Caesar*... for the fourth year in a row... and the argument shifts to who gets which role. Hastings, the self-appointed leader of the club, insists on being Caesar. He's a typical rich kid, the blond-haired, blue-eyed grandson of a *Watergate* attorney. He wants to be the hero. He scowls as some of the others disagree, instead suggesting *you* do it.

"You're awfully popular with the drama crowd," she says, pausing when Hastings calls you, 'at best, an amateur'. "Well, with *most* of them."

"I played Caesar three years in a row," you say. "Besides, I'm the only one here with an IMDb page."

Her eyes are glued to your face. "You're a real actor?"

"At best, an amateur," you joke. "I've had a few minor roles. Played a dead kid once on *Law & Order*."

"Wow," she says. "Remind me to get your autograph later."

You laugh at her deadpan. "Mostly, I've done local theater. Started taking acting classes as soon as I was old enough. Haven't done anything lately, though, unless *this* counts."

The words seem to be just falling from your lips, like talking to her comes natural.

"It counts," she says.

"Does it?" you ask, and you're serious about that. "Am I still an actor if I don't have an audience?"

"Is a writer still a writer if nobody reads what they wrote?"

You consider that. The arguing on stage is growing louder, almost to the point of coming to blows. It amuses you, on one hand, but mostly it fills you with a sense of sadness that *this* is what you look forward to. Your art is belittled down to a fight over who gets to be the hero in a high school production. Your dreams were always much bigger than that.

"I should intervene," you say, standing up, "before somebody does something stupid and gets us shut down."

"Well, if that happens, the '*eff your clubs*' club is here."

"Make sure you hold my spot," you tell her before heading up on stage to say, "You know, I'd much rather be Brutus this year."

"Is that right?" Hastings asks.

"Absolutely." You poke him dead center of the chest with your pointer finger, hard enough that he takes a step back. "It would be my pleasure to be the one who takes you down."

The others divide up the rest of the parts. They took so long making decisions that there's no time to get the scripts today. You have the entire thing memorized, though. So does Hastings. The two of you spit lines back and forth for a bit, things growing heated.

The girl remains seated in the back of the auditorium, no longer reading her comic book. She watches your every move, absorbing every syllable. You have an audience today, as you act your heart out, and she's captivated.

When the day ends, people leave, but you're in no hurry. You stroll down the aisle to where the girl still sits. She watches you approach and says, "If what I just witnessed is any indication, you might've been the best dead kid *Law & Order* has ever seen."

You sit down with her, laughing. There's no space between the two of you now. "It was a 'parents are monsters behind closed doors' storyline. I had a handful of lines. I was five."

"Wow," she says. "When I was five, I couldn't even remember how to spell my own name, and you were already memorizing dialogue."

"Ah, well, I have a good memory," you say. "Besides, it's easier when things are relatable."

You don't elaborate.

She doesn't ask you what you mean by that.

She's fidgeting with her comic book, thumbing through pages. Silence surrounds you but it isn't awkward. She's nervous, though— nervous sitting so close to you.

"So, you like comic books?" You pluck the one from her hand. "Breezeo."

Breezeo: Ghosted
Issue #4 of 5

"Have you read it?" she asks.

"Never heard of it," you say, flipping through the thing. "Looks shitty."

She snatches the comic right back. "How *dare* you! Blasphemous."

"Okay, fine, I retract that." Laughing, you grab the comic book again. She reluctantly releases it. "So, what, he's some kind of superhero?"

"Something like that," she says. "He was a normal guy, but he caught an experimental virus that's making him disappear."

"Like a ghost," you say, glancing at the pictures.

"Yeah, so he's just doing what he can to save the girl he loves while he has the chance."

"Huh, let me guess—they find a cure and live happily ever after?"

"It's not over yet. There's still one more issue left."

"But you have the others?"

"Yes."

"Bring them to me," you say. "Let me read them."

She gives you a horrified look. "Why in the world would I do *that?*"

"Because we're in '*fuck your clubs*' club together."

"You didn't join."

"I still might."

She rolls her eyes as she gets up to leave. You walk her to the front of the school. Nearly everyone is gone, just a handful of students remaining. A maroon-colored Honda is parked along the right-hand side of the circular driveway, a man approaching the building.

She tenses, feet stalling, when she notices him. "Dad! You're early."

"Figured you'd appreciate not having to hang out here on a Friday," the man says, smiling until his gaze shifts to you, standing awfully close to his daughter. His eyes narrow as he holds his hand out to introduce himself. "Michael Garfield."

"Jonathan," you say, shaking his hand, leaving it at that, but it's a pointless omission.

"Cunningham," her dad says. "I know who you are. I work for your father. Wasn't aware you knew my daughter, though. She hasn't mentioned it."

Disapproval is evident in every syllable of those words. You have a reputation with the people who work for your father, and it's not a good one.

"You knew he went here, Dad," she grumbles, face reddening with embarrassment that he's making this a *thing*. "It's a small school."

You don't say anything as she drags her father away. She's about to climb into the passenger seat of his car when you step forward, calling out to her. "Hey, Garfield..."

She stalls, turning to you.

Her father glares from behind the wheel.

"You forgot this," you say, holding up her comic book.

She grabs it, but you don't let go right away, hesitating as she says, "Please, don't call me that. Call me anything *but* that."

You release your hold, and she gives you a smile before climbing into the car and leaving, taking her comic book.

You don't know this, but that girl? She gathers up her Breezeo comics as soon as she gets home. All fourteen issues in all three storylines—*Transparent, Shadow Dancer,* and *Ghosted.* She spends the weekend re-reading them, just so they're still fresh in her mind, so when she brings them to school for you to borrow, she remembers every single line.

FIVE

KENNEDY

"In entertainment news, Breezeo star Johnny Cunning was involved in an accident last night in Manhattan…"

I'm halfway to the kitchen when those words strike me, my footsteps stopping. I turn around, looking at the television across the living room, thinking I must've heard them wrong, but no… there he is, stock footage playing from some red carpet, his smiling face on the screen, bloodshot eyes staring right through me.

"The twenty-eight-year-old actor was struck by a car near the set of his latest film. Eyewitnesses say Cunning stepped into traffic during an altercation with the paparazzi."

I approach the TV as the image on the screen changes, a video of the aftermath playing. The first thing I see is blood streaming down his face. He's alert, though. He's *alive*. The relief that floods my body nearly buckles my knees.

"A spokesman for the actor says he's currently stable and in good spirits. Filming for the movie has been temporarily suspended as Cunning heals from his injuries."

"Mommy?"

The second that I hear Maddie's voice, I press the button to turn off the TV, hoping she hadn't seen it. I turn to her, my hopes dashed right away. *Oh crap.* She looks shocked. "Yes, sweetheart?"

"Is Breezeo okay?"

"Sure," I say, giving her a smile. "He had a little accident, but he'll be okay."

"You mean like he's sick?"

"Something like that," I say.

Her expression shifts as she thinks about that, her face lighting up. "I can make him a card!"

"Uh, yeah, you can," I say, not letting my smile falter. "I'm sure we can find an address to send it to."

His agency accepts fan mail for him. I'm pretty sure he doesn't personally open it, so there's no harm sending something, if it'll make her feel better.

Maddie runs off to her bedroom to get to work on some art while I get busy making dinner, booting up my old piece-of-crap laptop while a frozen pizza cooks. For the first time in well over a year, I type his pseudonym into the search bar.

I take a deep breath when the results pop up. Pictures and pictures—*whoa*, so many pictures—along with a video of the accident. My heart drops as I stare at it. I press play and watch. Thirty seconds. I hold my breath, expecting the worst from him—drunken staggering into traffic with no regard for his life, maybe. But instead, I see him shove a man, telling him to back off when a girl gets caught between them. The girl goes into the road, and his reflexes are fast, *so fast*, as he grabs her and shoves her back onto the sidewalk before—

Cringing, I slam the laptop closed the second the car strikes him. He saved that girl from being hit.

I sit there in silence, stunned. My nose starts twitching, the smell of something burning tickling my nostrils. It takes a moment—too long of a moment—before my eyes start to burn and it strikes me. *Dinner.*

I run for the oven, turning it off, and open the door. The smoke detector starts blaring, and I make a face, fanning the smoke away. The pizza is charred.

"Mommy, what's stinky?" Maddie asks, strolling into the kitchen with a stack of paper and her box of crayons, her nose scrunched up.

"Had a bit of a mishap," I say, glaring at the burnt pizza. "Maybe we'll just order some pizza for delivery."

"And chickens!" she declares, climbing onto a chair at the table. "And the breads, too!"

"Pizza, wings, and garlic bread—got it."

I pick up the phone and call the closest pizza place, ordering the whole gauntlet. Can't afford to splurge, but what the hell, right?

After hanging up, I sit down with her, staring at her paper as she draws Breezeo. She's good. Talented. She could be an artist. She could be anything she wanted.

I know, because she's not just my daughter.

His blood flows through her veins, too.

He was the dreamer. The doer. The believer.

When he wasn't high, when he wasn't drunk, when he wasn't so utterly screwed up, I saw something in him, something I see when I look at Maddie. The two of them, they have the same soul, they live with the same heart.

And that scares the daylights out of me.

"Mommy, what kinda sick is Breezeo? Where does it hurt?"

"Uh, I'm not sure," I say. "All over, maybe. Johnny—you know, the real guy that plays Breezeo—got hurt by a car when he was helping a girl."

"But he'll get better?"

She looks at me, her eyes guarded.

She's worried about her hero.

I've tried to explain the difference between reality and the movies, to prepare her, just in case, but I'm not sure if she *gets* it.

"He'll get better," I tell her. "Don't worry, sweetheart."

✤ ✤ ✤

"I just… I can't believe this," Bethany says, standing beside me in the aisle as I restock canned goods. She leans against the shelf, nose buried in the latest edition of *Hollywood Chronicles*. The entire thing is dedicated to Jonathan.

Story after story, speculation and theories. Drugs. Alcohol.

Maybe he was feeling suicidal. I have no interest in reading any of that nonsense, but Bethany insists on spilling every nitty-gritty detail while on her lunch break.

"You know, you're supposed to pay for that before you read it," I tell her. "This isn't a library."

She rolls her eyes, flipping the page. "You sound like my mother when you say that."

I make a face. "I'm not that old."

"You sound it."

"Whatever," I mumble. "I'm just saying…"

"You're saying either put up or shut up." She closes the magazine as she pretend-gags. "I've already read about as much as I can take, anyway. Who even buys this junk?"

She does, I think. I've seen her buying copies.

She's quiet for a moment as I work before she asks, "You don't believe any of it, do you?"

"Believe what?"

"Any of this," she says, waving the paper around.

"I believe my opinion doesn't really matter."

"But where Johnny Cunning is concerned, anything is possible, right?"

I cut my eyes at her when she tosses my own words at me. "Right."

She frowns, defeated, and goes back to her register.

I finish what I'm doing, trying to shove all of it out of my mind. When three o'clock comes, I clock out, grabbing a few groceries and heading to checkout. I have to be back here in an hour for inventory, giving me just enough time to see Maddie after school and get her settled at my father's. I pay and am about to leave when I notice the *Hollywood Chronicles* paper tucked beside Bethany's register, meaning she bought it.

"Look, you met Johnny Cunning, right?" I ask. "And he was nice to you?"

"Yes."

"Then that's all that matters, isn't it? Whatever that trash says about him being horrible, you felt different. Don't let some guy sitting behind a computer spinning sensational stories change what you believe."

She smiles.

I don't linger.

I cringe, honestly.

As if to make the moment worse for me, Cher's *Believe* starts playing on the supermarket radio, and I figure that's my cue to leave. The soundtrack to my life needs a serious update. Getting into my car, I drive to my father's house, pulling into his driveway as the school bus arrives. My father's sitting on the front porch in his rocking chair as he stares out at the neighborhood.

"Ah, there's my girl!" he says, shoving to his feet, holding his arms open. Maddie runs to him for a hug, dragging her backpack along the ground.

"Guess what, Grandpa!" she says, not giving him time to guess before she continues. "I seen that Breezeo got sick in an accident, so Mommy told me I could draw him a picture!"

My father's eyes go wide as he shoots me a look.

"I told her we'd find an address and mail it to him," I explain. "You know, like fan mail."

"Makes sense."

"You wanna draw one, Grandpa?" Maddie asks. "I bet mine would be better, but you can try, too."

He scowls at her. "What makes you think yours would be better?"

" 'Cuz I'm best at drawing," she says. "You're good, too, but Mommy can't draw."

"Hey," I say defensively. "I can draw some seriously cool stars."

Maddie dramatically rolls her eyes, making sure I see it, announcing, "That don't count!" before making her way inside.

"You heard the girl," my father says, grinning and nudging me when I join him on the porch. "Your stars don't count, kiddo."

After I get Maddie settled in, sandwiches made for her and

my father as they hunker down at the kitchen table with paper and crayons, a fresh chocolate cream pie sitting on the counter (don't think I didn't notice), I press a kiss to the top of her head. "I've gotta go back to work, sweetheart. I'll see you tonight."

It's starting to drizzle when I head outside. *Ugh*, what is it with all this rain lately? Pulling out my keys, I start off the porch when I sense movement. I turn in the direction of my car, my footsteps coming to an abrupt stop.

My heart drops right to my toes, my stomach knotting. I lose my breath in that instant, caught by surprise when I see the familiar face. *Oh god.* Everything in me says run... run... run... get away while you have the chance... but I can't even move.

He's wearing jeans and a black t-shirt, a hat on his head. A black leather jacket is draped over his shoulders, his right arm tucked into a sling. His skin is battered and bruised, but it's him.

Jonathan Cunningham.

He's wearing sunglasses, so I can't see his eyes, but I can feel his gaze clawing at my skin. He doesn't speak, looking about as tense at the moment as I feel. My insides are wound tight. My chest hurts as I inhale sharply.

"Hey," he says after a moment of strained silence, that simple word enough to make me woozy.

"What do you want?" I ask, sparing a greeting, my tone harsher than I mean it to be.

"I just thought..." He glances past me, at the house. "I thought maybe—"

"No," I say, that word flying from my lips.

He sighs, his chest rising and falling as he lowers his head. "Can we at least talk?"

"You want to talk."

"Just a conversation," he says. "That's all I'm asking for. Just a minute of your time."

"To talk."

"Yes."

So much of me wants to say no again. The bitterness that

72

has rooted deep inside of me yearns to shut him down. But I can't, as much as I might think I want to… I can't say no without at least listening to him. Because this isn't about me, regardless of how personal it all feels. It's about that little girl inside the house, pouring her soul into a picture for a man she still thinks is a hero.

"Please?" he asks, encouraged by my silence, by the fact that I haven't told him to leave yet. "Take pity on a banged up guy?"

"You want my pity?"

"I want anything you're willing to offer me."

"Look, I can't do this right now," I say, stepping off the porch and onto the walkway. "I'm going to be late."

"Then afterward," he says. "Or tomorrow. Or the next day. Whenever you decide. Whenever is good for you. I'll be there."

I'll be there. How many times have I yearned to hear those words? I don't even know if he means them.

I slowly approach, pausing beside my car, a mere few feet separating the two of us. "I get off work tonight at nine. If you've got something to say to me, you can say it then, but for now…"

He takes a step back, nodding. "You need me to leave."

"Please."

I slip past him, climbing into the driver's seat of my car, watching in the rearview mirror as he hesitates before walking away. He leaves on foot, his steps slow. I don't know where he came from. I don't know where he's going. I don't know what he expects from me.

I don't know why my heart's racing.

I don't know why I feel like crying.

I drive to work after he's gone and get there a few minutes late, but nobody says anything about it. I'm lost in my head, distracted, wondering what he's doing and what he could be planning to say. I'm not sure words exist that can make any of this better, but there are a few that could make things worse.

"Kennedy!"

I flinch and turn toward the sound of Bethany's voice in the doorway to the stockroom. "What?"

"I've been standing here talking to you for like five minutes and you weren't even listening." She laughs. "Anyway, I just wanted to say goodnight."

"Leaving early tonight?"

"More like late."

"I thought you got off at nine?"

"I did," she says, glancing at her phone as it starts ringing. "Well, my ride is here, so I'm out!"

Confused, I glance at the clock. It's almost nine-thirty. I lost track of time. Shoving everything aside, I clock out, avoiding conversation with Marcus. I need to get back to my father's house before Jonathan shows up.

Halfway to my car, my footsteps falter when I spot him. He's here. Jonathan is perched on the hood of my car in the darkened parking lot, his head lowered, the hat shielding his face from view.

He hasn't seen me yet. I approach, studying him as I do. If you want to see someone's true colors, take a peek at who they are when they think they're alone.

He's fidgety, can't seem to sit still. Nervous, I think. Anxious. Or maybe he's just high. I'm almost right in front of him when he finally notices. He tenses as he stands up.

No sunglasses this time, but he's not meeting my gaze.

"How do you know where I work?"

His eyes lower, like he's ogling my chest, so I glance down and roll my eyes at myself. Work uniform. Duh. I'm a walking advertisement for the Piggly Q.

"I probably shouldn't have shown up here, but I was worried you might try to avoid me," he admits. "That you'd blow me off."

"So you weren't going to give me the chance?"

He laughs awkwardly. "Guess you can say that."

"Yeah, well, that's not me. I told you we could talk, so here I am."

"I appreciate it," he says, still fidgeting, his attention on the parking lot. "I, uh... I didn't really think I'd make it this far. I

74

figured you'd shut me down right away, run me out of town with my tail tucked between my legs like every other time."

"Don't do that," I say as I cross my arms over my chest. "Don't act like I'm the bad guy here."

"No, you're right, I didn't mean…" He sighs as he trails off, rubbing the back of his neck with his left hand. Silence festers between us for a moment. It's so quiet I can hear crickets chirping in the distance. "Do you think we could go somewhere? Sit down for a bit somewhere more private?"

"Look at me," I say, ignoring his question, because he hasn't made eye contact with me *yet*. "I need you to look at me, Jonathan."

He doesn't.

Instead, he sits back down on the hood of my car, mumbling, "Jonathan. It's been a long time since anybody has called me that."

"Oh, right," I say, unlocking the driver's side door, because I don't have it in me to stand here and play games with him. "Johnny Cunning. Almost forgot that's who you are now."

"I'm still the same person," he says quietly.

"And who exactly *is* that?" I ask. "Are we talking about Speaker Cunningham's son? The dreamer, the believer, the one who never let anything hold him back? Or maybe we're talking about the alcoholic. You know, the cokehead."

"I don't do that anymore."

"Why should I believe you?"

"Because it's the truth." His left hand slips into his pocket to pull something out. It reflects the parking lot lights as he holds it up—a shiny bronze coin, not much bigger than a quarter.

A sobriety chip.

I don't know what to say. Everything gets quiet again. My fingertips brushing against his when I take it from him. It's solid metal, a triangle etched in the face of it, the Roman numeral I in the center with '*recovery*' written along the bottom.

One year sober.

"People saw you coming out of a bar last week."

"That doesn't mean I drank. I wanted to, but I didn't. I won't." He pauses, his voice quieter when he says, "I can't."

I want to believe him.

I wish I could.

Once upon a time, I believed everything that flowed from this man's lips, but it's hard to give his words any weight after what we went through.

"Then why won't you look at me?" I ask. "You say that, you want me to believe it, yet you won't even look me in the eyes."

"Because I've fucked things up with you," he says. "Do you know how hard it is to face you right now? I know nothing can erase what I've done, but I need you to know how sorry I am."

Sorry.

It isn't the first time he's apologized. He does it every single time. But he was messed up then, *always*, and I'm not sure if he is right now, because the sobriety chip weighs heavy in my hand but his eyes still won't meet mine.

"I'm sorry for the way I hurt you," he says. "Sorry for everything I did that led us to this point. And I get it, you know, if you hate me. Wouldn't blame you at all. But I just need to tell you… I need you to know… that even when I was completely fucked up, I never once stopped loving you."

Those words, they rip the air from my lungs. I clench my hands into fists, the bronze coin digging into my palm.

"I don't expect you'll believe that." He shoves up from my car, his eyes finally meeting mine, and they're bright blue and so clear, but it only lasts a few seconds before his gaze returns to the ground. "But that's not the point. Point is, I'm not perfect, but I'm doing the best I can. I don't know shit about being a father, but I hope you'll give me the chance to try. Tomorrow… the next day… someday… whenever it is, I'll be there."

He starts to walk away with that, like he's said all he can and he has nothing more to offer.

"Jonathan," I call out. "Your chip."

"Keep it."

"What?"

"I know how I'm doing. I don't need a token to tell me, but maybe you do, so keep it."

I stare down at the coin in the glow of the streetlight. I don't know what to think. I don't know what to say. I don't know where he's going or how long he really plans to stay.

At the moment, I don't know much of anything, except that he's here, in front of me, telling me everything I've yearned to hear for a long, long time, and I'm letting him walk away like it all means nothing.

"Jonathan," I call out again.

He pauses and glances over his shoulder at me.

"I, uh… I'm glad you're okay," I say. "I saw about the accident, about what you did, helping that girl, and I just… I'm glad you're okay."

He smiles slightly, a familiar smile, one that's filled with so much sadness. "I'm going to stick around for a while, lay low in town. I'm staying over at the Landing Inn."

"Mrs. McKleski's place?" I ask. "She rented to *you*?"

A light laugh escapes him. "She wasn't thrilled about it, but I needed somewhere private. Took some convincing and one hell of a security deposit to get her to go along with it."

"I bet," I say, imagining how the woman must've looked when he showed up, seeking out sanctuary.

"So, that's where I'll be," he says. "If you're looking for me."

He doesn't wait around for a response, limping away. It's a little over a mile from where I work to where he's going. Memories of my mother's voice nag at me, the angel on my shoulder, telling me I should've offered him a ride, but instead, I listen to the devil, sounding a hell of a lot like my father when he says, 'Never get in a car with a stranger.'

I'm still not sure who he is right now.

✾ ✾ ✾

Maddie's asleep when I get to my father's house, sprawled out on her back on the couch. My father is sitting at the kitchen table, sipping a cup of coffee—decaf. He looks up when I walk in, eyes following me until I drop down in a chair across from him.

Crayons and papers are scattered along the tabletop, an envelope dead center of it all, addressed to *'Breezeo'* in bright red. The return address says *Maddie at Grandpa's*. It's not sealed, but I can tell she tried, a stamp crookedly slapped in the corner, upside down.

I pick the envelope up and pull out the sloppily folded paper, gazing at it. It's a 'get well' card, the words written in capitals up top, a frowny-face drawing of Breezeo below it. She drew herself beside him, smiling, handing him what looks like a bunch of yellow flowers, a short message written below that.

I saw you got sick in a accident. You should get better! And you should come back cuz Mommy says nobody always is gone. It will make you happy and me too. Love, Maddie

Sighing, I fold the paper back up, shoving it away, setting the envelope down on the table. My father's watching me, still sipping his coffee. Waiting me out, I can tell. He probably spent all evening helping her make that, telling her how to spell all the words.

"Jonathan showed up tonight," I say. "Wanted to talk."

"And did you?"

I reach into my pocket for the coin he gave me, sliding it across the table to my father. He picks it up, letting out a low whistle, a peculiar look flickering across his face as he stands up. *Pride.* That probably shouldn't surprise me. I shouldn't be surprised about any of this, but I am.

Strolling across the kitchen, he sets his coffee cup in the sink before leaning back against the counter, staring at the coin. Not far from where he stands, a set of keys hang on a hook, a similar coin affixed to them, converted into a keychain. *Twenty years sober.*

My father spent the first few years of my life struggling with alcohol. I only have vague memories of that time. He got clean before it was too late to be a dad, he always said, and I know that's

78

what he's thinking about right now.

"You're looking lost again, kiddo," he says as I start cleaning up the mess on the table, shoving the crayons back into the box.

"I'm feeling it," I admit.

He doesn't offer me any advice. I've never been good at listening to it. Had I taken his advice years ago, I would've never ended up in this situation. But I have no regrets, despite everything, and he knows that. Regardless of what happened, Maddie came out of it, and she's worth every moment of heartache.

"We all do what we have to," my father says, setting the coin down on the table in front of me. "I'm heading to bed."

"Thank you," I say, "for watching Maddie."

"Anytime," he says. "My girls are my everything. Wouldn't have it any other way."

SIX

JONATHAN

There's this thing about paparazzi—they're everywhere. Airports, stores, sitting outside of houses, lurking around hotel hallways and scoping out sets. I've caught them climbing trees to look in windows and digging through bags of trash. For *what?* Who knows? But it's a fact of life for someone like me—they're always around, always watching, and nine times out of ten, they're fucking *mean.*

I've been in Bennett Landing for twenty-four hours now. It's the first time in a long time I've gone an entire day without being ambushed. But as I step through the door of Landing Inn after ten o'clock in the evening, I get that intuitive feeling that eyes are watching.

Glancing through the foyer, I see McKleski coming out of the kitchen. Her stern expression aims my way. "Mr. Cunningham."

I nod in greeting, warding off a cringe when she calls me that. "Ma'am."

"It's late," she says. "Have you eaten dinner?"

I shake my head.

"Well, don't expect *me* to cook for you," she says. "You want to eat, show up at a decent hour."

"Yes, ma'am," I say quietly as she stalks off to do whatever it is she does when she's not tending to guests, since I'm her only one. Convincing her to let me stay here had been hard enough. When she realized I was renting the *entire* inn, indefinitely, meaning she wouldn't have anybody else, she nearly threw me out on my ass.

Only reason she didn't was because I look pathetic.

"And keep the noise down," she hollers. "I'm heading to bed."

"Yes, ma'am," I say again, strolling to the kitchen. I don't flick on the light. There's enough of a glow from a few nightlights for me to see where I'm going. I haven't eaten much since the accident. Hell, if I'm being honest, I haven't had an appetite in years.

Opening the fridge door, I see a small platter on the top shelf, holding a few sandwiches, covered in plastic wrap. A scrap of paper rests on top, the words 'you're welcome' scribbled on it.

Grabbing a sandwich, I head upstairs, taking a bite as I go, hearing McKleski shout from her room, "You get crumbs on the carpet, you're vacuuming!"

"Yes, ma'am," I mumble as I shake my head, still chewing. I've never been one to worry about things like karma, but I have a damn funny feeling I'm being hit with a hefty dose of it here.

It's morning.

The sun is shining.

Bright light spills through the open blinds covering the windows, streaming through the thin white curtains, warming the room. I haven't slept more than a few minutes here or there, short bursts that felt like mere seconds as my eyes fell closed, before reality shook me back awake—the reality of being back in this town, the reality of having seen *her* again.

There's a knock on the bedroom door, but I ignore it. It's just shy of eight a.m., too early for me to deal with whatever bullshit is on today's agenda. Another knock, and then the door flings open. I drape my left arm over my eyes and let out a groan when McKleski barges in.

"You've got a visitor," she says.

"Nobody even knows I'm here."

"Somebody does or they wouldn't be here to see you, huh?"

She walks out, leaving the door open. I lay in silence for a moment before moving my arm. *Visitor.* Only one person knows

I'm in town.

Kennedy.

Shoving to my feet, I stagger from the room and make my way downstairs. She's standing in the foyer, dressed in a work uniform, looking nervous. She glances up at me when she notices I'm here, a look on her face that makes my chest feel so fucking heavy. Distrust shines from her eyes, always guarded now, like she's just waiting.

Waiting for me to fuck up.

Waiting for me to hurt her.

"Hey," I say, pausing in the foyer in front of her. "I didn't expect to see you again so soon."

"Yeah, well, you know," she mumbles, not finishing her thought, averting her gaze and looking all around me, like she searching for some sort of *out*.

"Do you wanna sit down?" I offer, motioning toward the den area, pretty sure McKleski wouldn't mind.

"No, I can't stay. I just have something to give you."

"Okay."

She stands there, quiet for a moment, biting the inside of her cheek like she used to do when we were kids. *Kids.* I still think of us that way sometimes. Or well, *me*, anyway. She grew up way too fast, but me? Never quite made it past being that stupid eighteen-year-old with little morals and big dreams.

Reaching into her back pocket, she pulls out an envelope, red crayon scribbled along the outside.

My stomach drops. "Is that…?"

She nods. I don't even have to finish the question. Carefully, she holds the envelope out, her voice soft when she says, "I told her we'd mail it, but since you're here…"

"Thank you," I say, staring down at it. It's addressed to *Breezeo*. "Does she…?"

"No," she says, picking up what I can't bring myself to finish. "She doesn't know you're her father. She, uh… she thinks heroes are real, no matter how many times I explain they're just people, and she looks at you like you're one of them. She's too young to see you any other way. Which is why..."

She trails off. I know where it's going. Which is why it's so hard for her to give me that chance, because if I turn out to be anything *but* that hero, it's going to crush her. And I know she doesn't mean that in a theatrical sense. Nobody expects me to wear the suit and turn fucking invisible. But I've got one hell of a track record when it comes to disappointing people.

"I get it," I say. "And I know it's a lot, asking for your trust..."

"But you're not going away this time."

"No."

I figure that might piss her off, me pushing for this, but she lets out a deep breath, her posture relaxing. "Well, I should get to work. I just wanted to drop that off."

"Oh, yeah, okay."

After she's gone, I open the envelope and pull out the piece of paper, looking at it. She drew me a picture. I read her words and can feel my chest tightening, my eyes burning, but goddamn it, I'm grinning like a fool. I can't help it.

"You look like the cat that caught the canary," McKleski says, popping up in the foyer, eavesdropping.

"Yeah, she dropped this off," I say, waving the paper at her. "It's from Madison."

"Ah, little Maddie," she says. "A bit of a handful, that kid, but what do you expect? Look at her parents."

She gives you the comic books on a Wednesday afternoon.

It's after school, and you're standing out front, waiting to be picked up, when she pulls the thick stack of comics from her bag. She's been carrying them around with her for three days, gathering the nerve to approach you.

You're different this week. She senses it. You're quieter, withdrawn—yet, somehow your presence feels larger than ever. There's anger in your eyes and tension in your jaw. You've barely even looked at her. You barely look at *anyone*.

She shoves the comics at you, and you stare at them, confused. A moment passes before there's recognition. You mumble, "Thanks."

That's it.

You're gone a minute later.

You don't come to school the next day.

Friday afternoon, you show up at lunchtime. You walk right through the front door of the school, not bothering to check-in at the office. You stroll through the halls, bypassing the cafeteria, instead heading for the library, where *she* is. She always spends her lunch hour among the tall stacks of books, never eating or being with other people.

She's sitting alone at a long wooden table, nose buried in her notebook. You approach her, asking, "What are you writing?"

Right away, she slams the notebook closed, dropping her pen on top of it. She stares at you, not answering that question.

You drop the stack of comic books on the table. Her attention turns to them as she asks, "Did you even read any of them?"

"Read *all* of them," you say, pulling the chair out beside her, but you don't sit down in it. No, instead you slide up onto the table, sitting there with your sneaker-clad feet planted on the chair. You're not wearing the black shoes that go with your uniform. "They were better than I expected. Kind of pissed I have to wait to see how it ends."

"Now you know how I feel," she says, fiddling with the comics, putting them in order. "I'm surprised you read them."

"I told you I wanted to."

"I thought you were just humoring me."

"Why would I do that?"

"Because that's what everyone does," she says. "I don't know if you've noticed, but I don't fit in around here. People aren't mean, but they aren't nice, either. They just tolerate my presence."

"Well, I don't know if *you've* noticed," you counter, "but I'm not their favorite person, either. Some of them hate me. Most ignore me. Used to be they humored me, but now? Hell, look at me. I could sit here like this all day and nobody would say a word, like I'm invisible."

"Like Breezeo," she says. "You've disappeared."

You nod. "That's how it feels."

She smiles. "I don't know if it makes a difference, but I see you."

Silence falls between the two of you. It isn't awkward. It almost feels *comfortable*. She starts tinkering with the pen on top of her notebook. You stare at it for a moment. "Are you not going to tell me what you were writing?"

She shakes her head.

"You write in that notebook all the time."

It isn't a question, but she answers, anyway. "Almost every day."

"What, is it a journal? Like a diary or something?" you ask, and her cheeks turn pink as she lowers her head. "Ha! It is, isn't it? Have you written anything about me?"

You reach for the notebook, but she snatches it away. The pink on her cheeks is full-blown red now. "It's not a *diary*. It's a story."

"A story," you say. "What kind of story?"

"The kind you write," she says. "Or, well, the kind I do. Because I am. I'm writing a story."

She fumbles her way through that explanation.

You laugh. "Yeah, but what *kind*? Drama? Action? Mystery?"

"All of that," she says. "It's a bit of everything."

"Does that include romance?"

She doesn't answer, throwing a question back instead. "Why are you so interested?"

"Because I am," you say. "Would you rather I just humored you?"

"No."

She's quick with that answer.

She's blushing again.

There's noise outside the library. Students roam the halls. Lunchtime is coming to an end.

You shove off of the table, getting to your feet. Looking around, you sigh deeply before your eyes meet hers. "You want to get out of here?"

Her brow furrows. "Get out of the library?"

"No, I mean get out of this hellhole," you say. "My car's parked outside, if you want to go."

She gives you a look, one that says she thinks you're joking, but once you pull a set of keys from your pocket, she realizes you're serious.

"Club meetings are starting," you say. "It's not like you're missing anything. Besides, what's life without a little adventure? Might give you some inspiration for your story. We'll call it a *'fuck your clubs'* field trip."

You walk away.

She hesitates, just a moment, before grabbing her things and following, falling in step beside you. Her eyes dart around the parking lot. "We won't get in trouble, will we?"

"No promises," you say.

Despite your answer, she doesn't waver.

You drive a blue Porsche. It's not as flashy as some of the other cars, but it's enough to make her pause. "Wow."

She's fidgeting as she gets in the car.

You don't waste time driving away.

You head into Albany, going through a drive-thru to grab some lunch. You buy her a sandwich and a chocolate milkshake, although she insists you don't have to—she has no money. Food in hand, you head to a theater in town. You lead her inside, slipping through a back door.

People are everywhere.

A dress rehearsal is in progress. Looks are cast your way, a few people greeting you as they rush past. This isn't your first time coming here. They're confused, though, when they look at her, like her presence is something they can't fathom. She hesitates, so you grab her hand and pull her through, letting go once you're clear of the crowd.

She stares at her hand as the two of you take seats out in the empty theater. You eat and chat and watch the rehearsal. A Dr. Seuss musical. She sips her milkshake, laughing at the *Cat in the Hat* causing chaos on stage, and you get so lost in the moment that time slips away.

"We need to go," you tell her. "It's three o'clock."

Even rushing, you barely make it back to the school before the day is over. You park your car, but you don't get very far. An administrator is lurking. Hastings saw you leaving together and tattled.

"Cunningham. Garfield." The man looks between you. "My office. *Now.*"

Twenty minutes later, the two of you are sitting in that office when both fathers show up. They walk in together, neither man smiling as the administrator explains the situation.

Your father says nothing. He just stands there, listening.

Her father, on the other hand, is fuming. His nostrils flare as he yells, "What the *hell* were you thinking? *Skipping?* Do you know what it costs me to send you here? And how many times do I have to tell you never to get in a car with a stranger? Are you crazy?"

She stares down at her hands, biting her cheek, not answering his questions.

Three days of detention. That's the punishment.

You all walk out together.

It's sudden, out of nowhere, as your father's calm mask slips. Right in front of the school, he says not a word, but he swings, hitting you in the chest with a closed fist. It's hard enough that the girl hears it from a few feet in front of you. Hard enough that her father hears it, too.

They both turn to look.

The blow knocks the air from your lungs. You fight to catch your breath, grabbing your chest, but you're not surprised at all. This isn't some fluke.

"Go straight home," your father says, his voice calm, even as he gets right in your face. "I hope you know this isn't over. We'll deal with it later."

With that, he walks away.

You linger a moment, your gaze drifting to her, before you leave.

You don't know this, but that girl? She cries the entire way home from school. She isn't crying because she got in trouble. It isn't out of guilt or shame. Her tears have nothing to do with herself. She cries for you, because of the look she saw on your face when you walked away. There's anger in your eyes again and tension in your jaw, and now she knows what that means.

SEVEN

KENNEDY

"*Surprise!*"

I'm caught off guard as that word rings out behind me, startlingly close in the aisle. Spinning around, eyes wide, I nearly slam right into a lurking body, all six-foot-three of him wearing a straight black suit, looking the epitome of tall, dark, and handsome. "*Whoa.*"

"Didn't scare you, did I?" he asks. "You looked like you were in your own little world. Almost didn't want to interrupt."

"Oh, no, I'm just... surprised to see you," I admit, gazing at him. *Drew.* "What are you doing here?"

"Came to see you," he says. "Haven't heard from you since you cancelled our last date. I tried calling, but figured you were busy with work, so I thought I'd stop by, maybe buy you lunch."

I frown. "I just took a break."

"Pity," he says. "Maybe dinner?"

"Maybe," I say. "I'll see if I can get somebody to watch Maddie."

"Or you could bring her," he suggests, holding his hands up defensively when I cut my eyes at him. "Or not."

"I'm sure my dad won't mind," I say. "If he's busy, I know Meghan will be happy to do it."

"Meghan," he says, making a face at the mention of her.

"Oh, don't be that way." I nudge him, laughing. "She's been a life-saver. I don't know what I'd do without her."

"I do," he says. "I know what *I'd* do without her."

"Be nice."

He mock salutes me.

Drew is, well… what can I say about him? He isn't the easiest person to warm up to, but once you get to know him, he can be kind of charming. Sarcastic, a bit rash, but unshakably determined. We've been acquainted for years, but it wasn't until recently, when I ran into him while out somewhere with Meghan, that I opened myself up to the possibility of anything happening between us.

It makes sense, you know. I'm busy. He's busy. He's one of the few people that I don't feel compelled to hide my secrets from.

He hates my best friend, though, so that's a big strike against him, and the feeling is mutual, but that might have something to do with the fact that Meghan's as protective as bulletproof armor.

"I'll call you," I tell him, "as soon as I know."

"Good." Reaching over, he nudges my chin. "I'll see you."

I wait until he's gone before pulling out my phone, shooting a text to Megan quickly, since I'm on the clock. **Any chance you're free to watch Maddie tonight so I can steal some adult time?**

The bubble pops up, her response coming through. **I can be there by 6. Who's the lucky prick?**

Laughing, I type '**Who do you think?**' before shoving my phone back in my pocket, not bothering to look at it when it vibrates with a message, knowing it'll be a stream of disgruntled emojis with a few choice curse words thrown in—you know, *for emphasis.*

☆ ☆ ☆

There's a knock at the apartment door, but before I can answer it, the door flings right open and in waltzes Meghan. She's nearly six feet tall in her shiny red stilettos, at odds with the drab gray dress suit she wears, like she's not sure if she's going to work or heading out to a party. *That's Meghan for you.* Bright red lips and perfectly messy blonde hair, the kind that looks like she's doesn't care, but I know she spent an hour in the bathroom getting it that way.

Her blue eyes narrow, pointed right at me. She's trying hard to look mad, but she doesn't have it in her, cracking right away as she makes a face. "Really? *Andrew?*"

"Could be worse," I say.

"Could also be better," she counters. "Wouldn't be hard, you know. Few people are *worse* than Andrew."

Before I can argue, Maddie runs out of her bedroom. "Aunt Meghan!"

"Hey, candy-doodle pumpkin-bread," she says, scooping Maddie up and swinging her around in circles as she slathers kisses all over her face. "How's my favorite little munchkin doing today?"

Maddie giggles, trying to ward off the kisses. "Guess what, Aunt Meghan?"

"What?" she asks as she stops twirling, now swaying. *Dizzy.*

"Breezeo got in a accident, so I made him a card and Mommy says she got it to him!"

"Is that right?" Meghan asks, raising her eyebrows as she regards me, setting Maddie back down. "Mommy gave it to *Breezeo*, did she?"

"Yep." Maddie turns to me. "Right, Mommy?"

"Right," I say, giving her a smile, knowing I'm about to have to explain in a few seconds, so it's best she gets out of here. "Why don't you go draw Meghan a picture? I'm sure she'd love one. Wouldn't want her getting jealous."

After Maddie runs off, I head for the kitchen, Meghan tromping along behind me. "You gonna spill or do I have to call for a special prosecutor?"

"I think she summed it up nicely," I say, scouring through the fridge and the cabinets, pulling out stuff to throw together a quick dinner. "She drew him a picture. I gave it to him."

"How?"

I cut my eyes at her and continue what I'm doing.

"*Son of a bitch,*" she growls, dropping down into a chair at the kitchen table. "He showed up again, didn't he? He actually had the balls to show his face."

"He said he wanted to talk."

"So you talked to him?"

"Yes."

Meghan covers her face with her hands. "You're right. It could be worse. Could be much worse, so go and enjoy your night. Because compared to *that*, Andrew is perfect."

"I wouldn't say all that," I mumble.

She shakes her head, eyeing me warily as I preheat the oven. "What are you doing?"

"Throwing something together for dinner."

"Why? Don't you have a *date*?"

"Yeah, but Maddie hasn't eaten yet, and Drew won't be here for an hour, so…"

"So that gives you just enough time to get ready," she says. "I can handle dinner, no big deal."

"Are you sure?"

"Positive," she says. "Go put on something that'll make him want to ravish you, you know, if you're into all that. *Gag.*"

Laughing, I head to my bedroom to change, throwing on a pair of jeans and a pink blouse before taking it right back off. *Ugh.* I change three times before settling on a pair of black leggings and a purple tunic, heading back out to the kitchen to Meghan. "How's this look?"

She casts a glance my way before saying, "Unless he's taking you to *Planet Fitness* for some Pilates, it's a *no* from me."

Rolling my eyes, I head back to the bedroom to try again, putting on some flared khakis and a flowery flowing top.

The second that Meghan sees me, she makes a face. "Time-traveling to Woodstock?"

"Funny," I mutter, going back to my bedroom yet again, putting on skinny jeans and a black top.

"Now you're not even *trying*." Meghan glares at me. "Don't you have that dress still? You know, that black one with the lace?"

"This isn't a big thing, Meghan. He's taking me to dinner."

"Yeah, well, if you wear the black dress, you might end up being dessert."

I stare at her for a moment before shrugging. *What the heck?* Heading into the bedroom, I pull the dress out from the back of my closet, not giving it too much thought before yanking it on. I run my fingers through my hair, letting it do whatever it wants, and am in the bathroom putting on a bit of makeup when Maddie pops up in the doorway. "You look pretty, Mommy."

"Thank you, sweetheart," I say, gazing at her in the reflection of the mirror as she watches me, her expression curious. I pat the counter beside the sink, inviting her to join me, and she climbs up to sit on it as I grab a tube of lip-gloss, strawberry flavored. She puckers up, and I put some on her, smiling as I do it. "You know I love you, right, pretty girl? I love you more than *everything*. More than the trees and the birds and the sky. More than even pepperoni pizza and *Harlequin* novels."

"What's a Harley-Quinn novel?"

"Nothing you'll need to know about for a long, long time," I say, putting the lip-gloss away. "Just know that I don't love them nearly as much as I love you."

She kicks her feet, grinning. "I love you, too."

"More than chocolate ice cream and Saturday mornings?"

"Uh-huh," she says. "More than colors and money!"

"No way."

"And the Yoo-Hoo drinks and *Happy Meal* toys."

"Whoa."

"And even more than Breezeo!"

Eyes wide, I look at her. That's some serious commitment coming from my superhero-loving girl. "You know, you can love us the same."

"Nuh-uh," she says, shaking her head. "You're my mommy, so I love you more."

I press my pointer finger to the tip of her nose. "Well, I sure appreciate it, but remember that it's okay if you ever do."

Pulling her off the counter, I set her on her feet and glance at the time—five minutes until six. "I've gotta get going soon, sweetheart."

"Can I come?"

"Not tonight," I tell her, "but maybe next time. You get to hang out with Aunt Meghan instead."

She pouts her lips, the sight of her expression making me want to call Drew and cancel, because screw doing *anything* that makes her look so disappointed. But she recovers, wrapping her arms around me in a hug before running off.

I make it out to the kitchen just as there's a knock on the door. Seven o'clock on the dot. I'm still barefoot.

"Here," Meghan says, kicking her shoes off in my direction. "Nothing says *fuck me* quite like red stilettos."

I slip them on, almost tripping as I scurry to the door. I pull it open when he again starts to knock, coming face-to-face with Drew, still in that black suit from earlier.

"Hey," I say, "you're right on time."

"Always am," he says, offering me the faintest hint of a smile before he glances over my shoulder into the apartment. "Hello, Meghan. Nice to see you."

Her voice is curt as she responds, "Andrew."

"You ready?" he asks, looking back at me. "I thought we could try that new Mexican place in Poughkeepsie."

"*Chipotle?*" Meghan calls out. "That place isn't new, but I totally wouldn't mind if you brought me back a burrito bowl."

His face flickers with annoyance. "I'm referring to the restaurant on Main."

"Ah, the one with all the margaritas," she says with a laugh. "You know what they say about tequila…"

I shove Drew further outside, joining him, shouting goodbye to Meghan before she can say anything about getting naked. Drew starts to walk away, glancing over his shoulder to make sure I'm following.

"You want me to drive?" I offer.

He laughs at that. Yeah, he *laughs*. "I think I can handle it."

Drew drives a brand new Audi, shiny black with pristine leather. Quiet indie rock plays from the speakers as he fills the silence, talking about work. He finished up an internship somewhere and was hired to... do something.

I don't know. I'm not really listening.

Something to do with politics and the law.

It's not that long of a drive across the river. The restaurant is busy, but we're able to get a table without having to wait. Drew pulls out my chair, pushing it back in when I sit down, being a chivalrous gentleman. I laugh when I think about that.

"What's so funny?" he asks, sitting down across from me.

"Just remembering how much of a jerk you were when we first met."

"I wasn't that bad, was I?"

"You *never* spoke to me."

The waiter approaches, and I ask for water, while Drew orders a beer.

Once the waiter walks away, Drew says, "Pretty sure you didn't speak to me, either."

"Because you were a jerk."

He laughs.

Then he starts talking again.

I do my best to pay attention, chiming in at all the right places. I know the conversation like the back of my hand. *Politics.*

It makes things easy, though, but Drew's already easy. Things feel simple around him. *Familiar.* He's easy, and he's kind, and I keep thinking that he's handsome, but beyond that, nothing.

No tingles. No butterflies. No goofy grins.

He doesn't make me feel like I'm in a tailspin.

We eat.

Drew drinks.

I stick to water.

"Come on, let's get out of here," he says after he pays the check, refusing my money when I offer to pay my share. *Thank god,* because I couldn't afford it.

He takes my hand, and I let him. He leads me out to the parking lot, and I don't put up a fight. But the moment he tries to get me in the car, I resist. I wouldn't say he's drunk, but he's been drinking, and that'll never be something I risk.

"It's late," I lie—it's barely nine o'clock. "I can take a taxi home and save you the trip."

He looks confused, not sure how to react. I know he was hoping for more out of this night, and I could go along with it, but...

"Go home," I tell him, "but drive safe. I'll never forgive you if you wrap your car around a tree."

"You sure about this?" he asks, looking conflicted. "I can take you home."

"Positive." Leaning over, I kiss him, the tiniest peck. "Don't worry about me. I'll be fine."

EIGHT

JONATHAN

"How does that make you feel?"

The million-dollar question, one I've heard countless times this past year. I get asked some infuriating shit, day after day, night after night, but nothing gets under my skin quite like that one. "How do you *think* it makes me feel?"

"Deflection helps no one, you know," he says. "It's a defense mechanism that keeps us from acknowledging our problems."

"Don't shrink me, Jack," I say. "If I wanted to be psychoanalyzed, I'd be talking to my actual fucking shrink right now."

"Yeah, okay, so you feel like shit," he says. "*Less* than shit. You're dog shit on the bottom of a shoe that's being scraped off on a curb because nobody wants anything to do with shit on their shoe."

"Pretty much."

"That sucks."

I laugh at the casual way he says that. "Remind me again why I called you?"

"Because you'd give your left nut for a drink right now and you need someone to call you on your bullshit."

Sighing, I run my left hand down my face.

How right he is…

It's a quiet night in Bennett Landing. Most nights seem to be. The sun goes down and the town gets dark, and I'm left with nothing but my thoughts, which is a damn dangerous place to be. Last time I felt this isolated was back in rehab when I was struggling to get clean. I like to think I've made some big strides since then, but some nights test me.

I've been wandering around outside for the past hour, strolling toward the waterfront, through Landing Park beside the inn, spilling my secrets through the phone to a jackass that sums them up as 'sucking'.

"We all have bad nights, man. You know that," Jack says. "Try to remember why you're there. Drinking sure as hell won't help you make amends."

He's right. Of course he is.

But Jesus Christ, I *would* give my left nut to drown in a bottle of whiskey right now.

"I'm trying," I say, walking along, glancing up when I reach the small picnic area. My footsteps stall when I catch sight of movement, someone sitting on top of one of the picnic tables, staring out at the water.

I blink, getting a glimpse of her face in the moonlight as Jack starts rambling, telling me to go find a meeting.

I didn't expect anybody to be out here at this hour, but certainly not *her*. "Kennedy?"

She turns my way.

She doesn't look as surprised as I expect her to be, her eyes guarded as they watch me, but her posture is relaxed, so I guess that's something.

"You listening to me, Cunning?" Jack asks. "Or am I wasting my breath?"

"I hear you," I tell him. "I'll see what I can do."

"Good," he says. "I know it's not easy, trusting people, but I think it'll help you."

"Yeah," I mumble. "Look, I gotta go."

"You sure? You okay?"

"Yeah, I'm okay."

"Call me back if you need anything."

"I will."

I end the call. Kennedy is watching me, but she's said nothing yet, so I'm not sure if I should stick around. I'm not sure why she's out here or what she's doing, if she's even *alone*. I don't see anybody else, but that doesn't mean she's not waiting for someone to show up.

"Let me guess," she says after a moment. "Your manager?"

"No." I shove the phone in my pocket. "My sponsor."

"That's nice... I think." She pauses before adding, "Not really sure what to say to that."

"It is what it is." I take a few steps closer, gauging her reaction. "He's a good guy. Doesn't treat me like I'm a star, which I appreciate. He actually thinks my movies are shitty."

She laughs at that—genuinely *laughs*.

"Sorry, I don't mean to laugh at you, but well, that's kind of funny," she says. "I mean, you have to admit they can be a little hokey at times."

"*Hokey.*"

"I've only really watched the first Breezeo, but come on, some of the dialogue they added? *I think there's something wrong with my eyes because I can't take them off of you.* What kind of cheesy crap?"

"Yeah, that one was pretty bad."

"And what was it Maryanne said to him in the hospital, when he first got sick and they were looking for the cure?"

"*Our love will make you better.*"

"That's it!" She rolls her eyes. "*Because it's the most powerful thing in the world.*"

"I liked that one," I admit, taking a chance and climbing up on the picnic table, sitting down beside her. There's some space between us, so we're not touching, but she's so close I can feel her warmth and smell a hint of her perfume. "Their love didn't save him, but it did make him a better person."

"It doesn't matter," she says. "He was laying in a damn hospital bed, he thought he was dying, and *that's* what she says?"

I smile at the cynical tone in her voice, letting her have that one. She has a point. It grows quiet. She's staring out at the water, arms wrapped around her chest like she's holding herself together. She's shivering, so maybe she's cold, or she might be shaking because *I'm* here. I don't know.

"Do you want me to leave?" I ask.

She doesn't answer, eyes flickering to the ground in front of us. It's not a 'no', but it isn't a 'yes', either. I know I should probably leave her alone, not risk pushing her too far, too quickly, but I've missed the fuck out of her these past few years. I don't deserve her time, not in the least, but I'm so desperate for some part of this woman back that I'll steal every second that I can get.

"What are you doing out here, anyway?" she asks quietly. "You don't really have a good streak being in this park after dark."

"With *you*, no less."

She smiles at that.

"Just needed some air," I say. "Couldn't keep sitting in that house, staring at those walls, with that woman always there. Needed to take a break. It's late, so I figured I'd be alone out here."

"Sorry about that…"

"Don't apologize to me," I say, shaking my head. "So, you still hang out here?"

"Sometimes," she says. "Not usually after dark, though. Maddie likes it here, likes playing on the swings, hanging out by the river."

Maddie.

This makes twice in one day she's talked to me about her, twice she's brought up our daughter. I'm trying to not get my hopes up, but after years of slamming face-first into a brick wall, I feel like I might finally be headed in the right direction.

"So she likes the water? I seem to remember you hated it."

"I never *hated* it," she says. "I'm just not a fan of bugs."

"And ducks."

"And ducks," she agrees with a shudder. "Which is funny, because Maddie loves them. She loves coming down here and feeding the ducks every chance she gets. She always worries they're not eating enough. She's, uh…"

"She sounds perfect."

"Yeah," she whispers, "she is."

I don't know what to say, afraid to push her so I just sit here, my eyes scanning her in the darkness. She's wearing a little black dress, a pair of red heels kicked off on the ground by the picnic table.

"You look nice," I tell her.

She glances down at herself, making a face. "I had a date."

"A *date*."

That word is a thump to the chest.

I'm not a fool. I know she probably moved on, and I'd be the worst hypocrite to be upset by that after some of the shit *I* did these past few years in an attempt to numb my feelings for her. She has an entire life outside of me, *without* me, a world she built for herself where I don't even exist, and I don't blame her for it. Not a bit. It's not like I could expect her to sit around and wait. I never asked her to. Never gave her a *reason*. I haven't just been a shitty father; I was also a terrible boyfriend.

But still, there's a flare of jealousy burning in my gut, my shame dousing it like gasoline on a fire.

"You do a lot of that now?" I ask. "Dating?"

She cuts her eyes at me. "Not as much as *you* seem to do."

Touché.

"You've had, what… six, seven girlfriends? Hell, they say you've even got a wife now."

"*They* say, do they?"

"Yes."

"Tell me you don't read that shit, Kennedy. Tell me you don't actually *believe*…"

"I don't know what to believe," she says. "Not that it matters. Your life, it's yours. You'll do whatever it is you want to do. You made that clear a long time ago. But Maddie? *She's* what matters. And I can't have you around her if…"

"I'm not going to hurt her," I say when she trails off. "I

know that's what you're afraid of."

"Yeah, well, didn't think you'd hurt me, either, but the moment I became an inconvenience…"

I want to tell her it's different now. I want to tell her that I've learned my lesson, that I've grown up. I want to tell her that I'll never make those same mistakes again. *I want to tell her she's never been an inconvenience.* I want to tell her a lot of shit, but none of it will make a difference. They're just words, and I've said a lot of words over the years, including a few that have hurt her.

"I'm here," I say. "I'm sober. And for the record, I'm *not* married. I'm not sure where they even got that story, but there was no wedding. Most of what they print is bullshit."

"It doesn't matter."

"It does," I argue. "You're never going to let me see Madison if *that's* the kind of man you think I became, if you believe the shit they say about me is real. I mean, I don't even know what she looks like now. I could pass my daughter on the street and I wouldn't even recognize her. And that's my fault. But the shit they print, if that's what I'm up against? I'm *fucked*."

Closing my eyes, I run a hand through my hair, gripping onto the locks as I let out a long exhale. She says nothing, and after a moment I reopen my eyes, seeing the glow of her cell phone lighting up her face.

I start to say something, to tell her I'll stop bothering her tonight, when her eyes meet mine. She holds the phone out to me. My gaze flickers to the screen.

My heart nearly stops.

It's a picture of a little girl with big blue eyes, dark hair and chubby cheeks, flashing the brightest smile I've ever seen. She's posing, hands on her hips, head cocked to the side. She's a spitting image of her mother, *fuck*, but those eyes are all mine.

"She looks just like you," I say.

"Yeah, well, she acts like you."

I smile at that, grabbing her phone.

"There are a few more pictures on there," she says, "if you

want to look at them."

"You sure?"

She nods.

A *few more* turns out to be one hell of an understatement. It feels like hundreds as I scan through them. I'm getting a brief glimpse of the time I lost—birthdays, holidays, the first day of school. A flipbook of memories I'll never have, the what-could've-been, the what-*should've*-been, the time I would've had if I hadn't been so fucked up. She looks happy. *They* look happy, both of them.

I flip to another picture and pause, stumbling upon another familiar face.

Meghan.

"You see Meghan?" I ask, surprised—although, I shouldn't be. If anybody would be there throughout the years, loyalty unwavering, it would be Meghan.

"All the time," she says. "She's babysitting right now."

"Meghan babysitting? You sure the kid's still alive?"

She laughs and snatches the phone back, pressing a button so the screen goes dark. "I'll have you know, your sister's great with children."

"My sister," I mumble. "Don't let her hear you call her that."

My sister. Another amend I have to make.

She won't make it easy.

"On a scale of one to ten," I say, "how pissed off at me would you say she still is?"

"One to ten? I'd say she's about a seventy-three."

I cringe. "Figures."

"Anyway, I should get going," she says, standing up from the picnic table. "Need to get home before it gets too late."

"Did you drive?" I ask, realizing I haven't seen a car anywhere out here.

"I got dropped off. Figured I'd walk." She hesitates, looking at me, like she isn't sure she wants to continue. "I have an apartment. It's just a few blocks."

"Oh."

Oh. That's all I say, like a fucking idiot, as she grabs the shoes from the ground, not bothering to put them on. She takes a few steps away, barefoot, eyes still guarded.

"Can I walk with you?" I ask.

"I can make it there myself."

"I don't doubt that, but…" I hesitate. "Do you mind? I'd like to walk with you. Not to be some misogynistic asshole, but I just…"

"It's fine," she says. "But you don't have to."

"I know."

We're dancing around the fact that I *want* to, that she's doing me the favor here and not the other way around, but she motions with her head for me to come along, so I shove to my feet and fall in place at her side.

"So, this sponsor of yours," she says as we start to walk.

"Jack."

"Jack," she repeats. "Must be one hell of a guy if he's kept *you* clean."

That should probably offend me, but I laugh. "I wouldn't say he's kept me clean. He helps, but he's not why I'm sober. You are."

"Me?"

"And Madison," I say. "*This.* That's what has kept me clean, not some twenty-five-year-old recovering addict."

She's quiet, her face twisted in concentration, like she's considering my words, but she doesn't seem to be buying it. After a moment, her footsteps stall. We haven't even made it out of the park and she's already stopping.

"What did it?" she asks.

"What do you mean?"

"What makes this time different?"

"I, uh…"

"Most of the stories they print about you might be lies, but I know you've been to rehab a few times, I know they've held interventions and detoxed you but you went right back to it. And we were here. We've *been* here. That hasn't changed, so what did?"

"I don't know," I admit. "The last time I came here... last year... when your mom died, I wanted to be there for you, but I showed up drunk and I knew you were grieving, and you looked at me like..."

"Like what?"

"Like nothing had ever hurt you as much as me being there did," I say. "Up until then, I only saw your anger, but that day I saw your fear, like you were afraid of how much more pain I was going to cause you, when I wanted nothing more than to make it all better."

She starts walking again, her voice quiet when she says, "I wish I could believe you."

"Yeah," I mumble. "Me, too."

"I'm glad, though," she says. "Whatever did it, I'm glad you're sober, and I hope you stay that way. For Maddie's sake, yeah, because she deserves to know her dad, but for your sake, too. I know I was never enough for you, Jonathan, but I hope you find something that is."

You're back in Drama Club.

You've been back at it for a month.

This is the fourth week in a row you've shown up and participated. *Julius Caesar* bores you, but it's better than nothing. An addict will take whatever hit he can get. Besides, you find becoming someone else for a while therapeutic.

Maybe that's why you love acting so much. Maybe you're tired of being yourself.

The girl still sits in the auditorium every week. Sometimes, she writes. Mostly, she watches. When she's not watching you, you find yourself watching her. Your eyes meet on occasion in the middle, and she always smiles. *Always.*

Somewhere, within the past month, things changed. The two of you grew closer. She kissed you for the first time last week. In the library, during lunch, she just leaned over and did it, making the first move. It was unexpected.

You've stolen kisses from her every day since then.

Well, except *today.*

You're having a bad day.

You mess up a few lines. You're distracted. You've had this look about you all afternoon, like you're not quite there.

"Christ, Cunningham, get it together," Hastings says, running his hands down his face. "If you can't *handle* being Brutus—"

"Fuck you." You cut him off. "Don't act like you're perfect."

"I don't make rookie mistakes," Hastings says. "Maybe if you weren't so preoccupied with trying to screw the new girl, you might—"

BAM.

You shut him up mid-sentence with a punch to the face, your fist connecting hard, nearly knocking him off his feet. He stumbles, stunned, as you go at him again, grabbing the collar of his uniform shirt and yanking him to you. "Shut your fucking mouth."

People come between the two of you, forcing you apart. Hastings storms out, shouting, "I can't deal with him!"

Drama Club comes to a screeching halt.

You stand there for a moment, fists clenched at your side, calming down. You flex your hands, loosening them as you approach the girl. She's watching you in silence, expression guarded.

You sit down near her. There's an empty seat between you today. It's the first time you've not sat right beside her in *weeks*. You're giving her space.

It doesn't take long before Hastings returns, but he isn't alone. The administrator waltzes in behind him. The man heads for you, expression stern. "Cunningham, give me one good reason why I shouldn't expel you."

"Because my father gives you a lot of money."

"*That's* what you have to say?"

"Is that not a good reason?"

"You punched a fellow student!"

"We were just acting," you say. "I'm Brutus. He's Caesar. It's to be expected."

"Brutus stabs him. He doesn't throw punches."

"I was improvising."

The girl laughs when you say that. She tries to stop herself, but the sound comes out, and the administrator hears it, his attention shifting to her.

"Look, it won't happen again," you say, drawing the focus back to you. "Next time, I'll stab him and be done with it."

"You better watch yourself," the administrator says, pointing his finger in your face. "One more incident and you're gone for good. Understand?"

"Yes, sir."

"And rest assured, your father *will* be hearing about this." The administrator's attention shifts back to the girl. "Garfield, some advice? If you want to be successful here, find yourself a new friend, someone with their priorities in check... someone more like Hastings."

Hastings stands in the aisle, rubbing his jaw. Despite the fact that it's going to bruise, he's grinning. *Gloating.*

"Because Cunningham will cause you nothing but trouble," the administrator continues. "And you can do better."

The man walks away. Hastings follows suit. He's afraid to be near you without backup. The two of you have some longstanding rivalry, like Batman and the Joker... *or Breezeo and Knightmare.*

Which one are you, though?

The hero?

The girl shakes her head, doodling on the front of her notebook. "That was awfully rude of him."

"Yeah, well, it's true," you say.

"Is it?"

"I've already gotten you in trouble once," you remind her. "I can pretty much guarantee it won't be the last time it happens."

"Huh, and what about the other part?" she asks. "Is that true, too?"

"Which part?"

"The part where you might be trying to get the new girl

111

naked."

You just look at her. She's still doodling.

"Because if you *are*," she says, "you're doing a pretty crappy job of it. I mean, you haven't even *tried* yet, so..."

She's avoiding looking at you, her cheeks pink. Her doodling is more like absent-minded scribbling, anything to distract herself. She's biting her cheek.

Reaching over, you cover her hand with yours, stopping her before the pen tears a hole through the notebook. She anxiously cuts her eyes at you.

You say nothing right away, holding her gaze, before you lean over, closing the distance, and you kiss her. It's soft, and sweet, and it's *right there*, in front of the entire Drama Club, but you don't care who watches.

"You want to hang out?" you ask, your voice quiet. "Spend some time together outside of this hellhole?"

She nods.

"How about this weekend?"

Tearing a piece of paper from the back of her notebook, she scribbles her phone number down for you to call her after school.

You don't, though—not right away. Your life descends into chaos that afternoon. You don't even have a chance. Your father confronts you about the incident at school, and when you finally get away from him, you have something important to do.

But later that night, long after the sun goes down, you send her a text, asking if there's any way possible you can see her right now. You tell her it's important. It's so late there's a chance she's already in bed, but you get a message back a few minutes later with the location of a park near her house. *I can meet in thirty minutes.*

It takes you about that long to drive there. She's sitting on top of a picnic table when you arrive, staring out at the water, the park edging the bank of the Hudson River. It's the first time you've ever seen her out of her school uniform, so used to the knee—length skirts with the thick tights.

She's wearing pajama pants tonight.

It's dark where she's sitting, the glow of the moonlight surrounding her. You approach, your hands hidden behind your back. "I have a surprise."

"Is it the answers to Monday's Math test? Because if so, you're going to *at least* get to third base for that."

You laugh, standing in front of her. "Which base is third base?"

"Pretty sure it's dry humping."

"Shame," you say. "Could use a good dry hump, but no, that's not it. Although, you could always copy my answers. Just mark a few wrong on purpose, since they might get suspicious if you get a perfect score."

"Right, since you never miss *any*." She playfully rolls her eyes. "So if it's not the answers, what is it?"

You pull your hands out from behind your back. It's a comic book, tucked in a plastic sleeve. Her expression changes as she takes it.

Breezeo: Ghosted
Issue #5 of 5

"Is this...? *Oh my god*, is this what it says it is?"

"The last issue of Breezeo."

"But *how?*" Her eyes meet yours. "This isn't even out yet!"

"Ah, well, I knew a person who knew a person who knew a person," you say. "You know how it is. Pay enough money and you can get anything."

"You must've *really* hated waiting," she says. "*Oh my god,*

Jonathan. I seriously can't believe this. Is it good? Have you read it?"

"No, I didn't read it. I got it for you. Figured you might let me borrow it later, if I'm good to you."

"This is for *me?*" she asks, holding it against her chest. "Like, for real, it's *mine?*"

"Yes," you say. "It's yours."

As soon as you confirm that, she flings herself at you, a full-blown flying leap right off of the picnic table, into your arms. You don't expect it, and she nearly tackles you to the ground. You manage to stay on your feet as she wraps herself around you, legs around your waist, arms around your neck.

She kisses you.

You kiss her back as you take a few steps over to set her down on the edge of the picnic table, but she doesn't let go of you. If anything, she's more encouraged. She drops the comic onto the table and runs her fingers through your hair as she grinds against you.

You groan, pressing into her. You're so hard she can feel it. "Guess I hit third, after all."

"*That?* You knocked that one right out of the park."

You laugh against her lips, still kissing her. "Yeah? You already giving me a home run?"

"It's worth it," she whispers. "You can slide home anytime you want. It's all yours."

The baseball metaphors, yeah, they're stupid, but the meaning behind them gets you worked up. She's giving you the green light to go all the way, and well, what hormone-driven teenage boy is going to say no to *that* invitation?

Your hand slips down the front of her pants, and she gasps, throwing her head back. Your mouth goes to her neck as you drive her wild with your fingertips, asking, "How do you like it?"

She stammers. "I, uh... I don't know..."

"You want it just like this?" you ask, whispering in her ear as she grinds against you, making her own friction, nearly getting herself off. You help her, rubbing harder where she needs it. "I could bend you over the table, hit it from behind. Or we could go to my car, if you want, maybe have you ride me in the passenger seat. Tell me how to make you feel good."

You're a dirty talker. It makes her blush.

"I don't know," she says again. "I, uh... I haven't ever..."

"You mean you've never...?"

She shakes her head.

"Seriously? This is your first time?"

That catches you off guard. You pause what you're doing. You didn't realize she was a virgin.

She groans, shifting her hips. "Oh god, don't stop... *please*..."

You start rubbing again. She's close, so close it would be cruel to stop. Just a few more seconds before she gasps, an orgasm sweeping through her. You don't stop until she relaxes again, but once you try to pull away, she won't let you.

"I want to," she says. "I know you've done this before, and I haven't, but I want to... with *you*."

"Your first time can't be out here," you say. "It can't be bent over a damn picnic table."

"The car, then."

"It's not going to be that, either," you say. "Not with *me*. It needs to be in a bed. Nobody's first time should be a ten minute quickie in a park."

"What was your first time?"

"It was a fucking quickie in a park," you say, and she laughs. "So I know what I'm talking about. It lasted like two minutes in my case, but still."

"Sounds rough," she says, still laughing, but her amusement fades when she presses her palms to your cheeks. She looks at your face in the moonlight. The faint beginning of a bruise paints your jawline with discolored hues. She runs her fingers lightly along it. "Are you okay?"

"I'm fine," you say, pulling her hands away. "Nothing to worry about."

"Does that happen a lot?"

"What?"

"You know what," she says. "Your father hits you."

You laugh, but it's not a happy sound. "I can take care of myself. I'm not a little kid."

"But you're still *his* kid," she says. "And you're only seventeen. Besides, I'm guessing this isn't something that just started."

You don't say anything right away. You don't want to talk about it. She's not going to drop it, though. So you sit down beside her on the picnic table and say, "I turn eighteen tomorrow."

"Seriously?"

"Yeah, and you're right," you say. "It isn't new."

So you tell her. You tell her how he's always been hard on you, because you were a *mama's boy*. Your mother had been an aspiring actress, and that's how you got involved at such a young age, but your father never liked it. You were supposed to follow in *his* footsteps. It was a source of contention between your parents, and as your father rose in political ranks, your mother stepped away from her dream.

The first time he hit you, you were twelve, but it didn't become a regular thing until a year later when your mother swallowed a bottle of pills and never woke up from a nap. Your father blamed her career for killing her, but you blamed *him*.

That's why you can answer any question thrown at you in

116

class. He drills it into you every chance he gets. He seems to think he can beat your mother out of you and fill the hollowness left behind with more of him.

She sits beside you as you talk, her head on your shoulder. Afterward, you're both quiet, before she says she needs to get home.

Her parents don't know she's gone.

"Tomorrow night," she says as she picks up the comic book. "If you've got nothing better to do, come hang out with me."

"What time?"

"Eight o'clock," she says. "My house."

"Your house, huh? I'm starting to think you might *like* trouble."

She grins as she kisses you, just a soft peck, before saying, "I'll see you tomorrow, Jonathan."

"I'll be there," you say as she walks away.

You don't know this, but that girl? She's always been a bit of a plotter, and at the moment, she's devising a plan. You see, her parents are going out of town tomorrow night. She's supposed to go along, but she's starting to feel like she might be coming down with something. *cough* *cough*

NINE

KENNEDY

Before I can take even one more step, I'm yanked to a stop, a hand grasping hold of my wrist.

Turning, caught off guard, I look at him. *Jonathan.* We're still in the park, not far from where we started. There's a look on his battered face. I'm not sure how to read it, not sure what he's thinking or how he's feeling.

That's the thing with him, though.

He's an actor. His talent comes natural. He's never had to work very hard at it. He can switch moods in a moment, change scenes in an instant, flip the script without anybody even realizing it's happening. It's hard to tell if he's just playing a character or if you can trust that he means things.

"*Don't,*" he says, his voice low but pointed. "Don't do that."

"Don't do what?"

"Don't act like you weren't enough for me."

"I wasn't."

He shakes his head, his expression flickering with something else. Anger? Hurt? Frustration? "I don't know how you can say that, how you can even *think* that."

"Because it's true," I whisper, glancing down at where his hand is wrapped around my wrist. He isn't letting go. "I'm not saying that to be spiteful, but it's obvious I wasn't enough for you."

"How is it *obvious*?"

I can't believe he's asking that, that he's pretending to not understand what I mean. *Is* he pretending? I don't know. Either that or he's spent way too long ignoring reality.

"You wanted so much more than you ever had with me," I say. "I couldn't keep up. I tried, but I couldn't. The late nights, the parties, all those different places and faces... I got lost somewhere in the middle of it all, but you never stopped to look to make sure I was still with you. And then with the drinking, the drugs... the *women*."

He cringes when I say that. "I never cheated."

He's told me that before, but it's not the point. Good for him for keeping his pants on, for keeping his hands to himself, but still, time and again, he chose *them*. He left me behind, all alone, in a city where I only had him, so he could be with *them*.

Actors. Models. Socialites.

I fought *so hard* for him and his dream. I gave up everything. But by then end, he wouldn't even give me a minute.

A *minute* was all I asked for.

"It doesn't matter," I say. "It's over now, anyway."

He lets go of my wrist, and I start to walk again. He strolls along beside me. I can tell he wants to argue his point, and every so often his lips will part, like he's found the words he needs to convince me, but he stops himself.

When we reach my building, I come to a stop in the parking lot not far from my door.

"Thanks," I mumble, awkwardly not knowing what to say in this moment.

"You're wrong," he says when I turn away, his voice just loud enough for me to hear. Should've known he wouldn't let it go.

I shake my head. "I'm not."

"You are," he says again. "And I hate that I ever made you think otherwise, Kennedy."

He walks away. I watch him go, ignoring the tiny sliver of me that doesn't want him to leave.

Maddie's already tucked into bed when I go inside, but Meghan's on the couch, flipping through channels so fast I'm not sure how she can tell what's on. She looks at me, pausing as she sits up.

"Wow, you look…" she starts, waving toward me.

"I look *what?*"

"I don't know," she says, "but you look something."

"I feel something," I mumble, plopping down on the couch beside her, dropping her shoes on her lap as I kick my feet up on the coffee table. My dress is tugged up damn near to my waist. I'm probably flashing her my underwear, but I don't care. *What a night.*

"Oh god, was it that bad?" she asks, her voice dropping low as she clutches her chest. "Is it little? Does he have a needle-nose plier dick? Oh god, this is gold… *please* tell me Andrew's packing a pinky in his pants."

"No," I say with a laugh, pausing before adding, "Well, I don't know. Never seen it, but I doubt that's the case."

"What do you mean you've *never* seen it?"

"I mean I've never seen it. We've never… you know."

"What?" She looks at me with shock. "You've gone out a few times and you haven't even played with it? What the hell? I mean, I don't blame you, because *gross*, but why do you keep going if he's not sticking it to you? What's the point?"

"Maybe because he's nice."

"Nice? You know who else is *nice?*"

"Don't even start."

"Mister Rogers," she says. "He wants you to be his neighbor. Bob Ross, he's nice, too. He'll paint you a happy little cloud. Hell, how about one of the Cleavers? Why not go out with one of them?"

"Pretty sure they're all dead."

"Yeah, well, so is your vagina at this rate."

Laughing, I shove her, nearly pushing her off the couch. "It is *not.*"

"Fine, whatever, so Andrew's nice." She pretends to gag. "If you didn't get naked, what did you do tonight?"

"Went to dinner."

"Dinner," she says, eyeing me. "You've been gone four

hours. How much did you eat?"

"Why are you asking so many questions?"

"Just making sure you didn't run off and do something stupid, like get naked with *someone else*."

"Of course not," I say. "My dress stayed on all night long."

"But you ran off, didn't you?"

"I didn't do anything."

She waves her finger in my face. "You saw him."

Guilty.

I don't have to say anything. She knows.

"Jesus Christ, Kennedy…"

"I know, I know. You don't even have to say it."

"Oh, but I will," she says. "I'm not going to tell you what to do. I mean, I *want* to. I want to tell you to get a restraining order, but I won't. I know he's her father…"

"He's also your brother."

She shoves her hand in my face, pushing my head away. "*Ugh*, don't remind me."

Standing, she slips her shoes on, smoothing the creases from her clothes.

"You can stay, you know," I tell her. "You don't have to rush off."

"I know," she says, playfully roughing up my hair until I smack her hand. "But the universe demands balance. You didn't give it up tonight, which means it's up to me, so I'm off to do my civic duty."

"Ah, to be young again."

She flips me off.

Truth is, Meghan's got me beat by a few years. She's on the cusp of turning thirty and isn't anywhere close to settling down. She's so carefree that she makes me feel like an old fogy.

"Love you," she says.

"You, too, Meghan."

"Love you, cinnamon-sugar apple-fritter!" she yells as she opens the front door, her voice carrying through the apartment.

I don't expect her to get a response, but a sleepy voice calls from the bedroom, "Love you!"

Meghan looks at me, trying to appear serious, pointing to her eyes before pointing at me, warning me she'll be watching.

Before I can respond, she's gone.

I didn't really know Meghan until Maddie came into the world. We'd spoken a few times, saw each other in passing, but she had a life pretty far removed from her brother. She wanted to know her niece, though, and we grew close after that.

Sighing, I turn off the television, locking up before heading for bed. I stall outside Maddie's bedroom, lurking in the doorway, those blue eyes shining out at me. "Hey, sweetheart. You have fun tonight with Aunt Meghan?"

She nods. "Did you have fun with your date?"

"Sure," I say. "It was nice."

"Did he say you were pretty in your dress?"

"Uh, no." I glance down at myself. "I don't think he noticed."

"Why not?"

"Sometimes people just don't notice things like that."

"I did," she says. "I don't think you should like them as a date if they don't notice pretty dresses. 'Cuz you can see it, but if they don't see it, then they don't look. And they should look at you on dates when you're pretty."

"You're right," I say—she's too smart for her own good. "That's some really great advice."

She smiles as I stroll over, leaning down to kiss her forehead.

"Get some sleep," I tell her. "Maybe we can do something special tomorrow."

"Ducks! Ducks! Ducks! Ducks!"

I shake my head as Maddie snatches the pre-packaged bags

of kale off of the platform beside the cash register, excitedly chanting that word, hardly giving Bethany a chance to even scan them, much less toss them in bags with the rest of our stuff.

"You going to see the ducks today?" Bethany asks with a laugh, taking my money when I pay.

"Yep!" Maddie says. "Picnic with the ducks! Right, Mommy?"

"Right," I say—if *Lunchables* with juice boxes count as a picnic, which I like to think it does.

Bethany dramatically frowns Maddie's direction. "Lucky girl. I'm stuck working all day, unlike your mama, so no feeding ducks for me."

"The ducks eat all the time," Maddie tells her. "Every day, too, so you can feed them when you're not working!"

"You know, you're totally right," Bethany says. "I'll have to remember that."

Maddie smiles, satisfied, as she starts dancing around like she's playing hopscotch, jumping from square to square on the checkered floor.

Bethany counts out my change as she switches topics, rambling about schedules and days off and *blah, blah, blah...* precisely everything I don't want to talk about, but I humor her before making my escape. I look around for Maddie, spotting her at the end cap of the checkout lane, looking right at the exact thing she shouldn't be seeing.

Hollywood Chronicles.

"That's about enough of that," I say, pressing my hand to her back, steering her away from it. She doesn't fight me on it, and I'm instantly grateful she's just now learning how to read, because that means she didn't understand half of what I saw on that cover.

JOHNNY CUNNING REHAB SHOCKER!

Alcohol, Drugs, and a Sex Addiction Tearing Breezeo Star's Life Apart!
Friends concerned he's knocking on death's door!

I lead her out of the store, carrying our picnic stuff as she drags along the bags of kale. I'm digging my car keys from my pocket, trying to keep an eye on her, when she digs her heels in, dropping one of the bags.

I nearly step on it, hearing her as she whispers, "Breezeo."

"I know, sweetheart," I mumble, snatching up the bag of kale, about to hand it back to her when she yanks away from me.

"Breezeo," she says again, a little louder this time, gone from my side in a blink. *Running.*

"Madison!" I call out, darting after her. "*Stop!*"

Maddie doesn't stop, but *I* damn sure do. She's barely ten feet away, heading for someone approaching the grocery store. She runs right up, blocking the path as she says it again. "Breezeo!"

Oh god.

Oh no.

No, no, no…

Breezeo.

Jonathan stands there, blinking down at her, confusion clouding his face. I'm not sure how she recognized him, with scruff covering his jaw, still all banged up. He looks like a battered version of the actor, not the character.

My chest tightens as I hold my breath. He doesn't recognize her right away, but I can tell the moment it kicks in. There's a flicker of shock he can't conceal before his expression straightens out. He might be panicking, but he isn't showing it, not that I can see.

Yet, he says nothing.

He stares at her in silence.

I've imagined this moment so many times, in so many different ways, none of which I'm even remotely ready for, but it was never like this. I have no idea how he's going to react, no idea what he'll do. It's so far out of my control that I want to just grab her and run.

Jonathan's eyes meet mine, widening, pleading. *There's* the panic. Carefully, I step toward them.

"Breezeo?" Maddie says again, standing right in front of him, drawing his attention back to her. She sounds hesitant now, conflicted by how he's acting, a fact that seems to spur him into action.

"Hey there," he says as he kneels down, eye-level with her. "Don't say that *too* loud. People might hear."

"Mommy says she got my drawing to you," she says excitedly, whisper-shouting. "Did you see?"

He smiles slightly. "I did."

I can barely hear his voice. He stares at her like he's committing her face to memory, like he fears this may be the only time he ever sees it.

"Did you like it?" she asks. "Did it make you better?"

"I loved it," he says. "And it made me feel *a lot* better. Thank you."

"You're welcome, Breezeo!"

His gaze meets mine. He cocks an eyebrow. He's waiting for me to do something, but *what*?

"Maddie, sweetheart, we've talked about this," I say. "He's not *really* Breezeo, remember?"

"I know that." She rolls her eyes dramatically, like I'm being crazy. "He's Johnny, like on the TV and the papers and stuff, but he's still Breezeo too, right?"

"Right... I think."

"Sounds about right to me," he says, holding his left hand out to her. "My name's Jonathan, though. It's a pleasure to meet you."

She grabs his hand, shaking it wildly. "Mommy calls me Maddie. You can call me Maddie, too!"

"Maddie," he repeats.

It's a sweet moment—or well, it *should* be sweet. Tears sting my eyes that I blink away, a lump in my throat that I force down, not wanting to confuse Maddie with my reaction.

"What are you doing here?" I ask quietly when Jonathan stands back up.

"McKleski sent me to get milk," he says. "She told me to make myself useful."

126

"Yeah, uh…" I glance toward the store. "You're not going to want to do that. The cashier that's working, well, she's a bit of a Breezeo fangirl."

"Me, too!" Maddie says.

I grasp Maddie's shoulder, pulling her back to me. "Yes, but *you*, little one, know how to keep a secret."

"I do," she says, smiling widely as she looks up at me. "Like that one time when you told me that secret that you didn't like—"

I don't even know where she's going with this, but I don't let her finish, clamping my hand down around her mouth to muffle her words, hissing, "*Secret*, remember?"

Jonathan laughs. "Well, then. I guess no milk for McKleski today."

Maddie yanks my hand away from her mouth, too excited to stay quiet. "I can get her milk!"

"No, I, uh…" *Crap.* "I can do it. It'll only take a second. Just…" *Crap.* "Uh…" *How did I get myself into this?* "Just wait here. Do you think you can…?" *Crap. Crap. Crap.* I wave between him and Maddie. "For just a second?"

His eyes widen when he realizes what I'm asking, like he can't believe his ears, which is funny, because I can't believe it came from my own freaking lips. Did I seriously ask him to watch her for me?

"Sure," he says hesitantly, like he expects me to change my mind, and I *want* to, but I can't, not when I've already said it. "If *you're* sure."

I nod. "I'll be right back."

I try to be calm about it, to not raise any alarms, my footsteps determined as I head back into the store. I make my way to the back, grabbing a gallon of milk, before heading for the register with it, my heart racing the whole time. I can't believe I'm doing this. I can't believe I just did *that*. I left her with him, just left her there—with him—just like that. He could take her. He could run. For all I know, that was his plan all along. Maybe he doesn't even need milk.

"Forget something?" Bethany asks when I set the milk in front of her.

"Yeah," I mumble. "Stupid me."

She rings it up, and I pay for it, snatching up the gallon of milk before she can make conversation.

Stepping out of the store, I exhale shakily, spotting them still standing there together. Maddie is talking nonstop, while he's grinning down at her like he's mesmerized.

His smile dims a bit when I approach. He almost looks disappointed that I'm back. I try to brush that off as I shove the milk at him, but my stomach knots.

"Thanks," he says. "Maddie was telling me all about the ducks."

"Is that right?" I glance at her. "We should probably get over there."

"I told him we got kale!" she says, squeezing the bags. "He says that's crazy, 'cuz they eat bread! But he's the crazy one, 'cuz bread is bad for the ducks, but he doesn't believe they eat the kale!"

"Well, then," I say when she pauses to take a breath. "Guess he doesn't know much about ducks."

"Guess not," he agrees, lingering there like he doesn't want to leave.

"He should come!" Maddie declares, looking at him with wide eyes. "You can feed the ducks!"

"I'm not sure about that, sweetheart," I say.

"Why not?" she asks.

Why not? It's a good question, one I've got no answer for—at least, no answer she'll understand. "I'm sure he's busy."

"Too busy for *ducks*?" she asks incredulously, looking at him with disbelief. "You don't wanna feed them with me?"

I'm screwed. That's it. I know it instantly. The way she asked that, the way she worded it? There's no way he can say no.

He mumbles something, not answering her question, and looks to me for help. It's strange, seeing him so vulnerable. He's drowning right now.

"We'll be over at the park," I tell him. "If you want to come by after you drop the milk off."

"Are you sure?"

He's asking me, but Maddie answers. "*Duh.*"

He laughs. "Well, then, I guess I'll see you."

After a moment of hesitation, a moment of staring at Maddie again, he finally leaves. Maddie watches until he slips out of sight. Turning to me, she grins. "Mommy, it's Breezeo. He's *here*!"

She's got stars in her eyes, my dreamer girl, and I return her smile, even though I'm terrified that all this is going to inevitably crush her. He's here, and he's trying, but how long can that last? How long until he blows out of town again and goes back to his life, leaving everything behind? How long until my lovesick little girl becomes an inconvenience to him, too?

TEN

JONATHAN

The park is quiet this early in the afternoon, a few families hanging out, minding their own business. Nobody pays me any attention as I stroll toward the picnic tables, hat pulled down low, sunglasses on to avoid eye contact.

I've done live press conferences and walked red carpets, sat through depositions with high-powered attorneys who never hesitated to tear me apart. I went to rehab once... twice... okay, more like *five* times, sat through countless AA meetings and spilled my soul to the best goddamn shrink over on the west coast. Audition after audition, meetings and negotiations, interviews on press junkets where reporters seemed to not understand what '*no personal questions*' meant. I've been around some important people in my life. Even met the president once.

But never, through all that, was I ever as nervous as I am at this moment.

My palms are sweaty. My arm is itching. My wrist hurts like a son of a bitch—I can feel it throbbing along to the beat of my heart.

I think I'm going to be sick, but I suck it up as I head toward the water, where Kennedy lingers with our daughter.

I feel like shit, yeah, but nothing's going to get in the way of this... whatever it is. I'll take anything I can get.

"You're here!"

Madison's voice is loud, excited, as she runs up to me, still lugging around bags of kale. Her dark hair falls into her face, her braid coming undone. She blows it away, shoving it out of her eyes, smiling up at me.

"Of course," I say. "Couldn't miss seeing these ducks."

She shoves one of the bags at me, damn near punching me with it. I wince when she hits a bruised rib. It hurts like hell, but I make not a sound as she says, "You can feed them that one, 'cuz I got this one."

I take the bag, hesitating, before pulling the sling off my arm. I'm supposed to keep wearing it for a few more days, but *fuck it*. Can't do this one-handed. I toss it on the grass, watching as Madison rips her bag open, splitting it down the side and damn near losing all her kale. It starts to spill, and instinct kicks it. My hand darts out, and I grab ahold of it, wincing again as pain stabs up my forearm. "Careful."

"I gots it," she says, matter-of-fact, although she doesn't, leaving a trail of kale around us like Hansel & Gretel with breadcrumbs. None will make it to the ducks at the rate we're going.

"Here," I say, struggling as I open the second bag. "Let's trade."

She shrugs, like she doesn't see what the big deal is, but she trades bags with me before heading toward the water. "Come on, I'll show you!"

Met her less than an hour ago and she's already bossing me around. I follow her to the riverbank, where a family of ducks swims in the water.

"What about your mom?" I ask, feeling guilty, like I'm stealing Kennedy's morning.

"Mommy doesn't like the ducks. She says I can feed them but I gotta keep them over here 'cuz they might eat her."

I laugh at that, my gaze seeking out Kennedy as she sits at a picnic table, watching us. "Guess some things never change."

"Like what?"

I look at Madison. "Huh?"

"What things never change?"

"People," I say. "Or *some* people, anyway. Your mom hasn't changed much."

Still the beautiful, savvy woman she always was. Even at

132

seventeen, when she first came into my life, she felt so much more put together than everyone else, but her quirks are still there.

"You know my mommy?" Madison asks, her brow furrowing.

"Yeah," I say. "We used to know each other well."

Madison seems to mull that over as she closes the rest of the distance to the river, grabbing a handful of kale from her bag and launching it overhead, into the water. The ducks don't hesitate, rushing right for it. It's gone in an instant, and she throws another handful as they flood up onto the riverbank, making a ruckus.

"*Jesus Christ*," I say when the ducks surround us, trying to rip the bag out of my hand as Madison giggles, throwing handful after handful, not bothered in the slightest.

Panicked, I turn the bag over and fucking dump it out, right on the ground, taking a few steps back. Madison does the same, watching me, sprinkling her kale on top of them.

"You're right," I say. "They like it."

"Told you so," she says, crumbling the bag up into a ball as she looks for somewhere to put it.

I take it. "I can throw it away."

"Thank you, Breezeo."

That's all she says before darting away, running around, playing as some ducks follow her, even though she doesn't have the kale. I grab my sling and toss the empty bags into a trashcan before approaching Kennedy. She doesn't look at me, doesn't say a word, sipping juice as she watches Madison from afar.

"Crazy," I mumble. "It's like she's just this tiny *person*."

"She is," Kennedy says. "Were you expecting something different?"

"I don't know that I expected anything. I just—"

"I know."

She cuts me off before I can finish. Does she know? Maybe. But there's sharpness to her voice that tells me she doesn't want to talk about it, so I don't finish that sentence.

"Thank you for inviting me," I say. "I know this isn't easy for you."

"It doesn't matter how I feel," she says. "You and I are long over, Jonathan. All that matters is Maddie."

The way she says that stings. "Well, still, thank you."

She nods, whispering, "Don't make me regret it."

I hope like hell I don't.

Madison runs over, breathing heavily, waving her hands all around as she stammers out some half-sentences. Kennedy grabs a juice box, poking a straw in it before handing it to her. The girl sucks it down in one gulp.

"Do you have your suit?" she asks suddenly as she squeezes the empty box, crushing it.

The question catches me off guard. "What?"

"For Breezeo. Do you have the suit or no?"

"Uh, no," I say. "Not with me."

"Where is it at?"

"In a wardrobe trailer somewhere, I imagine. Why?"

She shrugs, giving the juice box to her mother. "Does it work? Does it go all invisible for real?"

"No, it's a normal costume."

"And you don't go all invisible?"

"No," I say. "I'm normal, too."

She scowls. I feel like I'm telling the kid Santa isn't real.

"But you're a hero," she says. "I seen it on the TV, so maybe you don't gotta disappear, so then you can stay and don't have to go away now."

Those words are a punch to the chest. I blink at her, not sure if she means that how it sounds, but I'm verbally getting my ass kicked this afternoon.

"We read part of *Ghosted* the other day," Kennedy chimes in. "She isn't happy that Breezeo leaves at the end."

The explanation doesn't make it much better. Sighing, I sit down on the edge of the picnic table. "Yeah, I always thought that sucked. Sure, he thought it was for the best, but I figured they would've given him a happy ending."

"He should come back," Madison says. "Then he can get

134

better and they'll be happy."

She's hitting way too close to home with this shit, and she doesn't even know it. "Huh, maybe *you* should've written the story."

Madison's eyes widen, her face lighting up with a smile. Her expression makes my goddamn heart act up. She's beautiful, this kid—even more beautiful than I ever could've dreamed of. There's a spark inside of her, one that echoes inside of me, the kind of spark I haven't felt in a long time.

"I can do that!" she says. "I can fix it!"

Kennedy laughs. "I'm sure you can."

Madison is off again, running around. I sit there in silence, watching her play. A few minutes pass before my phone rings in my pocket. I dig it out. *Cliff.*

"Yeah?" I answer flippantly.

"Hey!" Cliff says, sounding *way* too enthusiastic. "How's our hero feeling this afternoon?"

"Depends."

"On what?"

"On what you want."

"Just checking in to see how you're holding up."

"In that case, I'm doing fine."

"Good," he says. "Any less of a moody prick?"

"Maybe a bit."

"Well, every little bit counts."

He laughs.

Cliff doesn't laugh.

"Anyway, I didn't get the chance to check in with you after you got discharged," he says. "You back home in LA now?"

"No, I decided to, you know... stick around."

"Stick around," he says. "You're still here in the city?"

"Uh, close to it."

It doesn't take him long to realize what I mean. "You *didn't.* Seriously, tell me you aren't where I think you are right now."

"I am."

He huffs. "We go through this every time you go there. *Every single time."*

We do. Usually, I spiral after showing up in Bennett Landing. I'd go on a bender and binge my heart out and not stop until I was so fucking numb someone could've shot me and I wouldn't have felt it. And after I pulled myself together, the lecture would come—I'm playing with fire, it's a PR nightmare, *imagine what will happen if word gets out…*

Imagine if the paparazzi show up there. Imagine if they invade her life the way they do yours. Imagine them stalking your daughter at school. Imagine the stories they'll print about the kid you abandoned. Imagine what it'll do to you when they call you a deadbeat father.

"It's fine," I say. "Nobody knows I'm here."

"You're supposed to be taking it easy."

"Stop worrying. I'm not going to do anything stupid."

"You better not," he says. "Serena's causing enough trouble right now."

I sigh, lowering my head. "What now?"

"She checked into rehab."

That isn't what I expected him to say, but I'm not surprised. "Was it voluntary?"

"Sure," he says, "if you consider all those times *you* went to be voluntary."

Not even close.

"She was getting out of hand," he says. "Figured it was a good time for her to get some help."

"Good," I say. "Hope it works out."

"You and me both."

"So, that's it? Nothing else?"

"No," he says. "Unless you have anything to share?"

I end the call without humoring that and shove the phone in my pocket, looking over at Madison. I'm not going to jinx myself. Today was a happy accident. I'm not sure what happens next.

"Let me guess," Kennedy says. "Your wife?"

"I told you I don't have one of those."

"I bet you tell people you don't have a daughter too, huh?"

I cut my eyes at her. Bitterness drips from every one of those words. "Nobody ever asks."

"But you don't offer the information up, either."

"I would," I say. "I *will*, if you want me to. I'll call up a reporter right now and give them an exclusive. But just know, by tomorrow morning, they'll be banging down your door. They'll be hiding in the bushes, climbing trees, looking through windows, clambering to get pictures. *Hollywood Chronicles* will have you on the front page by next week. Is that what you want?"

She doesn't answer.

Of course it's not.

It's inevitable. Someday, they'll find out. I just hope we have time to figure things out before that happens, time for me to get to know my daughter and earn Kennedy's trust before the vultures swoop in and try to fuck it all up.

"Maddie!" she hollers, standing up. "We need to get going, sweetheart!"

"Don't," I say right away. "Please don't leave."

"I have things to do," she says.

"Just twenty more minutes," I say. "*Ten* minutes."

"I would, but…"

Kennedy trails off as Madison runs up to us, her hair wild now. "Do we have to leave, Mommy?"

"We have to go to Grandpa's, remember? We told him we'd come over."

"Can he come, too?" Madison asks her before turning to me. "Will you come?"

"To your grandfather's house?"

"Yep! Grandpa will like you, 'cuz he watches Breezeo, too!"

Kennedy laughs under her breath as she gathers their stuff.

"I don't think that's a good idea," I say. "Maybe another time."

She looks disappointed, *pouting*. I want to take it back. I want to tell her I'll go anywhere she wants me to go, even if that means visiting a man who once said he'd cut off my nuts if I ever stepped foot in his house again. I've shown up a few times since then, never brave enough to go inside, but I'd do it for her.

I'd grow big enough balls to risk him taking them. *Snip, snip.*

"Oh, don't even try those puppy dog eyes on him," Kennedy says, playfully grasping Madison's chin, her fingers squeezing her chubby cheeks. "He's way too smart to fall for it."

"But he can come next time?" she asks.

"Maybe," Kennedy says. "We'll see."

I open my mouth to say goodbye, but Madison lunges at me before I can. She wraps her arms around my neck, and my heart fucking *aches* as I hug her. It's over quickly, *way* too quickly, as she pulls away. "Thank you, Breezeo!"

"Jonathan," Kennedy corrects her.

"Jonathan," Madison says, "but still Breezeo, too."

"You're welcome, Maddie," I say. "Thank you for letting me feed the ducks."

Kennedy grabs Madison's hand, lingering there for a moment. I can tell she wants to say something. Her lips part, but all that comes out is a sigh before she walks off.

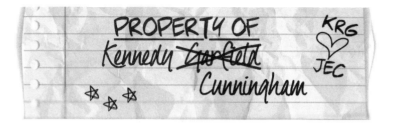

PROPERTY OF
Kennedy ~~Garreta~~
Cunningham
☆ ☆ ☆

KRG
♡
JEC

On Saturday evening, at a few minutes past eight o'clock, you pull your blue Porsche into the driveway of the modest two-story house.

The girl meets you out on the porch. She's barefoot, wearing a simple gray dress, the kind that looks like a long t-shirt.

You step onto the porch in front of her. You aren't sure what to expect. Your gaze scans her. It's blatant you're checking her out, your eyes lingering on her smooth, bare legs.

"So, my parents aren't home," she says. "I swore I wouldn't leave the house while they were gone."

She's nervous as she tells you that, fidgeting with the hem of her dress. It distracts you. Your eyes keep darting to it as the material inches up further and further. "How long will they be gone?"

"Until tomorrow," she says. "So it's just me, home, alone, all night long... whatever shall I do with my night?"

You meet her gaze. You smile.

You don't have to say a word.

She pulls you into the house. She's bold, again making the first move, kissing you as soon as you're inside. Her lips express confidence, but her hands are shaking. You grab them, *holding* them, and kiss her back.

"Happy birthday," she whispers. "I have something to show you."

"Can't wait to see it."

She takes you upstairs.

She takes you to her bedroom.

It's dimly lit from a small lamp and looks like the typical room of a teenage girl—cluttered, a lot of color, flowery comforter. There's a Breezeo *Ghosted* poster on the wall above her bed. There's a candle lit on a nearby desk. It smells like vanilla.

"You sure about this?" you ask when she kisses you again, but there's no doubt that she's *sure*. "I figured you'd want to watch a movie or something first."

"Do you?"

"Do I *what?*"

"Do you want to watch a movie?" she asks, kissing along your bruised jawline. "I mean, I guess we can, if that's what *you* want..."

"Fuck that," you say as you move her to the bed. "What *I* want is to find out what it feels like to be inside of you."

She blushes, and laughs, the sound morphing to moans as you kiss her neck. You waste no time pulling off her dress, leaving her in front of you in a lacy black thong with a matching bra.

"Fuck, you're beautiful, K," you say as your gaze scans her. "*So goddamn beautiful.*"

She dramatically rolls her eyes.

"I'm serious," you say, tugging her down onto the bed. "Don't you ever doubt that. You're the queen, baby... I'm just a commoner."

"Did you just...?" She stares at you as you push her onto her back and hover over her. "*Oh my god,* you seriously just quoted *Breezeo* to me."

"Foreplay," you say. "Besides, it's a good line."

She's speechless.

You yank off your shirt and kick off your shoes. You only have one condom stashed in your wallet, not thinking you'd actually get this far, and who knows how old the thing is, but she's on the pill, so you roll with it. *No stopping now.*

The rest of the clothes disappear.

You move slowly, your touch gentle, giving her time to adjust. Your fingers are inside of her, and your mouth is *on* her, as orgasm rips through her. You go easy, as you take her virginity, pushing in carefully and pausing. She's trusting you, giving herself to you. You don't want to hurt her.

You make her feel good.

Over and over.

You stay all night long.

It's nearing dawn when you finally slip your clothes back on. She's laying there, the blanket wrapped around her, watching as you sit down on the edge of the bed to put your shoes on.

As you tie them, she sits up, wrapping her arms around you from behind. She hugs you, her head resting against your back. She stays that way for a few minutes before she pushes away from you. "Crap, almost forgot to show you that thing for your birthday!"

"I thought that thing was *you.*"

"What? No." She laughs, blanket still wrapped around her. She almost trips on it as she drags you downstairs, forcing you onto the couch in the living room. "Sit."

She sits beside you and turns on the TV. You think maybe she's trying to watch a movie now, but no, she goes to something that she recorded—*Law & Order.*

"No way," you say when she presses play.

It's *your* episode.

"It was on a few days ago," she tells you. "Luckily, cable plays the same things over and over, and I caught it on a rerun."

You laugh, putting your arm around her.

The two of you sit together and watch it.

Not just your parts. You watch the whole thing. When it's over, she looks at you and says, "I don't care what else you do in the future, even when you're the biggest movie star in the world... the dead kid on *Law & Order* will always be my favorite part you've played."

You leave not long after that.

It's seven o'clock in the morning.

And you don't know this, but that girl? She realizes, as your car speeds away, that she's desperately falling in love with you. Her body's sore, and her chest aches, her heart pounding wildly. She hasn't had a moment of sleep, but that matters not a bit. She's sky-high, and nothing can bring her down from this euphoria—not even when a nosy neighbor tells her father all about the blue Porsche that spent the night parked in the driveway. Not even when he notices the love bites around her neck from your frantic lips. Not even when he threatens to take your manhood and tells her she's grounded for the rest of her life. Because the night that girl just spent with you? *Worth it.*

ELEVEN

KENNEDY

"Grandpa! Grandpa! Guess who I saw!"

Maddie starts yelling the second she's out of the car, running up onto the porch of the house. My father sits in his rocking chair, stalling his movement. "Who?"

"Breezeo!" she says, stopping on the porch in front of him, flailing her arms as she launches into her story. "He was at the store, and then he didn't believe that the ducks like kale, so he came to the park to see and he fed the ducks, too! But I think he got scared, 'cuz he didn't feed them good, but they ate it anyway."

My father blinks at her as he absorbs those words. "*Breezeo.*"

She nods. "But not real Breezeo, 'cuz he's not real, so he's Jonathan."

"*Jonathan.*"

Another nod. "I told him he should come here, too, 'cuz you like Breezeo, and he said maybe he would the next time."

My father lets out a laugh of disbelief. "Ha! I'd like to see him come here."

"*Dad,*" I warn.

"Me, too!" Maddie says, not realizing that's a borderline threat. She runs inside, leaving me alone with my father. He says nothing, but yet his expression says it all.

"It kind of snowballed," I say, sitting down on the porch beside him. "We need to have the *stranger danger* talk because she took to him right away."

"Like mother, like daughter," he says. "I'm guessing you

didn't tell her who he is to her."

"Yeah, no… not sure how to explain it."

"You just tell her."

"I don't think it's that simple."

"But it is," he says. "She's a smart girl. Besides, do you really think she'll take the news bad?"

"No, I think she's going to be the happiest kid on the planet, which is half the problem. Because what happens if he lets her down?"

"Hate to break it to you, but that's not something you can control. Will she ever be disappointed? Probably. But he'll love her, because who wouldn't? And if he's making an effort, she deserves a chance to love him in return."

He's right, of course, but he makes it sound so simple when it feels anything but at the moment.

"You realize we're talking about the same guy that you once called *the worst thing that could ever happen to anyone's daughter*?"

He laughs.

"Grandpa, can I have this?" Maddie asks, bursting out onto the porch, holding a banana Popsicle. She licks it, not waiting for permission, a bite already taken off the top.

"What? You want my Popsicle?" He scrunches up his face. "No way! I was saving that for later!"

She freezes, wide eyes flickering between the Popsicle and him. "*Uh-oh.*"

"I'm kidding," he says, nudging her. "Of course you can have it, kiddo."

It's after dark when we make it home. Maddie's fast asleep, so I pick her up and manage to carry her into the apartment. Her shoes are already off, abandoned in the car, so I set her in bed as she is, covering her up and kissing her forehead. "Love you, sweetheart."

She sleepily mumbles something back that sounds like '*crazy ducks*'.

Exhaustion weighs me down, so heavy in my bones that my

144

insides feel brittle, pieces of me already broken. I take a hot bath, trying to relax, but nothing can shut off my thoughts. They're a jumbled mess.

I don't know how I'm supposed to feel anymore.

Getting out of the tub, I throw on my robe and settle in my bedroom. Reaching into my bedside stand, I pull out the old business card and lay down in bed with my cell phone.

Johnny Cunning

Beneath his name is his contact information, along with his management on the other side. The cards are tucked into the envelopes that show up with the grotesque checks. I never accepted a single penny of his money, but once, long ago, I kept one of the cards. *Just in case.*

Opening my text messages, I type his number in, hesitating as I stare at the blank screen. What to say?

Hey, it's Kennedy.

I hit send without letting myself think too much about it, knowing if I give myself time to second-guess this, I'll never go through with it.

A response pops up within seconds.

Hey. Everything okay?

Is everything okay? *No.* Everything feels so out of control.

Just wondering if you're busy tomorrow.

No, what's up?

What's up is I don't know what the hell I'm doing, but I do it, whatever this is, while I still have the nerve.

Thought we could get together to tell Maddie the truth.

His response isn't as quick this time, a minute, maybe two, before a message pops up.

The truth?

Is that a problem?

A few more minutes pass of nothing. I'm starting to wonder if I'm making a mistake when my phone rings, the California number flashing across the screen. He's calling. My stomach churns. "Hello?"

145

There's a moment of hesitation before he says, "I didn't think you'd actually answer."

"Yeah, well, I did," I mumble, thinking I should've let it go to voicemail. "So, is there a problem?"

"No, I'm just wondering what the truth means to you."

My brow furrows as I stare up at my ceiling. "What?"

"You said you want to tell her the truth," he says. "*All* of it?"

I'm not sure how to answer. How much do I want to tell her? How much does he need to prepare for? I wonder how much he's even faced himself.

"I don't know," I admit.

It grows eerily quiet, but I know he's still on the line. I can sense him, faintly detecting his breathing. After a moment, he lets out a deep sigh. "What time?"

Noon.

The sun is shining outside, light streaming through the open apartment windows, warming the place with a soft glow. A breeze flows through the screens, ruffling the thin white curtains as some current pop boy band plays on the radio in the living room. Maddie dances around, wearing her *Sunday best*—meaning she's dressed like some sort of rambunctious little superhero, with a tutu and rainbow-striped tights, a too-big black Breezeo t-shirt, complete with a fuzzy purple blanket flung around her like a cape. She's all over the place, a ball of energy this morning, while I'm... well... I'm a *mess*.

My eyes burn. I didn't get much sleep, staring at the ceiling in the darkness, conjuring up hypothetical conversations, playing out years worth of *what if's*. This morning, my hands are shaking as I busy myself cleaning, trying to distract myself from reality, but it isn't working. No matter how much I sweep and mop and scrub, I keep thinking about how big of a disaster this could become.

The song on the radio changes... a girl band this time... as a soft knock sounds from the apartment door.

"I got it!" Maddie shouts, heading for the door as I tense, in the middle of wiping down the kitchen counters for the third time.

"No, wait, hold on a second," I say, but she isn't paying me any attention. The clock on the wall reads 12:01. I told him to come by anytime in the afternoon, and it's after *noon* now, which means...

"Breezeo!" she announces, flinging the door open, excitedly spinning around to look for me. "Mommy, look, it's—"

"Jonathan," I say, stepping out of the kitchen, nervously rubbing my palms on the thighs of my jeans.

"Jonathan," she repeats, standing in the doorway in front of him.

He stares down at her, smiling. "Maddie."

"Come in!" Maddie says, grabbing his arm—the injured one—to tug him into the apartment. He grimaces, not resisting, but his smile wavers when his eyes meet mine.

Sighing, I close the door behind them, my back pressing against it. Maddie's rambling away—about what, I don't know. I feel like I'm slipping underwater, my heart feverishly racing, but Jonathan seems to understand. He's smiling at her again, listening, as she seems to give him a quick tour of the apartment.

He pauses near the small hallway that leads to the bedrooms, his gaze meeting mine again. I know what he's thinking. I'm not sure how, or even why, but the moment our eyes connect, it's like being shoved back in time—to another place, a different apartment, one somehow even smaller, but it was our home for a while.

"We can go play in my room!" Maddie says, trying to pull him that direction.

"Oh, whoa, whoa," I say, coming out of my stupor as I shove away from the door. He comes around and *stranger danger* seriously goes right out the window. I know he's her father and all, but *she* doesn't know that. Not yet. "Slow your roll for a second, little girl. We need to have a conversation."

Her eyes widen. I glance between her and Jonathan, their

147

expressions nearly identical. *Worried.*

"I didn't do nothing," Maddie says, shaking her head.

"I know," I say, pointing to the couch. "Sit."

She sits, finally letting go of Jonathan. He carefully sits down on the edge of the couch beside her. I linger a moment before perching myself on the coffee table in front of her.

"I, uh…" I have no idea how to even begin. "I mean, *we*…"

"Maybe I should…" Jonathan starts, pausing before saying, "You know."

"It's fine," I say. "I got it."

"Got what, Mommy?" Maddie asks.

"We wanted to talk to you about something," I tell her. "About why Jonathan is here."

"To play with me?" she asks.

"No," I say, shaking my head. "Well, I mean, *maybe*, but that's not really it. You see, I've known him for a long time, since before you came into my life, sweetheart."

"Oh." She stares at me. "So he's gonna play with you, then?"

"What? *No.*" I scoff, making a face. Ugh, I can feel my cheeks heating. "It's nothing like that. It's just… look, you know your friend Jenny that lived beside Grandpa? You remember how she went away, and I explained that her parents decided not to live together anymore, because some parents don't live together, so she had to go stay at a different house?"

Her eyes widen again. "Do I have to go away?"

"What? No! You don't have to go anywhere."

"You promise?"

"I promise. It's not like that. I'm just saying, you know, sometimes parents don't live together, and that's okay, and it doesn't make them any less of a family. Everyone has a mom and a dad."

She shakes her head. "Not everyone."

"Yes, sweetheart. Everyone."

"Nuh-uh, Noah at my school doesn't got a dad. He's got two moms!"

"Oh, well… okay, but still, that's what I mean. Everyone has *two* parents."

"But Jenny doesn't got two now. She's got *three*, 'cuz her dad got married, so she has another different kinda mommy, right?"

"Right." Man, I'm screwing this all up. "But she still has her dad, too, so what I'm saying is—"

"I'm your dad."

Jonathan's voice is quiet as he cuts in, but it still packs enough of a punch to make me inhale sharply.

Maddie looks at him. "You wanna be my dad?"

"I do," he says. "I already am."

Her mouth falls open in shock. "Did you get married to Mommy?"

He blinks rapidly, caught off guard, while I choke on thin air, coughing at that question.

"Oh, no, we didn't…" His eyes cut my way before he continues. "It's not like that. I've always been your dad."

"How?"

"How?" he repeats. "Well, I just am. Your mother, she's your mom, and I'm your dad."

"But *how?*" she asks again.

He looks to me for help, like he's not sure what she's even asking, so I chime in again before he takes that *how* literal and starts spilling about the birds and the bees.

"Moms and Dads aren't always together, remember? So he's still your dad even if he wasn't around."

"But where was he at?"

She's asking me, not him. I know it's because she trusts me implicitly, and as much as she adores what she believes he is, she doesn't yet know Jonathan. But I don't know how to answer that, or if I even *should*. I don't know if I should be the one to explain his absence, to make his excuses.

"I wasn't where I should've been," he chimes in. "I should've been with you, but I was…"

"Sick," I say when he struggles for words.

"Sick," he says.

"Did you have the tummy bug?" she asks, looking at him.

"No, it was worse than that," he admits, "and I'm to blame, nobody else. I made some really bad choices. I—"

"Did you disappear?" she asks.

"I messed up," he says. "I know I haven't been here for you, but I want to be here now, if you'll let me."

She sits in silence for a moment, thinking that over, before shrugging. "Okay."

He looks stunned. "Okay?"

"Okay," she says again, standing up from the couch as she grabs his hand to pull him along with her again. "But you have to sleep in Mommy's bed, 'cuz mine can't fit you."

"Uh…" He laughs awkwardly as he follows her. "What?"

"He's not going to live with us," I say. "Remember Jenny's parents?"

She nods, looking at me. "But can he play now, Mommy? *Please?*"

"Of course," I say, giving her a smile. "He can stay and play as long as he wants."

She drags him away before I say anything else.

I faintly hear her rambling about something from her bedroom as I try to busy myself again to keep from fixating on his presence. I clean some more. I listen to music. I watch a bit of television.

Hours pass.

Long, long hours, some of the longest hours of my life. I don't know what they're doing, not wanting to interrupt, but I can hear Maddie laughing, and I can hear him talking, the two of them playing.

It's near dusk and I'm in the kitchen, cooking dinner, when things grow quiet. I hear footsteps behind me, restrained on the wooden floor, heading my direction.

Jonathan pauses right inside the doorway. "She fell asleep."

"Not surprised," I say. "She's been wide open all day long."

150

I glare at the food on the stove. She ate breakfast, and she ate lunch, but I know now dinner is a bust. Even when I wake her up, I doubt she'll eat much.

"Yeah," he says, leaning against the doorframe. "I wish I had even half of her energy. Bottle it up and take it with me for those late nights on set."

"Guess it beats the coke, huh?"

His expression falls when I say that. Right away, I feel like crap. *Ugh.*

"Sorry," I say. "I shouldn't have said that."

"It's fine," he says. "I deserve whatever you throw at me."

"Maybe so, but I told myself long ago that I wouldn't do that whole *woman scorned* thing."

I finish dinner, putting everything together, turning off the stove as he stands there.

"Are you hungry?" I ask. "I can make you a plate."

"You don't have to do that."

"I know, but I'm offering."

"Well, uh... okay." He strolls over to the table. "If you don't mind."

I fix two plates of food. Spaghetti and garlic bread—nothing fancy, but we get by. I'm not a good cook, frankly. The noodles are still sort of crunchy and the sauce came out of a jar. We sit at the table across from each other. He waits until I take a bite before he even touches his fork.

I pick at my food, not hungry, but once he starts eating, he doesn't stop until the plate is empty. I wonder when he last ate a home-cooked meal. I wonder if he has a hired chef. I wonder if Serena cooks for him.

Serena. He told me they weren't married, but beyond that, he's avoided the subject.

"Does she know?"

The question flies from my lips before I even give asking it much thought.

His expression is guarded. "Does who know what?"

"Serena," I say. "Does she know about our daughter?"

He hesitates, like he has to think about it. "Pretty sure she does."

"*Pretty sure.*"

"I vaguely remember telling her," he says. "But we were both high at the time, so who knows if she believed me or if she even cared."

"Wow," I say. "That's nice to know."

"We're not…" he starts, scrubbing his hand over his face. "Look, about that…"

"It's not my business," I say. "Not anymore. Whatever you do and whoever you do it with, that's on you. But if it starts affecting Maddie—"

"It won't," he says. "It's not serious."

"Looks serious."

"Looks are deceiving. We're just friends."

"Friends," I say. "So you're telling me you've never had sex with her?"

He hesitates.

"That's what I thought," I mutter, twirling the uneaten spaghetti around on my plate.

"It wasn't serious," he says. "It was just a thing that happened."

"How long ago?"

"I don't know," he says. "It was on and off."

"When was the first time?"

I know I'm asking a lot of questions for someone whose business this isn't, but the door is wide open, and I can't stop myself from peeking inside for answers.

He hesitates again.

"Forget I asked," I say as I give up on eating, shoving out of my chair. *Conversation over.* I busy myself with putting the leftovers away and start cleaning up while he sits there.

"Can I help with that?" he asks when I fill the sink with hot water.

"What, you're gonna wash dishes one-handed?"

"Uh, I guess," he says. "Don't you have a dishwasher?"

"Nope," I say, glancing at the dishwasher. "Well, I do, but it doesn't work."

"What's wrong with it?"

"Who knows? Maintenance was supposed to fix it, but well, like my dad always says, they're about as useful as Congress. They never fixed my washer and dryer, either."

"What's wrong with your washer and dryer?"

"One leaks, the other doesn't heat."

He grows eerily quiet as I start washing dishes. When I glance at him, I see he's looking around, his brow furrowed. "Why do you live here?"

"Why wouldn't I?"

"It's not much."

"It's enough," I say, "for *us*, anyway. I work in a grocery store, you know. This is what it pays for."

"Why?"

"Maybe because I never went to college like I was supposed to, so I do whatever I have to do."

"But... why?"

Turning, I look at him again.

He's staring at me with confusion.

"I send money," he says. "It should be enough."

"I don't want your money."

"Why?"

"Why, Jonathan? You're seriously asking me *why*?"

"Look, I'm just saying—"

"I know what you're saying, but we do just fine without your money."

"Come on, don't be that way, K."

"What way?"

"*That* way. I want to help."

"So be a father, not a paycheck."

He's quiet, as I continue washing dishes. When I finish and

start draining the water, he stands up to go. He takes a few steps before hesitating, saying, "I never cheated on you."

Drying my hands, I turn to him, leaning back against the counter.

"I'm serious," he says. "The past few years are a blur, so I can't tell you what I don't remember, but I know we were over before anything ever happened with her."

I nod, looking down at my hands. "I wasn't accusing you of cheating. I just wanted to know how long it took you to move on."

"Oh, well, that's an easy one," he says. "It hasn't happened."

TWELVE

JONATHAN

Dim church basements aren't my favorite places, nor are they my idea of a good time. I tend to think of them as necessary evils, although Jack would flip out if he heard me say that. They're where we go to spill our souls, confessionals for the alcoholics of the world.

Meetings. I fucking hate them.

They're supposed to be safe, *anonymous*, but that isn't always the case. People tend to recognize my face, and well... next thing you know, pictures leak and it turns into a clusterfuck.

Metal folding chairs fill the basement of Hatfield Episcopal. I slip into a seat in the back, grateful that they're not arranged in a circle so I can keep to myself. New place, new faces, which means they'll want to hear my story, but I'm not planning to talk. I just need a reminder tonight.

People filter in, about a dozen of them, men and women, nobody I recognize until *him*.

Son of a bitch.

Michael Garfield.

He heads straight for the front. I avert my gaze, keeping my head down, my hat on, but it's pointless. He pauses in front of everyone, eyes landing on me as he calls the meeting to order.

Shit.

"Welcome,. My name's Michael and I'm an alcoholic."

"*Hello, Michael.*"

The chorus of voices echoes through the room, but I don't

say a word, sitting in silence and staring down at my lap as he continues.

"I've been sober now for over twenty years," he says before going into the usual spiel. I've been through so many of these meetings and they always start the same way—a rambling introduction before the floor is opened up to sharing. Nobody seems to be feeling chatty so he suggests, "Why don't we talk about forgiveness?"

I laugh under my breath. I can feel his gaze.

They talk. I listen.

The meeting lasts ninety minutes.

It feels longer than those ninety days I spent in rehab.

After it's over, I linger in my seat, letting everyone else filter out of the basement. Michael strolls toward the exit, his footsteps stalling beside my chair. He stares at me for a moment, his expression hard, before he walks away without saying anything.

He's gone when I make it out of the church. They're all gone, the parking lot empty. I'm alone.

Pulling out my phone to call Jack, to let him know I made it to that goddamn meeting like he asked, I notice I have a voicemail. *Kennedy*. She called an hour ago.

I press the button to listen to it as I head through the parking lot, my footsteps faltering when the voice clicks on. No, not Kennedy. *Madison*.

"Mommy said I could call you 'cuz when I woke up you were gone. She said you ate *spaghettis*, but then you had to go. And I'm gonna eat some now 'cuz it's my favorite other than cheese pizza with just cheese. Maybe we can have some tomorrow when I'm not at school! We can play again if my mommy says it's okay, but you should ask and not me, 'cuz it's a school night but she might say yes if you ask."

Kennedy laughs in the background, saying, "I can hear you."

"Uh-oh," Madison whispers. "I gotta go now."

Smiling to myself after she hangs up, I open my texts and send one to Kennedy. **Sorry I missed it, but thanks for letting** her call.

Her response comes right away. **Of course.**

I consider it a moment before typing: **Any chance we can do it again tomorrow? I'll supply the pizza if you'll supply the kid.**

As soon as I hit send, I type another. **Completely my idea, of course.**

There isn't a response—not right away, at least. I slip my phone in my pocket and make the trek to the inn, the neighborhood quiet.

Reaching the place, I step up on the porch as my phone vibrates with a message. I look at it, my stomach dropping.

I don't think so.

Before I can put the phone away, I see she's typing again. It goes on and on and on as I stand here, waiting, trying to not get my hopes up.

It feels like a fucking century before the message comes through.

I'm going to be busy at work, but Tuesday is better. Is that okay with you?

Sounds good.

I slip my phone away as the front door of the inn yanks open, McKleski appearing in the doorway. "You planning on coming in or are you going to spend the night out here?"

There's a bite to her words, but it doesn't get under my skin. I step past her. "Not sure which would be more comfortable."

"Porch, probably. I might even toss you a pillow."

"They always did say you were hospitable."

"And they always said you were a bit of a rascal."

"A rascal," I mumble.

"Indeed," she says, "but if you ask me, I'd say that's putting it mildly."

"Well, good thing we're not asking you, huh?"

She laughs at that, patting me on the back. "Certainly is, because if we were asking me, there's quite a bit I'd have to say."

"Like?"

I regret it the moment I ask that. This woman wouldn't hesitate to drag me to hell and back with venom of her words.

"Oh, no, I'm not playing that game."

"What game?"

"The one where I give you *more* reason to mope around here with that 'poor me' attitude."

"I'm not moping."

"*He says in a mopey voice.*"

I laugh as she mocks me. "I'll have you know I've actually had a good day."

"Well, good for you," she says. "If you're hungry, there's food in the kitchen, but I'm going to bed, so keep all the ruckus down."

"Yes, ma'am."

✿ ✿ ✿

Monday came and went.

I almost spent the entire day in bed, but McKleski wasn't having that shit. I woke up to pounding on the bedroom door sometime in the afternoon, a list of chores tossed at me.

Things to do.

"Since you're staying here," she said, "you might as well do something."

I did it all—or at least, what I *could*. Cleaning, hanging pictures, fixing a creaky door. It wasn't easy with my wrist fucked up, and I'm not used to manual labor, but I made it work, keeping busy, waiting for Tuesday.

Tuesday.

When five o'clock Tuesday evening comes, I approach the apartment, carrying two large pizzas—a cheese pizza with only cheese, like Madison requested, the other a monstrosity made with ham and pineapple.

Hesitantly, I knock, hearing a flurry of footsteps inside before the door yanks open, the little ball of energy in front of me, grinning.

"Madison Jacqueline!" Kennedy shouts, popping up in my line of sight. "What did I say about answering the door like that?"

"*Oh.*" Her eyes widen, and before I can say a word, she swings the door shut, slamming it in my face. I stand here for a moment before the door cracks open again, her head peeking out as she whispers, "You gots to knock."

As soon as it shuts again, I tap on the door.

"Who's there?" she yells.

"Jonathan."

"Jonathan who?"

I laugh, shifting the pizzas around when they start slipping from my grip. Before I can answer, the door opens once more, Kennedy standing there.

"Sorry," she mumbles, motioning for me to come in as she grasps Madison by the shoulders, steering her along. "We're working on this *stranger danger* thing. She's way too trusting."

"But I know it was him," Madison protests.

"You can never be too sure," Kennedy says. "It's always best to double-check."

I open my mouth to offer an opinion but stop myself, not sure if I'm at that place where my advice is welcome. I'm not trying to get kicked out before even eating any pizza.

"So, uh, where should I...?" I told up the pizza boxes as I trail off.

"Oh, right. Kitchen table's fine."

"I'll show you!" Madison announces, as if I don't know where it is, but I let her lead me there anyway. Kennedy shuts the door and follows behind us. I set the boxes on the table, and Madison doesn't hesitate, popping the top one open. She makes a face, looking horrified. "Gross!"

"What in the world are you—?" Kennedy laughs as she glances at the pizza. "Ham and pineapple."

"Why is that *fruit* on the pizza?" Madison asks.

"Because it's good," Kennedy says, snatching the top box away before opening the other one. "There, that one's for you."

Madison shrugs it off, grabbing a slice of cheese pizza, eating straight from the box. I'm gathering this is normal, since Kennedy sits down beside her to do the same.

"You remembered," she says plucking a piece of pineapple off a slice of pizza and popping it in her mouth.

"Of course," I say, grabbing a slice of cheese from the box Madison is hoarding. "Pretty sure I'm scarred for life because of it. Not something I can forget."

She laughs, the sound soft, as she gives me one of the most genuine smiles I've seen in a while. It fades as she averts her gaze, but goddamn it, it happened.

"You shoulda gots the breads," Madison says, standing on her chair as she leans closer, vying for my attention like she's afraid I might not see her. "And the chickens!"

"Ah, didn't know you liked those," I tell her, "or I would've gotten them."

"Next time," she says, just like that, no question about it.

"Next time," I say.

"And soda, too," she says.

"No soda," Kennedy chimes in.

Madison glances at her mother before leaning even closer, damn near right up on me, whisper-shouting, "Soda."

"I'm not so sure your mom will like that," I say.

"It's okay," Madison says. "She tells Grandpa no soda, too, but he lets me have it."

"That's because you emotionally blackmail him," Kennedy says.

"Nuh-uh!" Madison says, looking at her mother. "I don't blackmail him!"

Kennedy scoffs. "How do you know? You don't even know what that means."

"So?" Madison says. "I don't mail him *nothing*!"

I'm trying not to laugh, I am, but *Jesus Christ*, it's almost like she's arguing with herself. Kennedy was always stubborn as hell, but I've never been any better. It's why, when the two of us fought, things got ugly.

"You give him those sad puppy-dog eyes," Kennedy says, grabbing Madison by the chin, squeezing her chubby cheeks. "And you tell him you'll love him *'the mostest'* if he gives you some Coca-Cola to drink."

" 'Cuz I will," Madison says.

"That's emotional blackmail."

"Oh." Madison makes a face, turning to me when her mother lets go of her. "How 'bout root beer?"

"I'm afraid not," I tell her. "Sorry."

Madison scowls, hopping down from the table to grab a juice box from the refrigerator.

Silence surrounds the table, but it only lasts a moment before Madison decides on something else she wants to talk about. The kid can ease even the most awkward situations, I'm realizing, as she chatters away, telling some story about something somebody at school did for Show & Tell today.

"Go wash up," Kennedy tells her when she's done eating, pizza sauce all over her hands and face. "Finish your homework and then you can play."

Madison jumps down from the table to run off. I hear water running in the distance as Kennedy puts the leftovers away.

"Homework in kindergarten," I say.

"It's just drawing stuff," she says, sitting back down across from me. "Draw three things that start with the letter 'S'. Not hard, but she loves art, so she never stops at three. It always ends up like an entire picture book."

Sounds like someone else I know—her mother, who drums her fingers along the table, looking anxious. She always was fidgety, but she used to channel that energy into creating.

"Do you still write?" I ask.

"No."

"Why not?"

She shrugs.

I want her to look at me. I know that's hypocritical. It's selfish. I want a lot. I'm *asking* for a lot, more than I deserve after everything that happened. I hurt her, and I wish I could take it back, be the man she thought I was.

I reach across the table, my fingertips barely grazing hers before she pulls her hands away. They disappear beneath the table—clenched into fists, probably. Wouldn't doubt it. It does the trick, though, her gaze meeting mine.

"What can I do?" I ask. "I'll do it."

I'm sounding fucking desperate, I know, but I am. My therapist would tell me it's unhealthy, that I'm being co-dependent. Jack would probably tell me to stop being a pathetic son of a bitch. Cliff, he'd likely remind me that I have the whole world at my fingertips, but that doesn't seem to matter, not when the first person to ever truly believe in me looks at me like I'm the worst of the worst.

She hesitates a moment, but before she can say anything, Madison waltzes in, slapping her paper down on the table between us.

"I need more that's an S," she says, her paper filled with a dozen of them. *Overachiever.*

"Snowflake," Kennedy says, scanning the paper, her hands back on the table as she points to something. "You spelled '*scissors*' wrong. There's a C after the first S."

Madison scowls, grabbing the paper to run out.

As soon as she's gone, I try again, reaching across the table for Kennedy's hands. She doesn't pull away this time when I touch her, my hands covering hers.

"Why are you doing this?" she asks, her voice quiet. "It's been six years, Jonathan. *Six years.*"

"I know, but I just…"

"You just *what?* Assume I still love you?"

"Do you?"

She shakes her head, but it's not a denial. It's more exasperation that I have the nerve to ask her that question.

Madison runs back in, and I pull my hands away, dropping it.

"How did you spell scissors?" she asks, erasing the word on her paper. Kennedy spells it out, and she writes it before tossing her pencil down. "Done!"

"Good job," Kennedy says. "You can play now."

Madison turns to me. "Do you wanna play?"

"Of course," I say, following her to her bedroom, figuring it best to give her mother some space, lest I push her too far and she punch me in the face.

I'm secure in my manhood. I have no qualms playing with dolls. So when Madison shoves a Barbie at me, I don't even balk. I'll give her the best goddamn Barbie performance she ever saw, if that's what she wants.

I stare at the Barbie, though, as Madison digs through a toy box. It looks different than the ones my sister played with growing up. This Barbie looks more like a scientist than a stripper, fully clothed, her hair still intact.

"Found it!" Madison says, holding up another doll. I freeze when I look at it, seeing the familiar white and blue suit and the head of blond hair. *You've gotta be kidding me.*

They made me into a doll. Or *him*, rather. Breezeo. Not an action figure, no—a straight up collector's edition Barbie doll.

"I'll be Breezeo and Barbie can be Maryanne for you," she says, sitting down on the floor and patting the wood beside her.

"Wait, shouldn't *I* be Breezeo?"

"You're him all the time, so it's my turn now."

Well, can't argue with that logic.

"Barbie's got the wrong color hair," I say. "Don't you have a Maryanne doll?"

"No, 'cuz it costs too many dollars, but you can pretend, right?"

"Right," I say, although she suddenly looks skeptical, like she doubts my abilities. "Don't worry, I've got this."

163

She starts things off. I don't know what's happening, and she doesn't give me any direction, so I'm improvising. She switches things up on me, throwing in plot twists. We're on the run from some bad guys before suddenly we're in school. I graduate, we both become veterinarians to her stuffed animals, and next thing I know, I'm running for president of the world.

It's funny. *She's* funny. The girl is quick on her feet. She gets distracted eventually, though, and puts down the doll to draw again. She's intense about it, in a trance, and I excuse myself, but I don't know if she notices. Picking up the Breezeo doll, I stroll down the hallway, seeing movement in another room.

Kennedy's bedroom.

She's sitting on the edge of her bed, changed out of her work uniform, wearing sweats and a tank top, busy pulling her hair up. I stall when I reach the doorway, still lurking in the hall, not wanting to invade her space. She eyes me warily, her attention shifting to the doll I'm holding.

She laughs.

Yeah, she fucking *laughs*.

"Did she make you perform for her?" she asks, nodding to the doll.

"No, she actually made me be Barbie," I say. "I don't think she was that impressed with my skills, because she gave up and went back to drawing."

Another laugh.

I could listen to that sound forever.

"Don't take it personal," she says, brushing past me out of the bedroom. "I'm sure you did a better job than I do. I usually get demoted to an audience member."

Kennedy heads to the living room. I follow her, curious, as she settles in on the couch, turning on the television. She curls up, flipping through channels in silence, the room dim. The sun is setting outside, which means they'll soon be going to bed.

"Do you work every day?" I ask.

"Weekdays."

164

"So you have weekends off?"

"Usually," she says. "I work while Maddie's in school."

"And when you're not working? What do you do?"

She cuts her eyes at me like I'm stupid.

I'm guessing this is it.

"I should probably get going," I say, strolling back to Madison's bedroom, finding her still drawing. "Hey, Maddie."

"Huh?"

"I'm gonna go now."

She stops what she's doing. "Why?"

"Because it's getting late."

"But why can't you stay?"

Because I fucked up years ago and I don't know if I can ever make things right again.

"I just can't," I say. "But I'll come back."

"Tomorrow?"

"Uh, not tomorrow, but soon."

"*When* soon?"

"First chance I get, I'll be here."

"Okay," she says, turning back to her drawing. "Bye!"

"Bye, Maddie."

Kennedy eyes me warily when I walk back into the living room.

"I have to head back to the city in the morning," I say, hesitating near the front door.

"You're leaving already," she says, a sharpness to her words. It's almost accusatory. "Should've known."

"I'm coming back."

"I'm sure you are."

I don't think she believes me.

As much as I want to stay and convince her, I know she won't believe me until I prove myself, so I leave the apartment, closing the door, and stand there until I hear her locking up.

⚜ ⚜ ⚜

"Well, if it isn't my favorite client…"

I stall in the doorway of McKleski's kitchen the moment those words strike me. *Cliff.* Morning sunshine streams through the downstairs of the inn, already warming the place to uncomfortable levels, because the old broad doesn't believe in air conditioning. Cliff sits at the kitchen table, eating what looks like an omelet, eyes glued to the Blackberry beside his plate.

McKleski is busy doing dishes across the room, scrubbing a pan she obviously used to cook for him this morning. *What the hell?*

"Are you talking to me?" I ask, not entirely sure at this point.

"Who else would I be talking to?"

"I don't know," I mumble, sitting down across from him. "Could be anybody."

He looks at me, eyes carefully scanning my face. I know what he's looking for. *The signs.* I'm pretty sure I look like hell. I haven't even bothered to shave. But he's not going to see them today, not going to see the signs. I want to say *fuck him* for thinking he might, but I can't really blame him for the suspicion, can I?

I've fucked up plenty of times.

"How are you?" he asks.

"Sober," I mumble.

"I can see that," he says. "Otherwise?"

"Kind of tired." I glance at his plate. "Kind of hungry."

"I'm sure your lovely hostess would be happy to whip you up some breakfast."

"No," McKleski chimes in. "I wouldn't."

"Or not," Cliff says, taking the last bite of his omelet, not even fazed.

"It's fine," I say. "I don't need anybody to take care of me. I can fend for myself."

Cliff drops his fork. "If that was true, I'd be out of a job."

"Whatever. What are you even doing here? How'd you figure

166

out where I was staying?"

"It's a small town," he says. "There weren't many options. And I'm here because you haven't been answering your phone, so I wasn't sure if you remembered you had an appointment. Figured I'd tag along so you didn't have to go alone."

"I remembered," I say. "And thanks."

"But for the record, if you'd finally hire a new assistant, I wouldn't have to concern myself with your schedule. It's been over a year since you've had anyone helping you. I still don't understand *why* you fired the last guy."

"He was a crackhead."

"And you were a cokehead."

"He stole from me."

"What did he steal? Your drugs?"

I'm not going to dignify that with a response.

It's true, but still… fuck that assumption.

"Can we go?" I ask. "I want to get this day over with."

"Huh, thought you were *less* of a moody prick these days."

"I am. I'm just… I don't know."

"Sounds like you." Cliff grabs his Blackberry and shoves his chair back as McKleski takes his empty plate. "Breakfast was wonderful. Thank you."

"Anytime," McKleski says, smiling. "I enjoy cooking for those that appreciate things."

I let that one slide.

Cliff stands, motioning for me to follow him, waiting until we're outside before he says, "Man, does that woman give you a hard time or what?"

"Always has," I say. "First time I ever got arrested, *she* was the one who called the police."

Cliff laughs as we approach a sleek black sedan.

"Nice car," I say.

"I rented it," he says. "Didn't want to call for a car service and give away your location."

"I appreciate that."

167

"Just doing my job," he says. "Come on, I'll drive."

I climb in the passenger seat.

I have a car. It's parked in a private garage in the city. I had it hauled in when filming started, in case I needed it, but I'm not supposed to drive until the doctor clears me. *Stick shift.*

It takes over two hours to get to the city. Another hour in traffic. Cliff valets the car when we reach the medical center. Weill Cornell. *Orthopedics.* I lower my head as we pass dozens of people, making our way to the seventh floor, going straight to the orthopedic surgeon's office, where they're awaiting my arrival.

Look, I get it—it's bullshit. Not just anybody can walk in and be seen right away, bypassing the waiting rooms. It's a privilege I'm grateful for—especially today. I'm nervous enough, being here, dealing with this. Anticipation and paranoia would make it insufferable.

"Mr. Cunning, how are you?" the doctor asks, standing up and holding his hand out, expecting me to shake it even wearing the sling.

"Okay," I say, ignoring his extended hand. "Ready to get this over with."

"A man on a mission," he says. "I like that."

He doesn't waste any more time, sending me straight for X-rays. It hurts like a son of a bitch when they examine my wrist, burning pain shooting up my arm and down to the tips of my fingers.

"Well, the good news is the bones haven't shifted, so doesn't appear you'll need surgery," the doctor says. "Bad news, of course, is you'll be in a cast for the next few weeks."

"Awesome," I mutter, flexing my fingers.

"How many weeks?" Cliff asks, standing in the corner of the office on his Blackberry.

"Hard to say for sure... four, I'd estimate."

"So another month?" Cliff asks.

"Yes," the doctor says. "He'll likely need some occupational therapy afterward."

"But he'll be out of the cast?"

"Yes."

"Good to know," Cliff says. "Is there any way to speed up the healing process?"

"Well, there's no miracle treatment, but some things might help. Vitamins. Calcium. Exercises."

"So get a stress ball and drink milk?"

"Pretty much," the doctor says. "Leafy greens are good."

They talk back and forth about me like I'm not even here. I stare down at my swollen wrist in annoyance as I wiggle my fingers.

"Anyway, let's get you wrapped up," the doctor says, "so you can be on your way."

A white fiberglass cast. He doesn't bother with the frilly colored bullshit, keeping it simple before sending me on my way.

I climb into the passenger seat of Cliff's rental, and he immediately starts rambling. "If you're out of the cast in the next few weeks, you can probably film again sooner than expected."

"You think so?" I ask, watching him as he goes through his Blackberry, checking his calendar.

"You've got a stunt-double to handle the action, so all they need is your voice…" He cuts his eyes at me. "And that pretty face of yours, of course."

"Of course," I mutter, trying like hell not to let that bruise my ego, but *damn*. Acting is more than just reciting lines. "What about Serena?"

"What about her?"

"She's in rehab."

"So?"

"So how are we going to start filming again next month if she's gone for ninety days?"

He gives me a look like I've lost my mind. "You really think she'll last that long?"

"You don't?"

"You never lasted," he says. "Not until you hit bottom."

"And you don't think she has?"

"Not even close. The only reason she's there right now is

because the studio demanded it," he says. "But don't worry about that. I'll take care of her. You worry about getting better."

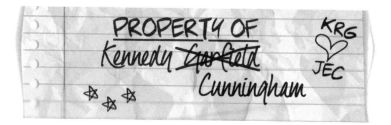

During the Revolutionary War, Aaron Burr had an illicit affair with the wife of a British officer.

You tell the girl that story.

You think it'll make her feel better.

She asks you who Aaron Burr is.

You laugh, because you can't understand how she's surviving at Fulton Edge when she doesn't even know the name of the man who killed Alexander Hamilton, but she is. She's surviving, maybe even *thriving.* She works hard and she's passing. Meanwhile, you barely pay attention and still ace every test.

But you show up to class now. Every single day.

Maybe you do it because you don't want to be expelled. You've made it this far. Might as well see it through. Or maybe you show up to be with *her.*

Both of you are on track to graduate in a month. The entire school year almost gone in a blink. You spent most of it sneaking around, whispered conversations and secret rendezvous, meeting under the cloak of darkness without her dad knowing. He forbid her from seeing you. He told her you would cause nothing but trouble.

Thing is, she already knew that.

That wasn't enough to stop her.

"So, Vassar, huh?" you ask, sitting beside her on the picnic table at the park near her house. It's dark, pushing midnight, and you just got done with a full rehearsal for *Julius Caesar.* The Drama Club is putting it on in three weeks as part of graduation festivities. "Liberal Arts. Bet your dad loves that."

"Yeah, he looked at me about the same way he did when he realized we were sleeping together."

Man, he hadn't taken that well *at all.* Full-blown rage to the point of taking his grievances to his boss. Your father shrugged it off, though, saying you've done worse things than *bedding a girl.* Needless to say, her dad isn't enjoying his job much anymore.

She's committed to attending Vassar College next year. Meanwhile, you haven't decided anything. You're not even sure you *want* to go to college. You have dreams but they don't include studying law at Princeton. You got accepted somehow. You didn't even apply. The whole thing reeks of your father.

"Congratulations," you say. "It's a great school."

The future isn't something you and her have talked much about. You've never even given this thing you have a title. No promises.

You don't promise things. *Ever.*

But the future is coming up fast. It's about to be *the present.* And whatever this is between you is going to be affected.

She nudges you with her shoulder. "Will you come see me?"

"I'm sure I'll pop up from time to time."

"You better," she says. "I'm going to miss you."

She's getting emotional, her voice cracking around those words.

"We've still got a few weeks," you say, shoving up from the picnic table as you grab her hand, pulling her to her feet. "Let's not waste tonight worrying about it."

You take a walk together, holding hands. There's an inn nearby, beyond the edge of the park. A cranky middle-aged woman runs it, one of the only people you've ever encountered your nights when you meet up here. The inn is dark tonight. Sheets hang out on a clothesline, left overnight.

You snatch one off.

Along the water, you lay it down on the grass. You lay her down on top of it. You know you'll have some privacy tucked back here, away from the picnic area. You don't want to waste any more of tonight. Every stitch of clothing is removed, and you take your time teasing her, and tasting her, before you make love to her.

You're going to miss her, too.

You don't tell her that, not with words, but she knows. She feels it in every kiss. In every thrust of your hips. You make her laugh as you're deep inside of her. You tell her she's beautiful as she moans beneath you.

You lay there after you finish, still on top of her, catching your breath as you kiss her neck. You're careful not to leave marks anymore.

There's a rustling nearby, along the water, shadows moving in the darkness. You only have the moonlight to see. Whatever it is comes closer... closer... closer. It's coming right for you.

The girl notices. She screams, the piercing sound shattering the silence of the night, when the thing in the shadows makes a noise beside her. *QUACK.*

She shoves you off of her. You're laughing too hard to calm her down. She scrambles away, shrieking, yanking the sheet out from under you to wrap up in it, scattering your clothes.

"It's just a duck," you tell her, sitting naked in the grass. You're still laughing as the duck veers toward her, quacking like crazy in reaction to the noise she's making.

"A *duck*?" she says. "What does it want? Oh my god, it's following me. Why is it following me?"

"It's probably hungry," you say.

"Do I *look* like duck food?" she asks, trying to shoo it away. "Go

173

home, Daffy."

You get to your feet and gather up the clothes, tossing hers at her. The duck waddles off, heading for the water. It's too late, though. She made too much of a ruckus.

There's movement again. More ducks are coming.

She runs away, toward the inn, carrying her clothes. You start to follow when a blast of light shatters the night. A flashlight. You freeze, alarmed. Someone is there. The girl hides in the backyard of the inn, but you hesitate too long. The flashlight finds you as a voice calls out, "Police! Let me see your hands!"

Your clothes drop. You stand there, in all your naked glory, and hold your hands up in front of you as a police officer approaches. He orders you to get dressed before putting you in handcuffs.

The girl starts to step out from the shadows. The police don't know she's there. But you do, and you shake your head, warning her not to do it.

The woman who runs the inn heard noises outside and called the police. Trespassers. She stands on her back porch, watching you get arrested.

Indecent exposure.

And you don't know this, but that girl? She runs the whole way home wrapped up in nothing but that stolen sheet, her clothes abandoned. Her mother is awake when she gets there and hears her come in. You see, the woman has known her daughter sneaks out at night for months, but she's never said a word about it. *A mother knows.* She knows what it's like to love the boy the world tries to keep you from. Her mother would lay awake at night, listening, to make sure she made it back home, but this morning is different. The woman senses it. The girl confesses. She tells her you were arrested. *'Don't worry,'* her mother says. *'I'll help him.'*

THIRTEEN

KENNEDY

You interested in going out tonight?

I absently tap my fingers against the screen as I stare at the text message on my phone, debating how to answer that. Yes? No? Yes? No? *Ugh.* I type out some long-winded excuse before erasing it with a groan, typing some more utter crap before erasing that also. I type out 'no,' straight to the point, but *ugh*, I feel guilty, so I instead type 'sure' and press send like an idiot.

The second that it says 'Delivered' beneath the text bubble, I want to slap myself. So many regrets already.

"*Ugh*, what is wrong with you?" I ask myself, making a face as I start to type an excuse to get me out of it.

A throat clears behind me. "Wouldn't know where to start."

That voice, it catches me off guard, so close I can feel his warm breath fanning across my skin. A chill shoots through me, my hands shaking as I spin around, losing grip of my phone. It drops, landing facedown on the hard epoxy tile of the aisle. I cringe when it hits, but I don't reach for it because of *him*.

Jonathan.

He's *right there*, standing here in the grocery store, a foot of space between us, so close I have to look up to meet his eyes. My heart stalls a beat, being a traitorous nitwit, before it hammers in my chest, aggressively battering my ribcage like my insides are declaring war on my sanity.

Jonathan picks up my phone as it makes a noise. Before I can stop him, he glances at the screen and freezes. Something flashes in his eyes. He looks horrified. *Oh god.*

"It's broken, isn't it?"

He blinks at me. "Huh?"

"My phone."

"Oh, uh... no." Shaking it off, he hands the phone to me, screen still intact. "Whoever *Andrew* is wants a time."

What time should I pick you up?

The text is prominently displayed. My stomach bottoms out. My hands are still shaking, and I shove the phone in my back pocket without answering that question.

"What are you doing here?" I ask. "I thought you left town."

"I did," he says. "I told you I'd be back, didn't I?"

"Yes, but I didn't know you meant *that* quick. I wouldn't have noticed you left. Why'd you even tell me?"

"Figured you should know."

"Why?"

He shrugs, like maybe he doesn't understand it, either. Before either of us can make sense of things, a feminine voice rings out in the aisle beside us, calling my name. *Bethany.* Panic flows through me. I don't give it much thought, acting in the moment, a knee-jerk reaction to her approach.

I grab ahold of him, gripping tight to his arm and take off in a hurry. He doesn't resist, doesn't put up a fight as I drag him down the aisle, away from the sound of her voice, and shove him into a small back stockroom. I dart inside and shut the door, casting us in near total darkness. I can't see Jonathan anymore, but I can feel him, right behind me, pressing up against me, his hand coming to rest on my hip. His touch heightens my panic. I shove away from him, putting space between us.

"Why are you here?" I ask, keeping my voice low. "You can't be here."

"I, uh…"

"Kennedy?" Bethany calls out from the other side of the door. "Are you back here?"

"Don't talk," I hiss at Jonathan. "Don't even *breathe*."

176

I open the door again and slip out, leaving it cracked behind me as I come face-to-face with Bethany. Her brow furrows as she looks into the pitch-black room behind me. "What are you doing?"

"Inventory."

"In the dark?"

"Yeah, I, uh… *yep*." I glance behind me before turning back to her. "Did you need something?"

"Marcus told me to find you." Her face twists into a fake pout. *Oh god*. "I asked for the Saturday off in two weeks, and he said the only way I can have it is if I find someone to cover."

"And you want me to do it?"

"Please?" She pokes her bottom lip out. "I wouldn't ask, but it's important!"

"Okay."

"Breeze-Con is that weekend, and they're having this big thing for the tenth anniversary of *Ghosted*."

"Okay."

"And I know it probably sounds silly to you but—"

"I said okay. Go. Have fun."

"You mean it?"

"Wouldn't say it if I didn't."

She lets out a squeal and hugs me. "Thank you, Kennedy! *Oh my god*, you're the best!"

"You're welcome," I say, prying her off. "I'm gonna get back to, you know, stuff."

I nod toward the stockroom.

Her eyes narrow. "What are you really doing?"

"Bye, Bethany."

I slip back in the room, slamming the door and leaning up against it.

Humor tinges every syllable of Jonathan's words as he says, "She sounds like you back in high school. How scary could she be?"

Rolling my eyes, I feel along the wall beside me, flicking up the light switch. It doesn't make it very bright, but I can see him

177

propped up against a crate, a smirk on his lips.

"She writes fanfic," I tell him. "The self-insert kind."

His smile only grows.

"I'm not taking about Breezeo. Oh no, I'm talking Johnny Cunning fanfic. *Erotica*."

The first flicker of concern shows on his eyes, but he still smiles. "So did you."

I roll my eyes. "That's completely different."

"Still, she's just a girl with fantasies," he says. "Nothing to hide from."

"True, but do you really think she'll keep it to herself? Come on, her idol shows up where she works? The only way it could ever be more fic-come-true is if we were working in a coffee shop here. Before you even made it out the door, it would be *all* over social media. But I mean, unless that's *what* you want…"

He shakes his head.

Didn't think so.

It grows quiet for a moment before he says, "Kale."

"Kale?"

"That's why I'm here. I needed to grab kale."

"Oh."

That's all I say.

It grows quiet again.

Awkward.

There are no windows in here, making the room feel impossibly small. Just him and I, confined together after all this time, breathing the same air, the room filled to the brim with strained silence. So much to say, but no words strong enough to clear the air between us.

"I wish shit wasn't so weird," he says eventually. "I wish you weren't so distant."

"Yeah, well, that's what happens when people break up."

"I know, I just wish there was a way we could…"

"Could *what?*"

He doesn't answer right away, looking away from me like

he's struggling to find a way to explain. *Forget? Move on? Start over?*

"Be," he says. "I wish we could just *be*."

For such a talented actor, he wasn't always good at expressing himself with me, but then again, I wasn't much better. Maybe that was why we worked so well. He spoke through the characters he played, and I... well, I used to *create*. The two of us always seemed to be on the same page until the day we just weren't anymore, and there was no way to get back to that place once we struggled so much to communicate.

But for a time, we just... *were*.

It's the most comforting feeling in the world.

When you lose it, though, it's the most confusing. It's like losing a piece of your soul.

"I'm sorry," he says, glancing at me again.

"How many times are you going to apologize?"

"As many as it takes until you believe me."

"I do," I say. "I believe you."

"You do?"

"Yeah, I do."

He stares at me when I say that. He doesn't respond, but I can tell he's holding back some reaction.

"Anyway, we should get you out of here before you get spotted," I say, pushing away from the door. "I can grab your kale for you."

I turn to leave but he stops me, grabbing my arm as he stands up from the crate. I tense, letting out a shuddering exhale when he pulls me to him. It's just a brief moment as he holds me there, a breath away, so close that if I stood on my tiptoes, I could taste his lips if I wanted to.

I do.

Or at least some part of me, deep down, does, a stirring in my gut that almost spurs me on. The moment he touches me, it's like I'm drunk. But the moment is over just like that when he says, "I also need milk."

His voice, those words—they sober me up. "*Milk.*"

"Yes," he says, letting go of my arm. "If you don't mind."

"Uh, sure, no problem."

I walk out, and he follows, diverting halfway through the store to head for the exit while I grab his stuff. I don't hear any frantic screams, so I assume he made it out.

Bethany lingers at her register, not paying attention to any of her surroundings, flipping through the latest edition of *Hollywood Chronicles*.

"Anything interesting?" I ask, setting the kale and the milk on the conveyer belt.

Bethany sighs, tossing the tabloid aside. "Not really. I swear it's like Johnny Cunning vanished into thin air. Nobody has seen him *anywhere*."

My eyes flicker to the exit, catching a faint glimpse of him lurking outside. "I'm sure he's... around."

"I hope so," she says. "Ugh, I hope he's not like, dead in a ditch somewhere. That would suck."

"Yeah, it would," I agree as she rings the stuff up.

After I pay for it, she picks the tabloid back up and continues reading. I make my way outside once she's distracted, carrying the bag to where Jonathan lingers.

"Here," I say, shoving it at him. "Your milk and your kale so you can go feed ducks or whatever you're doing with it."

He lets out a light laugh. "It's for me. Doctor's orders."

"That's horrible."

"Ah, could be worse."

"If you say so," I mumble, glancing at my watch. "I should get back to work."

I go to head back to the store when he calls out to me. "K?"

I glance at him, words on the tip of my tongue, but I don't get a single syllable out. The look on his face stuns me into silence, the vulnerability, like he's splitting himself open right now.

"Thank you," he says quietly.

I nod, hesitating before saying, "If you change your mind about eating the kale, I'm sure Maddie would be happy to help you get rid of it."

He smiles. It's a genuine smile, unconscious, like happiness is radiating from inside of him at that suggestion. I don't say anything else, nor do I wait for his response. Being around him is proving dangerous for my feelings. *Dangerous to my sanity.*

I head back into the store, strolling past Bethany at her register. She sets the tabloid down to look at me. "Didn't you just leave?"

"I stepped outside," I say. "I still have another hour until my shift is over."

"What did you do with your stuff?"

"Put it in my car."

"Even the milk?"

"Uh… yeah."

"But won't it go bad in this heat?"

"Probably."

She stares at me, mumbling, "I swear, you're *so* weird sometimes."

✿ ✤ ✿

"I should cancel."

"You should do no such thing." Meghan's voice is pointed, matter-of-fact, *don't you freaking argue with me* when she says that. "What you should do is take the guy for a ride, if you know what I'm saying."

"Meghan…"

"I'm serious," she says. "Just a quick spin around the block to see how he runs, make that engine purr for a little while."

"Since when are you pro-Drew?"

"I'm not." She makes a face of disgust. "I'm pro-orgasm, and I know it's been a long while since you've had one."

I laugh… until a little voice chimes in, asking, "What's that?"

Maddie sits at the kitchen table across from Meghan, swinging her legs as she draws her heart out on a piece of paper.

"What's what?" I ask, leaning back against the kitchen counter, arms crossed over my chest.

"What Aunt Meghan said," Maddie says. "What's the orga, uh…?"

"Organism," I blurt out, realizing she's about to ask us what an *orgasm* is.

"Organism," she says. "What's that?"

"It's from science," Meghan says. "It's what they call a living thing, you know, anything that's alive."

"You don't got one of those?" Maddie asks, looking up from her drawing, eyebrows raised. "Not for a long time?"

"Well, I have *you*," I say, pausing beside her chair as I ruffle her hair. "You're as alive as it gets. Don't need anything else… not even those crazy *organisms* Meghan's all about."

Maddie seems pretty pleased with that answer as she goes back to drawing, while Meghan shoots me a look, half-apologetic, half-pathetic. I roll my eyes, flipping her off out of Maddie's line of sight. "I guess I ought to get dressed."

"Something sexy!" Meghan shouts at me.

I go with something simple instead—skinny jeans, black flats, black shirt. I brush my hair, leaving the dark locks hanging loose, and put on a dash of makeup. *Done.* Meghan scrunches up her nose at me, but she keeps her opinion to herself.

"Mommy, can you do my stars?" Maddie asks, shoving her paper and pencil at me.

"Sure thing," I say. I'm not sure what it is she's making, but I can tell the skyline easily. I've showed her the easy way to draw stars a few times—*mountain, diagonal, across, connect*—but she always asks me to do them for her, since it's pretty much the *only* thing I can draw.

A knock echoes from the front door of the apartment. Meghan sighs as she shoves her chair back to stand, whispering as she passes me, "Sounds like your *organism* is here."

"I'll be right there," I mumble, finishing up the stars before handing the pencil back to Maddie. "I have to go, sweetheart."

"Where?"

"Out with my friend."

"Can I come this time?"

"Not tonight," I tell her, frowning when I see the disappointment in her eyes. "Someday, though."

"Is it your friend that didn't see you were pretty last time?"

"Uh, yeah, same one."

She makes a face.

I almost laugh.

But then I hear another knock on the door, Meghan's voice ringing out over the sound of it as she says, "Jesus, hold your damn ho—oh my fucking god. *No.*"

I tense at the sudden change in her tone, from flippant to shocked within half a word.

"No… no… no," she chants before saying, "Get the fuck out of here."

I look out of the kitchen, toward the front door, heart wildly racing. Jonathan stands on the small stoop in front of my apartment, a mere few feet in front of his sister.

"Meghan," he says, nodding to her in greeting.

The moment he says her name, the shock wears away, replaced by anger as her eyes narrow.

"No," she says, matter-of-fact, slamming the door right in his face.

Maddie jumps at the sound of the bang.

"Meghan," I groan. "*Please.*"

I don't need a scene, not one I'll have to try to explain. Meghan yanks the door back open. Jonathan still stands there, having not moved at all.

Maddie gasps, noticing him, and jumps down from her chair at the table, snatching up her drawing as she runs for the door. "Jonathan!"

"Hey," he says, avoiding looking at his sister, instead smiling at Maddie.

"You're back!" She shoves her paper at him. "I was making

you a picture!"

"Wow," he says, looking at it. "It's amazing."

"It's not done," she says, snatching it back from him, "but all I gotta do is the people now, because Mommy drawed the stars!"

"Well, they're some great stars," he says, meeting my gaze. "I'm sure it'll be perfect."

"You can have it when it's done," she tells him. "Are you gonna stay? You can play with me and Aunt Meghan!"

Meghan makes a noise.

"Not tonight," he says. "I just came by to talk to your mom for a minute."

Maddie frowns, mumbling, "okay," before she shuffles away.

Jonathan closes his eyes, letting out a deep sigh. I can tell he wants to change his mind.

"Maybe tomorrow," I chime in, stepping in Maddie's path so she'll stop walking. Grasping her chin, I tilt her head up, making her look at me. "It's kind of late to be playing tonight, anyway."

"Tomorrow," Jonathan agrees. "I'll be here."

Her eyes light up, disappointment fading.

"See you tomorrow!" she yells back at him before wrapping her arms around me. "Love you, Mommy."

"Love you, too," I say, "more than banana Popsicles and Hawaiian pizza."

"More than the dates with your friend?"

"Oh, *pfft*, of course." I playfully squeeze her cheeks. "More than dates with anybody."

Leaning down, I give her a quick kiss before she runs off to her bedroom. The second she's out of the room, the second she's out of earshot, Meghan's voice cuts in, a low growl as she says, "You *better* bring your ass back here tomorrow, little brother, because if you lied to her right in front of me, I swear to God…"

"I said I'll be here," he says, turning to look at Meghan, his expression hard. "I'm not going to lie to her."

"Oh! Is that right?"

"Yes," he says.

"Well, excuse me!" She throws her hands up. "Stupid me, should've known… I mean, you've only lied to every-fucking-body else. Forgot you were *daddy of the year.*"

"Now's not the time for this," I grumble, stalking over and coming between them. "Sort this out when there aren't little ears nearby."

I push Jonathan away from the apartment as I step outside, shutting the front door behind me to give us some privacy. Otherwise, Meghan might be inclined to add her commentary, like my life is an episode of *Mystery Science Theater 3000.*

"Sorry about this," he says, motioning toward the apartment. "I forgot, well, that you had *plans.*"

"It's fine," I say. "What did you need to talk to me about?"

"I just… I was thinking."

He's hesitating. *Stalling.* I can tell he's nervous from the way he averts his gaze. "About?"

"About something that girl said at your work."

My brow furrows, and it takes a moment before I figure out who he means. "Bethany?"

"Is that her name?" He stares off into space, mumbling, "Bethany."

"You met her once," I tell him. "She came to the set. Said she saw you outside of a bar."

He lets out a light laugh. "Ah, right. *Bethany.* She asked me about that time I got arrested."

She did. She told me about it. And all I can think is how incredibly happy she'd be to know he remembered her.

"Anyway," he says, that nervousness creeping back in. "Bethany mentioned wanting time off so she could go to that thing."

"The convention?"

"Yeah, you know, for the Breezeo shit, and I was thinking, and just wondering…"

"Wondering what?"

"If maybe I could take Madison?"

It takes a moment for those words to sink in, for what he's

185

asking me to register. I blink at him, at a loss for words, a sinking feeling in the pit of my stomach. I don't know what to say. I don't know what to *think*. A voice in the back of my mind is screaming out, on defense, terrified by that, but my heart—my stupid, *stupid* heart—is soaring at him wanting to do that with her.

"I, uh…" I shake my head, trying to clear my thoughts. "Wow."

"I know I'm asking for a lot," he says. "I'm asking for some trust, just a little bit, and I don't blame you if you won't give it to me, but I just… I'm asking. Can I take her?"

I open my mouth, still having no idea what to say, when movement catches my eye seconds before a voice cuts in. "Am I interrupting?"

Eight-thirty on the dot, I'm guessing. *Drew*. I don't turn, don't look at him right away, but Jonathan does. His back straightens, shoulders squaring, every inch of him rigid. I watch as his face clouds with confusion, hoping there's no recognition, but it's instant.

Confusion gives way to a raw sort of anger, the kind that has simmered for ages. He glares at Drew like he wants to tear his heart out, rip it from his chest and shove it down his throat.

Jonathan's voice is as scathing as his gaze when he says, "Hastings."

"Cunningham," Drew says, unfazed.

"What the hell are you doing? Why are you *here*?"

Drew points at me. "Picking her up."

I see it, as Jonathan connects the dots, realizing *he's* the plan I have tonight. *Andrew Hastings*. It's been a long time since I've heard somebody call him by his last name alone.

Jonathan turns to me, his expression hard as he tries to hold back his anger, but he's struggling.

"*Him*?" Jonathan asks. "*This* is who you're dating? *This* is the guy you're going out with?"

I start to answer, but he doesn't let me.

"Unbelievable." Jonathan shakes his head. "How *could* you?"

Those words send my defenses up. "Excuse me?"

"He's a part of your life? Madison's life? Jesus Christ, you let him around her? What the hell are you thinking?"

"Don't," I say, holding my hands up to stop him before he says anything else. "Don't even go there right now."

"You should listen to the lady," Drew chimes in, "and mind your business."

"This *is* my fucking business," Jonathan says, taking a step toward Drew, everything about him suddenly full of aggression. "We're talking about my daughter here. *Mine.* And I don't know what kind of shit you pulled to force your way into their lives, but you can't have her mother, either. You can't have either one of them. You can't steal my fucking life!"

"Stop it," I growl, stepping between them.

Jonathan shakes his head, furious, left hand clenched into a fist. I don't think he's going to swing, since his right hand is in a cast, but I can tell he wants to.

And it doesn't help matters a bit when Drew laughs. Amusement coats his voice when he says, "Can't steal what was up for grabs."

That sets Jonathan off. He comes at Drew, but I'm in the way. I shove him, hard, making him back up. "Just... leave, Jonathan. *Leave!*"

He looks at me, his expression hard as he says, "I can't believe you."

Turning, he walks away, leaving me standing here, fuming. *Unbelievable.*

He can't believe me? *Me?* After everything *he's* done? He wants to act as if I'm the one in the wrong?

"I see he showed his face again," Drew says. "How long has he been here?"

"Uh, two weeks, maybe," I mumble, watching as Jonathan disappears into the night.

"You haven't mentioned it."

"Didn't want to talk about it," I say. "Still don't."

"Fair enough." Drew grasps my shoulder, squeezing it gently. "How about we get out of here, forget this happened?"

"Sounds good," I mumble, giving him a smile, but I know that's a lost cause. Forgetting this is out of the question. I can feel my blood simmering. I want to follow that man right into the darkness and give him a piece of my mind.

FOURTEEN

JONATHAN

One step forward, fifty steps back.

That's how it feels, like getting knocked on my ass the second I find the strength to stand up.

My phone lays beside where I sit, on top of the old wooden picnic table, under the veil of darkness that earlier settled over the park. It's stupid. I'm stupid. No, worse than that—I'm *weak*. My contacts are open on the phone, the screen lit up, but I don't have it in me to press any buttons.

The glass bottle feels heavy in my hands. A fifth of whiskey. I don't recognize the brand. I grabbed the first thing I came upon in the corner store on my way here, something cheap and rough.

I can almost *feel* the burn.

I stare at it.

And stare at it.

And fucking stare at it.

The bottle's still sealed.

Would be so easy to crack it open and take a drink, dull the pain—the anger, the *anguish*.

Grasping the lid, I unscrew it, breaking the seal and getting a whiff of the strong, stringent liquor, when my phone vibrates against the picnic table. Jack's name flashes on the screen. Sighing, I ignore it, but he calls back.

Again.

And again.

"Goddamn it," I mutter, answering his fourth call, hitting the button to put it straight on speaker. "Always knew you'd be a pain in the ass, Jack. Didn't realize you were also psychic."

Jack laughs. "What can I say? I sensed a disturbance in the force. Figured I'd spit some Yoda-isms at you for a bit. *A fuck up, you are.*"

"Funny," I mutter.

"Truthfully, I was calling to congratulate you."

"For what?"

"For going a week without gracing the front of a single tabloid," he says. "Went to the grocery store earlier and didn't see your ugly mug *anywhere*. Made my day."

"I'm glad I could do that for you," I say.

"I appreciate it more than you know," he says. "Now tell me what I can do for *you*."

I hesitate, staring at the bottle. "Nothing."

"Bullshit," he says. "Try again."

"You know, you're supposed to be supportive and follow my lead."

"Again, *bullshit*. If you wanted to be coddled, you would've picked someone else as your sponsor. That's not me. I'm not babying a grown ass man when he's whining for a bottle."

"Yeah, well, fuck you."

"Spill it, Cunning," he says with a laugh. "Tell me how the big bad world hurt you."

I'm not in the mood to talk, but I know he's not going to drop the subject, so *fuck it*—I ramble, telling him all about the shitty day I've had.

He listens quietly, waiting until I'm done before he says, "Well, that sucks."

I laugh bitterly, because yeah, it does. It *sucks.*

"Your own fault, though," he adds.

"I know," I mutter.

"Do you? Because I'm guessing, and correct me if I'm wrong, but you're probably sitting alone somewhere, moping, about to drown your sorrows like you're the victim."

I glance around the park. It's like he's watching me. "Seriously, are you psychic?"

"Nah, I just know you," he says. "You're a self-sabotaging piece of shit some days."

"Thanks."

"You're welcome," he says. "But you know, most days, you're pretty okay."

"That's nice of you."

"Too bad your movies suck."

That makes me laugh. "Yeah, too bad."

"But anyway, if you're done bitching about the poor pitiful life of a Hollywood heartthrob, I'm gonna get back to my glamorous existence of trolling online and talking shit about your kind in the comments section."

"You do that," I say. "Thanks, Jack."

"Anytime, Cunning. Just call me next time. Sensing the force doesn't always work. I'm going to be pissed if you get drunk and I don't have the chance to yell at you about it first."

"I'll call," I tell him. "Next time."

�֍ �֍ �֍

Noise startles me awake, drawing me from a restless sleep, the sound of footsteps stomping up the creaky wooden stairs. I stare at the ceiling, trying to blink the grogginess away, as the sound grows louder, closer, shadows shifting outside the bedroom door.

No hesitation, the door flings open so hard it slams into the wall. Light streams into the room from the hallway, disrupting the darkness. I wince, sitting straight up, trying to get my wits about me as I shield my eyes. "What the hell?"

"You've got some nerve," a voice says, a sharp edge of anger to those words—so angry, in fact, that it takes a second for me to recognize it.

"Kennedy?" Caught off guard, I blink at her as she steps into the bedroom. Shadows mask her features, but it's her, all right... she's here, a few feet from the bed. I rub my eyes, trying to wake up. "Jesus, am I dreaming or something?"

"I can't believe you," she says, stepping closer. "That's what you said to me. *I can't believe you.* But I've done nothing wrong. *Nothing.*"

I blink at her, trying to make sense of that. "What?"

"What? Seriously? *What?*" She throws her hands up, coming even closer. "You act like I'm this horrible person, like I've done some horrible thing that you can't understand, but I didn't. I'm *not.* This isn't my fault! You left me, Jonathan."

"I didn't—"

"You did!"

She's standing right in front of me, so close that I can see her hands shaking as she clenches them into fists, tears swimming in her eyes. I glance around, trying to get some sense of the time, but I'm not sure where my phone is and there's not a clock nearby. It's dark, though—pitch black—so I'm guessing it's past midnight.

"You left me, Kennedy," I say, looking back at her, "not the other way around."

"You're wrong," she says. "I walked away. There's a difference. You left me long before that. I was pregnant, and you left me."

"I didn't—"

"You did!"

I stall a moment when she cuts me off before saying, "I didn't know."

"That doesn't make it any better!"

I want to argue, wanting to defend myself, but there's no defending this shit. "Look, I was wrong, and I'm sorry for that."

"So you keep saying, but sorry doesn't change anything, Jonathan, not when you keeping acting like, ugh... *that.*"

She waves toward me, and I glance down at myself. "What are you talking about?"

"You show up here, and have the nerve to try to weasel your

way into my life, into my *mind*, like you have any right to be there after all this time. You have the nerve to judge me for who I hang around… you have the nerve to question my parenting, like I don't know what's best for my daughter!"

Something clicks with me when she says that, some of the fog lifting. "Jesus… is this about him? *Hastings?*"

"No, this is about *you.*" She points at me. "You and your innocent act… and your money, and your things. The words you say—the jokes, the laughs, the smiles you give her that she eats right up, and ugh, your *face.*"

"My face?"

"Your stupid fucking face," she says, running her hands through her hair as she groans, those words startling me. Kennedy doesn't curse. "Your face is *everywhere*. I'm sick of it!"

"You're sick of my face."

"Yes!"

"There's not much I can do about that."

"You can get out of my head," she says. "Stop being there all the time!"

I laugh at that, because it's so damn absurd, but that's the wrong thing to do. Her eyes narrow as she stares me down, looking like she wants to hit me right now.

"I hate you," she says, her voice shaking. "I've never hated someone as much as I hate you, Jonathan."

Those words, they wake me right up. I'm no longer laughing. There's nothing funny about it. I got under her skin, and with the two of us already on shaky ground, I know that's dangerous.

She turns to leave, like she's going to walk away, but I grab her arm to stop her. "Come on, don't be like that…"

"Don't touch me," she says, ripping from my grasp.

I let go as I stand up, stepping toward her. "Just… wait a minute… talk to me."

"There's nothing left to say."

"I'll be goddamned." I grab her arm again before she can walk out. "You can't tell me you hate me and then leave. That's bullshit. You bust up in here while I'm asleep to yell at me..."

"You deserve it!"

"Maybe so, but still..."

"Still *nothing*," she says, turning to me again, getting right in my face. "I hate you. That's it. There's nothing else to say. I hate everything about you. Your voice, your *face*... I hate it. Why aren't you going away?"

"Because I can't," I tell her, "and I'm pretty sure you don't really want me to."

She scoffs.

"You're upset," I say, "but you're lying to yourself if you think you want me gone."

"I do."

"You don't."

"Leave."

"No."

"*Go away.*"

"I'm not."

As soon as that last word leaves my lips, she's on me, slamming into me, her lips pressing against mine. She's kissing me, and I'm so fucking stunned that it takes me a moment to react, a moment to consider kissing her back. She moans and wraps her arms around my neck, clinging to me damn near aggressively as she kicks the door closed.

There's a bitter tang on her tongue.

In a daze, it doesn't register right away, but the second that it does the world seems to stop.

I push away from her, breaking the kiss with a groan. "You've been drinking, K."

She's breathing heavily. Even in the darkness, I can tell her cheeks are flushed. Wide eyes regard me as she says, "It was just some wine."

She doesn't seem drunk, but well, there's no way in hell she's thinking clearly, not if what she's thinking about right now is kissing.

But before I can say anything, she's on me again, kissing, pressing against me and pushing me toward the bed. *Whoa.* She's not gentle about it. My ribs fucking ache. Her hands are all over, tugging at my clothes, a chill shooting down my spine when her warm fingertips reach bare skin.

"I don't think this is a good idea," I say. "We shouldn't—"

"Just *shut up*," she growls against my lips, hands winding through my hair, gripping it.

The back of my knees hit the mattress, and I fall back on it, dragging her down with me. Pain rips through my skull, damn near blinding, rivaling the burning happening in my chest.

I hiss. "*Fuck.*"

Her kiss grows harder, frenzied, desperation in her touch. She's not slowing down, showing no signs of stopping. Every stab of pain strikes deep, getting me all worked up. My heart is beating a million miles an hour.

"You sure you wanna do this?" I ask when she straddles me.

Her voice is a breathy whisper when she says, "No."

"Maybe we should stop."

"Shut up."

I laugh at that, shutting up, because I'm not going to argue. Maybe this moment is all wrong, and maybe it shouldn't be happening, but there's very little I want in this world more than I want this woman, so I'm not turning her down.

I drag her further onto the bed, struggling to keep a grip on her with one hand. *Damn cast.* Her hand slips down my pants, grasping my cock, and she strokes me, over and over.

"Fuck," I groan. "Fuck, fuck, *fuck…*"

If she doesn't stop that, I'm going to bust. Right here, right now, just like this.

I flip her over, climbing on top, fumbling with her pants as I try to pull them off. She doesn't hesitate, stripping out of her clothes, flinging them across the room. I don't bother getting naked, just freeing myself from the confines of my pants as I settle between her legs, between her thighs, *right there.*

Questions flow through my mind—so many questions, almost as many objections—until she whispers, "Make me feel good again, Jonathan."

I'm inside her then, not a moment of second-guessing, pushing in slowly with a deep groan.

So tight. So wet. *So goddamn beautiful.*

"Oh god," she whimpers, clinging to me.

I'm still dazed. Hell, maybe this is a dream. But it doesn't matter, because I'm not waking up from it. Slow, and deep, the way I know she always liked it, teasing to the point of agony.

It's *torture.*

Ten minutes, maybe an hour—I don't know. Pleasure rushes through me, my breathing haggard, parts of me brutally hurting, but I keep on going. Fucking her, making love—I'm not sure what this is, but her soft cries fill the room as her nails rake down my back, so I know she's all in. Sweat forms along my brow, a sheen coating her body, her skin slick and glistening in the dim moonlight from the window. I taste it, as I kiss her neck, the salty tang on my tongue.

I bite, and lick, and suck. I'm probably leaving marks, but the harder my mouth works, the more she squirms.

When she comes, her back arches, her face contorting and mouth falling open in ecstasy. She lets out a strangled cry, almost like she's choking, *suffocating,* before she dissolves into whimpers. Fuck, that sound does something to me...

I come, grunting, before stilling on top of her, trying to catch my breath, trying to clear my head. What the hell is happening? She's trembling beneath me, and I'm worried she's panicking. But when I pull back to look down at her, she smashes her lips to mine again, sending me reeling.

❀ ❀ ❀

Five o'clock.

That's what my phone says when I slip out of bed much later, finding it shoved in the pocket of the jeans I'd been wearing, the battery hovering down at ten percent. Notifications take up the screen, most of them messages from Cliff.

I can get those convention tickets. Why do you want them?

You remember they invited you, right?

You were supposed to be the headliner.

I know. I remember. I declined. Not that I didn't *want* to do it, but Cliff didn't think it wouldn't be wise considering when the invitation came, my sobriety was still on shaky ground.

Still is, asshole.

I sigh as I stroll to the door, glancing back at the bed at *her*.

Kennedy.

My eyes skim along her naked back, following the curve of her spine. She's curled up, cuddling a pillow, a flimsy white sheet draped over parts of her. She's sleeping, lightly snoring—in and out all night long.

The world is lightening as sunrise nears. I leave the room, my bare feet quiet as I make my way downstairs, replying to Cliff. **Forget about it.**

His response is instant, of course, because he doesn't sleep.

You sure?

I type a quick '**Yes**' before slipping the phone in the pocket of my sweats.

Heading for the kitchen, I grab a bottle of water from the fridge and crack it open when a voice chimes in behind me. "Have you lost your gosh dang mind?"

McKleski stands there in her nightgown and robe, clutching it closed and scowling at me.

"Uh, no."

"Where are your clothes?"

I glance down at my bare chest. No shirt. "Just haven't gotten dressed yet."

"You should do that," she grumbles, shuffling into the

197

kitchen past me. "Might give an old lady a heart attack running around like that."

I laugh, taking a sip of the water while she sets about making a pot of coffee. "I think, if I were to give you a heart attack, it would've happened that day at the park."

"Nearly did," she says. "Why do you think I called the police? All that *squawking* going on in my backyard."

She cuts her eyes at me, giving me a knowing look. Yeah, she knew what we were up to that night, and I'm pretty sure she also knows what was happening in the wee hours of this morning.

"Figured you were just a cranky old bat," I say. "Didn't realize you had the hots for me."

"Oh, don't push it, Cunningham," she says. "I'll throw you out on your ass."

"I know you will," I say as I stroll back out of the kitchen.

"Put on some clothes!" she shouts at me. "Make sure your guest does the same. No hanky-panky in public areas!"

"Yes, ma'am," I mumble, even though she can't hear me, making my way back upstairs to the bedroom. I reach for the door to go in when it flings open on its own, Kennedy appearing. She looks frenzied, hair a mess, clothes halfway on, and she loses her balance as she tries to slip on her shoes. "Oh, whoa… whoa… careful."

I grab her arm to steady her, but she pulls away, cheeks flushing like she's embarrassed. She gives me the briefest glance before averting her eyes, refusing to meet my gaze. "Sorry, I, uh… *ugh*."

"It's okay," I say. "No reason to apologize."

But there is. That's what her expression says, and I can guess why. She was trying to sneak out during my absence, to avoid seeing me, but I caught her.

My chest tightens at that. *Fuck.* Regret is written all over her, like she bathed in shame and can't get the stench off this morning. She straightens her clothes, and my stomach bottoms out when I realize a bottle of whiskey is tucked under her arm.

"I have to go," she says, ducking past me, out of the room.

"I didn't drink any of that," I say right away. "I know it looks bad, fuck, but I didn't—"

"And you won't," she says, "because I'm taking it."

"Okay."

"I'm pouring it out," she says. "You shouldn't even have it. It's stupid. *You're* stupid."

"Me and my stupid fucking face, huh?"

Her cheeks turn red as she stammers, "I shouldn't have... *ugh*, I should've been home hours ago."

"I understand," I say, crossing my arms over my chest as I lean against the doorframe, watching her scrambling. "You didn't plan on staying here last night."

"Or even coming," she mutters.

Coming. "Pun intended?"

She doesn't laugh. She doesn't find that funny. She just starts down the steps to leave, done with being here. I watch in silence as she hesitates halfway down.

"You, uh... you can take her," she says, her expression guarded. "I mean, if you were serious about it, if you wanted to take her, you can."

Those words stun me. "Yeah?"

She nods. "We're gonna have to talk about, you know, *things*, but if you meant it…"

"I did."

"Well, then, okay."

She's gone then. I hear the front door as she rushes out, probably running to get away from here.

Sighing, I pull out my phone, using the last bit of battery left to send Cliff another message. **I'm going to need those tickets.**

As usual, his response is instant. **Are you drunk? Because I swear, Johnny, you and these tickets…**

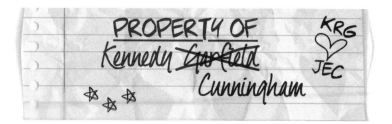

PROPERTY OF
Kennedy ~~Garfield~~ Cunningham

KRG
♡
JEC

☆ ☆ ☆

An audience is gathered in the auditorium of Fulton Edge Academy. Nearly every seat is filled. Students, families, administrators, *donors*. The girl sits in a seat along the aisle in the back, her parents beside her. Her father hadn't wanted to come, blaming the thirty-dollar cost of the tickets, but the girl knew he wanted to steer clear tonight for other reasons. *You.*

Saturday evening. Drama Club's production of *Julius Caesar*. There's a rumbling in the audience. People are growing restless. The play was supposed to start ten minutes ago. Hastings frantically runs around, dressed in his elaborate costume. They're scrambling as an announcement is made.

There has been a last-minute recast.

The role of Brutus will now be played by—

Not you.

The blue Porsche is parked in the parking lot. There's a reserved spot up front for your father. Although his seat is empty, the limo arrived earlier—which means you're both around, just not *here.*

The girl gets up from her seat as the play starts. Her father tries to stop her, but her mother doesn't let him, saying, "Let her go, Michael."

She runs out, heading toward the parking lot.

You're out there. So is he. The two of you are standing in front of your car, your father's security detail lurking as you argue.

The deadline to accept admission to Princeton was last night, so he accepted it on your behalf.

You tell him you're not going. Becoming *him* isn't your dream. He tells you to get your head out of the clouds—it's time to be the man he raised you to be.

You tell him he didn't raise you to be a man. He didn't raise you at all. He'd have to be a *father* to take credit for that, but he's not. He's nothing but an egotistical asshole that only cares about his job. You tell him you'll never be like him. Becoming him is your *worst fucking nightmare.*

The moment you say that, he loses his composure. He swings. He hits you. You're braced for it. You knew it was coming, but you don't expect the second hit... or the one after it.

He swings, again and again. You try to block the blows, but he's not stopping, so you shove him off. That gives you a moment of reprieve, but it doesn't last. He comes back at you, so you react.

You swing. You punch him right in the mouth.

It's the first time you've ever struck back. Your father is stunned, staggering. You hit him hard. Security rushes over, restraining you.

Your father's lip is busted. He runs his tongue along it. You're bleeding—blood runs from your mouth. He stands in front of you, staring you in the eyes as he says, "You'd never amount to anything without me. A waste of a life, just like your mother."

You spit in his face when he says that.

He blinks, pulling out a handkerchief to wipe the blood off. The girl, she's in front of the school, causing a scene as she screams for him to stop. Your father looks away, like he's about to leave, but then he turns back.

BAM.

He punches you again, one last time, a blow right to the chest. Security lets go of you to escort your father away as he calls back at you, "Princeton's nice, son. You'll like it."

You don't stick around. People are coming out of the school. *Julius Caesar* is a mess without its Brutus. So you get in your car and speed away, not wanting to be there. You can't face them right now.

You drive around.

You drive around for a long time.

Eventually, you end up in Bennett Landing.

It's three o'clock in the morning. You're standing on the sidewalk in front of the girl's house.

You're drunk. Not *that* drunk. Not drunk enough to forget. Not sure that's even possible when you're drinking champagne straight from the bottle. You swiped it from home before heading to the play. You thought you'd be celebrating with her tonight, but instead, it came to *this*.

She's still awake. She sees you from her bedroom window. She sneaks downstairs and slips outside.

"You're drinking," she says, looking around. It's the first time she's seen you this way. "Please tell me you're not driving like this."

"My car's at the park," you say. "Drank there."

"Without me?"

You hold the bottle of champagne out to her. "You can have some."

She takes it, dumping it out, before tossing the bottle behind her on the grass. "I meant you went to the park without me."

"Needed to think," you say, staring at the discarded bottle as you run your hands through your hair. "Been a rough day."

"I know." Her hands press gently to your cheeks as she examines your face. "Are you okay?"

203

"I'm fine," you say, kissing her, whispering against her lips, "I just needed to see you again... needed to tell you... that I, uh..."

I love you. You almost say it.

"Tell me," she says.

"I'm leaving."

Your voice is quiet.

She pulls away, blinking at you. "What?"

"I couldn't leave without saying goodbye," you say, caressing her cheek as you smile softly. "Didn't want to disappear on you. You'd never forgive me for pulling a Breezeo."

You're making light of it. You're trying to make her smile. You're trying to make this moment okay, but she's panicking inside. Her hands are shaking. She inhales sharply. Tears are filling her eyes. "What do you mean you're *leaving?*"

She asks that, but she knows what you mean.

"You can't leave," she says. "Where would you go? What would you even *do?*"

You're heading to California, you tell her. Or maybe you'll end up somewhere else. All you know is you have to follow your dreams and you have to do it now. It's time. You're going to go wherever life takes you, and as much as your chest aches at the thought of leaving her, at the thought of going through tomorrow without seeing her smile, at the idea of never again getting to hold her in your arms, you can't stay, not even one more day. Because every day you stay just makes it harder for you to go, and come tomorrow you may lose your courage. You'll end up at Princeton. You'll become your father.

She stares at you as you say all that.

She's starting to cry. "I'm not ready to say goodbye."

You wipe the tears from her cheeks. "Do you think you'll ever be ready?"

No, she won't.

She grabs ahold of you, hugging you tightly. "I know you have to go... *I know*... and you have to follow your heart, but how can I follow mine if you're gone? I love you, Jonathan. I love you *so much*."

You wrap your arms around her, holding her as she cries. Always making the first move. *I love you.* A long moment passes before you say, "Come with me, K."

She inhales sharply. "What?"

"You have a life here. You have a family. Fuck, you have *finals* on Monday. You're about to graduate and go to college. And I'm probably about to fuck up my entire life, but I love you."

She pulls back to look at you. "You love me?"

"More than anything," you say. "More than drama club and dress rehearsals and *Julius Caesar*. More than annoying the shit out of Hastings. More than the goddamn park down the road. Hell, even more than I loved punching my father. I didn't stick around here so long for any of that. I stayed for you. And if me loving you is enough—"

"It is," she says.

"So come along," you say. "Run away with me, baby."

You don't know this, but that girl? As she stands there, staring at you, seeing the light in your eyes and feeling so much love in her heart, she would've done anything you asked. *Anything.* She would've climbed any mountain and dug any hole. She would've lied, cheated, and stolen. That girl would've promised you forever. As long as you love her, for as long as you care, she's yours. So walking to the park with you and climbing in that Porsche? Easiest decision she's ever made.

FIFTEEN

"Come on, we've got to go!" I yell, shoving stuff around in a junk drawer in the kitchen, looking for my car keys but finding them nowhere. *Ugh.* I check the counter, and the table, before moving on to the living room. Not on the coffee table, either. Certainly not on the hook by the front door, where they're supposed to be. I pull the cushions up on the couch, checking under them. *Nothing.* "Maddie, have you seen my keys?"

No answer.

I look all around, my eyes skimming along the floor as I make my way down the hallway toward the bedrooms, in case I dropped them. *Nope.* I'm trying to remember the last time I saw them. The door was already unlocked when I got home this morning, so yesterday sometime?

"Maddie?" I call out, her silence concerning. "Are you listening?"

No, it turns out, she isn't. She's sprawled out on her bed, dressed and ready to go, her hair already messed up, even though I fixed it a few minutes ago. She's fast asleep, not hearing a word I say.

"Maddie, we need to get going," I say, shaking her awake, waiting until she sits up before asking, "Have you seen my keys, sweetheart?"

Rubbing her eyes, she shakes her head.

Even if she has seen them, I don't think she's awake enough to remember it.

"Get your bag ready for school," I tell her, walking away,

heading to my bedroom. I search around for a moment, now looking for my cell phone, going so far as to rip the blankets off my bed and dump out the hamper. *Nothing.*

Annoyed, I give up. I don't have time for this.

I'm already going to have to walk to work.

I go back to Maddie's room.

She's lying down again.

"Up, up, up," I say, picking her up and setting her on her feet before grabbing her backpack, shoving some stray papers into it, not sure what she needs. I put it on her back before taking her hand and pulling her to the door.

"I don't wanna go," she whines, dragging her feet.

"Sorry, school is a necessity."

"But why can't I stay home with you?"

"What makes you think I'm staying home?"

"Because you don't got no uniform."

"That's crazy, I—" Glancing down, I realize I'm not wearing my work shirt. *Crap.* "Wait here. Let me change my shirt."

She just stares at me.

"Seriously, don't move," I say, pointing at her. "I'll just be one second."

Any longer and she'll be right back in her bed.

Of course all my uniforms are dirty, so I shove through the pile of clothes I threw out of the hamper, finding the one that looks the cleanest. I'm pulling it on as a knock echoes through the apartment.

I tense, knowing Maddie's going to open the door even before she announces, "I gots it!"

"Wait!"

"Jonathan!"

My stomach drops as I walk back out, finding the door wide open—of course—with him standing there, grinning at her.

It's been a crazy morning. Waking up at dawn, naked in your ex's bed, body aching, covered in the scent of him, has a way of putting someone through the emotional ringer. Horror. Fear.

Dread. *Excitement*. I'm not sure how to feel about it, not sure about anything except the awkwardness, the guilt, the shame... and maybe I shouldn't feel that way, but it's unavoidable.

"What are you doing here?" I ask, more bite to those words than I mean. I can tell by the way he looks at me, the flicker of hurt in his eyes, that the question bothers him.

"He can come today, remember?" Maddie chimes in, looking at me like I'm being ridiculous. "He said since he couldn't stay and play with me and Aunt Meghan."

"Oh, I know that," I say, walking over, pressing a hand to the top of her head as I force a smile, hoping she doesn't sense the weirdness. "I just mean, why *right now*? Playtime is later."

"I thought you might need this stuff," he says, pulling something from his pocket and holding it out—keys and a cell phone. *My* cell phone, more specifically. My keys, too. "You must've forgotten it... somewhere."

"Ugh, thanks," I grumble, taking the phone from him as it starts ringing. *Work*. "It's been one of those mornings. I'm running late, and *ugh*... let me take this call. *Hello?*"

"Is everything okay?" Marcus asks when I answer. "It's ten after and you're not here."

"Yeah, sorry, I'll be there as soon as I can."

"Just checking, since this isn't like you."

I hang up, rolling my eyes, and turn back to Jonathan, about to apologize for having to cut this short when he says, "I can take Maddie to school, if you need to get to work."

Her eyes light up at that suggestion.

"I, uh... I don't know..."

"It's only, what—a couple blocks from here? I can get her there, no problem."

"Please, Mommy?" Maddie says, grabbing his hand like she's standing in solidarity. "He can get me there!"

Overprotective, paranoid me wants to say *no*, but how am I going to trust him to take her to a convention if I can't even let him walk her to school? I want to pick her up and shove her in my

209

pocket, shield her from everything for as long as I'm alive, but I can't do that, because the truth is, she's not just *mine*.

"Yeah, okay, fine," I say, those words earning a squeal of excitement from Maddie. I smile down at her. "Love you more than lunch breaks and paychecks."

"Love you more than recess."

"That's a lot of love, little girl."

"All of it in the whole world."

Leaning down, I kiss her forehead. "Go on, you don't want to be late for school."

She pauses, eyes widening. "Wait! I forgot!"

"Forgot what?" I call out as she sprints for her bedroom.

"Show & Tell!" she yells.

Sighing, I shake my head. "Can't forget about bringing something for Show & Tell."

"That would be a travesty," Jonathan says.

I look at him, frowning as I slip past, out of the apartment. "Can you lock the door for me? *Please*? I have to get going."

"Of course," he says. "Whatever you need."

I leave, not wanting to dwell, because if I do I'm liable to go back on all of it, and that wouldn't be fair. I get to work a quarter after eight, fifteen minutes late, and rush to clock in, flustered.

"You sure you're okay?" Marcus asks, eyeing me.

"Fine," I mumble. "Couldn't find my keys."

It's not a lie—not completely. It's more than that, of course, but I don't want to get into it. I spend the next few minutes in the back stockroom, watching the time.

At eight-thirty, I start to get nervous. Nearing nine o'clock, my anxiety skyrockets. Pulling out my phone, I text Jonathan. **Did you get her there okay?**

No response.

When nine-thirty comes, I can't take it anymore. I dial the number for the school, checking with the receptionist to make sure she made it, feeling like a fool when she confirms Maddie is in class and arrived on time this morning. I hang up, grumbling to myself when a message pops up on the screen. *Jonathan.* **Forgot to charge my phone. She made it safe and sound. No limbs lost.**

I stare at it, considering how to respond, but everything I truly want to say feels ridiculously sappy this morning. **So she still has all her fingers and toes?**

Ten of each, I'm assuming, but I didn't have a chance to count. Would've made us late.

I laugh at that as I type out a response. **Learn to multi-task, man.**

"What's so funny?"

Hitting send, I glance up and see Bethany in the doorway. "Nothing, just... you know."

I shake my phone at her as if that'll explain it.

"Boyfriend?" she guesses, raising her eyebrows. "Is it the guy that was here?"

My expression falls. "What guy?"

"You know, the one that came to see you."

Oh god. "How do you know about that?"

"Because I was here," she says. "Don't think I didn't see him lurking around."

"You saw him?"

"Of course." She laughs. "You seriously think I wouldn't spot that hottie? *Hello,* do you even know me?"

"Well, I mean, it's not what you think," I say. "He's not... we're not... you know... so I'd appreciate it if you didn't say anything."

"Oh, you don't have to worry. Your secret is safe with me."

"Really?"

"Of course!" She laughs. "I know you're, like, old or whatever, but I like to think we're friends. I'm not going to tell everyone your business."

Ignoring the fact that she just called me old, because *screw that,* I feel an intense sense of relief. She's taking this *so* much cooler than I expected. "Thank you. And I know you've met him, I guess, but if you want to meet him again, I can probably make that happen."

"Oh, no thanks." She waves me off. "He's a hottie, but he's not my type. I'm not really into that whole uptight authoritarian kink, if you know what I mean."

"What?"

"That guy of yours. What's his name? Andrew?"

"Oh, you're talking about Drew!"

"Who else would I be—*oh my god*, is there somebody else?" She lets out a shriek. "No way, you have *two* boyfriends?"

"Of course not." I scoff as my phone goes off. I glance at it, seeing a message from Jonathan. "I don't have a boyfriend at all."

You're the queen. I'm just a commoner.

Those words nearly take my breath away. It's been a long time since he's said them to me, so long that my heart skips a beat at the memories.

"Your face disagrees," Bethany says, motioning to me as I shove my phone in my pocket. "You're all blushy."

I roll my eyes. "Am not."

"Whatever you say." She turns to leave. "You look how *I* probably looked when I met Johnny Cunning."

"I heard a certain someone walked her to school this morning."

I stare at my father sitting on his front porch, casually rocking in his chair, wasting time before he heads off to lead a meeting later. It's nearing sunset. I ended up working over to make up for being late this morning.

"Yeah, I needed to get to work, and well, he was there."

"Lucky you," he says, "that he just *happened* to be there."

"Tell me about it," I mumble, leaving it at that. "Anyway, we should go before it gets dark."

"Because he's coming over to play?" he asks. "Heard about that, too."

I cut my eyes at him but don't respond to that, opening the front door to yell inside, "Maddie, sweetheart, time to go!"

Footsteps run through the house.

"I'm not judging you," my father says. "I just want to make sure you're being careful."

Careful. Squeezing his shoulder, I joke, "Don't worry, Mom had the '*safe sex is great sex*' talk with me as soon as I hit puberty. Took me to the clinic, put me on the pill and everything."

He cringes. "A lot of good *that* did. Should've taught you about abstinence."

"Spoken like a true conservative," I say as Maddie bursts outside with her backpack. "Besides, you know, say what you will, but it gave us that one."

"And she's plenty enough for all of us," he says, grinning at her when she throws herself at him to hug his neck. "Love you, kiddo. Have fun playing."

"Love you, Grandpa! Maybe you can play too next time!"

"Maybe," he agrees as she runs off the porch, skirting past me on her way to the car. My father waits until she's out of earshot before he says, "Be careful, and I don't mean, *you know...*"

"No glove, no love?"

Another cringe.

"That, too, but I think you already know that," he grumbles. "I hope you learned your lesson about going down that road with that boy. No good can come from it."

"*She* came from it," I point out.

He looks at me, eyes narrowing.

"Don't worry," I say. "I'm being *careful.*"

"You better be practicing abstinence."

"I'm twenty-seven, not seventeen."

"Doesn't matter. There's no ring on your finger."

"I'm not really a fan of jewelry."

"It's not about the jewelry."

"Not really a fan of archaic vows, either."

He scrubs his hands down his face. "Damn liberal hippies."

213

I laugh at that. He used to say that to my mother whenever she challenged him—which was all the time. "Bye, Dad."

"I'm serious, Kennedy," he calls out as I head for the car.

"I know you are," I tell him. "Don't worry."

"Don't worry? *Yeah, right.*"

I get in the car, wanting that conversation to be over before I slip up and give away just how deep I am. Sweat coats my back, my hands shaky as I grip the steering wheel and glance in the rearview mirror at Maddie, oblivious to it all as she plays with her Breezeo doll.

"Is he at home, Mommy?" she asks, glancing at me.

"Who?"

"Jonathan," she says, "so we can play."

"Oh, I'm not sure. I guess we'll see, huh?"

She smiles, nodding.

He's not there, though. He's not waiting when we get to the apartment. Disappointment radiates from her, her smile falling.

"He'll be here," I say, hoping I'm not lying to her.

"I know," she says.

She does her homework, practicing her spelling, and we eat dinner.

No Jonathan.

She takes a bath, putting on her pajamas, while I call him.

Voicemail.

Another hour or so passes before I finally change out of my work uniform. I check on Maddie in the living room, finding her fast asleep, the first Breezeo movie soundlessly playing on the TV, the lights all off. I glare at the screen, at his face staring back at me, making my insides twist up in knots.

"*Asshole,*" I grumble, reaching for the remote to turn it off, but a soft knock from the door stops me. I give Maddie a quick look—still asleep—before I head for the door, glancing out the peephole.

The face that's currently on the TV greets me.

Well, there are some differences, of course. The guy standing in front of my apartment looks like he's been through hell. He hasn't shaved in a while, and his skin is still peppered with faint scratches and bruises.

Sighing, I tug the door open. He starts to greet me, but I turn away, *walking* away, heading for the kitchen to clean.

Inviting himself inside, he shuts the door and follows, pausing when he glances at Maddie on the couch. "She's asleep."

"Yeah, well, that's what happens when you wait so late to show up."

"I came by earlier," he says. "Around four o'clock."

"I was still working. You should've waited or came back before now."

"I didn't have the chance."

"Oh? Something more important to do?" I glance at him when he doesn't answer. "I called you. You could've *at least* answered your phone."

"I had it turned off."

"What, didn't want any interruptions? You have a date or something? *Networking?*"

His expression hardens. "Don't be like that."

"It's just a question."

"No, it's more than that and you know it."

I turn away from him and start doing the dishes, trying to shove the bitterness down that's festering. He's right—it is more than that. I'm still angry. *So angry.* I try not to let it show.

He sits down at the kitchen table. "I had to go to a meeting."

I drop the plate I'm washing when he says that, hot sudsy water splashing up at me.

"So that's where I was," he says. "I tried to get here sooner, but the meeting ran a lot longer than I thought."

"A meeting," I say, shaking my head. I know meetings are the epitome of *what happens here stays here*, and they're supposed to be anonymous, but I'm not sure how that's possible in his situation.

"Yeah, the conversation veered somewhere unexpected," he says. "Being *careful* in relationships."

215

I turn to him, horrified. *Oh god.* "Please tell me you didn't say anything about us."

"Of course not," he says. "Not even sure what to say, if I wanted to, not sure... about us."

Us. There is no 'us'. There was an 'us' once upon a time, but now it's just me and him and whatever this mess is I've gotten into by throwing myself at him the way I did.

Drying my hands off, I sit down across from him.

He picks up the Breezeo doll that Maddie left on the table after dinner. "This is what she grabbed for Show & Tell this morning."

"I'm not surprised. She has probably taken it a dozen times."

He smiles, staring at it, but says nothing.

"Are you, uh, you know...?" I wave toward him, not sure how to word it. "*Okay?*"

He raises an eyebrow. "Am I okay?"

"You said you had to go to a meeting, so I wondered..."

"If I fucked up?"

"No, I didn't mean—"

"It's okay, you can ask it. I've fucked up a lot. But no, I haven't. Not this time. Not yet."

"Yet."

He laughs dryly. "Yet."

"Well, that's good to know, but that's not what I asked," I say. "I asked if you're okay."

He sets the doll down. "Yeah, I'm okay."

"Good."

"Are *you?*"

"Sure."

"Are you happy?"

It sounds like small talk, I know, but it's so much deeper than that and his expression shows it. Am I happy? I don't know. "I wouldn't say things are perfect, but I guess I'm happy. You?"

"No."

His answer is instant. He doesn't even consider it. He's living

216

his dream, but yet, he's not happy.

"I was happy this morning, though," he continues, smiling again. "Last night, too."

"Last night shouldn't have happened."

"But it did."

He reaches across the table, his hand grasping mine. I stare down at it, not moving, even though that voice of self-preservation begs for me to pull away, get some space.

He squeezes my hand as I meet his gaze. He's still smiling. He *looks* happy.

My anxiety flares.

"Let's go somewhere," he says.

"Where?"

"Wherever you want to go."

I shake my head. "We can't."

"Why not?"

"Because I have work and Maddie has school. We can't just *go* somewhere."

"We'll go for the weekend."

"And do what?"

"Whatever you want to do."

I pull away from him, his touch clouding my thoughts. He's saying pretty words, but I'm not sure I can believe any of it.

"I'll think about it," I say, afraid to say yes even though my stupid heart yearns to. "We should worry about next weekend first. You know, the convention. I mean, if you're still—"

"I am."

"Okay, but I need details—the where, the when, the *how*. When are you picking her up, when are you bringing her back, what are you feeding her, can you guarantee she won't be kidnapped?"

He laughs as he leans back in the chair, like I'm being funny, but I'm serious. That's a lot of people, a lot of strangers, and I'm already starting to regret telling him he could take her.

"I'll pick her up early Saturday morning. I'll bring her back late Saturday night. And to be honest, I'll probably feed her whatever she wants. As far as getting kidnapped, you don't have to worry. I'm not gonna let her out of my sight."

"But I, uh… *okay.*"

I don't know what else to say.

"Okay," he agrees, pulling his phone out when it rings, answering it quietly. "What's up, Cliff?"

Cliff.

I get up from the table, not wanting to listen to that conversation, but I catch parts of it as I finish cleaning the kitchen, something about timelines and schedules, meetings in the city and doctors appointments.

After he hangs up, he stands up, and I think he's about to leave, but instead he strolls over to where I'm standing and pauses behind me. He brushes my hair aside, and I gasp when he kisses my shoulder. It's soft, *so soft*, barely a graze from his lips. Tingles engulf me, a chill rushing through me that makes my knees go weak.

"We shouldn't do this," I whisper.

"We're not doing anything," he says, his right arm snaking around my middle, cast pressing against my stomach as he pulls me back against him.

He kisses my neck, and I close my eyes, gripping the counter tightly. He marked me last night, like we were some reckless teenagers, leaving love-bites all over. I spent most of the day trying to hide them from people.

"I've made so many mistakes," he says, his voice barely a breath against my skin, "but I'm not going to make those mistakes again."

"I want to believe you," I whisper.

I turn my head, glancing back at him, as he leans forward, kissing the corner of my mouth.

"I should get out of here," he says. "It's late, and I'm sure you've got better things to do than humor me."

I don't argue, nor do I try to stop him, although I think that's what he wants. He walks away, heading to the living room, where Maddie is still asleep. Curious, I follow, lingering near the front door as he kneels and brushes the hair from her face to kiss her forehead. "Sorry I fucked up tonight, little one."

He starts toward the door, eyeing me warily as I block his path. He brushes past me, but before he can go, I say, "They'll recognize you."

"What?"

"At the convention," I say. "People will know who you are. How are you going to shield her... how will you *protect* her?"

"That won't be a problem. Nobody will know."

"How can you be so sure?"

He laughs as he opens the front door. "That's what *cosplay* is for."

SIXTEEN

JONATHAN

Knightmare.

Breezeo's archenemy.

Where Breezeo is light, a breath of fresh air, the nice breeze on a warm summer day, Knightmare is the storm that rolls in and takes it all away. Darkness, thick and suffocating, the shadows you can't escape in the night in back alleyways.

Black leather framed with dark armor, head to toe, from the combat boots the whole way up to the oversized black hood with a metal mask covering part of the face, rendering him unrecognizable.

I've always been envious of the costume.

Beats the damn pseudo-spandex, that's for sure.

"I, uh, *wow.*" Kennedy stands in the doorway of her apartment with a look of awe as her eyes scan the costume. "That's just... *wow.*"

"Wow, huh?" I glance down. "Good or bad?"

"It's just, uh, you know…"

"Wow?" I guess.

She nods, fighting off a smile. "Wow."

I smirk. "It's the original."

"Seriously?"

"Straight from the second movie," I say, touching an armored chest plate with a fingerless glove-clad hand. "Well, except for these gloves. The real ones wouldn't fit because of the cast, so I had to improvise."

"It's, uh…"

"Wow?"

"Nice," she says, touching the costume, fingertips grazing the armor. "Kind of weird seeing you like this, but still, it's nice."

"Thanks," I say as she steps aside for me to come in the apartment. "I talked them into letting me borrow it. Might not give it back, though. I'm kind of enjoying it."

"You should keep it," she says, her eyes still scanning me as she closes the door. "It's, uh…"

"Nice?"

"*Wow.*" She smiles playfully as she walks away. "I need to finish getting ready for work. Maddie, you've got a visitor!"

A moment after Kennedy disappears, Madison runs in. She skids to a stop when she spots me, eyes wide, mouth popping open. "Whoa."

I push the hood off, shoving the mask up, her expression changing when she sees it's me, face lighting up. She runs right at me, slamming into me so hard I stumble.

I laugh as she hugs me. "Hey, pretty girl."

She looks up at me. "You think I'm pretty?"

"What? *Of course.*" I kneel next to her, grinning as I press a finger to the tip of her nose. "You look like your mom."

"You think Mommy's pretty, too?"

"I think she's the most beautiful woman in the world."

Her expression shifts rapidly when I say that before her eyes widen. "Even more beautifuler than Maryanne?"

I lean closer, whispering, repeating her words. "Even more beautifuler than Maryanne."

"Whoa."

Smiling, I hold a bag out to her. "I brought you something. Thought maybe you'd want to wear it today."

She grabs it, not hesitating as she yanks everything out, gasping. She discards the empty bag as she runs off to her bedroom, nearly slamming into Kennedy in the hallway.

"Careful," Kennedy says. "Where are you running off to?"

"No time, Mommy! Gotta get ready!"

"Well, then." Kennedy stares at her until she disappears, before turning to me as she runs her fingers through her hair, pulling it up. "You sure you can handle this?"

"I deal with vultures from *Hollywood Chronicles*," I say. "I can handle whatever she throws at me."

Kennedy doesn't look convinced. "I heard you caught an assault charge two years ago from punching one of them."

"Where'd you hear that?"

"The front of *Hollywood Chronicles*."

I shake my head. "Those charges were dropped."

"Because you were innocent?"

"More like they were just as guilty."

Kennedy rolls her eyes but doesn't have the chance to say anything. Footsteps run our direction, an excited voice screeching, "*Ta-da!*"

Madison stands there, grinning wildly, clad in the little white and blue getup—a *Breezeo* costume. They're bringing them out for Halloween but I managed to snag one early.

"Wow, look at you!" Kennedy says, smoothing Madison's hair. "Prettiest Breezeo I've ever seen."

"Jonathan thinks I'm pretty, too!" she says, smiling at her mother. "He told me so!"

"Did he?" Kennedy asks. "Smart man."

"And you, too," she says. "He says you're the beautifulest woman in all the world."

Damn. She ratted me out.

Kennedy seems taken aback.

"Well, that was nice of him," Kennedy says. "I have to get going. You have fun, okay? And be good."

"I will."

She kisses the top of Madison's head. "Love you more than Saturday mornings."

"Love you, too," Madison says, "more than even costumes and them other things."

Madison grabs my hand.

"I'll bring her back tonight," I say, "fingers and toes still attached."

Kennedy won't look at me. I can tell she's anxious, so I don't linger, leading Madison outside. The town car is idling in the parking lot, the driver leaning against it as he waits. He smiles when we approach and opens the back door, but Madison drags her feet.

"Is he your friend?" she asks, looking at me.

"Why?"

"Grandpa says not to get in cars with strangers."

"Oh, yeah, I know him," I say. "He's safe."

She climbs into the car, and I buckle her into a booster seat as I sit beside her. As the car pulls away, I see Kennedy watching us from the front door of the apartment.

Madison chatters the entire drive to the convention center, telling stories, and I listen dutifully. She's bursting with excitement by the time we arrive, but I'm somewhere on edge. While I was promised discretion, confidentiality agreements tossed around like candy at a parade, I know things don't always go according to plan.

The car takes us straight to the back entrance, past the awaiting crowds. A woman meets us in an attached garage, one of the event coordinators, along with a small security detail. She smiles when we get out of the car. "Mr. Cunning! And Miss, uh…"

Madison grins. "Maddie!"

"Miss Maddie," the woman says. "I'm so honored you could join us. My name is…"

Blah. Blah. Blah.

She launches into the spiel. It's expected. Always happens. I vaguely listen as she babbles on about the company's history, their record-breaking turnouts, laying the groundwork for me signing onto something in the future. Madison grows impatient and starts fidgeting, so I hurry the woman along, getting our wristbands for admission like everyone else so we can blend into the crowd.

"Security will be posted all around," she says. "They'll be keeping a lookout, of course, but should you need any help, don't be afraid to ask."

The woman leaves, and security takes us up a private elevator, straight to the main floor, letting us out inside the hall. The crowd is streaming through, rushing to get wherever they're going.

Panels. Trivia. Shopping. Autographs. The room is filled with booths, with comics, with artists, with writers and actors and cosplayers... the whole shebang. This isn't my first convention, you know, but usually I'm the one people line up for.

"So, whatcha wanna do?" I ask Madison. "It's up to you."

She clings to my hand, staring at it all with wide eyes. "Everything."

Everything. I laugh. "We can do that."

We start small, just walking around, taking in what we can see. Maddie's in awe, gawking at everyone in costume, and I think she might be intimidated by the crowd, but it doesn't take her long to warm up to things. I steer her away from autographs, since a lot of those people actually *know* me. She drags me from booth to booth, from table to table, excitedly announcing everything she sees, not lingering any one place long enough for me to buy anything.

"Whoa," she says, coming to a halt in front of one of those standees, a cardboard cutout of *yours truly*. "Look, Daddy! It's you!"

Daddy. Crazy shit goes down in my chest when she calls me that. It's the first time I've heard her say it. I blink at her, so astounded, so enamored, that it isn't until she repeats herself and people look her direction that I realize what she's saying.

"Daddy, it's you!"

Shit. I pull her away from it and kneel down in front of her when she looks at me in confusion, like she doesn't understand.

"That's not me today," I say. "I'm Knightmare, remember?"

Her brow furrows. "But it's still you for real?"

"Of course, but today we have costumes so we can play make-believe," I say. "So technically, that's *you* today."

Her expression lights up as she spins around, looking at the

225

booth. "Can I have me?"

"Can you have... *you?*"

She nods, pointing at the standee.

"Oh, you actually want one of those."

"Uh-huh."

"It's kind of big to be lugging around."

"I can carry it!"

I smile at the mental image of her dragging one of those damn things around all afternoon. "It's like three times your size."

"I can do it."

"I don't doubt it," I tell her. "How about we wait until the end of the day, after we do everything else, and if there's still one here, we'll take it with us."

"'Kay."

That was a heck of a lot easier than I expected it to be. I take her hand again as I glare at the standee. *Please let them sell out of those fucking things.*

Madison drags me around again, from place to place, before we make our way to the other side of the building where panels are happening. Madison acquires a schedule and picks where we're going. *Comics in the Movies. The Art of Fan Art. Metaphors and Themes.* I'm not sure she knows what half the stuff is. Hell, I'm not sure she can even read the words as she picks the panels, but she sits eagerly through them, eventually dragging me to a room with a sign that says '*Fandom Feud*'.

"I'm not sure about this one," I tell her. "I think they'll expect participation."

"Oh! Does that mean I can play?"

"Sure does!" a voice chimes in, a woman walking into the room behind us, dressed like Maryanne. "We're playing Breezeo trivia."

"That's me today!" Madison exclaims, grabbing at her costume to show it off.

The woman laughs. "I bet that means you're going to know all the answers, huh?"

Madison nods. "Yep."

The woman's eyes flicker to me, but I avert my gaze and say nothing. We find seats toward the back of the room. They play a few rounds of trivia, picking players to face off, before opening it up to everyone and calling on people in the audience.

"In the comics, Maryanne is a nurse," the moderator says. "What does she do in the movies?"

"Oh, oh, oh, me, me!" Madison yells, waving her hands wildly, trying to be seen, but the guy in front of her is too tall, so she climbs right up on the chair, standing on it. "Me! Me! I know!"

Muffled laughter flows around us when people notice her.

"The little Breezeo girl in the back," the moderator says, calling on her. "What does Maryanne do in the movies?"

Madison beams, shouting, "*Nothing!*"

More laughter.

"I'll accept that," the moderator says. "She's still in school. Come pick your prize, little Breezeo."

Madison jumps down, walking proudly to the front. People *ohh* and *ahh* over her, and she plays it right up. A lollipop, it turns out, is what she wins. Returning, she shoves it at me.

I open it for her and try to hand it back, but she makes a face at me, like I've fucked up. "What's wrong?"

"You gotta taste it first," she says.

"Seriously?"

"That's what Mommy does," she says, "in case it's poison, 'cuz it came from a stranger."

"Oh." I lick it before handing it to her. "Like that?"

She nods, popping it right in her mouth.

I blink a few times, watching her. That's one of the strangest things I've ever done in my life, taste-testing potentially poisonous candy.

Trivia is over after a few minutes. I lead Madison through the crowd, out of the room, fielding a few compliments from people about how adorable she is.

I probably look like an asshole, just nodding in agreement.

227

"Are you hungry?" I ask her once we're away from the crowd. "I'm sure there's something around here that you'll eat."

"Hot dogs!"

Hot dogs. I find them easy enough, but the line is crazy long. We wait damn near twenty minutes to buy some hot dogs and chips, and *goddamn it* she wants soda so I buy it, but there's nowhere to sit inside, so we make our way outside to a small amphitheater.

A crowd is gathered in Knightmare cosplay. They're putting on a show, having some sort of sword competition.

"What are those guys doing?" Madison asks before taking a bite of her hot dog.

"Looks like LARPing," I mumble.

She looks at me like I'm crazy. "Like *what?*"

"LARPing," I say. "Live-action role play."

"Oh, I wanna play! Can I?"

"I don't think so."

"Why not?"

"I don't know," I admit. *Because you're just a kid* sounds like a shitty excuse to deny her some make-believe fun.

She eats her lunch as the knights battle it out, getting into it like she's watching a movie, even picking a side—the one whose armor is trimmed in blue, unlike his opponent, who wears all black.

Picking up the schedule, I flip through it. "So, looks like we've got a choice—either *The Consequence of Alternate Universes* or *Exploring Headcanon.*"

"What do those mean?"

"I think they both deal with fan-fiction."

"What's that?"

"When fans make up their own stories," I say, shaking my head. We sat through a panel that explained that to her, but I'm pretty sure it went right over her head.

"Can we do that? Make the fan-fiction?"

"Thought you already were," I say. "You said you were going to fix the end of *Ghosted.*"

"I am."

"Well, there you have it. So which panel would you refer?"

"The consequences of the cannons," she says, mashing them together. I start to correct her, but she's not paying me attention, on her feet and cheering. "Go blue guy!"

The blue guy, in fact, loses—if there's such a thing as losing in what they're doing. The guy in all black takes a bow, celebrating, while Madison loudly boos, drawing their attention.

"You, young Breezeo," he says, still playing the part as he points his sword at her. "You have the gall to boo me? *Me*, the villainous Knightmare?"

"You're not the real Knightmare," she says, hands on her hips. "My daddy is!"

She motions to me, so there's no mistaking who she's talking about. *Shit.*

The man eyes me with a look of disgust. "Him? *Ha*! He's not the real one! He doesn't even have the gloves!"

Madison glances at my hands. "So? He doesn't always gotta wear them."

"Fair enough," the man says. "But if your father is the true Knightmare, perhaps he'd like to come down and stake his claim."

He points at me with his sword.

I shake my head. *Not happening.*

"He will," Madison says, contradicting me.

"It seems your father disagrees," the man says. "I suppose he's afraid of being exposed as a fraud."

"Nuh-uh! He's not!"

The man laughs.

Madison's getting heated, and seriously, *fuck this guy*. I'd never begrudge someone their act, wouldn't demand they break character, but I'll be damned if I'm going to let someone antagonize me in front of my daughter. Broken wrist or not, I'm defending her honor.

"Fuck it." I get to my feet, marching straight down to him as I say, "Someone give me a sword."

Right away, half a dozen guys offer theirs up. I grab the one

229

closest to me, trying to get a good grip on it with the cast. Mister Antagonizer has the nerve to look concerned, whispering, "You know we're just playing around here, right?"

"Are we?" I ask. "I wasn't sure."

Look, I'll be honest. Filming most of the second movie was a blur, but the lead-up to it, the endless hours of training for the fight scenes, is ingrained in me to the point that I could do this with my eyes closed. So while I'd probably die gruesomely if I lived back in the days of King Arthur's court, a fucking Knightmare LARPer is *nothing*.

"Feel free to kneel at any time," I tell him. "I'll accept your surrender."

He scoffs, those words setting him off. He takes the first swing. It's weak, easy to block. I let him try a few more times, picking up his pattern, before I put him on the defense, something he's clearly not used to.

BAM. BAM. BAM. Hit after hit, I go after him, following the same fight routine from the movie. It's like a choreographed dance, one the guy knows, but he's not quick enough on his feet to stop me. Five minutes maybe, I rail at him... he breaks a sweat, eyes wide like he's starting to think I might actually stab him. He puts up a decent fight, enough that a few blows nearly makes me lose it, my wrist stinging, pain shooting up my arm, but I don't stop until he kneels.

He drops his sword, dropping to one knee, and I hear Madison cheering, screeching as she runs for me. She wraps her arms around my waist, hugging me, and I laugh as I hand the sword off to whoever lent it to me.

"Man, you're good," the guy says with a laugh as he gets to his feet, holding his hand out. "Name's Brad. You are...?"

"Jonathan," Madison chimes in, answering for me. "Oh, wait, he's Knightmare today!"

"Well, *Knightmare*, if you ever decide to join a LARPing league—"

"I appreciate it, but it's not my thing," I mumble, steering

Madison away.

"Could've fooled me," the guy says.

I ignore that, leading Madison back inside the convention center. "So, did we decide what we're doing now?"

"More sword fighting!"

"Ah, I'm afraid that has to wait for another time," I say, "but there's still other fun to be had."

More panels. Some shopping. Even another trivia game. She eats ice cream, getting it all over her. I buy her the Maryanne doll, so she doesn't have to keep substituting with Barbie. It's nearing nightfall when things start coming to a close. I can tell Madison is running out of energy. She's quiet now, clinging to my hand.

"You ready to head home?" I ask. "I'm sure your mother must be missing you."

She nods.

We start toward the exit, but Madison hesitates halfway there, tugging on my hand. "Wait! We forgot!"

"Forgot what?"

She doesn't answer, instead dragging me straight over to the booth with all the standees.

"I wanna Breezeo one," she declares, telling the worker, pointing at the standee.

"They're $30," the lady says.

Sighing, I count out the cash and hand it over before grabbing the standee and hauling it along with us.

We make our way through the lingering crowd and out the exit. I lead Madison around the corner of the building, lingering there as I send a message for the car to get us. It's a minute or so out, so we wait as people wander past.

I shove the mask up off my face when I see the car coming and take a step toward it when a voice calls out, "*Johnny Cunning?*"

I turn, tense, and see a woman with her young son, the two of them gawking at me.

"Oh my god, it's really you!" the woman says, grasping the kid by the shoulders. "My son told me it was, you know, he kept saying it was you, but it didn't believe it."

It's always the kids.

They're intuitive.

No matter how much you disguise yourself, kids can sense it.

"Can I have an autograph?" she asks, holding out a comic book as she digs for something to write with. "Please?"

"Uh, sure," I mumble, taking the marker from her and scribbling my name, my eyes on the kid. He looks to be about Madison's age, the same look of reverence on his face that she had this morning. He, too, is wearing a Breezeo costume, but his is homemade... a lot of time went into it. It's strange, after everything I've done, having kids look at me like I'm some hero. "You want a picture, little man?"

He nods enthusiastically, like he's speechless, so I kneel down beside him, posing, letting his mother snap a quick photo.

"Take care of yourself," I tell him. "Make sure you always look out for your mother."

I stand up, grabbing Madison's hand and leading her to the car before anyone else spots me.

The drive back home feels like it takes forever. It's dark when we arrive, and Madison is fast asleep. I try to wake her, but she's not budging, so I pull her out of the booster seat and carry her. She grumbles, not waking up, arms wrapped around my neck. I drag the standee along under my arm as I head for the front door, prepared to knock, but it pulls open before I can.

Kennedy stands in the doorway, looking relieved to see us, still wearing her work uniform. She steps out of the way for me to come in.

I drop the standee right inside the apartment. Kennedy stares down at it before shooting me a peculiar look.

"I know," I mutter. "It's probably the last thing you want to have to look at, but she wouldn't leave without it."

Kennedy shakes her head, closing the front door as she says, "You can tuck her in bed, if you want."

PROPERTY OF
Kennedy ~~Garrett~~ Cunningham
KRG ♡ JEC
☆ ☆ ☆

As the students at Fulton Edge Academy take their finals, you're driving through the Midwest, on your way to California. The girl, she sits beside you, in the passenger seat of your blue Porsche, writing her heart out in her notebook.

It's one of the few things she brought along.

She slipped back into the house as you sobered up, filling her school backpack with clothes, packing her Breezeo comics and grabbing her cell phone before writing a note to her parents.

Mom & Dad,
I know you're gonna be upset when you realize I'm gone, but please don't worry too much. I'm okay. I'm with Jonathan.
Love you both,
Kennedy

Needless to say, over twenty-four hours later, they're pretty freaking worried. She's only seventeen. They've already called the police. She's officially a *teenage runaway*. Her phone started going off not long after you got on the road, bombarding her with messages, begging her to come home.

The phone died after a few hours.

She forgot to bring her charger.

You? You've got your phone, with nearly a full charge. The only person who has called you is your sister, to warn you that someone leaked the Fulton Edge Academy security footage. Your fight with your father is all over the news, playing on a loop. It's a political nightmare, Speaker Cunningham assaulting his own child. They're calling for his resignation.

Time keeps ticking away.

The miles between you and New York continue to grow as California edges closer. You offer to turn around for her. You don't want her to have any regrets. She tells you to shut up and keep driving west.

A few days later, you cross into the city limits of Los Angeles. The day you should've graduated. You find a small hotel that'll rent a room to an eighteen-year-old, just until you can get set up somewhere permanently.

"Let's go out," you say.

"Where to?" she asks.

"Somewhere nice. We're here. We made it. We should celebrate."

So you do just that. You take her out. She wears her graduation dress, the one her mother helped pick out—sleeveless, royal blue. She has to wear her everyday flats, because she forgot to pack extra shoes. It's simple. She feels so plain.

You tell her she's the most beautiful woman in the world.

Dinner is at a fancy steakhouse, the kind where portions are small and the bill is massive, but people don't complain because it's all about the atmosphere. Afterward, the two of you hit Hollywood Boulevard, seeing the handprints immortalized in cement before strolling along the Walk of Fame, looking at the celebrity stars as you hold hands.

"Someday, you'll be here," she tells you, smiling, as you pause and pull her to you. "You'll have your name on one of these stars."

"Yeah? You think I'm as talented as..." You glance down, to the nearest star by your feet, reading the name on it. "...*Kermit the Frog?*"

She laughs. "Well, now that I think about it, I'm not so sure. I mean, Gonzo maybe, but *Kermit?*"

"Maybe if I work hard," you say.

"Maybe," she agrees, kissing you.

You make out, right there, on Hollywood Boulevard. It's a beautiful moment. Nothing can ruin it—not even when a guy dressed like Darth Vader angrily tells you to *get a room*.

"We have one of those," you say. "How about we go make use of it?"

"Thought you'd never ask."

You make love to her, on and off, all night long. Now that those words are out, now that they exist between you, you can't seem to stop saying them.

I love you. I love you. I love you.

Your first night in California is one of the best of your life. You're hopeful for the future.

The next day, all your credit cards get shut off.

The day after that, your bank account is frozen.

It's a quick descent, from hopeful to despondent. You're not surprised your father cut you off, but it hurts. What you have is maybe a hundred dollars in your wallet and a notice to vacate the hotel in 72-hours. What you *don't* have is a job. You're going to have to do something drastic.

So you leave the next morning before dawn, to try to figure something out, and you don't make it back until later that night, well after sunset. You sleep for a few hours before you're back at it again.

You finish earlier this time, though, around three o'clock in the afternoon. The girl is sitting on the bed in the hotel, writing in her notebook. She greets you with a smile.

"What are you writing?" you ask, sitting down next to her, not expecting her to answer. You ask all the time, and she always tells you 'a story.

This time, though, she says, "Our story."

"Our story," you say. "That's what it is?"

"Sort of," she says. "It's my version of us."

"Can I read some of it?"

Her pen stalls. She hesitates. Carefully, she flips back to the beginning and hands it to you. "Just the first few pages."

You read, utterly fascinated, but you don't get far at all before you have a grievance to air. "See, now that's bullshit. This line right here. You said there was *nothing special* about you."

She snatches the notebook back. "About *her*, not me."

"But she's you. And I can assure you, the first time I saw you, I wasn't thinking..." You grab the notebook, and she refuses to surrender it, but you pull it close enough to read. "You're a commoner because not all girls can be royalty. That's bullshit. You're the queen, baby."

She yanks the notebook away, closing it and tossing it out of your reach. "I said it's *my* version. It's fictionalized."

"You should write my version."

"Which would be, what? Thirty pages of duck jokes followed by a whole bunch of smut?"

"Duck jokes," you say. "Or *dick* jokes?"

"Knowing you? Both."

"Funny, but no. It would be a story of struggle that leads to triumph." You stand up. "Come on, put your shoes on. Let's go for a walk. I'll show you."

"You'll *show* me."

Despite her incredulous tone, she listens, and the two of you walk around, strolling a few blocks. The neighborhood isn't the best, but it isn't too dangerous. Maybe a bit rundown, but it's quiet.

When you reach an old two-story white and blue building, you lead her around to the back of it, to a small outdoor staircase. You pull a ring of keys from your pocket. She looks at you with confusion.

Still, she follows you up those stairs, patiently waiting as you unlock a creaky door at the top. She steps inside, looking around the empty place.

It's an apartment. It's *small*. There's no other way to put that. The kitchen and living room merge together into one, beside a single bedroom just big enough to hold a bed. The bathroom is like a box, everything cramped together. The floor is made of old unfinished wood, scuffed and stained. The white paint on the walls is peeling, leaving patches of a peach color in places. There's only one window in the entire apartment, in the bedroom, blocked by an old air conditioner.

"I know it's not much," you say. "It's shitty, really. I know. But I'm eighteen, I've got no job and no credit, so it's the best I can manage right now."

"It's ours?" She looks at you. "You rented this?"

You hesitate, like your mouth doesn't want to admit that, before you nod. You're swallowing your pride. "It's ours."

"But can we even afford a place?" she asks. "How will we pay for it?"

"I got us some money," you tell her. "It won't last forever, but it should be enough to get us settled."

"Where'd you get money?"

You hesitate yet again. "I, uh... I sold my car."

You sold the blue Porsche. You tried to think of another way, but

237

it was the only thing of value you had, that you owned. So you sold it, for less than it's worth, but if you're careful, it's enough to cover living expenses for a few months.

"This place is great," she says, wrapping her arms around you. "Our very first apartment together."

"And hopefully, the last," you mumble. "It's only up from here. As soon as things start coming together, I'm gonna build you a house."

You don't know this, but that girl? She doesn't need a house. She doesn't even need an apartment. She would've slept in the car. She wouldn't have complained at all about it. You didn't have to sell it, but you did, and as grateful as she is for that, she already feels guilty. She's worried, and she's *scared*, that this won't be a story of triumph. Because she believes in you. She wouldn't be there if she didn't. But the world isn't always kind to good people. Sometimes it eats them alive.

SEVENTEEN

I fling my dirty uniform into the hamper in my bedroom and pull on a long white t-shirt, covering myself, when I hear a throat clear in the doorway, Jonathan's voice a gruff mumble when he says, "Shit, sorry, I was just, uh…"

I glance at him as he averts his gaze, forcing his eyes away.

"It's fine," I say. "You've seen me wear less."

"Yeah, well…" He looks my way again, hesitating, like he's not sure what he wants to say, if he should even say anything. "I wasn't trying to, you know…"

"I know."

Despite not trying to, he sort of *does*. His eyes slowly roam, and goose bumps coat my body, a chill creeping along my skin. Things are already weird, and he's making it more nerve-wracking by blatantly gawking. My stomach gets tied up in knots at the look on his face, the slack-jawed awe as he licks his lips.

"Anyway." He clears his throat. "I wanted to say goodnight."

"Goodnight," I whisper.

Jonathan lingers there, eyes continuing to roam. A moment passes before he turns away, making a move to leave.

"*Wait.*"

The lone word slips from my lips. I'm not sure why I say it. I don't even think about it. He hesitates again, meeting my gaze, eyebrows raised with questions I don't know how to answer as my heart thumps wildly with its own questions, like *what the heck are you doing?* I'm playing with fire, like I don't remember how much it hurts to get burned, but from here, where I'm standing, all I can seem to feel is the warmth.

I don't have to say anything else, which is good, because I'm not sure I could find the words if I needed to. He reaches for me, his fingertips grazing my flushed cheek and running along my jawline. He grasps my chin and tilts my face up as he leans down to kiss me. His lips are soft, *so soft*—so sweet and gentle.

He kisses me for a long time, not rushing, not pushing, just *waiting*. The breath leaves my lungs and all sense disappears from my head as I wrap my arms around him and pull him to my bed.

"You sure about this?" he asks quietly.

I shake my head, because *nope*, I'm still not sure about any of it, but I don't stop myself. I lay down and he's on top of me. I tug at his costume as he strips me of my clothes. My head is swimming and my heart is racing, and before I can catch my breath, his lips are on mine again and he's pushing inside, already settled between my thighs. I gasp as he lets out a guttural groan, filling me, holding me.

None of it feels real.

Not this time. Not last time.

He moves slow at first, and it's almost agonizing, before he increases his pace, thrusting harder, deeper, shoving my knees up and hitting that spot deep inside of me that makes my toes curl and my body quiver. I moan his name. "*Jonathan.*"

"Like that?" he asks, keeping his rhythm. "Is that how you want it?"

I nod, whimpering as he hits that spot again and again, unraveling the tight knots inside of me as I start to come apart at the seams. "Please."

"You're the queen," he whispers, not stopping as orgasm rocks me. I arch my back, gripping him tightly, nails raking along his shoulders.

Even when it subsides, he doesn't stop. He doesn't slow down. He knows what I want and he gives it to me, over and over, until I'm begging, pleading, and can't take another moment. Only then does he pull back, only then does he change his pace—hitting hard, *so hard* that my breath catches, a few rough, deep strokes as he groans, coming.

"Fuck," he curses, nuzzling into my neck. He kisses the skin, teeth nipping at my throat. "So beautiful."

The beautifulest woman in the world.

That's what he told Maddie.

That's how he described me.

Squeezing my eyes shut, I hold onto him, hoping he means those words, hoping I can believe him.

✤ ✤ ✤

"Mommy?"

That's all it takes to draw me out of a deep sleep, that lone word spoken nearby, the quiet voice calling out to me. *Maddie.* My eyes open, and I blink a few times, getting my wits about me. The room is starting to lighten, the sun rising outside, a soft glow streaming through the window and shining along the wooden floor around the bed.

I think maybe I was hearing things, because she's not in front of me, and I start to close my eyes again when I hear soft giggling. It strikes me then, pieces all coming together as panic floods my system. Clutching the blanket to my bare chest, I sit up abruptly and turn the other way, wide-eyed.

She's standing there, right beside where her father is sleeping in the bed. In *my* bed. Crap, he's asleep in my bed, not wearing a bit of clothing, the blanket draped over him. Thank goodness he's covered up—not that it makes this whole thing any better. She's much too young to know what any of this is, but she's got one heck of an imagination, that kid, which could prove dangerous.

I don't want her to get ideas in her head and think this is more than it is… whatever it is.

She pokes his cheek before sticking her finger in his ear, giggling again when he grumbles in his sleep and moves around, flailing his hand, trying to ward off the intrusion.

"*Madison*," I hiss, warning her. She pulls her hand away and looks at me with that '*oh shit*' expression, knowing she's busted. "What are you doing?"

"Nothing."

"Doesn't look like *nothing*."

A smile cracks her face.

She does it again, sticking her finger in his ear. His face contorts with annoyance as he shifts position, groaning, "I'm trying to fucking sleep, Ser."

Maddie gasps, yanking her hand back, looking at him with shock. I feel it, that same sensation stirring in the pit of my gut, but for much different reasons. *Ser.* Serena. He thinks it's her. "Daddy says bad words!"

The moment she says that, Jonathan's eyes snap open. He sits up so fast he rips the blanket right off of me. Gasping, I grab it, scrambling to stay covered, yanking it back onto me and almost exposing him in the process. He looks at me, wide-eyed, panicked, whispering, "*oh fuck*."

"See!" Maddie says, reaching over and poking him in the ear. "I heard it!"

He laughs and pushes her hand away as he turns to her. "Sorry, didn't know there were little ears in the room."

Grasping her earlobe, he playfully tugs on it.

"Maddie, sweetheart, why don't you head to the kitchen?" I suggest. "I'll be there in a second to make you some breakfast."

She leaves the room, and I try to slip out of bed, but well, I can feel Jonathan's eyes, and my clothes are too far away to reach. He tries to touch me, his hand on my back, fingertips grazing my spine. I move away from him, taking the blanket with me, wrapping it around my naked body as I snatch up some clothes.

"Kennedy? What's wrong?"

"Maddie's waiting for breakfast," I mumble, going straight for the bathroom. I close the door behind me, letting out a long exhale as I pull on my clothes, grumbling to myself. "Stupid, stupid,

stupid… could you be any more *stupid?* Sleeping with that stupid man after all the stupid crap he's done… what is wrong with you?"

Yanking the door back open, I nearly slam into a body blocking the doorway, lingering in the hall. He had the sense to put on his pants and is still struggling to button them.

"Excuse me," I mumble, averting my gaze, but he's not moving out of my way.

He grasps my arm before I can go past him, his brow furrowed. "Did I do something?"

"I don't know," I mumble. "Did you?"

I try to move away from him, but he steps further into my path. "Come on, don't be that way. Tell me what's wrong."

I hesitate. I want to make some snide comment and storm away, throw a tantrum like a petulant child because I feel so stupid, but that's not me. It's never been me. So whatever, it is what it is, so I say it, no matter how stupid it sounds. "You called her *Ser.*"

"What?"

"She woke you up, and you thought she was Serena."

He lets go of my arm as his expression shifts to something that looks like pity, and I don't like it.

I leave him there and head for the kitchen, sighing when I see a chair shoved over to the counter, Maddie standing on it, digging through the cabinets. "What do you think you're doing, little girl?"

"Looking for the Lucky Charms," she says as I pull her down and set her on her feet.

"I'm afraid we're all out." I grab a box of *Cheerios*. "How about these?"

She makes a face of disgust.

"Raisin Bran?"

Another face.

"How about some cottage cheese?"

She pretends to gag.

"Uh, well, how about—?"

"How about I take you out for breakfast?" Jonathan

suggests, stepping into the kitchen. "Pancakes, sausage, eggs…"

"Bacon!" Maddie declares.

"I don't know," I say. "I'm not sure that's a good idea, you know, with the whole *you being you* thing."

"Me being me," he says.

"Yeah, chances are you'll get recognized and then have to explain this whole thing and well, you know, I'm not sure it's worth it for some breakfast."

"But it might be *bacon*," Maddie whines.

Jonathan hesitates, thinking it over, glancing between us before he says, "I know somewhere we can go."

Mrs. McKleski's place.

Landing Inn.

That's where he takes us.

Maddie and I stand in the woman's foyer in our pajamas, while Jonathan wears just the leather pants from the Knightmare costume. Mrs. McKleski looks at us like we've gone crazy, and I instantly want to be anywhere else in the world, but it's too late, because Maddie's been promised some bacon.

"You want *breakfast*," Mrs. McKleski says. "That's what you're telling me?"

He nods. "Yes, ma'am."

She stares at him. *Hard.* I expect a denial, because this whole idea is absurd, but after a moment, she lets out a resigned sigh.

"Fine, but go put on some clothes," she says. "This is an inn, Mr. Cunningham, not *Chippendales*. I won't have you at my breakfast table looking like a gigolo."

He cocks an eyebrow at the woman. "Wasn't aware you knew what a gigolo was."

"Go," she says pointedly, "before I change my mind."

"Yes, ma'am," he says, flashing her a smile before turning to me and nodding toward the stairs. "Join me?"

I stare at him, not moving.

He steps closer. "Please?"

"Fine," I mumble, glancing at Maddie, not wanting to cause a scene. "Hey, sweetheart, why don't you have a seat in the living room?"

"Nonsense," Mrs. McKleski says. "She can come help me cook. Teach her some responsibility. Not sure her father ever learned any."

Jonathan scowls before again motioning for me to follow him.

"And no hanky-panky," Mrs. McKleski calls to us as we start upstairs.

"What's the hanky-panky?" Maddie asks, following the woman to the kitchen.

"She means the hokey-pokey," I yell down before Mrs. McKleski can answer, because there's no telling how that woman would explain it.

"Oh, I like the hokey-pokey!" Maddie looks at the woman with confusion. "Why don't you wanna play it?"

"Too messy," Mrs. McKleski grumbles. "All that turning yourself around."

Shaking my head, I go upstairs, stalling right inside the room as Jonathan sorts through his belongings to find some clothes.

"I didn't mean it, you know," he says as he strips off his pants, standing in front of me naked. *Oh god.* I avert my gaze, trying not to look, but I see from the corner of my eye as he tugs on a pair of black boxers. "The Serena thing... I didn't mean it."

I don't say anything. What am I supposed to say? He pulls on a pair of jeans before grabbing a plain black shirt.

"I'm serious," he says. "I was half-asleep and didn't know what I was saying."

"It doesn't matter," I say, trying to move away, but he stops me, one hand on my arm, the other cupping my cheek.

"It *does* matter," he says, making me look at him. "Serena

245

used to get fucked up on coke and stay awake for days and drive everyone on set *crazy*. And she'd do shit like that whenever we tried to rest. She played games. So it wasn't that I thought…" He trails off. "I *know* who I slept with last night. I know who I woke up beside this morning. And I'm sorry I said some shit in my sleep that made you think I didn't know."

I'm still not sure what to say, so I just go with, "Okay."

"Okay," he repeats me. "Just *okay*? That's it?"

I shrug.

He lets out a laugh. "I guess that's better than nothing."

He kisses me—softly, *sweetly,* his hand roaming from my cheek down between us, cupping a breast.

I pull away. "No hanky-panky, remember?"

He grins, moving his hand. "Okay, okay… breakfast."

We head downstairs, and as soon as we approach the kitchen I hear Maddie's excited voice rambling about the convention. Quietly, I sit down at the table and listen as she goes on and on about how much fun she had and how great her *daddy* is.

The whole time, Jonathan sits beside me, beaming.

When breakfast is finished, Mrs. McKleski hands out plates, slipping one in front of me on the table before Maddie settles in on my right with her own plate piled high with bacon. Jonathan's comes last, and I stifle a laugh as Mrs. McKleski shoves it at him, the food sloppily thrown on it, his toast burned and bacon extra-crispy.

"Uh, thanks," Jonathan says, picking up a piece of bacon and taking a bite, cringing as it crunches.

"Don't like it? Don't eat," Mrs. McKleski says. "Nobody likes a whiner, Cunningham."

She strolls out of the kitchen, and he watches her as she leaves, mumbling, "All I said was *thanks*."

"You didn't say it with *meaning*," she calls back at him. "It's no wonder you haven't gotten an Oscar. You're terrible."

I stifle another laugh as Jonathan glares at the doorway.

"Don't worry," Maddie says, munching on a piece of bacon. "You can get the Oscar someday."

246

He grins at her. "You think so?"

She nods. "All you gots to do is get better at it."

This time, I do laugh.

"Wow," he says. "I can sure feel the love."

Maddie smiles, not sensing his sarcasm. "It's 'cuz I love you."

His expression shifts. I see it as those words strike him. "You love me?"

Maddie laughs. "*Duh.*"

Duh. She says that like he's being ridiculous asking that question, like he's supposed to just know, but love isn't something he's had a lot of.

"I love you, too," he says.

"More than bacon?" she asks, munching on a piece.

"More than bacon," he says quietly. "More than everything."

She smiles at that and continues to eat her breakfast, satisfied by his answer. My chest aches, my heart feeling like it wants to burst. I sometimes wonder about his words, I question his feelings, his wishes, his wants, but from this moment on, I'll never doubt that he loves her, because I know he means it. I believe it.

We eat breakfast.

They chat. They laugh.

I mourn.

I mourn the years they lost, the time that was wasted, the love that maybe just wasn't quite enough to overcome his demons sooner. Every smile they share today is the product of years of tears, of years of fighting and struggling and hoping and mourning but never, ever, ever quitting or giving up, because we're here. And maybe it won't last, I don't know. Maybe tomorrow something will happen and the tears will come back, but I'm grateful for the moment, knowing he loves her more than anything.

"We should get going," I say after breakfast is through, the plates piled in the sink. "I have laundry to catch up on."

Maddie jumps down from her chair at the table and looks at Jonathan. "Are you coming? You can have another sleepover!"

"Not tonight," he says. "You have school in the morning,

and your mother has work."

Maddie frowns. "But will you come play tomorrow?"

"Yeah, sure, if you want me to."

Maddie nods. "See you tomorrow!"

"See you tomorrow," he says when she walks away, heading for the foyer. He turns to me as he says, "Thank you, K."

"What are you thanking me for?"

"Giving me a second chance," he says. "And a third, and a forth, and a fifth…"

"And a twentieth."

He laughs lightly. "And a twentieth."

"There won't be a twenty-first," I tell him. "I have to draw the line *somewhere.*"

"I won't need another," he says, his hand grasping my hip and pulling me closer, between his legs. "I'm going to get it right this time."

✿ ✿ ✿

"Aunt Meghan!"

Maddie takes off running for the apartment the second I park the car and let her out, heading straight for Meghan, who lurks by the front door.

"Hey, sugar-cookie, pecan-swirl!" Meghan says, snatching Maddie up and spinning her around. "How's my sweet niece doing, still in her PJs even though it's *noon?*"

Meghan's gaze shifts to me, suspicious. Yeah, it's practically the walk of shame, family-style. I haven't even brushed my hair. Ugh, I haven't *showered.* Her brother's DNA is all over me, all up in me, and Meghan's the human equivalent of a bloodhound.

The second I get close to her, she *knows.*

"My daddy took me to the convention!" Maddie says when Meghan sets her on her feet. "And then we had a sleepover, but he slept with Mommy, and then we went to have bacon!"

248

"Wow," Meghan says, shooting me a pointed look as she repeats herself. "*Wow.*"

I open the front door. Maddie runs inside, heading straight for her bedroom, but I linger there, knowing Meghan's about to pelt me with questions.

"You've gotta be fucking kidding me," Meghan says, stopping short and glaring at the cardboard cutout of Breezeo still in my living room. She cuts her eyes at me with disbelief. "*Really?*"

"I had nothing to do with that."

"It's in your apartment."

"Yeah, well…"

I have no defense.

"Unbelievable," Meghan says, shaking her head. "A sleepover? Are you… wow, you're *really* doing this with him again?"

"No, we're not. I mean, we're just… I don't know." I sigh, running my hands down my face. "I don't know what I'm doing."

"Clearly," she says, looking back at the cutout bearing her brother's face.

"I need to shower," I say, "I'll be back."

"Yeah, go do that. See if you can scrub him off of you."

Too late for that, I think, but I don't dare say it. He's all up inside of me right now—literally, figuratively.

I shower, and dress, and once I feel human again, I gather some clothes to take them across the street to the Laundromat, since my washer is still broken. Meghan comes by sometimes on Sundays and spends time with Maddie to give me a reprieve, a few hours so I can catch up on housework without interruption.

After the laundry is finished, I head to the grocery store and stock up on food, making sure to buy Lucky Charms for breakfast in the mornings. Afterward, I'm straightening up my bedroom and putting clothes away when my attention drifts to the ripped cardboard box hastily shoved back in the closet weeks ago. I pull it out again, shifting through the dusty mementos, and grab the old five-subject notebook. The cheap black cover is faded after all these years. I can only faintly make out my scratchy doodling.

I flip through it. Two hundred pages, college-ruled, most of them full of my messy scribble. The notebook feels heavier than one ever should, but I know it's not the paper weighing it down, but the memory of all those words. The notebook holds a piece of my heart, a piece of my soul, the piece I gave to him long ago.

"You're being an idiot," Meghan says, popping up in the doorway behind me.

I laugh to myself. "I know."

EIGHTEEN

JONATHAN

"You should buy a potted plant."

I laugh at that as I sit on the wooden picnic table at the park in the dark, listening to Jack ramble through the speakerphone beside me. "A plant."

"Seriously, hear me out—you get a plant. You nurture it, keep it alive, and *wham-bam*, that's how you know you're ready for this whole thing."

"That's stupid."

"No, it's not. It's a real thing. I saw it in that movie *28 Days*."

"The zombie one?"

"Nah, man, the Sandra Bullock one. You're thinking about *28 Days Later*."

"You steal your advice from Sandra Bullock movies?"

"Oh, don't you fucking judge me. It's a hell of a lot better than that shit you keep making. And besides, it's good advice."

"Buy a plant."

"Yes."

"Did you buy one?"

"What?"

"A plant," I say. "Did you buy yourself a plant to prove you're ready for a relationship?"

"No," he says.

"Why not?"

"Because I don't need a plant to tell me what I already know," he says. "I'm wearing a pair of emoji boxers and eating hot

Cheetos in my basement apartment. Pretty sure the signs are all there."

"Emoji boxers?" I laugh. "Talk about a stereotypical internet troll."

"Yeah, yeah, whatever," he says. "This isn't about me, though. We're talking about you."

"I'm tired of talking about me."

"Holy shit, seriously? Didn't think that was possible!"

"*Funny.*"

"Remember that interview you did on *The Late Show* two years ago?"

"I don't want to talk about it."

"You were stoned out of your mind, kept referring to yourself in third person."

"Fuck off."

"Pretty sure *that* guy would never be tired of talking about himself."

"You're an asshole."

He laughs. "True."

"You get on my nerves."

"You're welcome."

Sighing, I shake my head. "Thank you."

"Now go buy yourself a plant," he says. "I was in the middle of a game of *Call of Duty* when you called, so I'm going to get back to it."

"Yeah, okay."

"Oh, and Cunning? I'm glad you haven't drowned yourself in a bottle of whiskey."

"Why? Would you miss me?"

"More like your fangirls might murder me if I let you destroy yourself," he says. "I don't know if you've noticed, but they're *crazy*. Have you seen some of their fan art? It's insane."

"Goodbye, Jack," I say, pressing the button on my phone to end the call. I slip it in my pocket when a throat clears behind me, catching me off guard. I turn, wide-eyed, seeing blonde hair shining in the moonlight. "Meghan?"

"Your friend sounds like a real winner," she says. "Jack, is it? What is he, the eight-hundred pound, acne-riddled, misogynistic president of the Johnny Cunning fan club?"

I laugh dryly. "Not quite."

Meghan strolls closer, her expression hard, shoulders squared. She's on guard, rigid, like there's ice in her veins.

My sister and I weren't always so cold with each other.

"You can say it, whatever it is," I tell her. "Whatever you came to say."

She sits down on the picnic table beside me, staring out at the darkened water.

"This is where Kennedy had Maddie's first birthday party," she says. "If you could call it a *party*. It was just her, me, Kennedy's parents. No other kids, just family. Dad stopped by and it was… well, it was a disaster."

I tense. "I didn't think he had anything to do with Madison."

"He doesn't," she says. "Kennedy's father told him to leave, said he wasn't welcome, so Dad dropped off his gift and left, never tried again."

"What was it?"

"What?"

"The gift."

I'm not sure why it matters, why I feel the need to know, but I wonder what he gave my daughter on her birthday.

"A sterling silver rattle," she says, rolling her eyes, "because that's what a one year old wants. Kennedy threw it, plunked it right in that water over there."

"Good."

"Meanwhile, I bought her those little board books," she says. "And diapers and wipes, because that was what she needed. Well, actually, what she needed was a father, but she got her Aunt Meghan instead. I think I'm a good substitute, but I'm not *you*."

"I should've been here."

"You should've."

"I fucked up."

"You did."

"I'm trying to do better."

"That's what Kennedy says, but if you hurt her, I swear, I'll hurt *you*."

"I'm not going to hurt Madison."

"I'm not talking about Maddie. If you hurt her, you'll have a whole host of people ready to tear you apart. I'm talking about her mother. I've watched Kennedy try make a life for her and Maddie, and if you waltz your ass on in here and destroy that, if you knock her back down and then walk away, I'll string you up by the nuts."

Ouch.

I scrub a hand over my face. "You always were a ball-buster."

"I'm a woman in politics. I have to be."

❀ ❀ ❀

The apartment door yanks open before I can knock on it, Madison standing there, clutching a piece of paper and a stubby pencil.

"I need a T," she says right away, glancing at her paper. "I gots a turtle, and a triangle, and a truck, but I need more."

"A taco?" I suggest.

Her eyes light up, and she yells, "Tacos!" as she skips away to the kitchen. I hesitate before following, shutting the door.

Madison settles in at the table and starts drawing a taco.

"Table," I tell her. "That's another one."

"Table," she repeats.

"And tiger and teardrop and—"

"And I'm pretty sure I told a certain little girl that she could manage her homework by herself tonight and didn't need anyone giving her the answers."

My attention shifts to Kennedy when she walks into the kitchen, cutting me off mid-answer, giving Madison a pointed look.

Right away, by looking at her, I know something's off. Something has her in a bad mood.

Madison scowls and keeps drawing.

"Sorry," I say. "I didn't know."

"It's fine," she mutters. "Look, I know you were hoping to spend time with her tonight, but things have been crazy today, work's a mess—people are out sick and there's inventory to do, so I have to go back in for a few hours, which means she's going to have to go to my dad's."

My stomach drops.

"He can come," Madison says.

"I don't think so," Kennedy says. "Your grandpa doesn't like visitors."

"But he likes us," she says.

"We're family," Kennedy tells her.

"And he's my daddy," Madison says, "so that's our family, too, right?"

Kennedy hesitates. "Right."

She's stuck between a rock and a hard place here.

"It's fine," I say. "I get it."

"I'm sorry, really," Kennedy says, pulling out her phone and dialing a number, sighing dramatically as she mutters to herself, "Answer the freaking phone, Dad…"

He doesn't answer.

She tries again.

He doesn't answer that time, either.

Groaning, she hangs up before dialing for the third time.

"I could watch her," I suggest when she hangs up yet again, getting no answer.

"You don't have to."

"I want to," I say. "Besides, she's my daughter. I'm equally responsible for her."

"Never made a difference before," she mutters as her phone starts ringing. *Ouch.* Sighing, she glances at it, answering, "Hey, Dad."

255

She walks off to talk to him, while I sit down at the kitchen table across from Madison, resigned. She's busy drawing a table, her taco finished, the word written above it misspelled.

"It's a C, not a K," I say, pointing. "T-a-c-o, not t-a-k-o."

"Thank you," she says, erasing the whole damn word just to rewrite it properly.

"Anytime, kiddo."

Kennedy walks back in a minute later, shoving her phone in the back pocket of her work khakis. She doesn't even look at me as she starts rambling something about homework and dinner and bedtime, reciting rules that Madison soundlessly mimics the same time her mother says them. Clearly, she's heard this all before…

"Wait, you mean I'm watching her?" I ask, surprised.

Kennedy turns my way. "You wanted to, didn't you? If not, I can call my dad back."

"No, no, I did… I *do*. I'm just surprised."

"You shouldn't be. Like you said—she's your daughter."

She kisses the top of Madison's head and says something about being back as soon as she can, and then she's gone, out the door, heading to work, leaving me sitting here, having not absorbed *any* of her instructions.

Yeah, I'm going to fuck this up.

Madison finishes drawing her table and adds a tiger and a teardrop into the mix before declaring herself done with homework. She shoves the paper in her backpack before pulling out a beat up notebook and a pencil pouch jammed full of markers. She spreads them out along the table and opens the notebook, flipping through page after page of scribbles.

"What do you have there?" I ask, leaning over, trying to look at the pages, when she inhales sharply and throws herself on top of it, blocking me from seeing anything.

"No, don't look!" she says, shoving my face away. "It's not ready!"

"Okay, okay," I say with a laugh. "I won't look."

"Better not, 'cuz it's not ready yet for you to look."

"I won't look until you tell me I can."

Only after I say that does she settle back into her chair, satisfied her work is safe. There's so much of Kennedy in that girl that it's almost like déjà vu watching her.

Shaking my head, I stand up and look around the kitchen. "Any idea what we're supposed to do about dinner? I know your mother said something about it."

"She said no junk food, gotta have real food."

I glance in the cabinets. "Define *real food*."

"Pizza," she says.

"Ah, pizza I can do," I say, seeing a flyer on the refrigerator door for delivery.

"And chickens and the breads, too!" Madison declares, continuing to draw in her notebook.

"You got it."

I call the number, ordering a large pepperoni with chicken wings and breadsticks, even adding a ham and pineapple pizza to the order for Kennedy, in case she's hungry when she gets home— ordering way too much food for just us.

There's a knock on the door after about forty-five minutes and I start toward it, pulling out some cash from my wallet, but stop short. I didn't even think about the fact that somebody might recognize me and question why I'm here. Glancing back at Madison, I consider having her pay them, but well, that goes against everything her mother's been trying to teach her about not opening the door for strangers.

They knock again, and I take a deep breath before opening the door. It's a guy, mid-twenties, no older than me. He looks stoned out of his gourd, eyes blazing red, the dank woodsy odor clinging to his uniform, like the guy was smoking on his way to the door. He rambles off the price and I shove some cash at him, taking the pizza. Before I can close the door, though, his bloodshot eyes narrow, face contorting with confusion as he eyes me. "Hey, aren't you that guy? You know… that one from that movie? The, uh…?" He snaps his fingers, like he's trying to remember, before he points at me. "Breezeo!"

"Nah, not me," I say. "Get that all the time, though."

I shut the door before he can press it any further and watch out the peephole as he lingers. He shrugs it off, though, and strolls away, lighting something before he even reaches his car again.

Breathing a sigh of relief, I turn for the kitchen and nearly slam right into Madison standing there, just inches behind me.

"You told a lie," she says.

"I did," I admit, "but it was for the greater-good."

"What's that mean?"

"It means sometimes it's better we don't tell people who I am."

"Why?"

"Because people are nosey," I say. "If I admitted who I was, that guy would go back and tell his friends, who would tell their friends, and next thing you know, the whole world would be in my business and want to know what I'm doing here."

She's quiet, following me as I carry the pizza to the kitchen. She closes her notebook and sits there as I put some food on a plate for her, sitting down across from her with a plate of my own.

There's something wrong.

Something's bothering her. I can tell.

Just like her mother, remember?

"What's the matter?" I ask.

She shakes her head, saying, "Nothing."

"Ah, see, now I think *you* just told a lie."

"It's for the greatest-goods."

I laugh as she tries to throw my words back at me. "Come on, tell me what's bothering you."

She lets out the longest, most dramatic sigh, like I'm nagging her half to death here, before she says, "Do you not wanna be my daddy?"

That question is a punch to the chest.

"Of course I do. Why would you think that?"

" 'Cuz you don't want the people to know it," she says. "And

258

'cuz you weren't my daddy 'till now."

Man, I feel like an asshole. None of those little jabs from Kennedy hold an ounce of the pain that Madison's words contain.

"I've always been your daddy," I tell her. "I just wasn't good at it. I'm trying to be better. And I'd like for people to know, but it's complicated, and the pizza man really isn't the person to start with. But we'll tell everyone. We will."

She smiles, and eats, like my answer satisfied her, but I don't feel like any less of an asshole. This isn't fair to her—at all. I'm here, yeah, and I'm trying, but how much does it count if the entire time I'm sneaking around? Like I can only be her father behind closed doors.

I'm treating her like she's my dirty little secret.

This isn't the first time I've done this, either.

I did the same thing to her mother.

Cliff would tell me I'm overreacting, that it's about protection—protecting her, yeah, but protecting my image, too. My private life stays private. That's just how it goes. Jack would tell me to man the fuck up, because living a life in secret is a danger to sobriety. He'd tell me to do what's right, and stop being a self-centered asshole. But I don't know what's *right*.

"So, uh, now that we have dinner sorted," I say, "any idea what your mother said about bedtime?"

"Eight o'clock," Madison says. "And I gotta take a bath at seven-thirty, and then you gotta read me a book, but I get to pick which one."

"Fair enough," I say, glancing at a nearby clock—only six-thirty. "We've got about an hour. What do you want to do?"

She grins at me. "Draw!"

Today marks a year.

A year since that night you showed up drunk on the sidewalk in front of the white two-story house in Bennett Landing and asked the girl to run away with you, and she did. Your *Dreamiversary*, she calls it. The day you decided to follow your dreams.

But following dreams isn't easy, especially dreams like yours. You live in a city where thousands of people are chasing that same dream, and a lot of them have a head start.

They tell you that you've gotten lucky so far, but you don't feel it. You signed with a small agent, and your IMDb lists a few more minor roles, but 'Heroin Dealer' on *CSI* and 'Guy #3' on *Criminal Minds* isn't who you've dreamed of being since you were a child, nor does it pay the bills.

The money ran out long ago. It didn't even last three months. You've gotten a few odd jobs, but they always seem to get in the way of auditions, and every penny you manage to scrounge up disappears in a cloud of headshots and acting classes. So much has fallen onto *her* shoulders, but she doesn't complain. Because every single night, you tell her you love her. She knows you care, and that was the only promise you ever made her.

"Happy *Dreamiversary*," she says, popping up in the bedroom doorway of the tiny apartment. It's late, maybe one in the morning. Everything about her screams exhaustion, because she just got home from pulling a double-shift waitressing at the all-night diner around the corner. "I have something for you."

You're lying in bed, staring at the ceiling. You can't sleep when she's not here. She used to say you couldn't sleep because the two of you only had an air mattress on the floor, but you got a real bed a month ago and *nope*.

Can't sleep.

Well, not unless you let alcohol do the work, but she doesn't like that, so you take it easy. Not only does it upset her, finding you passed out, but it makes you an inconsiderate asshole to spend money you don't have getting wasted.

You sit up, gazing at the girl through the dim bedroom lighting. Though, she's not really a *girl* anymore. She's wearing the little pink button-up dress that is her work uniform, a white apron tied around her slim waist. She's lost weight lately, but she has more curves. She's a *woman*, one with an apartment and a job. One with her hands behind her back, hiding something.

"What is it?" you ask, and she whips out a business card, waving it at you as she approaches. She climbs right onto the bed, on top of you, straddling your lap as she smiles.

You take the card, looking it at. *Caldwell Talents*. Clifford Caldwell. You know who he is. You've been told dozens of times this past year that if you want to be someone in Hollywood, he's the man you need. But despite your best efforts, you can't get anywhere near him. He sees people by appointment-only, and it's *Battle Royale* trying to get one of those.

"You see the date and time written on the back?" she asks. "That's your meeting with him."

You look at her with shock. "How...?"

"He came into the diner tonight," she says. "He was with some clients... that guy in that new dance movie? *Step On In* or something.

262

And that guy from the vampire movies! And some girls, uh... oh, that model, the one that's on all those billboards? The young blonde? Her name is like Markson or something? Selena, maybe?"

"Kennedy, baby, focus," you say, laughing as she rambles on and on, your hands framing her face. "I don't give a fuck about some model. How the hell did you snag an appointment?"

"Oh." She blushes, grasping your wrists. "I kind of just asked."

"You *asked.*"

"Well, I mean, I worked up to it. He wouldn't even look at me at first, too busy on his phone, but I couldn't let him leave without getting his attention. So I spilled his coffee."

"You did *what?*"

"I didn't spill it *on* him. Just on the table. And some of it on the model, but it wasn't *that* hot, so whatever. She was mad, though. But anyway, when I was cleaning it up, Clifford put his phone down to look at me, so I went for it."

"*That's* when you asked?"

"What? No. That's when I flirted my butt off."

"*You? You* flirted?"

"Batted my eyelashes and everything. The whole damsel in distress act. *Oh my god, Mr. Caldwell, sir, I'm so very sorry... I just get so frazzled sometimes around such powerful men. I can barely contain myself when it comes to an utterly brilliant mind and uh, stunning body of work.*"

You laugh. "He believed that shit?"

"Yep." She grins. "I swear, they stayed for like an hour after that. He kept striking up conversation, asking me questions about my life. I told him all about you, and *wham–bam,* appointment!"

"Wow," you say, looking at the card again.

"Oh, I forgot the best part!" she says, shoving you back onto the bed, kissing you. "He left me a crazy big tip."

"Hmm, how big?" you ask, grabbing her hips, grinding against her. "*That* big?"

"Bigger," she says. "Much bigger."

"Are you trying to make me jealous?"

"Is it working?"

She squeals as you flip her over, onto the bed, and settle right between her legs. You shove material around, and she gasps with the first thrust.

"You changed our lives tonight, baby," you say. "Happy Dreamiversary."

You don't know this, but that woman? As you make love to her, whispering in her ear how much you love her, telling her with every thrust that things are going to be beautiful, she's believing every single word. And she's imagining it, how life is going to change, how so many doors are going to open for you. Your dreams are coming true. She lies there, with you on top of her, inside of her, and feels the weight on her easing for the first time in almost a year. Finally... *finally*... things are looking up. Finally, some good news.

NINETEEN

KENNEDY

"So, bad news…"

Sighing, I drop the small crate onto the floor of the store's back stockroom and shove it along the wall. I shake my head, refusing to look at Marcus, who stands in the doorway, the bearer of bad news. "Don't do that."

"Don't do what?"

"That whole *bad news* thing," I say, waving toward him. "I don't want to hear it."

"It's just a bit of a problem."

"Whatever it is, it's not *my* problem."

"But it is."

Groaning, I run my hands down my face. "Don't do this to me, Marcus."

"Bethany's feeling sick, so I'm going to send her home."

"I'm begging you," I grumble. "Don't do it."

"I need you to stay and run her register."

"Seriously?"

"Seriously."

"I *opened* this morning. I've been here since eight o'clock."

"You got off at three," he points out.

"And I was back here by five," I say. "I'll be back again at eight in the morning. Now you want me to stay until midnight?"

"I wouldn't ask you if I had another choice," he says before walking away, just like that, not waiting on a response. He didn't even actually *ask*. He assumed I'd stay, because that's who I am. It's what I always do.

"Look at me, *woo-hoo*, assistant manager of the Piggly Q," I grumble to myself, shoving more crates around before locking up the stockroom. "Doing amazing things with my life."

I head to the front of the store in just enough time to see Bethany scurry out, looking quite the opposite of sick, but hey, what do I know? The little dance she does, though, as she meets her friends out in the parking lot, is a pretty good indicator that I'm being screwed over.

Awesome.

I'm in a bad mood. I've been in one all day. I'm not sure what started it, but I'm on edge. My little quiet life of monotony is feeling more and more like some prank the universe is playing. The fact that LeAnne Rimes' *How Do I Live* is playing on the store radio pretty much proves that point, I think.

I run the register until the store closes, which means I stand around all night long, my feet angrily screaming from me being on them.

It's a quarter after midnight when I get to the apartment, slipping inside and locking up.

The lights are off, but the TV is on, playing quietly, the glow of it illuminating the couch, where Jonathan lays with Maddie snuggled up against him. He's fast asleep, while she's barely dozing, eyes open but zoned out so much that she hasn't even noticed me. She was supposed to be in bed *hours* ago, but I'm too exhausted to be upset about it. Colorful marker covers the white plaster on Jonathan's wrist. He let her draw on his cast.

Strolling over, I scoop her up in my arms, and she doesn't resist, already snoring by the time I tuck her in bed.

When I make it back to the living room, Jonathan is sitting up. He runs a hand over his face, groggy, as he asks, "What time is it?"

"After midnight."

"Jesus Christ," he grumbles, looking me over as I plop down on the couch beside him and kick off my shoes. "Did you *just* get home?"

"A minute ago," I say. "Cashier was sick, left early, so I had to close. Got home in just enough time to get some sleep so I can get up tomorrow and do it all over again."

"That's crazy."

"Yeah, well, that's what it's like in the real world."

"You don't think I live in the real world?"

"I think you live in your *own* world, Jonathan."

"You could quit," he suggests.

"And do what? Get a job somewhere else, making minimum wage again?"

"You could stay home," he says. "Maybe even write, whatever you want to do."

"That's not going to pay the bills."

"But I can."

I glare at him when he says that.

He stares back at me defiantly.

He looks like he doesn't even understand what's wrong with what he's suggesting.

"I'm not going down this road with you," I tell him. "Not again."

"But I should be supporting my daughter. I should be contributing."

"You should be doing a lot of things."

"Yeah, so, *let me*."

I shake my head. "What happens when I quit my job and you decide to stop *contributing?*"

He laughs at that question. He laughs, like I'm being funny, the sound getting under my skin. *Ugh.* I go to stand up, to walk away, but he stops me, pulling me back onto the couch. "Look, I get it. I've let you down, but just give it some thought."

"There's nothing to think about. I don't need you. I never did."

As soon as those words come from my lips, I almost choke on the flood of regret that flows through me. It might be true. I might mean it. I might not need him. But there's cruelty in every word of that, and that's not who I am. No matter what happened to us, I never wanted to be just another person who did things to hurt him.

"I'm sorry," I say, putting my head down as I rest my elbows on my knees. "I don't know why I said that. I'm all over the place right now. My emotions are a mess."

Before he has the chance to respond, there's a knock on the apartment door. I force myself to my feet to see who it is, brow furrowing when I look through the peephole and see Bethany. *Weird.* Jonathan mumbles something about saying goodnight to Maddie as he gets up, disappearing down the hallway.

Sighing, I unlock the door when there's another knock. Bethany tenses, her wide-eyes meeting mine when I open it.

"Kennedy?" Her voice is laced with confusion. "What are *you* doing here?"

"I live here," I say, brow furrowing as I glance around. She's with some friends, the girl who picked her up from work and a guy, maybe mid-twenties. "Did you need something?"

"Oh, uh, no," Bethany says, forcing a smile as her cheeks flush. "Sorry. We just thought, I mean… we were looking for someone else. Must've gotten the wrong apartment."

She elbows the guy beside her pretty hard, making him wince as he mutters under his breath, "I swear, this is where he was."

Those words make my stomach drop.

"Who are you looking for?" I ask. "Maybe I can help you find him."

"It's nobody," Bethany says. "It's stupid, forget about it."

She bolts away from the apartment, dragging her friends along, berating the guy as they walk. I make out a bit of their conversation as they flee, hearing that dreaded name.

Johnny Cunning.

Carefully, I close the door, making sure to lock it again, and turn off the TV in the living room before making my way down the hall. Jonathan stalls when I stop in front of him.

"You, uh… you might wanna consider staying," I tell him.

He raises an eyebrow. "Yeah?"

"Yep." I step toward him, flush against him, and rise up on my tiptoes as I whisper, "I think you've been *made*."

I head to my bedroom, and he hesitates before following, stopping in the doorway. "What are you talking about?"

"The knock on the door," I tell him as I strip, getting out of this uniform. "Seems they were looking for a certain someone they heard might be around here somewhere."

"*Fuck.*"

"I didn't tell them anything," I say, tossing my clothes in the hamper. "It was the cashier from the store—you know, the one that went home *sick* tonight—and her friends. Guess someone thought they spotted you and word got back to her at work that you were in town for some reason."

I turn to him, expecting a reaction, maybe an explanation, but he doesn't even look at my face. No, his eyes are drifting, scanning my body, as I stand in front of him in plain white cotton, a simple bra and underwear.

I wave my hand in the direction of his face. "Are you even listening to me?"

He meets my gaze, eyebrows raised. "What?"

I shake my head, walking over to the closet to pull out a t-shirt, putting it on. When I turn back to him, he's not looking at me again. No, this time his attention is on the top of the dresser right beside him, on the old notebook sitting there.

After a moment, he attempts to focus. "So I've been made, huh?"

"Seems so."

"Pity," he says, strolling over and sitting down on the edge of my bed. "I was enjoying anonymity."

"Yeah, well, real world, remember? You had to know it wouldn't last."

"Yeah," he mumbles, though he doesn't seem to like that fact, his attention now on the drawings covering his cast. He traces

269

the colorful lines with his fingertips.

Grabbing a black permanent marker from the drawer in my bedside stand, I push Jonathan back onto the mattress before climbing onto his lap, straddling him. I yank the cap off the marker with my teeth. Pinning him down, I find a spot on the cast that still has some white and carefully write the words, '*love doesn't know titles.*'

He watches me, reading it, and smiles.

"That line is in the movie," he says as I sign beneath it simply with a 'K' and put the cap back on the marker. "It wasn't when I got the *Ghosted* script, but I threw a fit so they wrote it in."

"They let you have input?"

"Of course," he says. "It's in my contract."

"Well, in that case," I say, "you ought to have them fix the ending for your daughter."

He laughs. "I'll see what I can do."

I kiss him. I shouldn't. We shouldn't be doing any of this stuff we keep doing, but I'm having a hard time stopping myself when it comes to this man. He makes me reckless again.

He kisses me back, hands roaming, pulling at clothes, touching, *caressing*. I moan against his lips when he starts rubbing. Even constrained by a broken wrist, he easily works his magic.

Breaking the kiss, I gasp as his mouth finds my neck. He's fumbling with his pants but hesitating for some reason. "You *are* on birth control, right?"

I pull back from him, enough to meet his gaze.

"We haven't talked about it," he says. "I wasn't sure, you know, and we should be careful."

He's trying to have a serious conversation. A legitimate one. One we *need* to have. One that would probably make my father proud. But he's still rubbing, he hasn't yet stopped, and everything is going hazy, because I'm getting closer and closer, pleasure tingling my body.

I force words out between breaths as orgasm tears through me. "I've got... *uh*... implant... in my... *uh*... arm." *Oh god.* "It's good... for another... year... *uhhhh...*"

He yanks me onto the bed beneath him, startling me, not hesitating anymore as he says, "Well, in *that* case…"

✿ ✿ ✿

"No, no, no…"

The screeching of the alarm startles me awake. The bedroom is still dim and my eyes are burning as I force them open, slapping at the bedside stand to silence the noise.

"Shut that thing up," a gruff voice grumbles, the words muffled, a pillow covering his head. I hit a button—some button, *any* button—to make it stop screeching, and try to sit up when arms wind around me, yanking me back down. "Hmm, *stay.*"

"I can't," I mumble. "I have to work."

"Quit."

"Maddie has school."

"She can quit, too."

Laughing, I try to break free from his grasp. "Seriously, Jonathan. I have to get up."

"I'd rather you not."

"Tough."

Sighing dramatically, he loosens his grip, letting me slip out of bed. I pause and stretch, cringing, my entire body aching this morning. Even my bones seem to hurt. I'm much too young to feel so old, but *real life*, remember?

I glance behind me at the bed, at Jonathan, as he peeks out from beneath the pillow. It's strange, so strange, him being here— exciting, yet terrifying. But just like his anonymity, I know this can't last forever.

"Guess I have to get up, too," he says, tossing the pillow onto the mattress beside him as he sits up. "Gotta go brave the public and get back to my grumpy ass landlady."

"You could stay here," I suggest right away—maybe too fast, based on the stunned look he gives me, but I'm just as shocked.

Did I seriously invite him to stay *here?*

"Are you sure?" he asks.

"No," I say.

He laughs.

"But you could, if you wanted to," I continue. "You know, stay and hide out. It would make it easier for you to see Maddie."

"Okay."

"Just don't snoop through my underwear drawer when I'm not home."

"Hasn't even crossed my mind," he says, grinning. "Does that mean I'm allowed to look when you're here?"

Rolling my eyes, I lean over the bed and kiss him—not dwelling, not lingering, and not answering that question—before leaving the bedroom. I shower and put on my uniform for work. Jonathan's already asleep again before I even wake Maddie up.

I'm exhausted, and the morning drags on and on and on. Maddie eats Lucky Charms before I drop her off at school, getting to work at exactly eight o'clock. Marcus is already there, bright-eyed, rambling on about schedules and vacation days and overtime pay. I barely pay him attention as I clock in until I hear the words 'Kennedy can cover the register this weekend'. *Oh, whoa, whoa...*

"Excuse me? I can do *what?*"

"You don't mind, do you?" he asks, not even looking at me, his attention fixed on some paperwork he's sorting through. "Bethany wants the weekend off, and we don't have anyone to cover for her."

"Here's a novel idea—*hire* somebody," I say. "The cashiers have been short-staffed for a while, even before Bethany started requesting all this time off."

"I could," he said. "I just figured you'd want the extra hours, being a single mom and all."

"Being a single mom and all, I'd like to have the chance to spend time with my kid, because I haven't had much of that lately."

"Fair enough," he says, still not looking at me. "Do me a favor when you go out there? Tell Bethany I have to decline her

272

request."

Hello, guilt trip.

Shaking my head, I walk away, heading through the store to get my work done so I can get out of here on time. I busy myself in the stockroom, figuring out what needs to be ordered, when there's a quiet knock and the door pops open, Bethany appearing. "Hey, Kennedy."

"Hey," I say, cutting right to it. "Marcus couldn't approve your weekend off."

She scowls but doesn't complain, just standing there, leaning against the doorframe, watching me as I shove crates around and finish what I couldn't last night because of covering for her.

"So, did you need something?" I ask after a few minutes, knowing she's supposed to be up front, running a register, and not back here.

"No, I, uh... I wanted to say sorry about last night," she says. "You know, about knocking on your door. Josh—that's my boyfriend, he delivers pizza, and he swears he delivered pizza to that apartment and the guy there looked like... somebody."

"Any somebody I might know?"

"Johnny Cunning."

She laughs awkwardly, and I cast her a look, seeing her cheeks are flushed with embarrassment.

"So your boyfriend told you he delivered pizza to Johnny Cunning at my apartment."

"Yeah," she says. "I thought it might not be so crazy, him being in town, since he's been here before, and nobody has seen him lately, but Josh must've been hallucinating or something. It must've been that Andrew guy you're seeing, because there's no way Johnny Cunning was hanging out at *your* apartment."

I stop what I'm doing to look at her. "Why's that?"

"Huh?"

"Why wouldn't he be at my apartment?"

She laughs. "Why *would* he be?"

"I don't know," I say with a shrug. "Maybe we go way back,

and he wanted to catch up on old times."

"Yeah, okay," she says, still laughing. "In that case, say hey to him for me."

"I will," I tell her, shaking my head as she walks away.

The afternoon drags just like the morning. Come lunchtime, I take my break locked up in the stockroom, wanting some peace and quiet. Sitting on a crate, I pull out my phone, seeing a message waiting from Drew.

Dinner this weekend?

I stare at it before clearing the notification and sending a message to Jonathan. **Bethany (your local fangirl) says hello.**

He responds right away. **Nice. Tell her I said hey.**

Will do. ;)

I hesitate after sending that before typing another one. **Drew asked me out to dinner.**

I feel like an idiot the moment I hit send, desperately wishing I could take it back. "Stupid, stupid, stupid," I mutter. Why did I just tell him that?

His little reply bubble pops up and then disappears again, over and over, for at least a minute, maybe two, before a call comes through. *Jonathan.*

Panicked, I almost hit decline, my finger bouncing between the buttons, before I answer it. "Hello?"

"You tell Hastings he can suck my cock," he says.

I laugh quietly. "Before or after dinner?"

"Either way," he says. "Though, I prefer the dinner not happen."

"Good to know," I say. "I'll be sure to pass on that message."

"You do that," he says, a gritty edge to his voice as there's a rustling on the line, the sound of springs squeaking.

"Wait, are you still in bed?" I ask. "*Seriously?*"

"Hey, don't judge me," he says. "You could still be in bed, too, but you chose to go to work. You made your choice. Don't hate on me for mine."

I glance at the time—nearly one o'clock. "All I know is I get off work in two hours and you better be out of bed by then."

"Or what?" he asks. "What are you going to do?"

"I guess we'll find out, won't we?"

He laughs and says something, but I don't hear what it is, because the storage room door pops open again. This time, Marcus appears, holding the week's schedule. He taps a pen against his lips in contemplation, and I know right away whatever he's about to say isn't going to be something pleasant.

"I have to go," I say quietly. "Work crap."

I don't give Jonathan a chance to respond, hanging up as Marcus starts talking. "So I did some finagling, moved some others around to cover the weekend for Bethany…"

"Lucky her," I say.

"Yeah, so I need you to work a double on Thursday, if you can manage that," he says, cutting his eyes at me. "Unless that's too much of a problem."

I want to tell him it is, but I'm too nice. Besides, you know, *money.* "Not a problem at all."

"Good, good," he mutters, walking out as my phone vibrates with a message. I look at it, seeing a text from Jonathan.

Work? Too bad you can't just… quit.

Shaking my head, I don't respond to that, instead going back to Drew's message. I need to reply while I have the nerve. **I don't think it's a good idea for us to go out with everything else that's going on.**

I send a string of frowny-faces, already wrecked with guilt, because hanging out with him is easy and he's been so nice, but I know it'll just cause problems, and the fact that my feelings for him haven't evolved past *acquaintances* is a sign that added complication isn't worth the trouble. I shove my phone into my pocket so I can get back to work, hoping the next few hours go faster, but no such luck. Every second seems to drag and drag and drag. By the time three o'clock comes, I feel like I've been at this place for days.

On my way out of the store, I run into Bethany, lingering by the register, face buried in the latest edition of *Hollywood Chronicles*. There's nothing about Jonathan on the cover. "Anything interesting?"

She scowls, closing the tabloid. "Nothing."

"I told him you said hey, by the way. He said hey back."

She laughs. "Yeah, right."

I give her a smile. *Poor girl.* She's going to kick herself. "Anyway, heard you got your weekend off. Big plans?"

"Just the usual," she says, shrugging.

"The usual, as in, knocking on apartment doors at one a.m. looking for Johnny Cunning?"

"Pretty much." She's blushing again. "Josh is such an idiot."

"Well, good luck with that," I say, leaving before I take pity on the girl and start spilling my secrets.

I get to my father's house the same time as Maddie's bus, meeting her in the front yard as my father rocks in his chair on the porch.

"Grandpa!" Maddie says, running right for him, digging through her backpack to pull out a drawing. "I made you a picture!"

"Well, look at that!" he says, grinning. "A dinosaur!"

She laughs. "No, it's not, silly! It's a alligator!"

"Ah, and it's by far the greatest alligator I've ever seen," he says. "Absolutely perfect!"

She runs inside to hang it up somewhere, like usual. I linger outside, waiting for her to resurface, as my father stares me down.

"So," he says.

"So," I repeat.

"So how's it going?"

"Okay," I say.

"Okay," he repeats.

It's silent for a moment as we stare at each other.

"You've got mail again," he says. "It's on the kitchen table."

"Thanks."

"Of course."

I head inside, passing by Maddie as she runs back out. I grab my stack of mail, sorting through it. Mostly junk, as usual, that I toss right in the trash, but I pause as I reach the last envelope.

Cunningham c/o Caldwell Talents

I stare at it for a moment before folding it, shoving it in my back pocket and heading outside, where Maddie sits with my father, rambling on and on about the fun she's been having with her *daddy*.

"Are you ready, sweetheart?" I ask. "We need to get home."

"Okay, Mommy," she says, snatching up her backpack to lug it off the porch.

"Thinking of having a cookout this weekend," my father says. "Nothing big, but I hope you can come. Haven't seen much of my girls lately."

"Sure," I say, hugging him. "We'll be here, Dad."

"Can my daddy come, too?" Maddie asks, swinging her backpack as she spins in circles.

"I don't—" I start, because I don't know about all that, but my father cuts me off.

"Of course," he says. "If he's up for a visit."

Oh, boy.

We head home, and as soon as we reach the apartment, Maddie bursts inside, screeching, Daddy! You're here!"

Jonathan is in the kitchen, wearing only a pair of pants. Food is cooking on the stove. I can hear it. I can smell it. He's frying something, and it's not currently burning, whatever it is. That's a step up from what dinner is like when I make it.

"I am," he says, waving the spatula toward Maddie when she heads right for him. "Figured you might be hungry."

"What is it?" she asks, trying to look.

"Fried chicken," he says. "Tater-tots. Mac & Cheese."

I shut the front door, locking up, before strolling to the kitchen. The latter came from a box, but still, it's impressive. *Huh.*

"Get started on your homework," I say, steering Maddie away from the stove. "We'll let you know when the food is ready."

She leaves the kitchen, dragging her backpack along.

"So dinner, huh?" I look over his shoulder as he pokes at the chicken. "Have you ever fried chicken before?"

"Nope," he says, "but I found a recipe and thought, *what the hell?* How hard could it be?"

Pretty hard, I think, but I let it go, pulling myself up onto the counter to sit on it.

I take out the envelope I got from my father's house and fiddle with it, running my fingertips along the edges before tracing the writing on the return address.

"What's that?" Jonathan asks, waving the spatula toward it.

I laugh dryly and hold it up for him to see.

It takes him a moment to recognize what it is. He plucks it right from my hand and tosses the spatula onto the counter, so he can open the envelope. Peeking inside, he lets out a low whistle, shoving his way between my legs and tapping the envelope against my chest as he says, "If I didn't know any better, I'd say that's more than enough to justify quitting."

It is. I know it. I don't even have to look.

"Well, if I didn't know any better," I say, "I'd say you were gloating about how much money you're making now."

"Who, *me?*" he says, feigning innocence.

"Nobody likes a braggart, Cunningham. It's unattractive."

"Is it?" He leans closer, tilting his head. "Does it turn you off, Garfield, hearing about my success?"

I dramatically roll my eyes as I shove his face away. "*Ugh.*"

Laughing, he grabs my hand and pulls it down, yanking me to him, snatching me right off of the counter, but his body pins me there, flush up against him. He kisses me, teasingly, again and again, whispering against my lips, "I think you're in denial."

"Am not," I say, pulling my arm from his grasp.

"I think you like it. I think you're proud."

"And I think you're full of yourself," I say, wrapping my arms around his neck, kissing him back. Deep. Rough. *Passionate.* It doesn't last long, though, just a few seconds, before a loud gasp rocks through the kitchen. Jonathan breaks the kiss, pushing away, leaving me breathless.

Maddie stands in the doorway, staring at us, her eyes wide and jaw slack. "Did you kiss my mommy?"

"Uh, yeah," he says. "I did."

"Are you gonna take her on dates now?" she asks.

"Sure, if she wants," he says, cutting his eyes at me before turning back to her and saying, "I mean, if that's okay?"

Maddie's face splits with a wide grin. "Okay, but only if you see when she gets all pretty, 'cuz sometimes people don't see."

"She's always pretty," he says.

"But you gotta tell her, and maybe pick her some flowers, too, 'cuz it makes her happy when I do that," she says, strutting over to him and grabbing his hand, trying to pull him with her out of the kitchen.

"Where are we going?" he asks, brow furrowing.

"To get ready, *duh*. You can't date with no shirt."

I laugh, hopping off the counter. "We're not going tonight, sweetheart. Daddy's a little busy right now. He's cooking dinner."

"Oh shit," he says, pulling his hand from Maddie's as he bolts for the stove, turning off burners and shifting pans around, groaning. "I hope you like your chicken extra crispy."

"I do!" Maddie says. "That's how Mommy makes it."

TWENTY

JONATHAN

It's strange how easy it is to fall into a routine, how simple it is to find a sense of normalcy. It's almost *instinct*.

Kennedy goes to work. Madison goes to school. I sit around, and well… I wait for them to get home. The apartment is small, but it isn't as cramped as that first one we lived in together. I get restless, yeah, but it's not unbearable. I distract myself by cooking, and I call Jack whenever I'm feeling antsy. I'm starting to think I might be cut out for small-town domestic life.

Okay, okay, so it's only been three days, but they're some of the best days I've had in years.

There's a knock on the apartment door. Three o'clock on Friday. Kennedy and Madison won't be home for another hour.

Quietly stepping over to the door, I look out the peephole, to see who's knocking, when I spot the familiar, crotchety lady. *Son of a bitch.* Opening it, I come face-to-face with McKleski, standing on the doorstep, holding a duffel bag.

My duffel bag.

Before I can greet her, she drops it at my feet.

I stare down at it. "You evicting me?"

"Thought you might want your *things*," she says, emphasizing that word, like whatever is in the bag might be scandalous, but it's just clothes. "You haven't been to your room in days. *Days!* I'm all alone out there!"

"Yeah, uh, sorry about that."

She scoffs. "You're not sorry."

She's right. I'm not. "So, you've missed me?"

"Like an alcoholic misses Happy Hour."

That might've been meant to offend, but it makes me laugh. "Will it make it better if I promise to visit?"

She makes a face at that.

"I'm re-renting your room, so don't come crawling back," she says, matter-of-fact. "*And* I'm keeping the money you paid for it. No refunds."

"I wouldn't expect any less."

She waves toward me flippantly as she turns to leave. "Good luck with all *this*. Don't run out on them like you abandoned me."

Ouch. That jab does sting a bit, but I suck it up and grab the duffel bag, closing the door again.

I shower and put on a fresh pair of clothes, the best thing I have with me—black slacks, blue button down, black shoes. I stare at myself in the bathroom mirror after I'm dressed. It's been about a month since the accident, so the bruises have all faded, the scrapes and cuts all gone. Except for the cast, it's almost like it didn't happen. *Almost.*

But I still see it, sometimes, when I close my eyes. The flash of headlights. The blood. I still hear it, even when it's quiet. The screech of tires. The screams. The pain might be gone, but the memory is embedded inside of me.

I hear the door unlock, hear Madison burst inside with Kennedy following. I greet them, and Madison runs past, saying, "Hey, Daddy," as she drops her backpack on the way to her bedroom. She's gotten used to me being here.

"Well, well, well," Kennedy says as she approaches, grasping my chin and scratching at the scruff I still haven't bothered to shave. Another layer of protection, privacy. Not quite as recognizable with facial hair. "You *almost* clean up nicely."

"Thought we could go out," I tell her. "You know, like a date."

"A date," she repeats.

"Date!" Madison screeches, running right back out of her

bedroom. "A date!"

I laugh, glancing at her. "Yeah, a date."

"Do I get to go, too?" she asks with wide eyes. "*Please?*"

"Of course," I say. "What kind of date would it be without you?"

"A sucky one," Madison says. "Right, Mommy?"

"Right." Kennedy grins down at her. "Guess we ought to go find something to wear, huh?"

Madison runs off again, just like that, yelling, "Come on!"

It takes them a while to get ready, but I don't mind. Madison changes her clothes about a billion times, settling on a yellow dress. She's a ball of sunshine, that girl.

And her mother? *Jesus Christ.*

The moment I lay my eyes on her, it feels like my guts get all twisted up. Little blue dress. *Goddamn*, she's beautiful. It reminds me of the one she wore our first night in California. I don't remember everything from those years, but I'll never forget that night.

I'll never forget how much she believed in me, how much she loved me, even though I did a terrible job showing her it was mutual.

"You look... *wow*," I say, pulling her to me. "So beautiful."

I lean down to kiss her but don't get the chance. The second my lips meet hers, Madison yells, "Wait! Not that yet! Don't do that 'till the end!"

"What?" I ask, glancing down at her as she shoves between us, pushing me toward the door.

"Guess you don't get to kiss me until the end of the date," Kennedy says.

Madison opens the front door, forcing me through it. "You gotta knock."

"Uh, okay."

Before I can say anything else, she slams the door in my face, leaving me standing on the doorstep.

I glance around to see if anyone is lurking before raising my hand to knock, but the door flies back open, Madison still there.

"Get some flowers," she hisses.

The door slams again.

Even through the thick wood, I can hear Kennedy laughing inside the apartment.

Flowers. I look around. There isn't a single goddamn flower in the vicinity, so I jog over to a patch of grass and rip up a few stray dandelions.

I knock.

No answer.

I knock again.

"Who is it?" Madison asks from the other side of the door.

"It's me," I say. "Jonathan."

"Jonathan *who*?"

This kid... she's trying to kill me. I glance around again before saying, "Cunningham."

The door flings open, and Madison stands there, grinning, so I hand her most of the dandelions, keeping only one of them.

"They're my favorite!" she says, taking them.

"Figured you might like them," I say. "They're the same color as your dress."

Kennedy strolls over, and I hand her the last dandelion. She takes it, trying not to laugh.

My phone chimes in my pocket—a message from the car service. "Our ride is here."

It pulls up—a simple black town car, nothing fancy, the same one that took Madison and me to the convention—same driver and all.

We settle into the car for the drive into Albany. Nobody questions where we're going until we arrive and the car drops us by the curb. The sun has gone down, giving us a cover of darkness, enough that I can hopefully fade into obscurity for a few hours.

"A movie," Kennedy says. "In a park."

"Not just *any* movie," I tell her, putting my arm around her and pulling her to me. "Quite possibly the greatest super hero movie ever made."

"Breezeo!" Madison says excitedly.

Kennedy stops short. "No."

"Yep," I say. "The sequel."

"Tell me you're joking."

"Nope."

"You took us to see your own movie. *Seriously?*"

"Well, in my defense, I've never actually watched it," I admit. "And I knew Madison would enjoy it, so I figured, you know, who better to watch it with than the two of you?"

Madison's ecstatic, jumping around, while Kennedy looks at me like I've gone insane. "You never watched it?"

"Not the whole thing," I say. "Hell, I barely remember *filming* it. They say it's good, though, despite… well…"

Despite me being so fucked up through the entire process that we're lucky it even happened.

"I've heard it's decent," Kennedy says.

Decent. From her, I take that as a win.

I didn't do a very good job at the whole planning thing. I have a blanket but have to buy hot dogs from a vendor, because what's a picnic without food? We settle into the park away from most of the others, giving us a bit of privacy.

The theme song comes on. Yeah, we've got a theme song. Think *Spider-Man*, just with different words, way too cheery for the scenario. Madison dances around, singing along as the movie starts.

Madison's enthralled from the very first moment. I'm sitting on the blanket, my legs stretched out, while Kennedy lays down, her head in my lap. I cringe my way through the movie, absently stroking Kennedy's hair.

I glance down at her after a while, realizing she's not watching the screen, her attention fixed on me. "What's wrong?"

"Nothing," she says. "It's just strange."

I caress her flushed cheek. "Being here with me?"

"Yes," she says. "Just when I was starting to doubt I'd ever see you again."

"You didn't think I'd keep popping up every so often?"

"Oh, sure, but that's not *you*," she says. "I knew that guy would keep coming back. I thought I'd be dealing with him for the rest of my life. Drunk, high, out of his mind... but I never thought I'd see you again, *real* you, yet you're here. I thought it would always be *him*."

I know what she means as she motions toward the screen. I can tell I was strung out. It's painful.

"I'm here," I say, "and I'm not going anywhere."

"I want to believe that."

"You can."

She smiles, and I don't know if she believes it yet, but she looks content in the moment. I brush my thumb along her lips as they part, and I want to kiss her so fucking bad right now, but I know I'll catch hell from my daughter if I try.

"Ohhhh, Daddy!" Madison says, grabbing my attention, catching me off guard as she launches herself my way. Laughing, Kennedy sits up, moving out of the line of fire as Madison damn near tackles me, leaping on my back and trying to cover my face with her hands from behind. "You're not supposed to do that!"

"What?" I laugh. "I didn't do anything!"

"You're kissing her!" she says as I pull her hands away from my mouth when she tries to cover it. I playfully pretend to bite her, making her squeal. "Stop, Daddy!"

She flings herself on me, falling into my lap, as I glance up at the screen, realizing Breezeo is kissing Maryanne. I scowl, tickling Madison. "It's just a movie. It's not real."

She giggles, slapping my hands away. "You didn't really kiss her?"

"Well, yeah, but it doesn't count."

"Why not?"

"Because it's Breezeo, not *me*."

"It's still yucky," she says, making a face.

"You think kissing me is yucky?"

I tickle her again, and she struggles, laughing, trying to get away, but I'm not going to let it go that easy. Grabbing ahold of her, pinning her to me, I nuzzle against her cheek as she shoves my face. "Help, Mommy!"

"Oh, no, you're on your own there," Kennedy says. "You got yourself into that one."

"Ugh, no fair!" Madison says, slapping her hands over my mouth. "No kissing 'till the end!"

"Fine." I let out a long, exaggerated sigh. "You win."

She sticks her tongue out at me.

The girl seriously sticks her tongue out, gloating, as she leaps at her mother and kisses on her—planting big, sloppy kisses right on Kennedy, making sure I see it. She's gone again then, right back to her movie now that the love scene is over.

"Unbelievable." I shake my head. "I get no love."

Grinning, Kennedy lays back down with her head in my lap. She stares at me, reaching up, her fingertips brushing across my lips. "You be good, and I'll make it worth it for you later."

I cock an eyebrow at her. "Is that right?"

"Yep," she says. "I'll—"

She's cut off before she can elaborate by my cell phone ringing. *Cliff.* I decline the call, but he calls back again right away. I decline that call, too, but then comes another, this one from an unknown caller. After that number calls twice, I turn the phone off and put it away, turning my attention back to Kennedy. I'm not dealing with that shit tonight. "So, you were saying…?"

She gives me a sly grin, shaking her head, shifting position to face the screen.

I try to pay attention to the rest of the movie, but that's harder than it sounds. I'm relieved when it's over. We stand up as the credits are rolling, though I know we can't leave until the post-credit scenes play. I grab the blanket, folding it up, and the moment Madison gives the okay, we're walking away.

Our ride is waiting by the curb to whisk us home.

Madison jumps out when we make it back to the apartment. She's twirling in circles, her dandelions crushed in her fist as she holds onto them, so not to lose them, as she runs ahead of us. I put my arm around Kennedy, pulling her to me, no hesitation, and kiss her—softly, sweetly at first before trying to deepen it, but she pulls back, grinning, pressing her pointer finger to my lips.

"We see one movie and suddenly you think I'm putting out?" she says. "What kind of girl do you think I am?"

"I think you're the kind of girl that would usually put out *before* the movie."

She gasps, playfully shoving me away, before grabbing my shirt and pulling me right back to her, whispering, "Maybe I'll even let you bend me over a table."

My footsteps stall, and I laugh at that as she walks away, pulling out her keys as she makes her way to the apartment door. I stand back, staring at her and Madison, smiling. It feels like my chest wants to fucking burst with all these feelings building up inside of me.

I can't believe we're here, that I'm with her... with *them*. Can't believe I'm getting another chance to love her. Can't believe I'm finally a father to my daughter.

Hell, I can't believe I made it all night without being bothered.

I start to say something—to say just that—when a voice cuts through the silence... feminine, and familiar, and *oh fuck*. "Johnny?"

I turn, tensing, and see her a few feet to my right in the parking lot of the apartment building.

Serena.

"Johnny!" She runs, flinging herself at me, and I stagger a few steps as she wraps her arms around me, squeezing. "I've been looking for you *everywhere!*"

Madison gasps. "Mommy, it's Maryanne!"

"I know," Kennedy says, her voice a whisper. "I see."

Serena turns, loosening her grip, like she's just now realizing I'm not alone out here. She plasters a smile on her face, zeroing right in on Madison. "Oh, who might you be, cutie?"

Madison stares at her. She looks conflicted, fidgeting,

tinkering with her dandelions as she says, "I'm Maddie."

"Well, hello, Maddie," Serena says. "It's always nice to meet a fan."

Madison fidgets even more.

"Come on, sweetheart," Kennedy says, grasping Madison by the shoulder to lead her into the apartment. "Let's go inside so they can talk."

Madison resists. She looks confused, like she doesn't want to go, but she eventually gives in. Kennedy casts a look my way, and it only lasts a second, but it's long enough for me to see the concern in her eyes, mingling with something else. *Hurt.*

The moment they're gone, Serena's expression changes, her smile dimming. She turns back to me, groaning, shoving against my chest. "Johnny, what the hell? I've been looking for you all night!"

"Why?"

She lets out an incredulous laugh. Her eyes, Jesus Christ, they're like saucers—completely black. "Why? I haven't seen you in over a month!"

"I know, but..." I shake my head, taking a step away from her as I run a hand down my face, trying to put a bit of space between us. "I thought you were in rehab."

"I was," she says. "But I couldn't stay there. It was hell, Johnny, and those people didn't get me. Not like you always did. And I missed you. I couldn't take it anymore. I needed to—"

"Don't do that," I say, cutting her off. "Don't try to make you leaving rehab about *me*."

"You were hit by a car! I was worried!"

"You're worried now? But not worried enough to check on me the night of the accident?"

"You know I hate hospitals," she says.

"So do I," I say. "And I know rehab feels like a glorified hospital, but sometimes a person needs help."

"I'm fine," she says. "I'm better."

"You're high *right now*, Serena."

She rolls her eyes. "So?"

"So how the hell are you *better* if you're still using?"

"I can handle it," she says. "I don't know if you've noticed, but this town is fucking depressing. I needed *something*. Honestly, I don't know how you're even surviving. I know Cliff sent you off somewhere to recover, but *here*?"

I'm having a hard time looking at her. My gaze fixes on the closed apartment door, at the splotches of yellow on the doorstep. Madison's abandoned dandelions. "I have family here."

She scoffs. "You hate your family."

"I hate my father. That doesn't mean I hate my family."

"So, whatever, *family*." She uses air quotes when she says that word, waving toward the apartment. "Is that who that was?"

"That was my daughter."

"Your *daughter*."

I can feel her gaze, piercing, judging. So damn angry. I don't even have to look at her to know she's fuming about that.

"I told you I was a father."

"You told me you knocked up that girl from back home, that she kept the kid."

"Yes."

"That doesn't mean you're a father," she says. "So, what, while I was off suffering in some hellhole, you've been here, playing house?"

"I'm not *playing* anything. I got clean so I could be a part of her life."

Serena lets out a bitter laugh. "No, Johnny, you did it because they made you."

"They made me go to rehab, but that's not why I'm still clean."

She shakes her head, running her hands through her hair—still dyed dark for the movie. "I just... I don't know what's going on with you, but this isn't the *you* I know."

I shake my head. Even if I tried to explain it, she wouldn't understand. "Look, I don't want to get into this with you. Tell me what you're *really* doing here, Ser."

"I told you—I miss you. And since we've had some time apart, I thought maybe you'd miss me, too. Maybe we could give things a try. Maybe—"

"It would never work."

"It *could*," she insists.

"It wouldn't."

She looks hurt by that. "We were good together."

"No, we weren't," I say. "We've been over this before. It was a fucking mess. When we got high, it was fine, but the moment we came down, we couldn't even stand to be in the same room."

"That's not true," she says. "I'm here right now."

"You're high."

"Oh, *fuck you!* So, I'm high. That doesn't have anything to do with how I feel about you."

"It does," I say. "It has everything to do with it."

She glares at me.

This conversation isn't going anywhere.

It never does. We've had this same argument half a dozen times this past year, ever since I stopped using. She doesn't understand why things had to change, why I started treating her differently.

But she and I have a history that isn't healthy. She's part of the cycle I had to break. I was numbing myself, killing myself, but it wasn't just the drugs and alcohol I'd been indulging in. Thousands of dollars in psychiatry bills taught me the real problem was my behavior. Go the same places as before, with the same people as before, and you end up doing the same shit you always did.

So I cut it all off. *All* of it. Even the sex.

Sober and celibate, everything felt different.

"Are you fucking that woman, Johnny?" Serena asks, her voice scathing. She's losing her high. "Did you come here and start fucking again? Fucking *her*?"

"That's none of your business."

SMACK

Stinging rips through my cheek as she slaps me, *hard*, my

head jarring. I take a step back, moving away from her.

"I'm not doing this with you," I say as she crosses her arms over her chest. "Call Cliff. He's probably worried."

I start to walk away, to head for the apartment, when she calls out to me, her voice cracking. "Wait, Johnny. *Please.*"

"Take care of yourself, Serena."

I stall in front of the apartment and look down at the discarded dandelions, ripped to pieces. Sighing, I glance behind me and find the parking lot empty, Serena gone.

I feel like an asshole.

I can't get anything right.

Strolling over to the patch of grass, I pluck a single dandelion from the ground. I'm grateful to find the apartment unlocked. Kennedy lingers right inside and eyes me warily.

I glance around.

I don't see Madison.

"She's in her room," Kennedy says.

I head that way, finding her sitting on the edge of her bed, swinging her legs as she picks off the polish on her little fingernails. I stall when I glance in the trashcan beside the desk in her room. Usually full of paper from discarded drawings, I see a familiar doll on top. *Maryanne.* She threw her away.

I pull the doll out, carrying it as I crouch down in front of Madison. I hold the dandelion out. "I know your flowers got messed up, so I picked you another one."

She takes it carefully. "Thank you."

"You're welcome," I say. "Do you want to tell me what made you upset?"

She shrugs.

"Did you have fun tonight?"

She nods.

"I had fun, too. You looked pretty in your dress."

She smiles, staring at the dandelion.

She won't look at me.

Sighing, I sit down on the floor. "I know this whole thing

must be confusing. I wasn't around, but now I am, and I'm Breezeo, but I'm also your dad. You see me kiss your mom, but Breezeo kisses Maryanne. And then it looks like Maryanne shows up and hugs me in front of your mom. Hard to keep up with what's real, huh?"

She nods.

"Well, like Breezeo, Maryanne's a story. The woman outside, her name is Serena. I work with her. I'm not going to be kissing her like I kiss your mom. When I kiss your mom, it's real."

She meets my gaze.

"So I don't think you should take it out on poor Maryanne." I shake the doll at her. "Breezeo loves her, just like I love your mom."

She takes the doll. "Does Mommy love you?"

"She did."

"But not no more?"

"I don't know," I answer honestly. "But it's not her fault. I took her love for granted."

"What's that mean? Taking her love for granite?"

I smile at her mix up. "It means I didn't show her how much I loved her, like I should've."

"You can do it now," Madison says. "Just pick her more flowers and tell her she's pretty, and then she can love you."

If only it were that simple.

"I'll have to remember that," I say, getting to my feet and ruffling her hair before turning to leave. I make it a few steps before she calls out to me.

"Wait, Daddy!" she says, springing to her feet and running over, grabbing my arm to tug me down to her level. I crouch down again, surprised when she presses her lips to my still-stinging cheek. "You almost forgot your kisses!"

Clifford Caldwell, it turns out, is an inconsiderate, egotistical jerk.

You show up for your appointment. You're early, but not *too* early. You have everything they request—headshots, resume, and demo reel. You spent money you shouldn't have spent buying a new outfit, and you look *good!*

When the time comes, the secretary leads you to Clifford's office. It's clean, classy, with glass walls and a view that overlooks Hollywood. Clifford sits behind a sleek metal desk, typing on his phone. The secretary hands him your folder as you sit down across from him.

He doesn't greet you, opening the folder and glancing inside. Thirty seconds, that's all he takes before shoving the folder back at you. "No."

That's it. He says no. He doesn't even watch your demo reel. You grab your things and get up to leave. "Can I ask *why?*"

Clifford looks up. "Are you certain you want to hear that answer?"

He tells you there's nothing to you. Your headshots are generic. Your resume reads like a thousand others that have crossed his desk. Sure, you can probably act, but what he's looking for is an attention-grabber, someone he can make a star, but you? *At most, you're just an amateur.*

Those words rip out a piece of your soul.

You've heard them before.

When you make it home, the apartment feels smaller than usual. You toss the folder in the trashcan in the kitchen and crack open the bottle of whiskey you spent your last few dollars on.

You drink. You get drunk.

You turn on the TV to discover the cable has been shut off. Neither of you paid the bill last month.

You drink some more. You get even drunker.

It's pushing ten o'clock when she gets home from a long shift at the diner. You've spent the past two hours sitting alone, in the dark, thinking about how disappointed she's going to be when she finds out.

Despite working all day, she's happy, and smiling, but that comes to a screeching halt when she turns on the kitchen light. She catches a glimpse of the folder in the trash and whispers, "No."

You've nearly drained the entire whiskey bottle. You guzzle the last of it when she looks at you. Shoving to your feet, you stagger over and drop the empty bottle in the trash, right on top of the folder. Your breathing is shaky. Your eyes are bloodshot. She looks at you with disgust. It's because you're drunk, because you can barely stand up, but nothing could convince you that she isn't disgusted because you're a failure. A waste of a life.

"I'm sorry," you say as you caress her cheek, but she smacks your hand away. She doesn't want you to touch her. Turning away, you stagger to the bedroom, saying, "I'll get a job tomorrow."

She doesn't come to bed. The next morning, when you wake up, she's already gone. She dug your folder out of the trash and set it on the counter.

You don't touch it.

You go job hunting. You apply everywhere. Weeks pass. *Nothing.* Because your pride hasn't already taken a big enough hit, she gets a second job since you can't seem to find anything.

She doesn't even tell you. You find out one night when she never comes home. You thought she was dead in a ditch somewhere. She says you're overreacting. It's just a part-time job at a corner store. You tell her it's dangerous, but she shrugs it off. Night shift pays more.

Three weeks later, she's robbed.

A guy points a gun at her. He wants everything in the cash register. Because that's not enough, he takes her purse, too. He could've taken her *life*, but after it's over, she's more worried about the money he stole from her.

Something happens to you in that moment.

You hit your breaking point.

You're sitting on your couch with your head down. She's in the bedroom, talking on your cell phone. She has to borrow yours since hers was in her purse. Her voice is hushed. She doesn't want you to overhear her conversation.

She steps out a few minutes later, handing you the phone back. Her eyes are bloodshot, face flushed. She's been crying.

"He's wiring the money," she says. "It's in your name."

She called her father. She asked him for help. The rent is due. So is the electric. She had all the money in her purse. She got paid that afternoon. She hasn't asked him for a single thing in over a year. He's barely spoken to her, except to tell her they'd be there when she realized loving you was a mistake.

You think it's coming. Your pride is gone. Your dream is fading. You think you're losing her, too.

It's hard to say when you make the decision. Hard to pinpoint the moment you fall so far.

Can you remember the first lie you told? The first time you smiled in her face while deceiving her?

You tell her you found a job. You didn't. But you're an

extraordinary actor, so you convince her. You tell her you're valeting cars, and money starts coming in. Tips are nice, you say. Some nights, people are extra generous.

In reality, you're stealing. Stealing money. Stealing things. It weighs heavy on your conscience, so you start drinking more.

Liquid courage.

You're caught one night, though—caught rifling through a car by none other than Clifford Caldwell. Happenstance put you there. You don't run. No, you start talking. You tell him he left his headlights on, and you were just turning them off before they killed the battery. You're so convincing he thanks you. He pulls out his wallet and *tips* you. You turn to leave when his voice calls out.

"Have we met before?" he asks. "You seem familiar."

You hesitate before telling him, "We met once."

"Refresh my memory."

"My girlfriend was your waitress. She got an appointment for me. You called me an amateur after thirty seconds."

"Ah, the girl from the diner?" he asks. "I remember her. She spoke highly of you. I could tell she believed every word. Made me want to meet the actor she said was, and I quote, '*way too good* for even you, *Mr. Caldwell*.'"

You laugh. "She said that?"

"She did," he says. "And I must say, you're a decent actor. You're a natural, very convincing when you speak. So convincing, in fact, you almost made me forget my headlights were automatic."

You know you're busted as soon as he says that.

You pull the money from your pocket—the twenty he tipped, as well as the thick stack of cash you found in a Manila envelope hidden in the car's glove box. You hold it all out to him. He looks quite surprised, but he waves it off. "Keep it, if you need it."

You pocket it once more.

"Monday morning. Eight—thirty. My office."

"Excuse me?"

"We'll give it another try," he says. "Be there."

You go home to share the news, but the apartment is empty—she's working tonight at the diner. So you wait until she makes it home in the middle of the night, and you tell her he's giving you another chance. You tell her you ran into him when you were working. You pick her up and swing her around, excited. You're happy, and you're sober. It's been a while since those things coincided.

You don't know this, and it's something she'll never dare admit, but that woman? She already knew your news. She knew Clifford Caldwell decided to give you another chance, because he showed up at the diner for coffee afterward. He told her everything, including how he caught you stealing. And then he told her if she wanted you to be successful, if she wanted to help your chances, he knew a way to make that happen: all she had to do was take off her clothes. And that woman? She didn't hesitate... nope, not at all... didn't hesitate to pour hot coffee right on that pig's crotch. *Seriously, what a jerk!!!*

TWENTY-ONE

KENNEDY

"I, uh… *crap.*"

I pull the car in along the curb and put it in park, staring at the house down the block. Apparently when my father says '*just a few people, nothing big,*' he really means '*everybody I've ever met and whoever they want to bring.*' People surround the place, socializing.

I cut the engine and pocket the keys as Maddie flings off her seatbelt, already climbing out of the car before I can think of something more to say.

I look at Jonathan in the passenger seat. He's been quiet today, subdued. I'm not sure he got any rest. He stayed at the apartment last night, but he didn't try to sleep in my bed. He was still sitting on the couch when I woke up at dawn, tinkering with his phone.

The first words he spoke?

'*They know.*'

By morning, it was all over the Internet… *Johnny Cunning has been found!* It started with just his location, *Hollywood Chronicles* reporting that he'd been hiding out in a sleepy little New York town, but as the day progressed, so did the speculation. It was only a matter of time now before someone figured it all out.

His sunglasses are on, his hat pulled down low. Although it's warm outside, he's wearing jeans and a hooded sweatshirt with the sleeves shoved up to his elbows. He's shielding himself, *hiding*, as much as he possibly can, which isn't much.

I get out of the car before Maddie can run off, and he follows us to my father's house. As soon as we reach it, Maddie goes right inside, while I hesitate on the sidewalk.

"You don't have to do this," I say, looking at Jonathan. "Maddie will understand."

He sighs. "It's fine. I made this mess. I have to face it."

"Yeah, but…"

"But…?"

"I don't know," I say. "Feels like there ought to be a *but*."

Jonathan laughs under his breath as my father steps out onto the porch, wiping his hands on the grilling apron he wears.

"Hey, Dad," I say. "Nice party."

"It's not a party," he grumbles. "It's just a little thing."

More like a test, maybe. A welcoming committee, except not quite as friendly as one of those might be.

"Mr. Garfield, sir." Jonathan clears his throat. "I appreciate the invitation."

"It's what my granddaughter wanted," he says. "Whatever it takes to make her happy. I'm sure you get that."

"Of course," Jonathan says.

"Well, then, I should get back to my grill." My father looks at me, eyes suspicious, as he says, "Join me, Cunningham. We can catch up."

Jonathan offers me a small smile, trying to be reassuring, but I know without a shadow of a doubt that the world is about to be turned upside down.

Gravity, don't fail me now.

I mingle, avoiding certain conversations, dodging questions, sticking to simple pleasantries with the neighbors. Maddie, she's running around, telling anyone who will listen about her *daddy*. I try to steer her elsewhere, but she's a kid. She doesn't understand why it's all such a big deal. She just wants to share her happiness, while I can't shake my unsettling feeling.

It's growing, deepening, like a bottomless pit.

It's about to hit us like a storm.

Every time I see Jonathan, he's near my father, the two of them talking, both men tense like they're on edge from the conversation. But when my father announces that it's time to eat, Jonathan's missing.

I fix Maddie a hot dog, settling her into a chair on the back patio, telling her to stay there while I go on a hunt for her father. He's not outside, so I head into the house, hearing his voice—quiet, *so quiet*, bordering on despondent.

He's talking on the phone.

"Just do whatever you can," he says. "Try to get ahead of this before it spins out of control."

He's standing at the front door, alone, looking out.

"I know, I hear you, but I just… I *can't*," he says after a moment. "I get it, and you're right, but I can't do that, so do what you can to stop this."

Sighing, he hangs up, slipping his phone into his pocket. I absorb those words, the sound of his voice, as I take a step closer. The creaky floor alerts him to my presence, and he glances over his shoulder, a flash of panic showing.

"Everything okay?"

"Everything's fine," he says. "Had to talk to Cliff."

"What are you going to do?"

"Have PR put out a statement, asking for my privacy," he says. "Not sure it'll make a difference. Cliff thinks the only way to stop this from snowballing is if I leave, go make myself visible somewhere else to draw the attention away from here, so the story looks made up."

"Are you going to?"

"No," he says, hesitating. "Unless that's what you want."

Before I have the chance to tell him what it is I want, he pulls me in front of him at the door, wrapping his arms around me, my back flush against his chest.

Leaning down, he whispers, "Look across the street."

I do as he says. Everything seems quiet.

I'm not sure what he wants me to see.

The house directly across from us is old, and brick, with way too many potted plants surrounding the place. The couple who live there long ago retired. They're currently in my father's backyard, eating hot dogs with my daughter.

"What do you see?" he asks.

"A bunch of ugly plants."

"Is that it?"

"Uh, a house, trees… there's a mailbox and a flag and…" I trail off when movement catches my attention. Somebody's lurking. "Who's that?"

"He called himself a reporter."

I glance back at Jonathan, surprised. "You talked to him?"

"No, but your father did. He knocked on his door this morning, wanting to talk to you."

"*Me?*"

"Said he heard a girl might be around here that knows something about me," he says. "Your father told him to get the hell off of his property, but then he spotted the guy lurking around the neighbors, so your father invited the neighbors over here."

"Wow." I'm not sure what to say. "Why my father's house? Why not come to the apartment where I live?"

"I don't know," he says quietly, "but I'm sure they'll make it over that way eventually."

The reporter slips out of sight, trying to go undetected.

"The food's ready," I say, still trying to process everything. "You should eat something."

"I'm not hungry."

"But still, you should eat," I say, turning around to face Jonathan, patting his stomach playfully, trying not to dwell on the fact that our lives may be about to change. "Gotta keep your strength up, since I'm pretty sure the entertainment portion of this party is gonna be your interrogation."

We head out back and fix ourselves plates. Jonathan barely eats, but he seems more at ease, even as the questions start.

They're not personal. No, people don't ask about our situation. Instead, they ask if Hollywood is glamorous. They ask if he knows their favorite celebrities.

He takes it all in stride.

He's charming and witty.

He's so much like that boy I fell in love with back at Fulton Edge Academy, no pretense at all.

He loves on Maddie, making her laugh as she sits on his lap, drawing pictures for neighbors to pass the time. She soaks up the love like it's sunshine, and I know, without a shadow of a doubt, that not a single one of these people are going to say a bad word about him to that reporter.

"This was smart," I say, approaching my father as he sits along the side of the patio, on the outskirts of the gathering.

"I'm not sure what you mean," he says.

I perch on the edge of his chair and look at him. "Yeah, you do. The whole *'get the neighborhood on his side'* thing you orchestrated here. How'd you think of it?"

"I worked in politics," he says. "I've got plenty of tricks up my sleeve."

�֎ �֎ ✖

"The second amendment exists for a reason," my father says. "*The right of the people to keep and bear arms shall not be infringed.* That's what it says. There's no 'but' to it, no stipulations or qualifications."

"With all due respect, that's bullshit," Jonathan says. "Nobody wants a lunatic running around with an AK-47. That's not what the Founding Fathers intended."

"Oh? Does that mean you've spoken to them? Enlighten me—what did Thomas Jefferson say when you asked? Because I hate to break it to you, son, but watching *Hamilton* on Broadway doesn't make you an expert on their intentions."

"It's common sense," Jonathan says. "Better safe than sorry."

"Now *that's* bullshit," my father says. "You can't infringe on a constitutional right because you think someone *might* do something."

Jonathan opens his mouth to respond, but I clear my throat loudly, interrupting, gathering their attention. I'm not sure how it even got started, but the two of them are sitting in the living room, arguing politics—my father's favorite pastime—while Maddie sleeps on the couch.

"While this conversation is absolutely riveting," I say, "it's getting late, so can you just agree to disagree?"

They stare at each other.

Neither wants to be the first to concede.

I have to say, it's kind of nice to see the two of them having a conversation that has nothing to do with *me*.

"Blah, blah, blah, we're never going to agree but I respect your viewpoint even though I think you're an idiot," I say, waving between them. "There, I covered it for both of you. Time to go home now."

My father grumbles, something about me ruining his fun, as I lean down to hug him. Night has fallen. It's dark outside. We've spent the entire day here, and I'm tired.

I scoop Maddie up. She mumbles in her sleep, her body heavy as she rests against me, her head on my shoulder. Jonathan stands, holding his hand out toward my father. "Mr. Garfield, sir."

My father stares at his extended hand for a moment before waving him off, saying, "Cunningham."

That's about as close to a truce as I think these guys will ever get. Just Jonathan walking out of here without being castrated is progress, and he takes the brush off in stride, laughing to himself.

We leave, and I head to the car, my footsteps hurried. I set Maddie in her booster seat and am buckling her in when I hear a voice call out way too close to us. "Who's the kid, Johnny?"

"Get the hell away from us," Jonathan says, and I look up, my heart racing when I see a guy there. *The reporter.*

He's holding his phone. He's *recording.*

"Come on, don't be that way," the guy says, coming even closer. "I'm just doing my job here."

"Back off," Jonathan warns.

I shut the car door. The guy isn't backing off. Instead, he starts firing off rapid questions, each one worse than the one before it. "So, who's the woman? Is that her kid? Have you been screwing around with her? Huh? How long have you been seeing her? How long have you been cheating on Serena? Wait... is that *your* kid? Did you get her pregnant, Johnny? Knocked her up and what, paid her off so she'd keep her mouth shut? How much did it cost you? Why'd you do it? Don't want anyone to know about the bastard?"

That's it.

That's what it takes.

The second that last word is out, Jonathan snaps. I see it, his expression hardening as anger takes over. He swings, cast and all, slamming the guy in the face, stunning him. Staggering, the guy drops his phone, and Jonathan stomps on it.

"I told you to *back off*," Jonathan says, getting in the reporter's face. "I'm not going to tell you again."

"Jonathan, stop!" I run over when he shoves the guy, grabbing his arm to try to drag him away, but he resists. "Please, just... get in the car."

He takes a few steps back as the guy shouts at him, something about *getting what's coming to him*, but Jonathan isn't fazed.

"Stay the hell away from me," he says, "and stay away from my fucking family."

"You'll regret that!" the guy yells. "I got it all on video!"

Jonathan pulls away from me and grabs the cell phone from the sidewalk, the screen now cracked. It's still recording. Jonathan presses the button to stop it, and I think he's going to delete the video, or maybe *take* the phone, but instead, he hurls it at the guy.

The reporter tries to catch it, but it slips from his grip and clatters to the sidewalk by his feet.

"Fuck you and your *video*," Jonathan says. "Don't let me catch you around here again."

He gets in the car. I hurry to get behind the wheel when the reporter snatches up his phone and says, "Still the same old Johnny

Cunning."

I speed home, my eyes flickering to the rearview mirror the entire drive. Maddie stays fast asleep. She missed the whole thing. Jonathan says nothing, flexing his fingers in and out of a loose fist around the cast, cringing the entire time.

I whip into a parking spot when I reach the apartment building, cutting the engine, my eyes scanning all around us, expecting an ambush.

Something touches my leg, and I jump, yelping. Jonathan's hand is resting on my thigh.

"Are you okay?" he asks.

"I think I should be asking *you* that."

"I'm fine."

"Your hand is hurt."

"It's been hurt."

"But still, that guy... he was a *jerk*."

"I'm used to it," he says, hesitating before adding, "as much as a person can get *used* to that. But he said some shit, and I know you're not used to it."

"I'm okay."

He nods, but I don't know if he believes me.

I don't know if I believe me.

I'm shaking. Trembling.

His hand on my thigh is steady.

"We should go inside," he says, nodding toward the building, "in case anybody shows up here."

He carries Maddie this time, taking her into the apartment and straight to her bedroom while I lock up. Frazzled, I head for the kitchen, peeking in cabinets and groaning before grabbing a glass and filling it with water from the tap, taking a drink before mumbling to myself, "I'd kill for some alcohol right now."

Why'd I have to pour that perfectly good whiskey out?

A light laugh echoes behind me. "I know the feeling."

Jonathan stands in the doorway.

I give him a sheepish smile. "Shouldn't have said that."

308

"You don't have to watch your words. I'm a big boy. I can handle it." He pauses, shaking his head as he slowly approaches me. "*Usually*. Spent a lot of rehab working on that. *Bad words don't need to lead to bad deeds.* Guess I'm still a work in progress."

"We all are."

"I don't know about that," he says, eyeing me. "You seem pretty well put together."

"Who, *me*? Assistant Manager at the *Piggly Q*?"

"You aren't your job."

"Good thing, because I don't know if I'll be working much longer. If they found my father, they probably found my job."

"Sorry."

"Not your fault. I would've quit eventually. Just planned to be stubborn for a bit longer."

He laughs at that, leaning against the counter beside me. "You always were the most hardheaded person I knew."

"Yeah, well, you gave me a run for my money on that one. I met my match with you."

"Match made in heaven."

"Or hell. Depends on who you ask."

"You," he says. "I'm asking you."

"I'd say a bit of both, then. We were fire and gasoline. We burned hot for a long time."

"Past tense."

"What?"

"You said that in the past tense."

"Guess I'm used to talking about us that way."

It gets quiet.

My hands are still shaking.

I'm tinkering with the glass, sipping on the water, trying to wrap my mind around what's happening.

"I can go," he says quietly. "I'll understand if you'd rather me not be here."

"Why wouldn't I want you here?"

"I don't know," he says. "I don't really know where your

head is, Kennedy. Sometimes I think I do, but other times…"

Setting the glass down, I grab his hand. "How about I show you?"

"Show me?"

I nod.

I pull him into the bedroom.

I push him down on the bed.

The clothes disappear, scattered along the floor, as our bodies tangle up in the sheets together. I'm on top of him, and he's inside of me, my hands pressing flat against his bare chest, feeling the heat of his skin.

The fire? It still burns.

Something tells me it always will, no matter who tries to put it out.

Footsteps pad around the apartment when I wake up. It's early. I try to slip out of bed, but Jonathan grumbles and clings to me.

Laughing, I pry myself out of his arms and throw on some clothes. I'm halfway down the hall when I hear a clatter in the kitchen before a small voice says, "*Uh-oh.*"

"What in the world?" I say, seeing Maddie sitting on the counter, holding the box of Lucky Charms, a bowl on the floor. "What are you doing?"

"Breakfast," she says.

I pull her off the counter and commandeer the box of cereal. "Why don't you go find some cartoons to watch? I'll bring you something to eat in a moment."

"Okay, Mommy," she says, skipping off to the living room. I pour her some cereal with milk and turn to leave the kitchen when a knock sounds through the apartment from the front door. *Crap.*

My heart drops.

I step that way, tensing when I see Maddie unlocking the door. "Sweetheart, wait!"

She yanks it right open. "*Whoa.*"

"Madison Jacqueline," I hiss, starting toward her. "How many times do we have to talk about not opening—?"

The door.

I don't get to say those words.

I stop dead in my tracks. A police officer stands there, on my doorstep, in full uniform. *Whoa* is right.

"Uh, hello," I say. "Can I help you, Officer?"

"I'm actually looking for somebody," the officer says, glancing past me, around my apartment.

"Who?" I ask.

A gritty voice chimes in behind me. "That would be *me.*"

I spin around. Jonathan stands there, still half asleep, only wearing sweatpants. "*You?*"

He nods.

I turn back to the officer.

He nods, too, confirming it.

It takes a second for things to make sense. When it clicks, I hand Maddie the bowl of cereal. "Take this to your room."

"But you said we can't eat in our rooms, 'cuz that's not what rooms are for."

"I'm making an exception. Go play."

I'm grateful she doesn't put up a fight.

I don't want her to see what I think is about to happen here. *I* don't even want to see it, even though it won't be my first time.

"You mind if I get dressed?" Jonathan asks, his voice casual. "I'm sure there are lurkers."

"Go ahead," the officer says. "Just don't take too long."

It only takes him a minute, maybe two, before he returns, fully dressed in jeans and a t-shirt, leather jacket, shoes on. I stand here in shock as Jonathan approaches the officer.

"What's the warrant for?" he asks. "Assault?"

The officer nods. "And criminal mischief."

Jonathan turns around, putting his hands behind his back. He's placed in handcuffs, but he doesn't seem bothered by it, nor

311

does he look *surprised.*

He kisses me, just a brush against my lips, before he says, "I'll be back when I can."

TWENTY-TWO

JONATHAN

Cliff is typing away on his Blackberry.

I've always hated that damn thing.

He's never been married, which is no surprise, considering so much of his life is spent glued to that screen. A string of flings is all he has time for. He always says his work is his wife.

It didn't take too long, after I called from the police station, for Cliff to make it up here from the city, where he was busy working.

Working on fixing my other messes, while I was busy creating more of them.

We're sitting in an interrogation room, just him and I. I've been free to go for half an hour, but Cliff wanted to talk somewhere private, so the police offered this space up—you know, in exchange for some autographs.

Problem is, Cliff hasn't said a word since we sat down, too busy typing whatever it is he's typing.

"So... good talk," I say after a long stretch of silence. "Captivating conversation we're having."

"Oh, am I *boring* you?" he asks, still not looking up. "Sorry, I'm a little busy talking to PR about coordinating a press release to explain your arrest. I'll try to do better next time."

"Not sure there's anything to explain," I say. "Video makes it all pretty self-explanatory."

He shakes his head. "What were you thinking, Johnny?"

"He called my daughter a bastard."

"So? They're just words. Don't punch the guy while he's recording. You just gave him grounds for a lawsuit, which means a settlement, which means more money out of your pocket." He sets down his Blackberry and starts shifting through his briefcase, pulling a stack of papers out and sliding them to me. "Your lawyer sent these for you to look over."

I glance at the top sheet.

Confidentiality Agreement.

"What's this for?"

"To ensure Miss Garfield's continued discretion."

I blink at it for a moment before looking at him. "You're kidding."

"Do I look like I'm kidding?" he asks as he picks the Blackberry up.

No, he doesn't.

"I'm not asking her to sign this," I say, shoving it all at him without even reading any of it.

"Would you rather *me* ask her?"

"It's unnecessary. She doesn't need one."

"I disagree. Better safe than sorry."

"It's offensive. There's no way she'd even sign that shit."

"Why wouldn't she? She signed the previous one."

I stare at him as those words sink in. "What do you mean she signed the previous one?"

"I mean she already signed an agreement. This is just an updated version."

"You had her sign one of these? *Seriously?*"

"Of course I did," he says. "I had it drawn up the moment I signed you."

I don't even know what to say.

He never mentioned it.

Hell, neither did *she.*

I give this man a lot of leeway when it comes to my affairs. He's coordinated damn near every part of my life for quite a few years now. I don't know everything he's done on my behalf. Pretty

314

sure I wouldn't *want* to know some of it. So I won't say I'm surprised he did that.

But I am surprised she didn't tell me about it.

"You also need to establish paternity… not that there's any doubt." His eyes flicker to me. "There isn't, is there?"

"No doubt at all."

"Regardless, legally, you need to do it. And then you'll need a custody arrangement drawn up with a visitation schedule."

"Things are working out fine."

"For now," he says, "but you don't want to find yourself in a position where you can't see your daughter when Miss Garfield runs you out of her life again."

When. Not *if.*

"That's not gonna happen."

"History tells a different story."

"You know, I'm pretty sure you're paid to manage my career, not judge my personal life."

"It's all the same with you, Johnny. Like it or not, your personal life affects your career."

"I *don't* like it."

He stares at me, grabbing that stack of papers and shoving them back in his briefcase. "I have other clients to attend to today, ones I've been neglecting lately because of you. Do you need a ride to the inn?"

"I'm not staying there."

"Where are you staying?"

"With her."

"At the address on Elm?"

I hesitate. *Elm.* That's where her father lives, the house she grew up in. "She doesn't live there."

"Are you sure? Because that's where the checks are still being sent every month."

"Positive," I say. "You don't know about her apartment?"

"How would I? You don't tell me anything."

He sounds genuinely frustrated by that.

"How'd Serena know? She showed up at the apartment."

"Who knows how anybody knows anything?" he grumbles, shoving his chair back to stand. "Come on, I'll give you a ride wherever it is you're going. I still think you're better off leaving town, at least until this blows over, but you're the one who has to live with it, so... you do you, Johnny, and I'll do what I can to work around it."

I stand in front of the apartment door, torn between knocking and walking right in. It's not my apartment, but I feel at home here. I go back and forth for a moment before reaching for the knob, my stomach sinking when it won't turn.

Well, that solves my problem.

Locked.

Hesitantly, I tap on the thick wood.

Footsteps approach, pausing there for a long moment before the locks jingle and the door flies open. *BAM.* Kennedy's on me, knocking into me with so much force I nearly fall backward. She hugs me, whispering, "You're back."

I laugh. "It's been like six hours."

"Felt like another six years," she says, dragging me inside so she can lock the door. "I keep forgetting to give you a key."

"A key."

"Yeah, so you don't have to knock next time," she says. "Unless you don't want it. I just figured..."

"Please," I say. "I'd like that."

She smiles softly, walking into the kitchen and digging a key out of a drawer. She holds it out to me, the key in her palm, but I grab her entire hand and pull her to me.

"Thank you," I say. "For still letting me stay, despite... *you know.*"

"Despite you beating up a reporter?" She kisses me, a soft

peck. "Despite you getting arrested?" Another kiss. "Despite your tabloid-wife showing up and blowing our chance at privacy?"

One more kiss, and I laugh against her lips. "Pretty much."

I slide the key from her palm, pocketing it. The moment I do, I hear Madison in her bedroom talking to someone.

"Oh, by the way," Kennedy says, "your sister is visiting."

I stall there, in the living room.

That's the last thing I need.

"She heard about the video," Kennedy explains, "so she came to see you."

"And what, yell at me about growing up? Lecture me on responsibility?"

A throat clears nearby, and I know it's her before she speaks. "More like I came to high-five you, but you know, *that*, too. You should do all that."

"Grow up and be responsible?"

"*Ding, ding, ding.*"

I shake my head. "I'm trying."

She looks like she wants to say something, but she bites her tongue when Madison bursts in. Madison gasps and runs over, slamming into me like her mother did, hugging my waist. "Daddy, you're here!"

"I am," I say, ruffling her hair. "Geez, I haven't had people *this* excited to see me since my last red carpet."

"Can I go to the red carpets?" Madison asks.

"Someday," I tell her. "If your mother says it's okay."

"Mommy? Can I?"

"We'll see," Kennedy says.

Madison looks up at me, grinning. "She said okay!"

I smile. "Pretty sure that's not what she said, but nice try."

Madison is off again to play, and I sit down on the couch, running a hand through my hair.

"I'll give you two some time to talk," Kennedy says before disappearing to her bedroom, leaving me alone with my sister.

"Oh, goody," I say. "Because jail wasn't enough fun, I get

some quality family time on top of it."

Meghan laughs, kicking my shin to get me to move as she squeezes past to sit on the couch.

"Speaking of *family*," she says, pulling out her phone.

I lower my head with a sigh. "Can we not?"

"Dad's who told me about the situation," she says. "He sent me a message this morning."

"Awesome."

She clears her throat, her voice dropping mockingly low as she imitates our father's voice, reading his message. *"My dearest Meghan, it has been brought to my attention that your brother was involved in yet another altercation with the media. As a staunch supporter of free press, a defender of the first amendment, someone will likely be contacting me for a comment. I felt it was only fair to warn you beforehand. Grant B. Cunningham."*

"Pretty sure James Madison wasn't all about protecting someone's right to verbally attack a child."

"James Madison didn't even really believe in the First Amendment," Meghan says. "For him, it was all about holding politicians accountable."

"There you go," I say. "Send him a message back and say James Madison would tell him to shove his opinion up his ass."

"Yeah, sadly, too late for that." Meghan waves her phone toward me, showing me an article before she reads part of it. "Former Speaker of the House Grant Cunningham issued a statement saying he's deeply troubled by his son's behavior. *Free press is essential to a free society*, the statement reads. *Violence against members of the media should not be condoned. While John has a history of outbursts, it is my hope that this situation will serve as a wake-up call for him.*"

"That's rich, coming from him. He probably doesn't even give a shit how any of this affects my kid."

Meghan continues to read. "When asked about his rumored granddaughter, Former Speaker Cunningham commented that he never speaks on family matters."

318

"Unless it's to drag me through the mud."

"Well, in his defense, you make it *so easy*," she says. I cut my eyes at her, not amused, and she holds her hands up. "I'm joking."

"Did they call you for a comment?" I ask.

"Of course not." She rolls her eyes. "I doubt they even called him. He probably contacted them, desperate to be relevant."

"Pity," I say. "You could've told them what an irresponsible asshole I am."

"That's not what I would've said." She shoves her phone in her back pocket as she stands up. "I would've told them to get off your ass. You're *trying*."

The second time you find yourself in Clifford Caldwell's office, he again gives your folder thirty seconds of attention before closing it.

He looks at you. *Really* looks at you.

"Tell me about yourself," he says.

You hesitate. "What do you want to hear?"

"I don't *want* to hear any of it, but I need to know all of it."

"It's all on my resume."

A slight smile touches his lips. "Not your work. I'm not an agent. I'm a manager. My job is *you*. So how about you tell me who you think you are, and I'll tell you who you're going to be."

You tell him the basics of Jonathan Cunningham. There isn't much beyond your dysfunctional family. You tell him about the woman waiting for you at home, even though he already knows all about her.

You talk for a few minutes, and when you stop, he says, "So now let's talk about *Johnny*."

Johnny Cunning.

That's who you become.

Johnny sounds more approachable than Jonathan. Cunningham makes people think of your father, so you drop the last syllable. The name tweak alone takes you from being the rich kid in a political family to the mysterious guy that somehow feels familiar. You keep them guessing, you don't answer questions... but you set out on a path that keeps you on their minds at all times.

That's the plan.

He tells you he can make you the biggest name in Hollywood. All you have to do is listen to him and do what he says.

A contract is drawn up before you even leave the office. You read it. You should've had a *lawyer* read it, but when opportunity knocks, you have a habit of just throwing open the door.

You sign it, right then and there.

Instead of going to the apartment afterward, you detour to the diner, where she is. She's working, flitting around in her little pink uniform, laughing and joking and *flirting*. You stand outside on the sidewalk, watching her. She notices you and smiles.

Slipping outside, she asks, "How'd it go?"

"You're looking at a man under *management*."

Her eyes widen. "You're joking."

"Nope."

She squeals, doing a flying leap right into your arms, wrapping her legs around your waist, clinging to you. You hug her and laugh as she frantically kisses all over your face.

"I'm so proud, Jonathan," she says. "And so, *so* happy for you."

"For us," you say. "This is for you, too."

She loosens her hold, her feet back on the sidewalk. "You better not forget that when you've got all these rabid fangirls trying to get in your pants."

"Don't worry, you'll always be the only rabid fangirl for me."

She grins, nudging you. "Well, Mister Big Shot, I need to get back to work... you know, just until you hit it big and I can quit my job."

She heads back into the diner. You go home.

And you don't know this, but a few minutes after you leave, Clifford Caldwell walks into the diner. He nearly stole your moment again. He sits down in her section, brazenly ordering coffee, and slides a paper to her. "Sign it."

Confidentiality Agreement.

She hesitates. "No."

"Sign it, or his career's already over."

She doesn't understand the point.

So she calls his bluff and he leaves.

She's not signing *anything.*

Everything goes back to normal. Weeks pass. You're getting worried. You don't know why your brand-new manager isn't taking your calls.

She knows why, though.

So she shows up at Clifford Caldwell's office and signs that stupid paper, swearing she'll never publicly disclose anything about you or any of *this.* Not that she ever would, but it worries her why the man is so fixated on keeping her silent.

The next day, your phone finally rings in the middle of the night, and things take off. Meetings. So many meetings. You need to sign with a new agent. You need to talk to some publicists. You need better headshots. There are classes to take and vocal coaches to see, not to mention prepping for auditions and creating a more appealing demo reel.

You get paid for none of that. No, you get *billed.* Clifford covers all the costs upfront, but it'll be charged to you. Long hours, day and night. Your schedule gets so crazy you can't keep up.

She does, though. A calendar on the wall in the living room has all of it scribbled down. She keeps you on track, even as she works overtime. She's covering the bills. She's buying the food. She cooks, and cleans, and she waits up for you the nights you're late, even though she's exhausted. Even when she just wants to get some sleep.

She smiles and tells you it's okay when your first big audition falls on her nineteenth birthday.

Months pass, months of chaos. The days all meld together. Time slips away. You miss holidays, but so does she. You celebrate Christmas in January.

You book your first movie. It's one of those teen romantic comedies. You play the best friend. No more *Guy #3* or *Heroin Dealer*. Your character has a name—*Greg Barlow*. It films locally. She visits you on set a few times, but you're both so busy that she can only stay a few minutes.

The movie wraps on your second *Dreamiversary*. You take her out to celebrate, but every penny you earned from the movie went to reimbursement, so celebrating entails hanging out in a park together.

"Do you still love me?" she asks, sitting across from you at a picnic table. You're holding her hands, gently stroking her skin with your thumbs.

"Of course I do."

"More than everything?"

"Anything," he says. "Why are you asking?"

"I just miss hearing it," she says.

You stare at her. It's been awhile since you've said it. It wasn't intentional. Life just gets crazy, but she understands. Even writing time has been scarce. Whenever she gets the chance, her thoughts are a jumbled mess, the words a blur. The poetry is all gone. The metaphors. The symbolism. They've disappeared. It's all become a hazy mass of stripped-down syllables on paper.

"I love you," you say. "More than everything in this park. More than every line of dialogue I've ever spoken. More than I love Hollywood. Is that still enough, K? My love?"

She smiles. "Of course."

You don't know this, but that woman? Even as she smiles, she's utterly terrified. Your love is more than enough for her, but she feels pieces of it slipping away. Something inside of her is disintegrating. *Her dream.* She's losing it. She came here with you, not quite realizing what you were going through. You felt invisible, and you were desperate for an audience, but where does that leave your love? Because the more people who see you, it seems, the less you see *her*. And she can't even tell her story now, not the way she wants, because her voice has been stolen and no one will ever get the chance to read her words.

TWENTY-THREE

KENNEDY

Marcus stares at me.

He stares. And stares. And stares.

An awkward silence fills the office, thick and suffocating. It's just after dawn. Nobody else is here yet. I wanted to do this before anyone showed up, thinking it would be easier, but no... *awkward*.

He keeps staring.

"So, yeah," I mumble. "That's it."

I put in my two-week notice.

How I'm going to last that long, I don't know. It's Monday morning, and the rumors had all weekend to spread. The video went viral in the first twenty-four hours. The guy, it turns out, works for *Hollywood Chronicles*.

Marcus clears his throat and says, "I'd like it if you'd reconsider."

"I know," I say, "but there's just no way it'll work out."

I can tell from his expression that he isn't happy, but it's for the best, and deep down, he knows it. Already, there's a police cruiser positioned in the parking lot, a new sign on the store door that says '*customers only*'.

"This whole thing will die down, you know," he says, waving toward the open office door. "They'll get bored and go away."

"I know, but still... it's time."

Time for me to figure out what the heck I want to do with the rest of my life, because this isn't it. This was never the 'something special' my parents wanted for me, nor was it my dream.

"Fair enough," Marcus says. "I'm disappointed, but I won't pretend to be surprised. I knew we'd lose you someday. Just hoped I'd be retired by the time you came to your senses."

"Tough break."

"It is," he says, waving me away, dismissing me—just like that. I slip out of the office and head to the back stockroom to get a jumpstart on work, pulling my phone out as I walk. So many notifications. So many missed calls. I clear them all and send Jonathan a text. **Any way you can get Maddie to school this morning?**

His answer comes quickly. **Sure.**

I stare at his response before adding: **WITHOUT assaulting any reporters?**

See, now we're going to need to have a talk about these unrealistic expectations.

You're totally right. What was I thinking, expecting you to be civilized?

I really don't know. But don't worry. I'll get her to school... by any means necessary.

He adds a grinning devil and a water gun emoji to his message, so I send him back the rolling eyes one in response.

Time ticks by.

I work on inventory.

I hear people moving around the store after opening, but nobody bothers me. I know it's coming, though. It's only a matter of time.

Nine o'clock comes, I text Jonathan. **Did you get her to school okay?**

Define 'okay'.

Nobody got punched and nobody cried.

Does the teacher's aide count?

What the...?

You punched the teacher's aide???

No, she cried. Asked for an autograph. Big fan of mine.

I send another rolling eye emoji before pocketing the phone. I try to focus on work after that, but I'm too distracted.

Ten o'clock comes, I text Jonathan again. **Did she eat breakfast?**

The teacher's aide?

Maddie. Did she eat this morning?

Oh yeah, a bowl of Lucky Charms.

Satisfied, I go back to inventory, but it doesn't last long.

Eleven o'clock comes, I send yet another text. **She remembered to brush her teeth, right? Sometimes, she forgets.**

No response.

Instead, the phone rings.

He's calling me.

I answer it. "Hello?"

"Don't you have something else you're supposed to be doing instead of playing twenty questions with me this morning?"

Sighing, I perch myself on one of the crates. "Unlike you, I can multi-task."

"She brushed her teeth," he says. "Brushed her hair, too. And she wore some kind of one-piece thing. A jumper? Romper? Blue, maybe? Might've been black."

"And she remembered her backpack?"

"Of course," he says with a laugh. "Even put shoes on before we left the apartment."

"Sorry, I know I'm asking a lot of questions, but *ugh*, I've always been around in the mornings. This is the first time I wasn't there to fix her breakfast or tie her shoes."

"She was fine," he says. "When I woke her up, I told her you had to get to work early, so she got Daddy. And I'm pretty sure, when I dropped her off, she *still* had all her fingers and toes."

"Thank you," I say. "I should get some work done now. I'll see you in a while."

I hang up, getting back to work when there's a knock on the door. It slowly opens, and Bethany appears, hesitating right outside.

She says nothing at first. She stares at me like Marcus did. Staring, and staring, and staring...

"Did you need something?" I ask.

She shakes her head as the stifling silence from the office weasels its way in here. "I was just..."

"Just what?"

"Just... is it true? Like, seriously, he *was* at your apartment?"

"Yes."

Her expression flickers with hurt. "You know Johnny Cunning? And you didn't tell me?"

"I did tell you," I say. "I even told you he said hello the other day."

"We were joking around. Or I thought you were joking. You were *serious?*"

I shrug a shoulder as guilt settles in, because maybe I'm being unfair. "He really did say hello. He remembered you."

Her eyes widen, face going pale. "Oh my god, really?"

"Really," I say. "And I'm sorry that I let you think it was a joke, but honestly, would you ever have believed I actually knew him? I don't think so."

"But you could've, I don't know, brought him around? Oh my god, Kennedy, I would've believed then!"

"I couldn't."

"Why not?"

"Look, it's complicated. I've known him for a long time, since I was younger than you. I knew him before there even was a Johnny Cunning to speak of. What we have... it's complicated."

"Have you...? Oh my god, have you and Johnny, you know? *Together?*"

"Have we *what?*"

"You know... have you done it?"

I give her an incredulous look. "You know where babies come from, right?"

"I know, but like... *oh my god.* It's true? She's his daughter?"

"Yeah."

"Oh my god."

"Bethany, I swear, if you say *oh my god* one more time."

"Sorry! I just can't wrap my mind around the fact that *you* have a baby with Johnny freaking Cunning! How is this real life?"

"Well, she's not really a baby anymore. And like I said, it was a long time ago."

"So you haven't, you know, since he's been around? The two of you haven't... *together*?"

I say nothing, because really, I don't want to answer that, but my silence is enough to give her what she wants.

She gasps, eyes somehow even wider as she lets out a squeal and yells, "You have!"

I cringe.

She squeals again, stepping into the stockroom. "No freaking way! You have to tell me *everything*. I need details!"

I can feel my face heating. "I don't like to kiss and tell."

"What? No! You *have* to! You can't tell me you're sleeping with Johnny Cunning and not give me more. Like, how is he? How big is it? What's it look like? Describe it!"

I laugh at that. "I'm not describing it. And he's, well... I don't know. He's not lacking, if that's what you're asking."

"Oh my god!"

I let that one slide.

"Just... *wow*," she says. "This is blowing my mind. I'm not being pranked, am I? This is real, right?"

"Right."

Pulling out my phone, I hesitate before opening FaceTime and dialing Jonathan's number. I've never FaceTimed him, so I'm not sure if he'll even answer, but after a moment he picks up, his face flashing on the screen in front of me.

All I see is skin—he's not wearing a shirt. His hair is disheveled. He still hasn't shaved. It only takes a second before I realize he's in my bed.

"Are you freaking kidding me?" I say right away. "Were you seriously sleeping?"

"Was trying to," he says. "But *somebody* keeps interrupting my nap."

"Unbelievable." I shake my head, shoving away from the crate to stroll over to a shocked Bethany. I know she's heard his voice. I know she recognizes it. I shove my phone at her, forcing it in her hand as I say, "Have fun with that one. Maybe he'll describe it for you."

I slip out of the storage room, hearing her squeal. "Oh my god!"

The store is busy for being a Monday afternoon. I need to walk the aisles so I can put out stock, but people are all around, shopping.

Or, well, *pretending* to shop.

I can feel eyes following me.

Marcus's voice comes over the loudspeaker, calling out, "Assistant Manager to Customer Service."

I groan. I'm the only Assistant Manager around. When I reach the front of the store, my footsteps stall, eyes going to a man standing at the customer service counter.

Clifford Caldwell.

His face is one I haven't seen in a while—a face I would've been okay never seeing again in my life. Fifties, sort of handsome in a *Mad Men* kind of way. He's always reminded me of a vintage ad exec. Confidence oozes from his pores, and it's probably deserved. He's good at what he does. The industry treats him like he's a god, but I long ago realized he was the devil in disguise.

Clifford leans against the counter, waiting for something.

Me, I realize.

"Mr. Caldwell," I say as I approach. "Can I help you with something?"

He smiles as he looks me over. It makes my skin crawl. "I was hoping we could chat."

"Chat," I say. "I'm not sure this is the right place for that."

"You can use my office," Marcus offers.

I've never wanted to strangle someone as much as I want to

strangle my soon-to-be ex-boss. A *chat* with Clifford won't be a conversation about the weather. I've been dreading him showing up, although I knew it was inevitable. Being a part of Jonathan's life means this man vying for control, and that's something I've avoided thinking about, because I'm not sure it's something I can accept. Not anymore. I tolerated a lot years ago, seeing it as a necessary evil of Hollywood, but things are different now.

"After you," Clifford says, motioning to the empty office.

I sigh so loud everyone in the store probably hears, crossing my arms as I shuffle into the office, sitting in the chair behind the desk.

Clifford closes the door.

He doesn't sit.

Instead, he towers over me, watching, like he's sizing me up, before setting a paper on the desk in front of me. "Sign it."

Confidentiality Agreement.

"I've already signed one."

"This is an updated version. He was a 'nobody' when you signed. Expectations are different when dealing with a celebrity."

"Does that mean the one I signed is no longer valid?"

He smiles tersely.

I take that as a disgruntled 'yes'.

"I should've updated yours years ago, but I honestly didn't see the need. I didn't anticipate you becoming a problem again."

"A problem… is that what I am?"

"Maybe *complication* is a better word for you, because yes, you complicate things. You did back then, and you do even more so now. So sign it, Miss Garfield. Get it over with."

I read through the agreement, to see what's so different. It's no longer about protecting his privacy and preserving his reputation. Now it's all about protecting his right to monetize the information.

His name has value. His story is worth money. Tabloids would pay quite a bit for it. No longer a person, he became a brand, trading his privacy for notoriety when he sold his soul to the devil.

And this little paper says I can't whisper a word of what I know because doing so is like stealing his *property* and pawning it off as my own.

"Does he know about these?" I ask, curious, because I can't fathom Jonathan being okay with his existence being equated to a *thing*, like he's a moneymaking puppet and not a human.

"He's aware," Clifford says. "His lawyer has enforced a few on his behalf."

Arbitration, it says, meaning there's no court, just a snappy judgment, the settlement kept private.

"Okay, but has he ever *read* it?"

Clifford doesn't answer that, instead saying, "I hope you know this isn't personal."

"Of course it is," I say. "It's always been personal. Otherwise, you would've made Serena Markson sign one of these."

"I make everyone sign them."

"Well, a lot of good that did, huh? Are you going to take her to arbitration for sending the tabloids to my father's front door?"

He stares at me.

I can feel his gaze.

I'm tired of people staring.

"Why are you so sure it's Serena?" he asks. "Could it be because you're trained to blame the *other woman*?"

"There is no other woman," I say, the way he worded that ruffling my feathers, so to speak. He's trying to get under my skin, and *ugh*, it's working. "He told me they're just friends."

"And what are you and him?"

I open my mouth to answer, but I haven't the faintest idea what to say. He's the father of my daughter. He's the man who sleeps beside me, who makes love to me, who swears he still loves me, but I'm not sure what all that adds up to.

"Johnny's talented," Cliff says, my silence enticing him to continue his little lecture. "But this business is ruthless, and it takes more than talent to get ahead. I work hard to keep him on top. He's not going to fade into obscurity on my watch. So again, this is nothing personal. I'm doing what's necessary to ensure he never again becomes a 'nobody'."

There's so much I want to say right now. He pulls out a pen, holding it out to me, but I ignore it. Instead, I crumple up the paper and shove the chair back to stand, saying, "The thing is, Mr. Caldwell, Jonathan has never been a *nobody*. I stand by what I told you years ago. He's too damn good for you."

I leave the office, making it a few steps into the store before I hear loud voices. Glancing at the registers, I see Bethany.

Standing beside her is Serena Markson.

"*Awesome*," I mutter.

Just what I need.

The pair take selfies like they're long-lost friends, and Bethany gushes over her as she signs autographs. Clifford steps out of the office behind me, clearing his throat, getting Serena's attention.

"Cliff, where have you been?" Serena asks, approaching the customer service desk.

"Taking care of a problem," he says. "We can go now."

I try to slip past them, try to go around them, wanting nothing more than to *exit stage left* before this gets ugly, but Serena notices my presence.

"Kennedy," she says, reading my nametag. "*The* Kennedy? You look different."

"Different," I say, wondering what she means by that, because it's not sounding like a compliment.

"From the other night," she says. "With Johnny, you were all dolled up, wearing a dress? I almost didn't realize it was *you*. You always look so different in your little work uniform."

Yeah, definitely not a compliment.

Even in a grocery store, she looks like she's prepared for a photo shoot, not a hair on her head out of place.

"Yeah, well, you know how it is," I mumble. "Real world and all that."

Her eyes narrow.

"A pleasure as always, Miss Garfield," Clifford says before pressing his hand to Serena's back and giving her a nudge. "I'm sure we'll be seeing each other soon."

"I look forward to it."

Man, I'm going to have to help a lot of old ladies cross the street to earn back some good karma for *that* big, fat lie.

Serena casts a look over her shoulder at me as the two of them leave the store. The second they're outside, she throws her hands up and starts ranting. I watch through the glass doors as Clifford forces her into an awaiting car before she can make a scene.

Sighing, I approach Bethany, who's so excited she's bouncing. As soon as I'm within arm's reach, she hugs me. "Oh my god! You're the best!"

"I take it you guys had a nice talk?"

"The best!" She gives my phone back. "Because of you, I got to talk to *both* of my idols!"

"Oh, well, I'm not sure the Serena thing was my doing."

"But when she showed up the other day, she was asking about you, so I'm totally giving you credit."

"The other day?" It strikes me when I ask—the night she showed up at my apartment. "Wait, she was asking about *me*?"

"Yeah, she asked if anybody knew a lady named Kennedy. It's kind of funny, because she didn't even know you worked here! She just knew you were from Bennett Landing, and the store was really the only thing open. She wanted to know where she might find you, so I sent her to the apartments." Bethany's eyes widen. "Wait, should I not have done that? I didn't know... I wasn't sure... I was just so excited, and she didn't even mention Johnny, so I didn't realize... *oh my god*, are you having any affair with her *husband*?"

I shake my head, my fist tightening around the crumbled up confidentiality agreement. I don't even know what to say to any of that, so I just walk away.

Before I can slip the phone in my pocket, it vibrates with a message.

I glance at the screen.

It's from Jonathan.

That girl is crazy. She asked me to describe my cock.

I laugh at that, despite everything else going on. **What did you tell her?**

Seriously? What do you THINK I told her?

I start to type 'that she's lost her mind' when another text comes through.

I told her it was the most beautiful nine inches in the fucking world, baby. ;)

"Daddy! Daddy! Guess what!"

Maddie runs right for him the second we're safely inside the apartment, too excited to even notice the police officer lurking outside, a patrol car parked cockeyed not far from my front door to keep everyone at a distance.

Jonathan's in the kitchen cooking again—or well, he's trying to. I smell something burning. I don't think he's any better at it than I am. He shuts a burner on the stove off, shoving the pan aside before looking at us. "What?"

"Today, at school, Mrs. Appleton said that we're gonna do a play!"

He raises an eyebrow. "A play?"

She nods excitedly. "It's about the weather outside and water and stuff! We got to pick parts, but we did it with a hat, 'cuz everyone wanted to be the sun, but not me! I get to be a snowflake!"

"Wow, that's awesome," he says, grinning at her. "I think I'd want to be a snowflake, too."

"It's not 'till the end of school," she says. "Will you come watch?"

"Of course," he says. "I'll be there."

She runs off, saying something about needing to practice, even though '*end of school*' is still over a month away. I lean against the kitchen counter beside the stove, my eyes settling on the food. "Hot dogs."

"Yeah, I fucked them all up," he says with a laugh. "I walked away for one second and all hell broke loose in the pan."

"We like our hot dogs like that around here," I say. "The more burnt, the better."

"Good," he says. "Because they're so burnt they're pretty much black."

He starts looking through the cabinets, pulling out a box of Mac & Cheese to make to go with them. Other than the stove, the apartment is scrubbed spotless. I can tell he's been cleaning, even though it wasn't messy to begin with. The domesticity, although appreciated, stirs up an unsettling feeling.

He's growing restless.

"Are you okay?" I ask.

"Why wouldn't I be?"

"Many reasons."

He starts boiling the macaroni and ignores my question for so long that I don't think he's going to answer it. Eventually, though, he says, "Been one of those days."

"You want a drink."

He cuts his eyes at me. "Don't get me wrong. It's not that I'm not okay. It's just…"

"You want a drink."

"Yeah." His eyes go back to the stove, like he doesn't want to look at me. "Disappointed?"

"Depends," I say. "Did you get drunk while I was working?"

"Of course not," he says.

"Then I have no reason to be disappointed."

"It doesn't bother you that I'm weak?" he asks. "Everything to lose, and *still*, I'd give my left nut for just a sip."

"That's not being weak, Jonathan. I've seen you weak. I've

338

seen you so drunk you couldn't stand, so high I doubted you'd ever come down, but here you are."

He looks at me again.

"The only way you're going to disappoint me is if you show up here drunk," I say. "Or, you know, if you don't show up at all."

"You don't have to worry about that," he says, switching the subject. "So, how was your day?"

My day? "Honestly, I'd give *both* your nuts for a drink after the afternoon I had."

He cringes. "That bad?"

Reaching into my back pocket, I pull out the paper I've been carrying around all day. It's folded into a small square now, wrinkled and torn. I've smoothed it out and crumpled it up multiple times, reading the words over and over to the point that I have passages memorized. I've agonized over whether I'm doing the right thing and I'm still not sure.

"What's that?" he asks.

I hand the paper to him.

Brow furrowing, he unfolds it, his eyes scanning over the unsigned confidentiality agreement.

"I'll sign it," I tell him, "if that's what you need."

"Don't worry about it."

"I hope you know I'd never sell you out," I say. "I'd never sell your story. I'd never even *tell* your story. It's not mine to tell."

He shoots me an incredulous look, one that stings, before he says, "It's just as much your story, Kennedy. You have every right to tell it."

"But I wouldn't do that to you."

The incredulous look gives way to something else. *Suspicion.* "Is that why you stopped writing? I know Cliff had you sign one of these a long time ago." He shakes the crumpled paper at me. "Is this what made you stop telling our story?"

I hesitate. I want to say no, because it isn't—not in the way he's thinking. But yet, it is. It's one of many things that veered our story the direction it went, making it end the way it ended. But I don't know how to explain that.

His expression changes again, my silence upsetting him. There's anger in his eyes and tension in his jaw, almost like someone hit him—someone he trusted, someone that's supposed to care for him, someone that's never supposed to cause him harm. My chest gets tighter as my eyes start to burn, my vision blurring. I'm trying not to cry, but his expression is breaking me.

He tears the paper up, ripping it to tiny pieces before throwing it in the trashcan. "I don't need you to sign it."

I reach for him, worried, because I've seen him do this before. I saw it so many times when we were younger, him withdrawing. I touch his arm but he pulls away, putting space between us.

"Jonathan…"

Before I can say anything else, before he can react, Maddie runs into the kitchen, announcing she's hungry. Jonathan's expression changes again, the shift so abrupt it nearly takes my breath away. He smiles, not letting her see he's upset, the actor kicking in. He gets her a hot dog, finishing making the Mac & Cheese, settling her in at the table and kissing the top of her head before turning to me, the shift happening again. *Anger.*

He walks past me, out of the kitchen, saying, "I need to take a walk," as he heads straight for the front door.

I follow him.

"Wait," I say quietly, not wanting Maddie to overhear. "Please, don't walk out when you're like this."

"I'm fine," he says. "I just need some air."

He's gone then, and I stand there, staring at the front door, until Maddie finishes her hot dog and walks out of the kitchen, asking, "Where'd Daddy go?"

"He had to do some grown-up stuff. He'll be back later."

Later. Much later.

I'm putting Maddie to bed, reading to her, and she's looking a bit worried that her father hasn't returned, when the apartment door opens. Maddie shoves right out of bed, abandoning me mid-

340

book to run to him. I hear his laughter echo through the apartment and see his smile as he carries her back into her bedroom. I watch as he tucks her in, not saying a word to me.

I suddenly feel invisible.

I hand the book to Jonathan, mumbling, "You can finish," before leaving the room.

I'm changing out of my uniform when Jonathan comes into the bedroom, sighing as he sits down on my bed. I can feel his eyes watching me as I put on pajamas. I'm no longer invisible. No, I feel startlingly naked at the moment, even covered by clothes.

"I shouldn't have brought it up," I say, needing to say something, because the tension is gnawing at me. "You were having a rough day. I only made it worse."

"You didn't do anything wrong," he says. "I told you not to tiptoe around me."

"You're upset."

"But not at you," he says. "I'm just... I'm pissed off at the situation. I'm mad because of what my bullshit has done to *you*. Whenever I try to make things better, you end up suffering."

"I'm not suffering."

He ignores that and keeps talking. "They say to make amends—it's the only way to be a better person, to have a better life, but not if fixing myself means hurting someone else. *Make amends, unless it causes further harm.* I spent the past year telling myself not to come here, not to do this, because I'd end up fucking up what you've built, but I thought maybe it would be okay. I thought, hey, maybe it'll work out, but here we are—you can't even go outside without being harassed, and my manager's throwing confidentiality agreements at you because *god forbid* you be free to exist in your own goddamn story."

"I'm not suffering," I say again. "You're not hurting me by being here. You're not hurting us by being a father. All you're hurting, Jonathan, is your *image*."

"I don't give a shit about my image."

But he does. He's been that person for a long time now.

"Johnny Cunning doesn't have a family, just like he didn't have a girlfriend," I say. "Johnny Cunning has a famous model-slash-actress that may or may not be his wife. Johnny Cunning doesn't hang out in small towns or go to school plays to see some little girl pretend to be a snowflake. The only white powdery stuff Johnny Cunning ever gave a crap about was *cocaine*."

He says nothing, staring at the floor.

"Maybe you don't see it, because you walk in his shoes every day. Maybe you're too close, but from the outside, where I am, it's obvious. You're two different people. You have two different lives. I share a story with *one* of them. And until you decide who you really are, who you want to be, nothing's going to change."

"I don't want to keep hurting you," he whispers. "I never wanted to hurt you."

"I know." I push him back on the bed just enough to crawl onto his lap. My hands frame his face as I make him look at me. "*I know*, Jonathan. You've always wanted to make me feel good."

"Because I love you," he says.

"More than whiskey?" I ask.

"More than whiskey," he agrees. "More than cocaine."

"More than models-slash-actresses?"

"I don't even *like* them most days. But I love you. I swear to fuck, I've loved you since before my eighteenth birthday when we sat on your father's couch and watched me play dead on television."

"My favorite thing you've ever done," I whisper, kissing him. "You still owe me that autograph, dead kid on *Law & Order*."

TWENTY-FOUR

JONATHAN

"Come on, sweetheart!" Kennedy yells, looking at her watch as she stands by the front door. "Time to go! I need to get to work."

"I'll take her," I say, "if you want."

"You don't have to do that."

Madison comes tromping through, dragging her backpack behind her. "I want Daddy to take me to school again! *Please?*"

Kennedy blinks a few times, mumbling, "Or maybe you do."

"I got it," I say. "No problem."

She hesitates before giving a resigned sigh when Madison grabs my hand. "You got everything you need?"

Madison nods. "Yep."

"It's Tuesday," Kennedy says. "You got something for Show & Tell?"

Another nod. "Yep."

"Breezeo?" Kennedy guesses.

A grin this time. "Yep."

"Of course," she mumbles, bending down to kiss Madison on the forehead. "Have a good day. Love you."

"Love you, Mommy," Madison says. "More than even Show & Tell."

"More than your daddy's burnt hot dogs," Kennedy says playfully, standing back up. Leaning over, she kisses me, lingering there as she smiles softly, whispering, "I'll see you after work."

She's gone then, out the door, as Madison tugs on my hand. "Come on, Daddy. Time to go to school."

It's tricky, taking this kid to school in the mornings. There's a cop parked in front of the apartment. There will be one in front of the school, too. But the in-between is where things are a bit sketchy. It's only a few blocks over, but in our situation it's like playing a fucking game of *Jumanji*.

Roll the dice and hope the bloodsuckers don't pop out and swarm your ass.

We got lucky yesterday, but today, not so much. A block away from the school, someone calls my name from across the street and jogs over, trying to get me to stop.

I ignore him and keep walking.

"Daddy, that guy's talking to you," Madison says.

"I know," I say. "Pretend he's not there."

"Like he's invisible?" she asks. "Like Breezeo?"

"Exactly like that," I say. "No matter what he says or does, act like he's nothing but air."

"I can do that," she says with a nod. "And now since I'm a snowflake, I don't even got ears. I don't hear nothing."

"Good girl."

The guy tries. *Jesus, does he try.*

More than once I want to haul off and punch him in the fucking mouth for what he says in front of my daughter. Are you drinking again? Still getting high? Why'd you assault that reporter? Are you pissed off the world has learned your dirty little secret? Cute kid, why'd you try to hide her? Are you ashamed of her mother or something?

My footsteps stall in front of the school, and I look down at Madison. "Go on inside."

I try to let go of her hand, but she resists, squeezing me tighter, tugging. "No, you gotta come, too."

"I have to come inside?"

"Yes."

"Why?"

"Just 'cuz," she says, pulling as hard as she can, trying to get me to budge. I concede, following her inside, letting her lead me to

344

her classroom.

"Shouldn't I have to sign in at the office or something?" I ask. "Show ID? They don't just let adults roam the halls, do they?"

"I dunno," she says, shrugging.

"Well, that clears that up…"

She pulls me into the classroom, stopping right at the doorway. "*Ta-da*!"

I glance down at her, confused, as everyone in the classroom looks at us. "Is it career day or something?"

"No, silly," Madison says. "Show & Tell!"

"What?"

"We can bring a favorite thing so we can show each other," she says, explaining Show & Tell to me, like she thinks I'm just not getting it. "But nothing too expensive, 'cuz it could get stole, but I didn't pay nothing for you."

"You brought *me* for Show & Tell?" I ask incredulously. "I thought you brought Breezeo."

The moment I say that, it clicks.

I'm the Breezeo she brought today.

"*Duh*," Madison says. "Mrs. Appleton, can I do my Show & Tell now? 'Cuz I can't keep him in my backpack 'till lunch."

The teacher doesn't seem to have any idea of what to say, so she just waves at Madison, giving her permission. Madison pulls me to the front of the classroom as the bell rings.

"This is my daddy, but he's not just my daddy. He's also Breezeo. The *real* Breezeo!"

There are a few *ohhs* and *ahhs*, but a little boy in the back scoffs. "He doesn't look like Breezeo."

"Well, he is," Madison says before looking at me. "Right, Daddy?"

Talk about awkward. "Right."

The teacher clears her throat. "Questions come afterward, guys. Not during the presentation."

I look at the woman with disbelief. "Questions?"

She nods, mildly amused.

"First, I got my daddy… I dunno when," Madison says, brow furrowing as she thinks about that. Guess I don't fit into the format. "When I was a baby, I think, but I didn't know 'till I was five. And, uh, I think my mommy gave him to me."

The teacher is trying very hard not to laugh.

"Second, he was made by his mommy and daddy, but I don't know them," Madison says. "And third, he's one of my favorite things 'cuz he's my daddy. And 'cuz he's Breezeo. So thank you for listening and raise your hands if you have questions."

Way too many hands shoot up, including the teacher's aide lurking in the back of the classroom. Madison grins, bubbling with excitement from being the center of attention.

"Can I get a chair?" I ask. "I have a feeling I'm going to be here for a while."

After my ass is planted in a seat, the questions start. *Is Breezeo really real? Can he go invisible? When did he become Breezeo? How come he doesn't look like him?* Madison answers them the best she can, but I chime in occasionally to clarify that I'm, in fact, not actually a superhero.

"But are superheroes real?" a little boy asks.

Madison looks at me expectantly, yielding to my expertise on that one, but I've got nothing. I'm not killing the imagination of a room full of kindergarteners with that reality. The paparazzi coming after me are bad enough. Moms with torches? *Hell no.*

"Heroes are certainly real," the teacher's aide says. "Mr. Cunning actually saved a young woman from being hit by a car recently."

There goes the *ohhs* and *ahhs,* a 'whoa' or two tossed in for good measure.

"Wasn't that big of a deal," I say, looking at my wrist. "I just happened to be standing there when it happened."

Mrs. Appleton chimes in. "I hate to cut this short, but we need to get started on today's lesson."

I seem to be the only one not disappointed by that. The teacher thanks me and Maddie hugs me and I'm out the door and heading down the hallway before the teacher's aide can cry this morning.

Stepping outside, I see the damn guy still lurking that followed us here. Lowering my head, I walk past him as he asks, "Johnny, what does your *wife* think about this whole thing?"

"I have no wife."

"You don't?"

"Nope."

I walk away, but he doesn't follow.

Guess his job isn't as fun without an audience, either.

The police car is no longer in front of the apartment when I get there, but a black sedan is. Cliff stands beside it, leaning back against it, busy on his Blackberry.

He doesn't even look up when I approach.

"Did you forget about your appointment today," he asks, "or did you decide you don't care?"

"Appointment?"

"For your wrist," he says. "You do *at least* remember it's broken, don't you?"

"Of course."

"Good," he says. "I was wondering—what, with you running around, punching people. Figured you forgot it was supposed to be healing so you could get back to work."

He's in one hell of a mood. He's even *typing* aggressively, his fingers slamming against the screen with so much force it wouldn't surprise me if it cracked.

"I called your doctor and told them you'd be late," he says. "Which is something your assistant should be doing."

"Haven't bothered getting another one of those."

"I'm aware," he says. "That's why I've been stuck doing it."

"Nobody said you *had* to do it," I point out. "My personal

life is my own problem."

"And I've told you many times, Johnny, there's no separating the two. You getting back to work hinges upon medical clearance, and if you can't be bothered to keep a damn doctor's appointment, well, the entire fucking movie is screwed."

I stare at him. In all the years I've know this man, I've never heard him say *'damn'* before now, much less that *'fucking'* he threw in afterward.

"Look, it slipped my mind," I say. "I walked my daughter to school. Wasn't trying to piss you off."

"It's fine," he says, shaking his head. "It's not *that* big of a deal. I was frustrated before I got here."

"What's got you so upset?"

"Your girlfriend."

"What?"

"Or your *ex*-girlfriend, I should say." He puts the Blackberry away before looking at me. "Serena, not Miss Garfield. *If* she's an ex—I'm still out of the loop as to what's going on."

"We're, uh… I don't know. But what did Serena do?"

"She overdosed."

My stomach feels like it drops to my toes when he says that word. *Overdosed.* "Is she okay?"

"She'll be fine," he says. "You know how she gets. Her assistant found her, called me… I handled it."

I know there has to be more to it, there always is, but Cliff isn't going to tell me.

"We should be going," he says, "before we have to delay your appointment *again*."

I climb in the passenger seat.

Cliff drives in silence.

"I'm surprised you didn't call me," I say, "remind me you were coming."

"I tried," he says. "Your phone is off."

Brow furrowing, I reach in my pocket and pull out my phone, pressing a button. Nothing. When I try to turn it on, the battery symbol flashes on the screen. *Dead.* With all the bullshit that went on last night, between the confidentiality agreement and me walking out, calling Jack and taking my ass to a meeting before going home and talking to Kennedy, I didn't even think about my battery. "You don't happen to have an iPhone charger, do you?"

He cuts his eyes at me.

Blackberry, remember?

"Should've charged it last night," he says.

"Should've," I agree. "Forgot."

"Been forgetting a lot lately."

"Must've been all those drugs I did."

He doesn't think that's funny.

He shoots me an annoyed look.

When we reach the medical building, Cliff valets the car, and we're ushered inside the building just like last time, bypassing the waiting rooms as we head up to orthopedics.

The doctor is waiting for me in his office.

"Johnny Cunning," he says, grinning, as he stands up and offers me his hand—again, like last time. "Good to see you."

People like him know my real name. It's written all over the paperwork. Jonathan Elliot Cunningham. I never legally changed it. But I'm always Johnny Cunning to them.

I shake his hand this time and we get down to business.

X-Rays. Examinations.

I mourn a bit when they cut the cast from my wrist, the saw slicing right through the spot where Kennedy signed it, annihilating her words.

"How does your wrist feel?" the doctor asks.

"Like shit," I admit as I bend it. Looks like shit, too. "It's stiff. Feels weak, like it might snap in half."

"I assure you that won't happen. It will ache for awhile, but I can prescribe—"

"No."

"Okay." The doctor laughs awkwardly. "Otherwise, it's healed nicely. No new damage. Must not have been a strong punch you threw."

Cliff, sitting in the corner of the office, shakes his head. "Just strong enough to make my life a nightmare."

The doctor finds that hilarious.

"So that's it?" I ask, flexing my fingers.

"I'm going to give you a brace. Wear it for a few weeks, until you get some strength back. But it can be removed as needed, so there's no reason you can't get back to things. Just no stunts."

"No punching, either," Cliff chimes in.

"No punching," the doctor agrees. "Take it easy until your strength comes back."

The doctor slips a black brace on my wrist, tightening it so it fits snug, and then we're gone.

"The studio will be happy," Cliff says as we pull away from the medical center in the car. "I'm going to make some calls, get things rolling tonight so you can get back to filming."

"What about Serena?"

"We'll give her a few days," he says. "Let her recuperate before pulling her onto set."

"She needs longer than a few days," I say. "She's a mess."

"I'm well-aware," he says. "I *just* had her sent to rehab. I'll send her again as soon as production wraps."

He says that so matter-of-fact.

Like that's just that.

"Do you even *care*?" I ask.

He cuts his eyes at me.

I touched a nerve with that.

"You're the last person that ought to be talking," he says. "You were living with your little runaway girlfriend and stealing from people when I signed you, and look at you now. So, do I care? Of course. But careers don't just *happen*. I have a job to do."

I don't know how to respond to that, wanting to refute it, but I can't. So I sit in silence as he drives, realizing something is off after a few minutes in traffic.

"You're going the wrong way," I say. "You're heading into

Midtown."

"I'm dropping you off at a hotel. I need to take care of things."

"Well, *I* need to get back home."

He swings the car up to the St. Regis hotel before looking at me. "*Home*? Where's that? LA? That's where your house is, isn't it?"

"You know what I meant."

"That apartment will still be there whenever you make it back," he says. "So will the people who live in it. But this movie has been delayed for *weeks* because of you, so I need a few hours, okay? Just a few hours of your time so I can get your career moving along. Is that too much to ask for?"

"Fine, okay," I say, getting out of the car. "Do whatever you need to do."

He drives away before I even make it into the building.

I check in, not bothering to use an alias. It's already late afternoon, working its way into early evening. I don't go upstairs. I don't have any luggage to drop off, so I pocket the keycard and walk out.

It's New York City. You can get anything here. But yet I can never seem to find what I'm looking for, lost in the chaos. It takes almost an hour to find a phone charger. I grab some takeout afterward, since I haven't eaten, and make it to the room at a quarter past five.

I plug my phone in and eat half a sandwich before the screen lights up. At once, notifications flood in, ping after ping after ping.

The first thing I see is a string of messages from Kennedy.

I've only been at work for ten minutes and this day is already a disaster.

How much of an a-hole would it make a person if they quit two days into a two-week notice?

Can you pick Maddie up from school? I have to work a double.

Ugh, are you napping?
Never mind.

351

Fuck this.

That last one came two-and-a-half hours ago. A *'fuck'* from Kennedy is never good.

Tossing down the other half of my sandwich, my appetite gone, I send a reply, because she probably thinks I'm ignoring her. **Sorry, something came up. Phone was dead. Just got all your texts. Everything okay?**

The reply bubble pops up right away, but it disappears again, over and over for damn near five minutes before a message comes through.

Define 'okay'.

She's using my words. That tells me all I need to know, but I answer anyway, giving her back her own definition. **Nobody got punched and nobody cried.**

Everything's fine.

It's clearly not, though, so I hit the button to send her a request to FaceTime, because the texting shit isn't cutting it. I want to look at her.

She doesn't accept right away. It feels like it rings forever before she picks up, her face popping up on the screen— surrounded by sheets, and blankets, and pillows.

"You're in bed?" I ask, confused. "I thought you were working a double."

"I quit."

"Oh wow."

"Yeah," she mumbles, staring at me from the screen. Even through the phone, the look she gives is piercing. "Seems I'm not the only one currently in a bedroom."

"Hotel room, technically."

"Looks like a fancy one. What's the occasion?"

"Had a doctor's appointment." I hold my wrist up so she can see it. "I graduated to a brace."

"Well, good for you," she says, pausing before adding, "I know that sounded sarcastic, but I mean it. Good for you."

"Thanks." I lower my arm. "So, everything's okay?"

352

"Everything's fine."

"It doesn't seem that way."

It feels awkward right now, like something is being wedged between us, slowly pushing her away from me when I've been desperate to find a way to bring her closer.

"Just having one of those days," she says.

"The kind where you want a drink?"

"More like the kind where I question everything."

"Let me guess—you quit your job only to come home to me gone, which freaked you out, because you don't like the idea of depending on anyone, much less someone so goddamn unreliable?"

"That's a pretty good guess."

"I thought so, too."

"I just think maybe we should've started smaller. Give you a cactus to take care of first."

I laugh. "Jack would've appreciated that. He told me to buy a plant."

"Jack's your sponsor, right?"

"Right."

"Did you meet him in a meeting?"

"No, I met him back in rehab. We had these group sessions, and he'd always call me out on some bullshit and get yelled at for *disrupting* the environment. I was struggling after I got out, and I looked him up. He reminded me of you."

She looks surprised. "*Me?*"

"Yeah, he didn't hold back with me like everyone else. I still sometimes feel like I'm stuck back in Fulton Edge, surrounded by all these fake smiles, all these perfect people in this perfect fucking world. But Jack doesn't pretend. You never did, either."

"I'm liking the sound of this guy. Is he handsome?"

"He's not your type."

"How do you know?"

"He looks nothing like me."

She makes a face. "Who says I like you?"

"*I* say you do," I tell her. "Also, your pussy seems to be quite fond of me lately, too."

Her eyes roll so hard that I laugh.

"Speaking of which, have we ever had phone sex before?"

She's trying not to smile, but I can see the amusement in her eyes. "I'm gonna go now."

"Ah, come on. Touch yourself for me."

The screen goes black.

I toss the phone down on the bed. Barely a minute passes before it rings, and I smile to myself.

Maybe she changed her mind.

Maybe she just didn't want me to *see*.

I scoop the phone back up to answer it, but freeze when I spot the name that greets me. *Serena*.

I almost answered without looking.

Hesitating, I hit the button to decline.

I run my fingers along the edge of my phone, something nagging at me, but I try to push it back. I haven't heard from Cliff yet. It's going to be a long night.

Opening my texts, I send one to Kennedy. **Tell Madison I love her, and that I said goodnight. I'm not going to make it back before she goes to bed.**

A response comes a minute or two later.

She says she loves you, too.

I smile as another text pops up beneath it.

My bad, she says she loves you more than she loves that creepy cardboard version of you in her bedroom. (She made me specify)

And another after that.

She says it's NOT creepy and wants you to know that I called it creepy, not her. She loves the thing.

And another.

But not as much as she loves you.

Laughing, I reply. **Good to know.**

So you're coming back here tonight?

It'll be late, but I'll be there.

She replies with a simple smilie-face. *:)*

I hesitate before I type: **I love you, K. I hope you believe that.**

Nothing for a few minutes. I stare at our back and forth in silence. Just when I'm about to give up, a response comes through. **I do.**

✿ ✿ ✿

BANG. BANG. BANG.

Startled, I sit straight up in bed as pounding echoes in my ears, pulling me from sleep. My blurry eyes scan the moonlit room. It takes a moment for me to remember where I am, for me to realize someone's knocking on my room door.

Shoving to my feet, I stagger that way, nearly knocking over a fucking lamp when I try to turn it on. I give up, navigating through the darkness. The knocking doesn't stop until I reach the door.

I glance out the peephole.

Cliff.

I pull it open, brow furrowing as I regard him. "How'd you know what room I was in?"

"I asked the front desk."

"And they told you?"

"Yes."

"Unbelievable," I mutter as he strolls in.

"What's *unbelievable* is you used your real name to check in," he says, turning on that lamp I couldn't quite figure out. "Took me half a dozen tries to figure it out. Tried every alias you've ever used, but no, *Jonathan Cunningham* it was."

"Yeah, well, didn't think I'd be sticking around long enough for it to matter."

"*Right*," he says, drawing out that word as he leans against the desk along the side of the room. "You were going home tonight."

"I am."

"I would've been back sooner, but I got busy dealing with Serena," Cliff says, pulling out his Blackberry, doing something on it. A moment later, my phone charging across the room chimes. "I sent you a tentative filming schedule. It covers next week."

Next week. "As in, just a few days from now?"

"That, indeed, would be next week," he says. "They're still working on the full schedule, but it's looking like it'll be a month of long hours and not much sleep for you, so get some rest while you can. You'll need it."

I stare at him as those words sink in. "A month."

"You can handle it," he says. "You've had worse schedules."

"Yeah, but I didn't have a kid to worry about then."

The second I say that, the moment that statement leaves my fucking lips, I feel sick. Because I *did.* I had a kid. I've had her for years. Through all my television guest spots, through those ridiculous teen comedies, through the critically acclaimed but didn't-pay-shit Indies, through the Breezeo movies… she was there. Living. Breathing. *Existing.*

I had a kid to worry about then, but I was too worried about myself to do anything about it.

Shaking my head, I scrub my hands down my face, *hard,* like I'm trying to wipe the fucking shame off. It makes my wrist sting and my head hurt, but the pain is almost a comfort.

"It's just a month," Cliff says, as if a month is *nothing.* "It's not the end of the world."

"I know it's not," I say, "but to my little girl, it might feel like it."

Cliff pushes away from the desk. He doesn't respond to that. Instead, he heads for the door, his voice all-business as he says, "Hire a personal assistant. And maybe call your therapist. Sort it out. Pickup is Monday morning at six, right out front of this building. Meanwhile, I need to figure out where Serena has gone, because while I was trying to find your room, she disappeared from *hers.* So if you happen to see her, let me know."

He leaves, clearly not going to take me where I want to go. Snatching my phone off of the bed, I glance at the time. *Midnight.*

Fuck it.

I toss the keycards on the desk, leaving them there, and walk out, heading down to the lobby.

I gave him a few hours. Time to go.

Strolling through the lobby, I order a car pickup. *Ten minutes away.* I glance around, stalling when I look inside the lobby bar. "You've gotta be fucking kidding."

Serena.

She sits on a stool at the bar, all alone, eyes fixed on a glass of something in front of her. It looks a hell of a lot like one of those fruity concoctions, the kind that's usually full of liquor.

I feel like an asshole doing it, but I text Cliff. **Serena's in the lobby bar.**

He replies, **Distract her. On my way.**

I grumble to myself as I walk into the bar, heading for her. This is the last place I want to be. Serena sips her drink as she looks up, spotting me. "Johnny."

"Have you lost your mind, Ser? You're sitting here *drinking*?"

A smile twists her lips as she holds the glass out, pointing the straw at me. "If you wanted a sip, all you had to do was ask."

"You know goddamn well I *don't* want any."

"Oh, relax," she says with a laugh, waving me off as she takes another sip from the glass. "It's non-alcoholic."

"Seriously?"

She offers it to me again. "Try it, you'll see."

"Thanks, but no," I say, "I'm not risking my sobriety for some shit with a tiny umbrella."

"Your loss." Serena shrugs. "But I'm telling you, it's just as *virgin* as that nerdy sober buddy of yours. What's his name? Josh?"

"Jack," I say. "And I'm pretty sure he's not a virgin."

"Someone slept with that guy?"

"Pretty sure."

357

"Well, then... my drink is *more* of a virgin, which really makes me wish it had alcohol in it."

I lean against the bar as I eye her.

She seems to be in a good mood.

"Did you use today?" I ask. "What did you take?"

Her smile dims, the good mood gone, a bitter edge to her voice as she says, "Why are you even here? Don't you have somewhere else to be?"

My eyes flicker past her, out of the bar windows lining the street, seeing a black sedan coming to a stop as my phone chimes. "Funny you ask that, because my ride just got here."

I leave her sitting at the bar and pass by Cliff in the lobby as I head outside to climb in the car. I give the driver an address in Long Island, and I make a few calls on the way over, making sure someone is meeting me there. When we arrive, a man stands right outside the massive fence surrounding the property. He greets me, opening the gates to let me inside, before handing over a set of keys. "First garage."

The garage is climate controlled, covered in layers of security like they're guarding the fucking Hope diamond—*luxury car storage*. The garage door opens and lights flick on as I stroll inside, running my hand along the glossy blue paint of the Porsche.

I bought it after rehab at Jack's insistence.

Well, I mean, Jack told me to give myself a celebratory gift to mark the milestone. It was my longest stretch of sobriety in a decade. So I bought myself a new convertible 911 Porsche, much like the one I sold when I moved to Hollywood.

When I told Jack, he called me a *filthy fucking cocksucker*. Apparently, for his celebratory gift, he'd just sent himself flowers.

I sign some paperwork to get the car released and climb behind the wheel. Less than a thousand miles on it, according to the odometer, and I'm about to add another two hundred.

It's a long drive. Tonight, it feels even longer. I get to the apartment just shy of four o'clock in the morning. The door is locked, but I use the key Kennedy gave me to get inside.

Quietly, I head down the small hall, glancing in Madison's bedroom along the way, seeing her peacefully sleeping. I keep going, not wanting to disturb her. The door to Kennedy's bedroom is cracked open, the dim light of a small lamp illuminating part of the room. My chest feels tight when I push the door open and see her, fast asleep in bed, clutching a familiar old notebook, the one that holds her version of our story.

I've read parts of it. The beginning. I've been too afraid to see how it all went to hell in California. She wrote it like it was meant for me, but I remember things differently. To me, she was the center of the universe, the sunlight that burned so bright, but she writes herself in the shadows, secondary in her own life. Instead, she made *me* the hero, the center of this alternate universe she invented around her.

I always knew it, yeah, but I never really understood that *I* was her Breezeo.

And then I slowly disappeared.

Carefully, I pull the notebook from her grasp and set it aside before turning off the lamp and laying down beside her. She stirs as the bed shifts, her eyes opening. She blinks in confusion before a small lazy smile plays on her lips, her voice a sleepy whisper when she says, "You're here."

"I said I would be, didn't I?"

"Yeah, well, you say a lot," she mumbles, shoving against me, snuggling up to me.

I put my arm around her, pulling her even closer as I unfasten my wrist brace, yanking it off to toss it somewhere in the darkness. My hand slides under her shirt, her skin warm against my palm as I stroke her back, fingertips tracing her spine. A soft moan escapes her.

The sound, *fuck*, it does something to me. Arching her back, she shifts her body, and it's instinct that I move, pulling her beneath me as I hover over her.

She stares up at me and lets out a shaky breath before I lean down and kiss her.

"I mean it all," I whisper against her lips as my hands roam, getting rid of those pesky clothes. "Every single word."

"You've said some horrible crap," she reminds me.

"That was the coke talking," I say, kissing her neck as she tilts her head. "The whiskey, too."

"Tell someone who fucking cares."

Her voice is quiet, unthreatening, but there's that *'fucking'* word. Pulling back, I look at her. "What?"

"Those were the last words you said to me."

"The day you left?"

She nods. "You were sober when you said it."

Tell someone who fucking cares.

If that was how our story ended for her, I seriously dread to know what's written in the last few pages of that notebook.

I try to sit up, but she wraps her arms around me. "Oh, no, I don't think so. You finish what you started, Mister Big Shot."

She kisses me, hard, and just like that, I give in, pushing my way between her thighs. In one stroke, I'm inside of her, and goddamn if I'm not *home* again, so I show her, over and over, as she writhes, that I didn't mean it when I said that bullshit.

Dreams aren't always just dreams. Sometimes, they turn into wide-eyed nightmares, the kind where you're screaming but nobody can hear you. They don't want to listen. They're drowning you out.

The first time you snort coke is at a club in LA. It's a present from the Markson model. Serena's her name. It's your twenty-first birthday. Clifford throws a party in your honor and invites the *who's who* of Hollywood, but the woman you love stays home. Clifford says she's not old enough to come. The venue is twenty-one and up. So you tell her it's nothing special, just networking. Part of your job is making connections. It's 'work'.

But the pictures that hit the tabloids don't much look like you're working, not when in most of them you're snorting powder off of a table. Clifford's whole entourage is there. Girls surround you. But some of them aren't twenty-one yet, either. A few are barely *legal.*

You apologize. It was a mistake. You ask for a second chance. But you only do that after the evidence comes out. And when you start filming your second movie—another teen comedy, where you play the lead this time—the world tilts a bit. Your first movie hasn't even released yet and there are already whispers. Clifford Caldwell's newest client might be someone to consider. You get more inquiries. You're juggling so much. Promo is soon starting. You need a little *pick me up.*

That's what you tell yourself. No harm in a tiny boost. And you believe it, because *my god,* it makes you feel so good. It makes you feel like you can take on the world. You come home at night, and those blue twinkling eyes are gone. She stares into a murky puddle and slowly slips into the void, but you smile and tell her everything is all right where you are. She wonders where that is and how she can get there, because you're not with her. You're disappearing.

When she tells you she's worried, you tell her you love her. You tell her you'll stop, you will, but *oh god,* if only she could feel it.

So you pour yourself into her. You make her feel good. When you're inside of her, when you're making love to her, she truly believes she can take on that tilting world.

But love is only as strong as the people who fuel it. And you? You're Superman, thinking Kryptonite makes you invincible.

And the woman you love? She... can't keep pretending any of this is normal. She can't keep writing this as if somewhere along the way the plotline will fix itself. She can't keep acting as if this isn't her story.

You're on a collision course, Jonathan. You're hurling toward something none of us can see in the darkness, but whatever it is, it's going to hurt. You think you're in control, that you're soaring, but you're in a free-fall, and you don't hear me when I try to warn you.

As I write this, you're 2500 miles away. You're in New York City, so close to home... or where home used to be. You're working on another movie. It's still dark here in LA, but the sun will have risen where you are by now, another day dawning. It was our third *Dreamiversary* yesterday. I spent it here without you.

It has been a bad year. There's no way to sugarcoat it, no pretty words I can conjure up to turn it into something sweet, not when I'm so bitter. You're the caterpillar that went into the cocoon and emerged a glorious butterfly, but I'm the reminder that butterflies don't stick around long, a few weeks at most before they're gone.

I'm not going to waste time detailing everything. I'll want to change too much to make it fit with my version of you, the one who walked into that *American Politics* classroom nearly four years ago and stole my heart, but that guy isn't here anymore. Where has he gone? He took my heart with him when he left, but I'm going to need it back. I'm going to need it for what's to come, so I can try to protect it, so it doesn't shatter when this new version of you hits bottom.

Because it's coming, Jonathan. Your dream has become my nightmare, and I'm begging you to let me wake up.

You don't know this, but the woman you love? The one you hung around for in New York when she was still just a girl, even though you were suffering, and wanting to go, but you stayed because of love? That woman, right now, is doing the same thing for you.

TWENTY-FIVE

KENNEDY

"Take a deep breath. Speak loud and clear. If you forget something, improvise. Got it?"

"Got it!" Maddie exclaims, bouncing from foot to foot and grinning at her father as he sits in front of her on the living room floor. The two of them are 'running lines', as Jonathan called it. She's dressed up like Breezeo at the moment—said if she was going to be an actor, she needed a *costume*.

"Okay," Jonathan says, glancing down at the small stack of papers in his hands, clearing his throat as he reads, "*The weather—*"

"Wait!" Maddie yells, covering the papers with her hands. "I'm not ready yet!"

"I thought you said you were."

"I was, but..." She pauses, brow furrowing. "What is improvise?"

He laughs. "It means make something up. Say anything. You just don't want there to be any awkward silence."

"Oh, okay." She moves her hands. "Got it!"

"Uh, you sure that's *really* what you want to suggest?" I ask, sitting on the couch, flipping through channels. The TV is on but turned down low. "I'm not sure that's the best advice."

Jonathan glances my way. "Hey, who's the actor here—me or you?"

"Me," Maddie says, motioning to herself.

"I'm just saying, you know, improv might be a little advanced for the situation."

"It's okay, Mommy," Maddie says, grabbing the sides of Jonathan's face, squishing his cheeks as she forces him to look at her. "I'm ready now, but don't do that part. Do *my* part."

Jonathan flips through papers, skipping ahead. "Once a beautiful, fluffy cloud, I'm starting to feel so heavy and cold. *Brrr.* Oh no! I think I'm going to snow!"

I try not to laugh as he delivers that line.

"Hey, guys!" Maddie says loudly. "What's got six arms and is like nothing else in the whole world?"

"A snowflake," Jonathan says.

"That's me!" Maddie throws her arms out at her sides and spins. That's not in the script. *Improvising.* "I'm falling and falling and falling. Where am I going?"

"Down," Jonathan says, "to the ground."

Maddie trips over her own feet as she spins, falling, but Jonathan catches her as she giggles, plopping down in his lap.

That's it. That's all the lines she has until the very end when she says, *Snowflakes aren't the only special things—you're all special!* She's spent all day memorizing them at school.

"Again!" she says, springing back to her feet.

"Later," he says. "Right now, we should do something about dinner."

"I can make something," I say, starting to stand up, but he stops me.

"I can take care of it," he says. "You just relax."

Relax. It's the first time I've not worked on a weekday in a while. I've spent all day doing nothing, sitting around. I even napped while Maddie was in school. I'm not used to having nothing to do. It's weird.

He heads off to the kitchen.

Maddie goes to her bedroom.

I flip through more channels.

I make it almost a complete cycle, back to where I started, when I flip to something that makes me stall. One of those evening entertainment shows, the equivalent of a TV tabloid. Jonathan's face is plastered on the screen from an old set photo.

"Breezeo is a-go! After being derailed when star Johnny Cunning sustained injuries in an accident, filming for the highly anticipated third Breezeo movie is scheduled to resume next week. Sources tell us Cunning will return to set on Monday, while his co-star and on-again off-again girlfriend Serena Markson is slated to join him when production moves to Europe."

"I, uh…" Jonathan's voice cuts through the living room, his eyes going straight to the screen. "I ordered pizza."

I flip the channel, a sinking feeling rocking the pit of my stomach. "Okay."

He slips his phone into his pocket before running a hand through his hair. I know he saw it. Heard it, too. Not that it matters, because he would've already known.

They would've told him.

I stop on another channel, some pointless sitcom rerun, as Jonathan lets out a deep sigh. "I was gonna talk to you about that."

"When? As you were walking out the door?"

"I would've done it before this weekend," he says. "I didn't know until last night. The doctor cleared me, and the studio wants to get a jump on it so they don't have to push back the dates."

I nod, so he knows I heard him, and pull my legs up, tucking them beneath me as I lay against the arm of the couch, staring at the television.

"You're mad," he says.

"I'm not."

"Annoyed."

"No."

"Then, what? Indifferent? Because you're sure not happy."

I look over at him as he stands there, watching me, brow furrowed like he's expecting some sort of reaction that I'm not giving him.

"I'm not mad," I tell him again. "I guess I'm just… sad. I knew it would happen sooner or later. I knew this couldn't last, that you'd have to go, but I thought we'd have a little more time."

He frowns, coming closer. "It's only a month. After that,

filming should be over and…"

"And what?" I ask when he trails off. "What happens then?"

"Then I'll come back."

"Then you'll come back," I mumble. "For how long? A couple days? Another six weeks, maybe? But then you'll be off again—shooting, promoting, doing interviews… meetings, auditions, classes… not to mention the red carpets, the studio parties, the *networking*."

He makes a face when I say that last one, reacting as if it's an accusation. And maybe it is, I don't know. Other than sad, I don't know how I'm feeling. I'm a twisted up mess, a broken once-hopeful romantic, holding my heart in a clenched fist and begging him to take it, yet I'm afraid to let go and give him that kind of control.

Because the last time I gave my heart to him, he crushed it.

"For however long I'm wanted," he says, "so that depends on you."

I shake my head. That's a cop-out answer. "You don't mean that. You might *think* you do, but you don't. We don't live in a box, Jonathan. The world still exists outside of these walls. And that world, it's never going away."

"I know that."

"Do you?" I ask, genuinely wondering if he understands what he's getting himself into. "When was the last time you stayed in one place for more than a week? When was the last time you slept in the same bed, night after night? Because I'm not sure you remember what that's like."

"Is that not what I've been doing? I've been here, haven't I?"

"This doesn't count."

"Why doesn't it?"

"Because it just doesn't."

He shakes his head, running a hand through his hair as he says, "This is ridiculous."

What's ridiculous, I think, is how much my chest aches when I look at him. How much my insides coil when I hear his laughter.

How much his smile sets my soul on fire. What's ridiculous is how *lost* I feel when I think about the future.

Jonathan always was a dreamer, walking around with stars in his eyes. Seeing that light dim as the drugs took over was one of the worst feelings in the world. There was nothing I could do to stop it. I tried and failed every single time.

But if there's one thing I've learned from it all, it's that we have to be our own heroes. No guy in a costume is coming to save us. We have to save ourselves.

"I forgive you," I tell him, not sure if he knows that, but I think he needs to hear it. "And I know you came here to make amends, but you don't owe me anything. The only person you owe anything to is that little girl in her bedroom. She deserves a father, and you leaving is going to scare her, because she's gotten used to having you around."

"Then come with me," he says. "*Both* of you."

"We can't."

"Why not? We can be together."

"I gave up everything to follow you once. I can't do that again."

Groaning, he runs his hands down his face. "I don't know what you want from me, Kennedy."

"I want you to be the man she needs you to be," I say. "Because when you tell her you're coming back, she's going to believe you."

He stares at me for a moment before asking, "What about you? Do you believe me?"

"Yes."

He looks surprised by that.

"That's not the question, though," I say. "I don't doubt you'll be back. The question is whether you'll still *want* to be here."

"Why wouldn't I?"

"Because the real world could never compete with what awaited you out there. And maybe you love me—"

"I do."

"But love doesn't give you a free pass to come and go. I can't live somewhere with a revolving door."

He sits down on the couch, his shoulders slumping as he covers his face with his hands. "Do you want me to quit acting? Is that what you want?"

"Of course not," I say. "I'm not asking you to give up your dream. I'm asking you to share it. Your work, it's important, I know, but *she's* important, too. You can't get caught up and forget she's sitting at home waiting for you. Because you live in a big, big world now, but hers is very small. A day without you is going to be like a day without the sun. Don't let her days go dark."

I get up, because I don't want to do this right now.

"Is that how I made you feel?" he asks.

"It is."

"I'm sorry."

"Don't be," I say. "It taught me something important."

"What's that?"

"Never make someone else the main character in your own story."

"I'm gonna go to work."

Jonathan eyes me peculiarly when I say that, stalling in the doorway of the bedroom as he slips on his jacket. "*Work*."

"Well, I mean, what used to be my work," I mumble as I fold the freshly washed uniforms. I woke up this morning to a brand new washer and dryer installed in the apartment, courtesy of the guy currently looking at me like I've lost my mind. I told him he didn't need to do that, but they were fancy, with their buttons and sounds and settings, so naturally, I spent all day playing with my new toys. *Ugh, I'm getting old.* "I need to turn these uniforms back in."

"I can drop them off for you," he says, glancing at his watch. "I've got some time before getting Maddie from school."

He comes toward me and tries to grab the uniforms, but I yank them away, clutching them protectively. "No."

He laughs, holding up his hands. "Fine, I won't."

"It's just... *ugh,* I haven't seen the outside world in a long time. I'm starting to forget what sunshine feels like."

"You're being dramatic."

"Am not."

"It's been two days."

He's right. It's only been about forty-eight hours, but I'm antsy doing *nothing.* "Still, I can take them myself."

Jonathan is trying not to laugh. "Kennedy, baby, I think you might be a workaholic."

"Am not."

"There are meetings for that, you know," he says, ignoring my denial. "It helps to channel your energy into something else— reading, maybe *writing.*"

I roll my eyes. "I'll keep that in mind."

"Come here," he says, reaching for me, pulling me toward the doorway. "Walk outside with me."

I don't resist, because that's exactly what I'm trying to do. *Go outside.* I carry the uniforms along, following him out the front door of the apartment. Just as I'm about to ask him where we're going, he pulls a set of keys from his jacket pocket and presses a button, making something *beep,* lights flashing in the parking lot.

I look past him, nearly tripping over my own feet when I see a blue Porsche parked right beside my Toyota. "*Holy shit.*"

Jonathan smirks, putting his arm around me as he steers me toward it. "Must be one hell of a surprise if it has you cursing."

"It's exactly like your old car."

"Well, it's a bit newer, but yeah..." He shoves the keys at me, dropping them on top of the uniforms. "You do know how to drive a stick, right?"

"I, uh, *what?*" I grab the keys when they start to fall. "I mean, I can, but I can't drive your car."

"Why not?"

"It's a freaking Porsche! What if I scratch it? Dent it? What if I wreck it? I can't fix it!"

He laughs. *Again.* He's been laughing a lot this afternoon. "I rarely drive, so you might as well use it. Otherwise, it's just going to sit in a garage in the city. Besides, no offense, but I'm not sure how much longer your piece of junk is gonna keep running."

I glance at my car, scowling, before I look at Jonathan. He means well, I know he does, and I'm grateful. But he's worrying me with this. "This is too much, Jonathan. You *just* gave me a washer and dryer this morning. Now you're handing me the keys to your car. I mean, what's next?"

"A dishwasher," he says. "It's supposed to be delivered tomorrow morning."

I blink at him. "You know I don't need *stuff*, right?"

"I know," he says before pushing me toward the car. "Now go, turn your uniforms in. And make sure you put the top down, you know, so you can feel the sunshine."

He goes back inside, leaving me there.

I stare at the car for far too long before giving in. It's not mine, but it *is* a new toy, and it's a little hard to resist when I'm overcome with a sense of nostalgia. It reminds me so much of when our dreams still felt beautiful.

So I get behind the wheel and I drive to the store. Or well, I drive past the store, circling the block a few times, before gathering the nerve to park and go inside, heading for the front office.

"Kennedy." Marcus's voice is all business as he sits behind his desk, greeting me as soon as I walk in. "What can I do for you?"

"I stopped by to turn in my uniforms," I say, holding the pile of clothes up to show him.

"You can put them over there," he says, waving toward me. "Thanks."

"Of course," I say, setting them down on top of a box by the door. I linger there, watching him sort through paperwork, feeling guilty because I know he's doing my job.

"Did you need something else?" he asks, raising an eyebrow

as he looks at me.

"No," I say, hesitating. "Well, I wanted to tell you I'm sorry."

"Sorry enough to want your job back?"

"Not quite."

He laughs, turning back to the paperwork. "Had to try."

"Anyway," I say. "Thanks for taking a chance on me when you did."

I walk out of the office, not wanting things to get too sentimental. The store is pretty busy, not unusual for a Friday.

I'm heading for the exit as the delivery guy switches out the magazines by the registers. Instinctively, my eyes turn toward them, drawn to a certain one—*Hollywood Chronicles*. My footsteps stall as I inhale sharply. It feels like I've been punched.

I snatch up the top copy. The world around me is trying to tilt. My heart pounds hard. As panic floods my system, my hands start to shake.

Turning away, I walk out of the store, taking it with me as I drive straight home. The apartment is quiet. Jonathan is walking Maddie home from school, so I'm alone for the moment.

I go straight to my bedroom.

Sitting down on the bed, I stare at the front page of the tabloid.

JOHNNY CUNNING'S DOUBLE LIFE

Along the top, there's a picture of *us*—me, and Jonathan, and our daughter. Our faces are plastered on the front of *Hollywood Chronicles*. It's unavoidable, I know. He lives his life beneath a scorching spotlight. We'd inevitably get drawn into it.

And it's strange, but he looks *happy*.

It's one of the only times they've ever printed a picture of him smiling.

Beneath that, though, tells a different story.

There's a picture of him in a bar, the caption claiming it was a few days ago. He's standing beside Serena, and she's holding her drink out, offering it to him.

I flip through it, finding more pictures. More of us. More of *them*. Close to midnight on Monday—the day of his appointment. It says they met up at a hotel in the city, when hours before, he finally broke his silence about their relationship while walking his daughter to school.

Closing the tabloid, I toss it aside.

A few minutes pass before I hear the front door, Maddie's laughter filtering through. She runs through the apartment, into the hall, yelling, "Hi, Mommy! Bye, Mommy!' before disappearing into her bedroom.

Jonathan comes to the bedroom, asking, "So, how'd it go at the store?"

I look at him in silence for a moment before saying, "It went about like I thought."

"Good? Bad?"

I shrug.

His brow furrows as he steps closer, noticing the tabloid on the bed. Grabbing it, he groans and sits down beside me. "You *bought* this shit?"

"No, I kind of just took it."

"You took it."

"Yes."

His eyes scan the cover before he flips through it, going straight to the article. He skims it, scowling, before tossing it aside.

"Since when do you shoplift?"

"I don't," I say. "It was a mistake."

"A mistake," he says. "I've made my fair share of those."

"You make any lately?"

"Maybe a few."

"Like?"

"Well, for one, that article I just read."

"Which part of it was the mistake?"

"The part where I wasted brain cells *reading* it," he says. "For the record, I didn't drink that night. I know it looks bad, but I was waiting for my car and she happened to be there. There's nothing going on between us, which is what I told that asshole when he claimed I broke my silence."

"Good to know."

Reaching over, Jonathan grabs my hands, placing his over mine. I'm fidgeting, I realize.

"Don't do that," he says. "Please. Don't ever doubt me over something *they* print."

"It's just, you know… the photos."

"It's a split second snapshot," he says. "Anything can be made to look bad if taken out of context. And they'll do it, every chance they get."

"I know."

"But back to the subject. Another mistake is spending even an ounce of energy entertaining their bullshit when there are much better things we could be doing."

I close my eyes as he pushes me back onto the bed. His mouth meets mine, and he kisses me, tongues mingling together. His hands roam, stroking my side, one slipping beneath my shirt. He palms a breast, squeezing it, sliding beneath my bra. I moan when his fingertips brush against the nipple, sending sparks through my body, but it's gone again, drifting south.

His fingertips trail along my stomach before slipping past the waistband of my pants. I inhale sharply when he starts rubbing, stroking me through the soft cotton of my underwear. Heat rushes through me. Tingles consume me. Just a touch from this man sets my world on fire.

"*Oh god,*" I whisper, arching my back as his fingers work their magic, sparks flowing down my spine. I'm getting close already. I can feel it building up, tightening in my gut. I bite my lip to keep from making too much noise.

So close…

So close…

Oh god, so—

"Daddy!"

Maddie's voice shouts down the hallway as footsteps head our direction. At once, Jonathan pulls away, standing up. "What?"

She bursts in as I force myself to sit up, still breathing heavily. I feel my face heating. I'm shaking, *aching*... clenching my thighs together to try to make it stop.

"I'm ready to do some lines!" she says, grinning, again wearing her Breezeo costume.

Jonathan laughs. "Ready to run lines, you mean."

Her brow furrows. "That's what I said."

"No, you said..." He trails off. "Never mind."

"You're running lines again?" I glance between them as Jonathan goes to the duffel bag he lives out of and starts digging through it. "That'll take, what... five minutes? Ten?"

I'm trying to gauge how long he's going to leave me hanging.

Jonathan pulls out a thick stack of papers, waving them at me. "Probably a bit longer than that."

The Breezeo script. *Ghosted.*

"Whoa," I say, reaching for it, but he yanks it back, away from my grasp.

"No touching," he says before handing it to Maddie. "It's top secret material."

"What?" I scowl at him. "How come *she* gets to read it?"

"Because I'm Breezeo, *duh*," she says before running off with the script, not letting me near it.

"Yeah," Jonathan says, leaning down to kiss me—just a brush against my lips. "*Duh.*"

He tries to move, but I'm not done with him, yanking him down on top of me.

Laughing, he kisses me some more, real kisses this time, and presses himself into me. He's *hard*. "Is that what you want, baby?"

Baby. Hearing him call me that makes me shiver in his arms. "Oh god, yes..."

"Daddy!" Maddie whines from the living room. "Hurry up!"

"Pity," Jonathan says, biting my bottom lip before he pulls away. "Guess we'll have to reschedule."

I gape at him as he heads for the door. "You son of a..."

"Bitch?"

He laughs.

"This is cruel," I say. "Cruel and unusual punishment!"

"Don't be mad, Mommy!" Maddie yells across the apartment. "Maybe Daddy will give it to you later."

She's talking about the script, I know, but dang it, I blush when Jonathan glances back at me from the hallway, cocking an eyebrow. "Maybe Daddy will."

I give him the middle finger.

He laughs *again*.

I'm flustered, no doubt about it, and parts of me still ache, but when I hear Maddie's excitement as they start reading, I'm overcome with this sense of peace.

I can't help but smile.

It's all I've wanted for years.

Getting up, I go to the kitchen and cook dinner. When it's finished, they take a break. The three of us eat together at the table. Afterward, they jump back into it, and I make my way to my bedroom.

Picking up the discarded copy of *Hollywood Chronicles*, I tear out a photo from the cover, the one where Jonathan is smiling. The rest of the paper, I throw in the trash. Pulling out my broken box of old mementos, I set the photo in. As strange as it may seem to keep, it's our first real picture together as a family.

✤ ✤ ✤

"You want to run some lines with me?"

It's after dark when Jonathan reappears in the doorway to the bedroom, leaning against the doorframe, holding the script. I'm sitting in bed, propped against the headboard, knees pulled up and notebook in my lap. "Don't you have a daughter for that?"

"She fell asleep," he says. "Must've bored her unconscious."

"Must've," I agree. "So, what, you think you can just come crawling back to me? Think I'll welcome you back with open arms? Give you yet another chance?"

"Was damn sure hoping so. I'm banking on the fact that some part of you actually likes me."

"Most parts of me like you."

"What part doesn't?"

"My brain, usually."

He laughs, strolling closer, his brow furrowing when he sees what I'm holding. "Are you writing?"

"Just thinking," I say, closing the notebook when he sits down beside me on the bed. I take the script from him, and he doesn't resist this time, letting me flip through it.

"*I used to wonder what could possibly be worse than being invisible,*" he says, and I know he's reciting a line, because it's word-for-word from the comic. "*What could be lonelier than always being by yourself?*"

"*I think I know now,*" I whisper, turning a few pages until I come to the scene.

"*Worse is loving someone who disappears and never knowing if they'll come back. Because how do you move on if you're not even sure they're gone? The answer is—you don't. When you spend most of your life chasing ghosts, eventually, you become one.*"

I smile. "I always liked that part."

"I know," he says as he moves closer, grabbing my legs. I yelp as he tugs me down the bed, climbing on top of me once I'm lying flat on my back. "That's the part we're filming Monday."

I want to ask him questions about that, but then he starts taking off my pants and I can't think of much other than his hands. They're all over me, followed by his lips as he kisses and touches and loves, going lower and lower and—

"Oh god," I gasp, tossing everything aside to fist handfuls of his hair when his mouth finds its way between my thighs. He doesn't tease. He's not playing around. He gets right down to the nitty-gritty, almost aggressive about it.

I'm writhing, gasping, moaning his name, feeling the tension building, gripping hard as I try to pull him closer. He hits that spot, the one I desperately need, and I feel the sudden rush of pleasure.

Back arching, my breath catches as orgasm tears through me.

He doesn't stop until I relax against the bed, the sensation fading.

Sitting back, he pulls off his shirt, stripping. In a blink, he crawls between my legs, hiking my knees up, his lips crashing into mine as he pushes inside. I cry out into his mouth, his kisses swallowing the noise as he thrusts deep, hitting hard, over and over.

My hands are shaking, the earth around us quaking, as every inch of me is consumed by him. Our bodies are tangled and my heart is so mangled that it doesn't know how to beat the right way anymore, but some part of me must know *something,* because everything about this feels so perfect. Me and him, here, like this, and I don't want to admit it, but *ugh…*

Ugh…

Ugh…

I love him.

He moves, pulling back a bit to gaze down at me, as if the man is psychic and knows I just thought the words he's been trying to hear, but I can't say them, not yet, not until I know this isn't a fluke.

I'm in love with this reckless, starry-eyed fool who, in two days time, is going to walk out my front door, and all I can do is trust he'll come back with that same look of love in his eyes, because if he doesn't, it's going to break more hearts than just my own.

And if he breaks *hers,* I'll never forgive him.

✣ ✤ ✣

Sunday night.

The sun is going down outside.

Every second that ticks by makes my chest feel tighter, my shoulders heavier as the weight of the outside world comes down on me. Jonathan has to go soon.

He hasn't told her.

Maddie has no idea.

She sits at the kitchen table, surrounded by crayons, making a card for her Aunt Meghan—it's her birthday tomorrow. Swinging her legs, she hums to herself, oblivious at the moment.

"Mommy, how old is Aunt Meghan gonna be now?" she asks, as I stand at the sink washing dishes... scrubbing the same glass for the past ten minutes.

"Thirty," I say.

"Whoa," Maddie says before mumbling, "That's *a lot.*"

I turn, glaring at her for that. I'm not far off from thirty. I don't say anything, though, because my eyes catch sight of Jonathan as he steps into the kitchen, carrying his bag.

Maddie looks up, hearing his footsteps. Her legs stop swinging. She blinks at him with confusion before asking, "Are we going away?"

He doesn't answer right away. He freezes, so she looks at me, like she trusts that *I'll* tell her since he isn't.

"No, sweetheart, we're not going away," I say, wanting to shake some sense into him, because silence isn't going to help. "But your daddy is."

"Daddy is *what?*" she asks, and I know she already knows the answer, because she clutches her crayon so hard it snaps.

"Going to work," he says, finally chiming in. "I have to finish making the movie, so I have to go away for a little while."

"How much is a little while?" she asks. "'Till tomorrow?"

"Longer than that," he says.

"The one that's after that?" she asked. "Will you be back on that day?"

"Uh, no," he says. "It'll take about a month."

"A month?" She gasps, looking at me again when she asks, "How many days is that?"

"About thirty," I tell her.

I see it, the panic that flows through her. That's a lot of days for such a little girl. She frantically shakes her head, throwing her crayon down. "No, that's too many! I don't want you to do that!"

"I'm sorry," Jonathan says, but '*sorry*' isn't what she wants to hear, so it does nothing but upset her more.

Shoving out of her chair, getting to her feet, she shakes her head again as she rushes toward him, grabbing his bag. She yanks on it hard, trying to rip it out of his hand. "No, don't go! I want you to stay!"

"I know you do," he says, "I want to stay, too, but I have to be Breezeo, remember?"

"I don't care!" she says, digging in her heels, pulling the bag so hard that he loosens his hold, surrendering it. She almost falls, but he catches her. The bag drops to the floor, and she tries to kick it away. It doesn't move, so she shoves *him,* wanting to put distance between him and that bag. "You don't gotta be Breezeo! You can just be Daddy, and it'll be okay! It's gonna be Aunt Meghan's birthday, and you can walk me to school, and we have to do the lines together so I can practice, 'cuz I'm gonna be a snowflake! And how can I be a snowflake if you don't stay?"

Her voice cracks as tears fill her eyes. She's still shoving against him, trying to get him to move, but he's not budging.

She's getting furious.

Sighing, he bends down to her level, gently grasping her arms when she angrily tries to shove his face away from hers.

I want so much to intervene. I want to grab her, and hold her, and make it all go away, but I can't. So I just stand against the counter, trying to keep myself together, because me falling apart isn't going to help anyone right now.

"You can still be a snowflake," he says. "You're going to be the best snowflake ever."

"But how will you know?" she asks, the first tears starting to fall. "Will you still come see?"

"Of course," he says. "Wouldn't miss it for anything."

"You promise?"

I inhale sharply, but he doesn't miss a beat.

"I promise," he whispers, wiping her cheeks. "I'll be back for it. It's just that, right now, the movie needs me to be Breezeo."

"But I need you to be my daddy," she says.

"I'll still be your daddy, even when I'm Breezeo."

"No, you won't!" she yells. "You're gonna go away, and then

you won't be here no more, and it'll be just like before!"

"It won't be like before," he tells her.

"It will! You didn't wanna be my daddy then, and now you don't wanna *again*! You wanna go away and you're not gonna live here no more, 'cuz you have all your stuff and it's gonna be gone and you won't be here to tell Mommy she's pretty so now she can't never love you!"

Whoa. She blurts all that out in one frantic breath before shoving past him and running off, her bedroom door slamming.

A strangled silence sweeps through the room in her absence before Jonathan slowly stands and says, "I probably deserve that."

Frowning, I shove away from the counter, stopping him before he can go after her. "Let me talk to her."

I head to her bedroom, pausing outside to tap on the door.

"Who is it?" she yells.

Now she wants to know who's knocking before she answers. "It's Mommy."

"Mommy who?" she mumbles.

I laugh to myself, straightening my expression out before I open the door, saying, "The only *Mommy* you've got."

"Just one Mommy," she mutters, "and no Daddy now."

Strolling over, I sit down beside her on the edge of her bed. "Is that what you *really* think?"

She shrugs.

"Look, I know you don't want him to go away, because you're going to miss him, but you know how special Breezeo is. And I know it's not fair to you, and it really sucks, because you finally got to have him as your daddy and now he has to go, but you can write him, and call him, and draw him all the pictures you want."

She swings her legs, eyes on her feet. "It's not the same."

"I know, but he promised he'd be back," I say, standing up. "Do you want to come say bye to him? Maybe wish him luck?"

She shakes her head.

I leave her there, in her room, leaving the door open when I walk out. Jonathan lingers in the living room, holding his bag. He frowns when he sees me. I don't take that personally.

"Is she okay?" he asks.

"She'll be fine," I tell him. "Don't worry."

He glances at his watch, sighing. "I have to get going. The car's here to pick me up."

"Okay," I whisper as he leans over, kissing me. "Be safe. And smart. No drinking. No drugs. No more jumping in front of moving cars."

"You sure know how to take the fun out of things," he jokes. "I'll see you when I can."

He opens up the front door, to leave, making it barely a step over the threshold when Maddie's voice screeches through the apartment, loud and frantic. "Wait, Daddy! Wait! Don't go yet!"

He pauses, and she runs right by me, nearly plowing me over as she rushes toward him, clutching the notebook she draws in.

She shoves it at him, hitting him in the chest. "You forgot to have this."

He takes it. "What is it?"

"The fan-fictions I made for you," she says. "Remember? I fixed it. If you're gonna be Breezeo now, you should have it, 'cuz it's better."

He smiles. "Thank you."

She nods, and hesitates, the two of them awkwardly staring at each other, before she flings herself at him, hugging him. "I love you, Daddy. More than *all* the Breezeo movies ever."

"I love you, too," he says, hugging her back. "More than everything in the world."

TWENTY-SIX

JONATHAN

It's strange how much perspective can change in such a short amount of time.

I've wanted to be an actor for as long as I can remember, but somewhere along the way, I lost the spark. Between the cocaine binges and rocky relationships, between the stints at rehab and the paparazzi confrontations, between struggling with sobriety and facing notoriety, I forgot what it was I loved about it all.

And it's funny that an almost six-year-old could remind me in just shy of two months.

I laugh, sitting on the steps of the Hair & Makeup trailer on set. It's barely dawn, and everyone else is gathered in the caterer's tent for breakfast, while I sit here, reading through Madison's notebook. It's funny, this story she came up with. It's mostly pictures with just a few words and reads like a Scooby Doo crossover, a literal ghost mystery getting solved by Breezeo. Because he's invisible, she says that means he ought to be able to hang out with ghosts. It's common sense.

So at the end, Maryanne gets blown up in the warehouse.

BOOM.

It's a happy ending, though, in a twisted way, because now she, too, is a ghost, and they live happily ever after, invisible together.

The logic of a child.

"Well, well, well... if it isn't Johnny Cunning." Jazz's voice calls out as she approaches the trailer. "Talk about a sight for sore eyes."

I glance at her, grinning, as I close the notebook. "Jazz."

"Is that...?" She grabs her chest, feigning shock. "Is that a *smile* on your face?"

"Maybe," I say. "What, can't remember the last time you saw one of those?"

"Oh no, I remember," she says. "Five years ago, your very first day on the set of Breezeo. Only time I saw you genuinely smile was the first time you put on the suit."

I stare at her blankly. "Jesus, what did you do, write it on your calendar like an annual holiday?"

"*Johnny Cunning isn't always a dick* day. We used to celebrate it with a bottle of hard liquor but now we just sleep all day and avoid being around assholes."

"Sounds nice."

She smiles. "So what's got you grinning at six o'clock in the morning?"

I hold the notebook up. "Somebody wrote me a story."

"Somebody, eh?" She shoos me away from the trailer steps so she can go inside, motioning for me to join her. "And who would that somebody be?"

"My daughter."

"Your daughter," she repeats, not sounding surprised. She pats a chair in front of her big mirror, wordlessly telling me to sit down. Hair, first, so Jazz leans against a vanity to watch as one of the hairstylists gets to work.

"So it's true?" Jazz asks. "What *Hollywood Chronicles* said?"

"Doubtful," I tell her. "Most of what they print is bullshit."

They get to work, because well, they've got their work cut out for them this morning. I need a haircut as well as a shave, and that's just the tip of the iceberg of how I've let myself go since the accident.

Haven't been to a single acting class. Certainly haven't gone on any auditions.

Can't remember the last time I saw the inside of a gym, and I damn sure haven't been sticking to the diet. Hell, I haven't even spoken to my therapist.

"They said you met a girl at some prep school you went to," Jazz says. "The two of you ran away together, and you were some sneaky little criminal until Mr. Caldwell discovered you."

My brow furrows. "It said I was a criminal?"

"Well, in other words." She laughs. "Said you were stealing to survive, which is unbelievable, since your family is loaded. But it said you got your big break and the girl, she got pregnant, but she resented your fame and left you without telling you about the baby, so you're just now learning about your daughter."

There's so much wrong with what she just said that I'm not sure where to begin. My mind keeps going to the stealing—which, ironically, is the true part. But few people know that. I kept that secret tightly guarded out of fear that it proved I was the failure my father said I'd be. So who the fuck told *them*?

Jazz doesn't wait for an explanation. I never give her one. So she looks damn surprised when I say, "I knew about my daughter."

She raises her eyebrows. "Yeah?"

"Yeah," I say. "And she didn't resent the fame—she resented what fame turned me into."

She stares at me. "So, wait, you *knew* you had a daughter?"

"Yes."

"The whole time I've known you, you've been a father?"

"Yes."

WHACK.

I flinch when she picks up a hairbrush and smacks me with it. "Jesus, Jazz, what the fuck?"

"Why in the hell were you wasting your life away with all those sleazes when you had a family you could've been with?"

I just blink at her.

I have no good answer.

"Unbelievable," she says, shaking her head. "So, what's your daughter like?"

"She's smart. Creative. Funny. *Beautiful.* She's a lot like her mother, actually."

"Her mother, huh?" Jazz grins. "Hate to break it to you, but it sounds like you might be smitten."

"No *might* about it," I say. "I love her."

Jazz gasps. WHACK. She smacks me again. "Shut your mouth!"

I don't have a chance to respond before someone clears their throat, stepping into the trailer. I glance over, seeing Cliff. Jazz is suddenly on high alert, completely professional.

"Johnny," Cliff says. "I'm glad to see you. You weren't at the hotel this morning for pick up."

"Couldn't sleep. Figured I'd get to set early."

"That's good," he says, an edge to his voice that tells me he doesn't think it's good at all. Any break in habit is concerning. "Just tell me next time."

He lurks, lingering, taking a seat to do some work on his Blackberry, so Jazz doesn't bring anything up again, everyone just doing their jobs.

"Well, would you look at that," Jazz says after half an hour. "You look like Johnny Cunning again."

I stare at my reflection.

"Wasn't sure it would ever happen," Cliff says. "He was becoming unrecognizable."

People come in and out of the trailer, greeting me and welcoming me back, being overly friendly. I don't mind it. It's kind of nice, being back at it, especially once I put on the suit. The material feels tighter than usual, and wardrobe works hard to get it to look how it should. I stand there, surrounded by mirrors, and smile.

"Boy, if you keep making that face, it's liable to get stuck," Jazz says, spinning around in an office chair as she watches.

"Don't you have work to do?" I ask her. "Someone else to be fixing up?"

"Nope, just *you*, superstar."

At eight-thirty, I'm called to set. We're filming inside today, so I don't have to worry about the gathering crowd. Excitement stirs inside of me. I feel hopeful. On top of my fucking game. I'm ready to take on the world and conquer it... until the camera starts rolling.

It moves in a blur. We have a lot to cover. Jumping from scene to scene, from moment to moment, trying to get my head right and channel the emotions. I'm out of sorts, out of breath, completely exhausted by the time we wrap for the day.

"Get to the gym tonight," Cliff says, walking beside me on the way back to wardrobe to take the suit off. "Build up that stamina, or you're going to have the longest month of your life. It's not going to get any easier."

"I know," I mutter, heading into the trailer.

It takes another hour before I'm back in my clothes, ready to leave, but I can't because the director is requesting a meeting and a producer wants a quick word and my script needs altered after my schedule gets updated. The excitement is wearing off as the pressure mounts. I grab a muffin from the caterer before he can pack up, and endure a few dirty looks because I'm supposed to stay in tip-top shape and that doesn't leave room for shit like *carbs*.

Cliff, meanwhile, is talking to PR, and I want to have a word with them myself, but they leave before I can.

"You ever tell anyone how you discovered me?" I ask Cliff when we head for the car. "You ever talk about it?"

"No," he says. "Why would I?"

"I don't know. Maybe it just came up."

"What's this about?" he asks.

"*Chronicles* mentioned something about me being a thief."

He sighs loudly. "How many times do I have to tell you not to read that? You shouldn't even be *looking* at it. Stop worrying about them."

"I'm not worried," I say. "I just found it strange they knew."

"This industry springs more leaks than the Titanic. People like to talk. That's why I push for the confidentiality agreements—so *we* can control the narrative as much as possible."

"But not many people knew what I did back then," I say. "Me. You. My therapist."

"Your girlfriend," he says, not even looking up from his Blackberry.

"I never told her."

"Come on, you think she didn't figure it out?"

"Even if she did, she wouldn't have said anything," I say, "and my therapist *can't.*"

"Okay, then, they made a lucky guess," he says, that edge back to his voice again. "They've accused you of a lot. Throw a bunch of darts and something is bound to stick. But I don't know why you're stressing. You have *people* for this. Let the grown ups handle it."

Few things are more infuriating as a grown man than having someone tell me to let the *grown ups* handle things.

✡ ✣ ✡

"Did you fuck up?" Jack's voice sounds incredibly hopeful. "I bet you fucked it all up, didn't you?"

"Sorry to disappoint," I tell him, "but even when I suck, I'm damn good."

He snickers, not bothering to hold back. I realize how those words sound the moment I say them, and Jack being Jack isn't going to let it slide. "Is that how you keep landing these roles? Blowing your way straight to stardom?"

"Fuck off."

"You know, now that I think about it, you do talk about people *riding your ass* a lot."

I laugh at that one, strolling through the hotel lobby, wearing an old white t-shirt and sweats, looking like I ought to be in bed. Wish I could, frankly. I tried calling Kennedy but got no answer, so instead I called Jack and well, you know how it is.

"Yeah, yeah, laugh it up," I tell him. "At least I'm doing

something."

"I'll have you know I'm doing something as we speak."

"What? Whacking it to tentacle porn?"

"Christ, are you spying on me, man? How the hell did you know?"

"I figured it was either that or you were trolling dating sites using my picture."

"Ha-ha, you're the last person I'd use to pick up ladies," he says. "I'm not sure how you even get them, running around looking like *that*."

"Like what?"

"Sweatpants," he says. "Pretty sure that t-shirt has holes in it. And those Nikes are filthy."

Brow furrowed, I glance down at myself. "Are you spying on me?"

"Would I do that?"

"Yes." I look around the lobby, my gaze shifting outside the front doors, spotting him standing along the curb. He waves. "That's creepy as hell, Jack."

"Creepy is my middle name."

Hanging up, I slip my phone in the pocket of my sweats before strolling out of the hotel, meeting him on the sidewalk.

I haven't seen him in a while. We've only hung out in person a handful of times. Our lives are so different that the opportunity doesn't happen often.

"Am I going to have to get a restraining order?"

"Probably," he says. "I was in the neighborhood, knew you'd be here, so I thought maybe you'd want to do something."

"Well, I was on my way to the gym, but any excuse not to work out tonight is good with me," I say. "What do you have in mind? Video games? Fast food? I'm going to have to draw the line at prostitutes."

He grins. "Something much more exciting."

"What's more exciting than that?"

A meeting, it turns out. *You've gotta be fucking kidding.* Thirty minutes later, I'm sitting in a dim basement, listening to another alcoholic's sob story. They take turns sharing before the room goes quiet. An awkward silence. Those are a nightmare for an actor.

Fuck it.

I stand.

"My name's Jonathan and I'm an alcoholic."

They welcome me. Half of them probably *recognize* me, but I don't care. As many of these as I've been to, this is the first time I've spoken, always too worried about my damn image.

So I tell my story, not sugarcoating. I tell them how much of a fuck-up I was. My daughter went the first few years of her life without a father because I chose it all over her. The drugs. The alcohol. The movies. The red carpets and the parties and the people I didn't even *like*, but I humored them because they were famous.

The meeting ends a few minutes after I finish.

As we're leaving, Jack turns to me and says, "So, how about a drink?"

I laugh, shoving him. "I don't think I could've chosen a *worse* sponsor."

"Yeah, you suck at making decisions."

"I'm getting better, though."

"Are you?"

My phone starts ringing. I glance at it. *Kennedy.*

"I'm gonna prove it right now," I say, shaking the phone at him, "by choosing my family over a drink with your dumb ass."

We go our separate ways as I answer the call. "Hello?"

"Hey, you," Kennedy says, her voice quiet. "How was your day?"

"Long," I say. "Yours?"

"It was okay," she says. "Sorry I didn't answer when you called earlier. I wanted to, but Maddie insisted I didn't."

My stomach drops. "Is she still mad?"

"No." She sighs. "She heard Meghan say you should always play hard to get, because it'll make a guy want you more if he has to wait. So she said not to answer yet and then you'll love us even

392

more."

"Well, who can argue with that?"

"Right? Which means I can't talk long. I just wanted to see how you were doing."

"I appreciate it," I say. "I'm actually heading back to the hotel to get some sleep. Just got out of a meeting."

"A *meeting*-meeting or like... a meeting?"

"Whichever of those is for alcoholics."

"Ah, well, that's good." She pauses. "I'm gonna go before she catches me. Have a good night."

"Goodnight, baby."

I look up when I reach the hotel, pocketing the phone, my footsteps slowing when I see a handful of people lurking. They spot me, so I stop, signing some autographs and chatting, taking a few pictures before going inside.

Instinctively, I look around, always on alert. And for the second time in a week, I see a familiar face in the lobby bar.

This time, though, it's Cliff.

He's sitting alone at a small table with what looks like a glass of scotch. Never have I known Cliff to drink alcohol. I take a few steps that direction, curious, when a guy slips into the chair across from him and picks up the glass.

Something strikes me as familiar about him, but I've seen *a lot* of faces in my life, so it's not always easy to place them. I watch for a moment, the two men casually chatting, before the guy downs the rest of the scotch and stands up to leave.

He makes it halfway through the lobby before his eyes flicker my way. He looks surprised to see me, which is funny, because in that moment I remember where I saw him.

He followed me that morning when I walked Madison to school. He works for *Hollywood Chronicles*.

The guy turns away and keeps on going, which makes this whole thing even funnier, because I've never known any of them to pass up the chance to provoke me.

✿ ✿ ✿

"Hey, Daddy!"

Madison's grinning face takes up my whole phone screen. Guess the self-imposed *'make him wait'* strategy has been abandoned, considering she's FaceTiming me at seven-thirty in the morning.

"Good morning, beautiful," I say. "You getting ready for school?"

She nods, shaking the phone as she does. "I already got my clothes all on, and Mommy said we had some minutes, 'cuz I got my backpack ready early."

"So you decided to call?"

"Uh-huh, to remind you so you didn't forget."

"Forget what?"

"Me, *duh.*"

"You don't have to worry about that, but I'm glad you called. I miss you."

"Miss you," she says. "Guess what! Yesterday it was Aunt Meghan's birthday and Mommy got her cupcakes, but Aunt Meghan didn't eat none, 'cuz she says cake don't like her thighs, but I dunno why. So we can have them all, and I saved one for you, but Mommy says it won't be good in thirty days so I ate it."

"You ate it."

She nods. "For breakfast."

I laugh, because I have no idea what to even say to that. Her eyes narrow, like she doesn't know what I find so funny.

In the background, I hear Kennedy yelling, something about it being Tuesday.

"Uh-oh," Madison says, her face flashing with panic seconds before she drops the phone to the floor and runs off.

I stare at a view of the ceiling. "Madison? *Madison!* Pick the phone back up!"

There's a knock on my trailer door behind me. It opens

without invitation. Cliff steps inside, looking at me incredulously. I'm sitting here with my feet propped up, relaxing.

"Wardrobe's waiting," he says. "You should be in costume."

"Tell them I'll be there in a minute."

"You know, maybe if you hired a personal assistant…"

He finishes that sentence, saying something, but I don't pay attention, because Madison returns. "Sorry, Daddy. I forgot it was Tuesday and I had to get some Show & Tell."

"It's okay," I tell her. "What did you pick?"

"Guess!"

"Breezeo?"

"Nope!" She whips out her Maryanne doll to show me. "*Ta-da!*"

"Wow, something new, huh?"

"Yep," she says.

"What made you switch?"

"I didn't want Mommy to be sad, 'cuz you're gone, so she got to have my Breezeo for now. He's in her bed, taking a nap!"

"Wow," I say, trying not to laugh at the fact that she's sleeping with a tiny doll version of me in my absence. "That was nice of you."

Kennedy yells again in the background, asking Madison if she's seen her phone.

"*Uh-oh.* Gotta go!"

She hangs up.

I shake my head, realizing Kennedy probably doesn't even know she called me.

Getting up to go to wardrobe, I see Cliff still lurking.

He glances at his watch. "You're due on set in fifteen minutes."

Shit. I'm going to be late.

They're making a Breezeo movie.

You whisper this as you crawl into bed with the woman you love for the first time in weeks. It's the middle of the night. You just got home from New York. You've been back and forth all summer, deep into the fall. You were due back days ago, the first of October, but you kept delaying your return.

Your arms slide around her from behind as you pull her to you, her back against your chest. You smell like your cologne. Too often, you come home smelling like booze or perfume. She makes you shower every time it happens before you can even touch her.

"Are you serious?" she asks. "A Breezeo movie?"

You hum in response as you tug at her clothes, moving just enough fabric aside to make her feel good. She's only wearing her underwear and one of your t-shirts. She moans as you slide into her from behind. Your lips are on her neck. It takes no time at all before she's crying out in pleasure.

You move then, laying flat on your back as you pull her on top. Sighing, you grasp her hips and slide right back inside, closing your eyes. "You feel so good, baby. I just want to lay here and feel you. I'm so fucking exhausted right now."

"And you think I'm *not?*"

You open your eyes again when she says that. There's a bite to those words. She's not moving, staring down at you. It's dark in the bedroom, but not so dark that she can't see your clear blue eyes. You came home sober.

"I didn't say that."

"Didn't think about it, either, huh?"

There's that bite again.

"Come on, can we not fight right now?" you ask, and you even *sound* exhausted. There's not a shred of anger in your voice. "I just got home ten minutes ago. I haven't seen you in over a month. I... fuck, I just want to be inside of you right now. We can fight tomorrow if you want."

She makes a face at you but slowly starts moving. You close your eyes again, relaxing. It doesn't go on long before you pull her down to you, holding her as you thrust. You whisper in her ear, whispering how much you've missed her, how you haven't been able to sleep without her beside you.

After you finish, she just lays there, still on top. Your hands roam beneath the t-shirt, stroking her back. It's quiet. Used to be, the silence between you felt comfortable, but now it's like an invisible barrier that's difficult to get around.

"I took some meetings for it," you tell her. "For Breezeo. They haven't announced it yet. I'm not even supposed to talk about it. It's still too early."

"Wait, you're doing it?" She moves, rolling over to look at you. "*You?*"

"I don't know. I'm supposed to spend tomorrow going over it with Cliff. But that's why I didn't come home right away."

"That's... wow. You have to do it! Or you at least have to *try*. You'd be brilliant as Breezeo."

"Now you're pushing it. If I go for the movie, there's no way I'd ever get the lead. I can't carry a franchise."

"What? Of course you can! You'd be perfect, Jonathan. I'm

398

serious! I mean, come on, nobody knows Breezeo like I do, and I'm a billion percent sure that it has to be you. So you have to *try*, okay? For me? *Please?*"

"You just want to see me wearing the costume, don't you?"

"Well, I mean, I don't *not* want to..."

You laugh, kissing her. "I'll see if I can make that happen for you."

"You promise?"

You never promise things. She expects you'll laugh, but instead, you say, "I promise. I'll try."

For the first time in a while, she goes to sleep with a smile... and that's the last smile she ever gets.

Ugh, that's too dramatic. It's also not true. What I really mean is it's the last time she smiles *with you*.

Look, I'm doing this wrong again. I can't keep distancing myself from reality... but then again, what happens after that last smile doesn't feel real.

When I wake up in that bed a few hours later, I'm alone. For a moment, as I lay there, I think I dreamed it, but the smell of your cologne is all over. As I breathe it in, I wonder where you are. It's not even dawn yet and you're already gone.

I find out that afternoon. You were spotted in the wee hours of the morning across town, sitting alone in a theater, watching a rehearsal for the stage debut of Serena Markson.

When you finally make it home that night, well after dark, the first thing you do is kiss me. But you taste like whiskey and you smell like a whore, and my chest is caving in on me because of it, so I push you off. Both hands pressed against your chest, I shove you so hard you slam into the wall. You look at me, and I can't tell if you're shocked, or hurt, or even confused, because you look *numb*. Your eyes are a void.

'You're overreacting,' you say when I confront you. 'It's nothing.' But it's not 'nothing,' I know, because that was me once. Don't you remember? I know what it's like to be somebody's lone captive audience. And maybe it would've been okay had you told me, had you not come home drunk, covered in perfume, when I worked all goddamn day to ensure you still had a home to come to. In three years, the only thing your dream seems to have paid for is *coke*.

I'm yelling, and the tears start falling, and you keep whispering, "I'm sorry," over and over and over, and when I tell you 'sorry doesn't cut it, you say, "I love you, more than anything, baby."

And I believe you, because you're *good,* Jonathan.

Something toxic grew between us. I thought the drugs were your Kryptonite, Superman, but I'm beginning to think it might be me. Am I destroying your dream? Are you free-falling because you're being weighed down by me? If I weren't here, would you be soaring?

We scream, and I cry, and you get high, over and over as the weeks carry on, a perpetual cycle fueled by all this stress. The tiniest things start triggering me, and it's making me sick, so sick that I can't get out of bed some mornings. And I just want to talk to you, *really* talk, and not argue. I miss you. I miss *us.* So I ask about the Breezeo movie, trying to bring us back to common ground, back to where we both still exist, and you say, "It's not happening now."

"They're not making it?"

"Oh, they are," you say. "I'm just not auditioning."

Cliff talked you out of trying. I cry when you tell me that, and you lose your temper, telling me to 'grow up' because it's 'just a shitty comic,' not realizing I'm upset because you promised, when you never promise, which means I don't know how much I can trust your words anymore.

I think it was that moment that doomed us. It gets so ugly

400

that we don't speak for days. You sleep on the couch. The barrier of silence becomes an unclimbable mountain.

All I do is cry... cry... cry...

I'm at work when I realize what's happening. I confirm it that night, but you're already passed out on the couch. I'll let you sleep. I'll tell you in the morning. You'll be sober. We'll be all right. I stay up all night, not sure how to feel. When I hear you stirring in the morning, I hesitate. I'm scared.

I shouldn't ever be afraid to talk to you. What happened to us?

You're sitting on the couch, putting on your shoes to leave. I stand in the bedroom doorway and ask, "Can we talk for a minute?"

"I have things to do," you say, no affection in your voice. You sound like your father at that moment, but I'd never say those words to you.

"It's important. I have something to tell you."

You stand up, and you're stone-cold sober, your blue eyes so clear, and I think maybe it'll be okay, but then you stare me in the eyes and say, "Tell someone who fucking cares."

And then you walk out.

You walk out on me.

And then I collapse.

My legs won't hold me.

And you don't know this, but that woman you once loved? The one whose world you just shattered? She's pregnant. She's having your baby, Jonathan. And you don't even know. *You don't even care.*

TWENTY-SEVEN

KENNEDY

It's raining.

It doesn't rain a lot here, no more than average, but it always seems to want to rain at the worst moments. It's as if the sky has a direct line to my emotions. When things get all twisted up inside of me, the world starts cracking and the sky comes apart.

It was storming when I woke up this morning, but now, early evening, barely a trickle falls. The rain has slowed enough for Maddie to splash around in the mud puddles in my father's front yard, while I sit in a chair on the porch. My father is beside me, steadily rocking.

"You look lost again," he says. "Like you don't know whether you're coming or going."

I glance his way. "I'm getting a déjà vu vibe here, Dad."

"You and me both, kiddo," he says. "Seems like every few months we go through this. He shows up, and then he leaves, and you're left behind to grieve."

"It's different this time."

"Is it?"

"He's coming back."

"Didn't he always?"

"Yeah, but…"

"But it's different," he says. "Yet, it's not."

I sigh, exasperated, which only serves to make him laugh.

"He wanted us to go with him."

My father looks surprised. "So why are you sitting *here*?"

I blink at him. "Are you not the same man who went ballistic last time I left with him?"

"And are you not the same girl who didn't care what anybody thought, you were going?"

"I was only seventeen. I didn't know what I was doing."

"Which is why I went ballistic."

I turn away, looking at Maddie. She's covered in mud and smiling. She doesn't look lost at all. She looks like she knows exactly where she belongs.

I wish I had her resilience.

I wish Jonathan's words alone were enough to calm my fears.

He's been gone for two weeks.

We're halfway through the month already. Two more weeks and he's supposed to be done. They're in Europe now, and the time difference makes it difficult. The calls are sporadic, thirty-second voicemails telling Maddie goodnight or saying '*I love you*'. I wake up to texts, and by the time I answer, he's too busy to read them.

"I can't live my life on his terms," I say.

"And he can't live his life on yours," my father says. "That's why there's such a thing as compromise. Your mother and I, we rarely agreed on anything. It was a matter of give and take. You win some, you lose some, and you keep on playing."

Maddie runs over to us, shoving her hair from her face. She jumps up onto the porch, trailing mud behind her, and instantly, without a single second thought, she flings herself at me. I gasp. She's *drenched*, the hug getting me muddy.

Giggling, she runs off again, yelling, "Got you!"

"You little…" I jump up, and she squeals as I chase her back off of the porch. She expects me to stop there, but I run out into the yard. The ground's slick, and I slip, and… "*Ah!*"

My feet come out from under me, and I go down, but not before I get my hands on Maddie, taking her along. We both land flat in the grass, stunned, covered in mud.

My father laughs from the porch.

"Got you," I say, sitting up, poking Maddie in the side when she gets to her feet. She jumps on me, trying to tackle me, as my pocket vibrates. I'm confused until I hear the muffled ringing. "Oh, hold on, *truce*!"

I hold a hand up to stop Maddie as I grab my phone. She gives me barely five seconds to look at the screen before she tries to take me down, just enough time to see his name on FaceTime. *Jonathan.*

"Wait! It's your daddy!" I say, but I'm too late, because the girl slams into me so hard the phone goes flying, landing on the wet grass.

Maddie grabs the phone as it goes silent. Eyes wide, she shoves it at me. "Fix it, Mommy."

"Is it broken?" I ask, pressing buttons, grateful it still works. Opening FaceTime, I call him back. It rings and rings and rings and my heart sings when he picks up.

He's in a bed in a dim room, looking like he's half-asleep. His brow furrows. "What are you doing? Mud wrestling?"

"I, uh… yep."

He laughs, a sleepy kind of laugh.

The sound does things to my insides.

"Hey, Daddy!" Maddie says, jumping on my back, choking me as she wraps her arms around my neck. "Are you napping?"

"Something like that," he says. "Kind of sad I'm missing all the fun."

"Is Breezeo not being fun?" Maddie asks, snatching the phone from my hand to take over.

"It's a lot of work," he says. "Not nearly as much fun as you seem to be having."

"Don't worry, we can have fun when you come home," Maddie says. "We can play in the rain, and you and Mommy can wrestle!"

"Promise?"

"Yep."

"Good," he says. "Can you put your mom back on? I can't

talk long."

"Okay," she says, handing the phone to me, yelling, "Bye!"

She's off, running up onto the porch, as I look at Jonathan.

"I'd ask how you're doing," he says, "but I think the sight of you right now probably sums it up."

"What, I'm a mess?"

He laughs. "No comment."

"Yeah, well, you look…"

"Like shit? I feel it. Long days and we're still falling behind. I'm going to be cutting it close on making it back in time."

In time.

My gaze flickers to Maddie before I go back to Jonathan, who looks incredibly nervous. "How close?"

"Depends," he says. "When's the play *exactly*?"

"Three o'clock on the second of June."

He hesitates. "We wrap that morning in New Jersey."

My heart drops the whole way to my toes.

"I'll be there," he says. "Don't worry."

"Kind of hard *not* to worry."

"I'll make it. I promised her I would. I just wanted you to know, in case…"

"In case you didn't make it?"

"In case I had to break a few laws."

I laugh at that. "I'll forgive you."

He gazes at me, like he wants to say more but he isn't sure of the words.

"Are you okay?" I ask. "You seem *off*."

"I'm just tired," he says. "Days feel like months without you."

Those words, they resonate with a deep part of me, a part that feels so much older and so much colder than it ought to be. "I know the feeling."

"I'm in Paris right now," he says. "Three days ago, I was in Amsterdam. I've been all over the world, but the only place I really want to be is Bennett Landing."

"You hate Bennett Landing."

"It's where you are. Where Madison is."

"We'll be here," I say. "And we'll see you at three o'clock on the second of June."

"You will." He smiles. "I need to try to get some sleep. I'm due on set in a few hours."

"Okay," I say. "Sleep well."

"I love you," he says, pressing the button to end the call, the screen going black as the words sit on the tip of my tongue in response. *I love you.*

Today makes ten years since the night we ran away. Our tenth *Dream*iversary. He didn't mention it. I don't know if he remembers, but I'll never forget. By choosing him, I changed my entire world, and looking at my mud-covered little girl, I know I'll never regret a single moment.

✿ ✿ ✿

There are only a few blank pages left in the back of my old tattered notebook. After Maddie came to be, the narrative changed. It was no longer a story about a brazen boy with stars in his eyes and a lovesick girl with her heart on her sleeve, no more '*you*' and '*her*' to speak of. The plotline fractured. That boy and girl still existed in the world, and occasionally their stories intersected, but their worlds were just too different.

It became the story of a wandering man, one whose dream was killing him.

It became the story of a heartbroken woman, one who found her purpose.

Both stories continued to be documented, just not like before. One played out on the cover of tabloids, while the other was scribbled in baby books.

I always thought the first story was finished, the original one, and maybe it is. Maybe this is just an epilogue, or maybe it's a sequel.

I run my hand along the tattered notebook cover. Maddie's asleep, lying beside me on the couch. *Breezeo* is quietly playing on the TV screen, still on that endless loop.

There's a knock on the apartment door. I set aside the notebook. It's late, pushing ten o'clock at night. Glancing out the peephole, I see someone standing there—a guy, about my age, with shaggy blond hair, wearing jeans and a black *Call of Duty* t-shirt. He's holding something, looking nervous, mumbling to himself.

He knocks again, so I open the door a crack, just enough to greet him. "Can I help you?"

"Uh, yeah, I'm looking for Kennedy?"

"That's me."

His brow furrows. He looks me over. "*Seriously?*"

"Yes, seriously," I say. "And you are…?"

I'm about two seconds from slamming the door in his face, because he looks at me like there's no way *I* can be who he's looking for. I'm wearing pajamas, my hair in a messy bun, still damp from the long hot shower I took to wash off the mud.

He shakes his head. "I know your boyfriend—or, uh, whatever you wanna call the dude. My name's Jack."

"Jack," I say, and I know my expression must mirror his. "*Seriously?*"

"I'm guessing you've heard of me."

"He's mentioned you," I say. "The way he talked, I guess I didn't expect you to look so normal."

"He calls me a *troll*, doesn't he? That fucking undeserving jackass…"

I laugh, opening the door further. "So, what can I do for you, Jack?"

He holds something up—a gift box. "Just doing a favor for the asshole and dropping this off."

I take it from him, surprised. "This is from Jonathan?"

"Jonathan," he says with a laugh. "Never heard anyone call him that. But yeah, *Jonathan* asked me to get it to you, said it was important it be today. He would've mailed it, but he's busy making another shitty sequel... *my* words there, not his... and he didn't trust anyone else, so here I am."

"Wow, you came this whole way for him? Did he pay for your gas, at least?"

"Better than that—he *hired* me."

"Really?"

"Said he needed someone to *lighten his load* and keep people off of his ass. I told him I wasn't blowing anyone for him, but if he pays me enough, I've got no problem being his errand boy and yelling at him when he's supposed to be somewhere," he says. "And who am I kidding, for the obscene amount he offered me? I'd *probably* blow somebody."

A personal assistant. Wow. I have no idea how the two of them are going to work together, but I can tell already it's going to be interesting. "Well, thank you. I appreciate it."

He mock salutes me. "Sure thing. Have a good night."

"You, too," I say, closing the door as he leaves. I lock up again before opening the box to find a spiral notebook inside. It's simple, college-ruled, with a blue cover, a glittery blue gel pen on top of it. Couldn't have cost him more than a dollar. When I take it out of the box, a note slips from the front of the notebook, falling to the floor by my feet. I pick it up to read.

Ten years ago, you ran away with me so I could follow my dream.
It's time you follow yours. Wherever it takes you, I'll be there.
Happy Dreamiversary.
Jonathan

My eyes sting. *Ugh*, I'm crying. My vision blurs, and I blink away tears as I sit back down on the couch. I open the fresh notebook, staring at the blank lines for a moment before I start writing, glittery blue ink flowing across the page:

Rain fell from the overcast sky in sporadic bursts, quick manic showers followed by moments of nothingness. The weatherman on channel six had predicted a calm day, but the woman knew better. A tumultuous storm was rolling in. There was no way to avoid it.

TWENTY-EIGHT

JONATHAN

"Love abroad."

I pull my arm from across my tired eyes to glance at the door of my trailer, where Jazz stands, holding what I guarantee is the latest edition of *Hollywood Chronicles,* reading from it.

"I don't want to hear it," I mutter, covering my eyes again, trying to block out the world and steal a bit of peace, but that's asking for a miracle. I've got a two-hour lull in the middle of filming, our first day back on American soil, and I've got the worst case of jet lag. I feel hung-over, that groggy 'day after a coke binge' sensation where I hate the fucking world and everyone in it—myself included.

"There's nothing like the *City of Love* to rekindle a fire between former lovers," Jazz says, ignoring me as she continues to read. "Sources on the Paris set of *Breezeo: Ghosted* tell us things are heating up again between Johnny Cunning and Serena Markson."

If by 'heating up' they mean she makes me so fucking angry I could spit fire, they'd be right about that. Being around her has been intolerable.

"The pair have been spotted together a few times recently," Jazz says. "Rumor has it Serena has chosen to forgive Johnny for his indiscretions after he begged her for another chance."

Laughing dryly, I sit up. I'm not even going to entertain that bullshit with a response. "Jazz, no hard feelings, but can you just... fuck off?"

"Whatever you say, grouchy pants." She skims the article as

she says, "I wonder who their source on set could be."

"You know they make shit up, right?" I shove to my feet, staggering over to the small fridge to find something with caffeine in it. "Or someone else makes shit up and feeds it to them."

"Yeah, but *somebody* takes the pictures," she says. "They sure aren't made up."

Bottled water. Vitamin Water. Some kind of fancy juice. *No caffeine.* Sighing, I grab some antioxidant pomegranate something before turning to Jazz. "There are pictures?"

"Of course," she says, holding it up to show me—a full spread of set photos. "So much for a closed set. *The call is coming from inside the house.*"

She laughs at her own joke, but I don't find any of it funny... probably since it's *my* life they're trying to destroy. It could be any number of people, but those who work in production tend to value their jobs too much to risk them.

Besides, there's plenty of legitimate dirt they could sell me out with, not this manufactured relationship bullshit.

Opening the juice, I take a sip and gag, spitting it back out. "That's disgusting. Where's all the fucking caffeine?"

"Mr. Caldwell had it removed," she says, closing the tabloid. "Something about you getting your life together."

I sigh, tossing the juice in the trash before running my hands down my face. "I need a new manager."

Jazz laughs, but she's cut off when the trailer door pops open and Cliff walks in. Jazz excuses herself, making a speedy exit.

Cliff watches her run out the door and asks, "Something going on between the two of you?"

I drop down on the couch. "I have a girlfriend."

"Do you? Did you make it official?"

"Haven't talked about it. Not sure it matters. Love doesn't know titles."

He blinks at me. "Did you just quote *Breezeo*?"

I shrug.

"Anyway," he says, whipping out a piece of paper. "I need to

412

go through a few things with you since you have the time. Production wraps in two days, and we'll want to keep momentum going."

I scan the paper when he hands it to me. A tentative schedule he coordinated with my agent. Meetings. Auditions. Offers. Not to mention entire weeks blocked off by PR for promotion. I glance back at the top and shake my head when I see the date. "Can't do it."

June 2 @ 4pm

"Excuse me?" Cliff says.

"I can't do the first meeting."

"Why not?"

"My daughter's in a play."

"A *play*."

"Yes," I say. "I promised her I'd be there, so I'm leaving the second we wrap."

Cliff stares at me. "Any other conflicts we should know about? Maybe some PTO meetings we need to work around? Chaperoning field trips? *Disney on Ice*, maybe?"

His voice sounds so condescending that I want to throw him out of my fucking trailer, but seeing as I *have* a trailer thanks to his hard work, that's probably not a good idea.

"I'll keep you posted," I say, setting the paper down.

"I'd appreciate it," he says before walking out, shutting the door harder than usual.

Sighing, I drop my head down low and close my eyes, exhausted. *Exasperated.* I barely get a minute of peace before Jazz peeks her head in. "All clear?"

"Yeah," I mumble. "He's gone."

She steps into the trailer, holding out a can of Red Bull. "Brought you a present."

"I could kiss you for that," I say, grabbing it, popping the top and taking a drink.

"I'd rather you didn't," she says. "I've read all about the places those lips have been."

⯐ ⯐ ⯐

Despite filming across the border, in Jersey City, we still stay at the usual hotel in Midtown. I meet up with Jack once I get to the city, the car service dropping me off at his basement apartment.

"Nice place," I say when I step inside, glancing around. It's tiny, and dim, and reminds me of a cave. Posters wallpaper the place, and my eyes go straight to a Breezeo one. It's not me. Not even the movie. It's a poster of the *Ghosted* cover—same poster Kennedy had on the wall as a teenager. "Thought you weren't a Breezeo fan."

"Never said that," Jack says. "I said the movies were shit and you didn't deserve to be in them. There's a difference."

Shaking my head, I hand him the paper from Cliff. "Got a schedule for you."

He takes it as he plops down in a computer chair. "Do they leave you any time to *sleep*?"

"Occasionally," I say. "My manager's a bit of a hardass."

"Why do you put up with that?"

"Because he's good at what he does," I say. "And because I signed a contract agreeing to do whatever he tells me."

"How long is your contract for?"

"It renews every year."

"How do you *un*-renew it?"

"That's not even a real word."

"Oh, just answer the question, asshole."

"I send a certified letter saying I'm not renewing."

He nods, setting the paper aside. "I'll keep that in mind for when you start bitching to me that you haven't slept in six months."

"You do that," I say. "Thanks, Jack."

I leave, making the trek to the hotel a few blocks away, managing to avoid any crowds. Stepping into the lobby, a loud disruption catches my attention, coming from the bar. Serena sits there, surrounded by people, socializing. She has a drink in her hand, empty shot glasses on the bar in front of her, so there's no question it's alcohol.

Tomorrow, on set, she's going to be hell.

I turn away, knowing talking to her is a lost cause, when a flash catches my eye across the lobby. A man is snapping photos, a man I recognize—the one from *Hollywood Chronicles*.

"Hey!" I start toward him as he moves through the lobby to leave. "Hey, you! Hold up!"

The guy doesn't stop, going straight outside.

I catch up to him on the sidewalk out front, trying to get his attention, but he isn't paying attention. *Seriously?* The vultures circle me every damn day trying to get me to talk, but the one time I have something to say, the jackass runs?

I fist his shirt and yank him to a stop before shoving him against the side of the building, pinning him there. He looks stunned, raising an eyebrow. "That's *assault*."

"And what you're doing is harassment."

"I'm just doing my job," he says. "Not my problem you don't like that my job includes taking pictures of you glaring at your drunk wife surrounded by men."

"I told you I didn't have a wife."

"Yeah, well, that's not what your people tell me."

I start to say I don't care what people tell him, before it strikes me how he worded that. "*My* people? Where are you getting your information?"

"Sorry, buddy, but I'm taking that to the grave," he says. "I swore my secrecy on the dotted line a long time ago. No going back on that. My sources are confidential."

He doesn't realize it, but as he says that, he just confirmed what I've been suspecting for a while. *No PR is bad PR.* That's Cliff's motto. He invented Johnny Cunning that morning sitting in his office, a *character* I agreed to play, and I've been giving him the performance of a lifetime without even realizing every moment of my existence has been scripted.

"How's my little snowflake doing?"

"The best!" Madison says, her excited voice rattling the speakerphone. I tried to FaceTime her, but she refused, saying I couldn't see her costume until show time. "Are you on your way now to come home?"

"Not yet, but soon," I say, sitting in Jazz's chair in the Hair & Makeup trailer, getting ready for the last day of filming. "I have to finish my work first."

"But you'll be there?"

"I promised, didn't I?"

"But promise *again*."

"I promise I'll be there."

"Okay, Daddy!" she says. "Bye!"

"Wait, Madison, don't hang up! I want to—" CLICK "—talk to your mother."

Jazz laughs as I let out a sigh.

She hung up on me.

Opening my texts, I send a quick message to Kennedy.

Madison hung up before I could tell you I love you, so this is me, telling you I love you.

Does it really count as telling me if it's being texted?

I send her back the emoji of the little yellow guy shrugging.

Well, in that case, I love you, too.

I stare at my phone.

I read that message over and over.

My fucking heart is battering my ribcage as I text her back.

Do you really mean that?

Her response comes right away.

The emoji of the yellow lady shrugging.

I want to continue the conversation, but the mood is disrupted when the trailer door yanks open and Serena storms in with her scrambling assistant. Cliff is behind them, nobody looking happy this morning. Serena wasn't around for pickup, and there was no answer in her room, so Cliff stayed behind at the hotel to find her.

Serena drops down into a makeup chair nearby, big sunglasses shielding her eyes. The stench of alcohol clings to her, making my nose twitch.

"I am *so* not in the mood for this," she says. "I don't see why we can't delay it. It's *one* day."

"They don't have one day," Cliff says. "They delayed it already too much because of Johnny."

"Johnny, Johnny, Johnny," she grumbles, swinging the chair to face me. "It's always all about *Johnny*."

"Well, he *is* the star," Jazz says.

Serena scoffs, still looking at me. "Why don't you go ask them to postpone it until tomorrow? I bet they'll do it for you."

"Not happening."

"Figures," Serena mutters as she takes her sunglasses off and turns to gaze in the mirror, leaning closer to examine herself. Her eyes are bloodshot, her skin sweaty, sickly pale. "Nobody ever cares how *I* feel."

I know she's taking a swipe at me with that, but I let it slide.

I get up to leave when Jazz is finished with me, about to slip my phone away, when I catch a glimpse of the screen, seeing two new texts from Kennedy.

(I mean it)

(I love you)

I want to stand here forever, absorbing those words. I want to bask in them, soak them up, but I don't have time to dwell. After going through wardrobe, putting on the suit for possibly the last time, I head to my personal trailer to steal a few minutes alone, hearing muffled yelling coming from Hair & Makeup. Serena is flipping out about something, and Cliff's trying to calm her down.

Her assistant paces around outside, so frustrated she's crying.

Once I'm in my trailer, I call Jack. It rings, and rings, and rings, and I'm about to give up when he finally answers. "Holy shit, man, it's not even eight yet! What could you possibly need at this hour? *Bacon?*"

"I need you to come to the set."

"Where's the set?"

"Jersey."

"*New* Jersey?"

"That's the one."

"But I don't like New Jersey."

He's whining.

I give him the address and tell him to be here by noon before hanging up and setting my phone down on a table. I make my way out onto set at call time, but Serena is running late again.

She puts us thirty minutes behind.

It's a long morning—take after take, screw up after screw up. I'm getting frustrated, while Serena's close to having a breakdown. I think, as I watch her make a mess of it all, that this must've been what it was like to deal with *me* over the years.

"Cut!" the AD yells, and half a dozen people groan when he adds, "Let's take a ten minute break to clear our heads."

Right away, Serena stomps over to Cliff, the two of them having a heated exchange before he pulls her into her trailer. Jazz approaches me, making a motion, tapping her nostril like she's snorting something.

Jazz isn't far off the mark, because Serena has a hell of a lot more pep when she resurfaces.

"You're high," I tell her. Not a question now, because I *know*.

Instead of being angry, Serena grins, pressing her hand to my chest. "You want some?"

"Are you crazy?" I grab her wrist and pull her hand away. "You just overdosed last month."

"*Shut up*," she hisses, yanking from my grasp. "Nobody knows about that. Cliff promised—"

"That he'd keep it a secret? Maybe he will, but that's not the point. You need help, Ser. You need back in rehab."

418

She glares at me. "I told you I was fine. I can handle it."

"Need I remind you again that you overdosed?"

"That has nothing to do with the damn coke," she growls. "So, what, I swallowed a bunch of sleeping pills and took a nap. Get off my ass about it."

Whoa. What the fuck? "You did it on purpose?"

"I was tired," she says. "I'm over it. It'll never happen again."

We're called for the scene before I can respond. A few more takes, that's all we need, but I'm struggling to stay focused after what Serena told me, while she's bouncing off the goddamn walls. Over and over and over, we go through it, before we finally manage to get it finished.

That's a wrap.

I breathe a sigh of relief. Everyone around me cheers. I try to go after Serena, to talk to her, but Cliff gets in my way, saying, "Congratulations."

I eye him warily as Serena escapes to her trailer. "Thanks."

"You don't look happy," he says. "Going to miss the suit?"

I shrug. I think I actually might. I won't miss the stress of trying to stay sober while surrounded by temptation, night after night, but I'm going to miss putting on the suit, miss playing the character that changed my life.

"Just bittersweet," I tell him.

"I bet," he says, smacking me on the back. "But there are plenty more opportunities in your future, Johnny. Since you can't make today's four o'clock, the producer wants to see you in thirty minutes, so head over to wardrobe and meet us in your trailer." He starts to walk away, but hesitates. "Oh, by the way, security told me earlier that some guy showed up, claiming to be your assistant."

"Already? What time is it?"

"It's almost one o'clock," he says. "Are you telling me you actually *hired* someone?"

My heart drops.

I shove past Cliff, ignoring him as he calls for me, wanting his question answered. I head straight for security, spotting Jack

419

standing along the side with a guard, looking somewhere between disturbed and amused.

"Strangest shit I've ever witnessed in Jersey," Jack says, looking me over. "And that's saying something, because I once saw a chimpanzee roller skating, and that was weird as *fuck*."

"I'm going to take that as a compliment, even though I know it isn't one," I say, grabbing his arm and making him follow me. It's about a two-and-a-half hour drive to Bennett Landing, but I barely have two hours. "Please tell me you drove."

Before he can respond, I hear Cliff shouting as he follows. "Johnny! Where are you going?"

"Oh, buddy." Jack glances behind us at Cliff. "Am I your *getaway driver?*"

"Something like that," I say. "You ever play *Grand Theft Auto?*"

"Every fucking day, man."

"Good," I say, continuing to walk, despite Cliff attempting to catch up. "If you can get me where I need to be, there will be one hell of a reward in it for you."

His eyes light up as he pulls out a set of car keys. "Mission accepted."

There's a crowd gathered around set. They figured out we're here. They know we're wrapping today. I scan the area, looking for a way around them.

"Where'd you park?" I ask, hoping it's anywhere but right across the street.

"Right across the street," he says.

Fuck.

I'm going to have to go through the crowd.

"You sure you, uh, don't want to change?" Jack asks, his eyes flickering to me, conflicted.

"No time for that."

The crowd spots me, and they start going crazy, making Cliff yell louder to get my attention, but I don't stop. I slip off of set, past the metal barricades and right into the street, as security tries to keep the crowd back, but it's a losing game. So we run, and I follow Jack to an old station wagon, the tan paint faded.

"*This* is what you drive?"

"Not all of us grew up with trust funds," he says, slapping his hand against the rusted hood. "This was my inheritance."

"Not judging," I say, pausing beside it. "It's just all very '70s suburban housewife."

"That sounds like judgment, asshole."

I open the passenger door to get in the car when Cliff catches up, slightly out of breath from running. "What are you doing, Johnny? You're *leaving*?"

"I told you I had somewhere to be."

"This is ridiculous," he says, anger edging his voice. "You need to sort out your priorities."

"That's a damn good idea," I say. "Consider this my notice."

"Your *notice*?"

"I'm taking a break," I say. "From you. From this. From *all* of it."

"You're making a big mistake."

"You think so?" I ask, looking him right in the face. "Because *I* think the mistake I made was trusting you."

I get in the car, slamming the door, leaving Cliff standing on the sidewalk, fuming.

Jack starts the engine, cutting his eyes at me. "So, where to? The unemployment office?"

"Home," I say, "and I need to get there as soon as possible, because somebody is waiting for me, and I can't disappoint her."

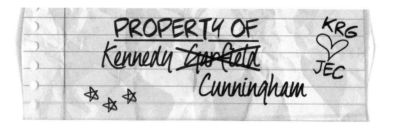

PROPERTY OF
Kennedy ~~Garfield~~
Cunningham

KRG
♡
JEC

✮ ✮ ✮

The only clock in the small one-bedroom apartment glows blue from the old microwave on the kitchen counter. The numbers are fuzzy, and it often loses time, a few minutes every now and then, like it sometimes forgets to keep counting.

It reads 6:07 PM when I leave. (Yes, *me*. This part of the story is all mine. There's no denying it.) I'm not sure what time it really is, but around twelve hours have passed since you spoke those bitter words. It took half a day for me to gather the courage to walk out, knowing once I did, I wouldn't be back. I spent most of those hours staring at the door, waiting for it to open, for you to walk back in, for you to tell me you didn't mean it.

I tear a piece of paper from the back of my notebook and stare at the blank lines, lines that were meant to hold so much more of our story.

Goodbye.

That's all I write. There are a million things I *want* to write, but I keep those words locked up tight. I leave the note on the kitchen counter, beside that microwave. I take only a few things, shoving some clothes and mementos in my backpack, before I go to the train station. I need time to think.

Three days later, I arrive in New York, no longer the lovesick seventeen-year-old girl that ran away with a boy all those years ago. I'm a heartbroken twenty-one-year-old woman now, one that doesn't know where to call *home*.

The taxi drops me off along the curb in front of the two-story white house in Bennett Landing. I pay the driver every last penny in my pocket. I'm queasy, and exhausted, and I want to cry but the tears won't fall.

Snow is falling, though. The world outside feels icy cold. My jacket is thin, and I'm shivering. The sun was still shining back in California.

As the taxi pulls away, the front door of the house opens. My father steps out onto the porch and stands there in silence. He's not surprised. He knew I was coming.

"Kennedy? Is that you?" My mother bursts out of the house and hugs me. "I can't believe you're here!"

Her excitement makes me lightheaded. Haze coats my vision.

She drags me into the house, straight past my father, who still says nothing, yet his eyes say enough. My mother wants to chat. I just want to stop feeling like I'm about to pass out. "Can I lay down somewhere?"

"Of course, sweetheart," she says. "You know where your room is."

My room is just how I left it, except the bed is freshly made. They expected me, and not just on some 'you'll come crawling back someday' level. Someone warned them.

I get under the covers, pulling them over my head, trying to find some warmth again. I don't want to think about who that 'someone' must be.

Another three days pass. I don't move unless I have to. I'm sick, and I'm weak, and my mother keeps checking up on me, bringing bottles of water and forcing me to eat crackers and smoothing my hair and telling me it'll be okay, doing all those things a mother does for her child. And I love her, and I know she does it because she loves me,

424

but I want to scream at her, because how is it possible to love someone so *unconditionally*? How can she look at me and smile and be so happy that I'm here, that I *exist*, when she has every reason in the world to be angry for the trouble I've caused? All the sleepless nights she endured, all the stress and worry…

"How far along are you?" she asks that third night when she finds me curled up on the bathroom floor. Her voice is gentle as she sits down beside me.

I just look at her.

She smiles softly. "A mother knows."

"I'm not sure."

"Do you want to talk about it?"

I open my mouth to say no, because talking is the last thing I want to do. But the denial dies on my lips and comes out as a sob, and once it starts, I can't stop. She pulls me to her, and I lay my head in her lap as I cry. And words spill out of me along with the tears, all the struggling and fighting, the lies and the broken promises, the resentment that grew when he got swept up in the hurricane and left me behind to battle the storm.

"He's been calling here," she says. "Drunk. Your father answered the first call. He wanted to know if we'd heard from you. Said he came home and you were gone, so he thought you might come here. And he kept calling back, but your father didn't answer again until tonight… when he told him if he knew what was good for him, he'd stop."

"I'm sorry," I whisper.

"You have nothing to apologize for," she says. "I know what it feels like. Your dad's the greatest man I know, but he was a terrible drunk. It changes people, and that doesn't excuse anything, but it means there's hope. They can get better, but *you* can't change them.

They have to want to change."

"He doesn't want to."

"Maybe not," she says. "Or maybe not yet. It took your dad a while. But no matter what *he* did, I knew I had to look out for myself... and for my kid. And I have no doubt you'll do the same, because you're my daughter."

I feel better hearing that. Not completely, of course, because life is scary and my heart is still broken and the boy I fell in love with is gone, but enough to pick myself up and keep going.

Days pass. A week. *A month.*

A new year comes.

I gather the courage to see a doctor. I'm still in the first trimester. My father and I haven't spoken much, but he knows I'm pregnant. He calls it the '*lovesickness*'.

More days.

I get a job at the grocery store, and I *hate* it, but they give me a lot of hours, and I need money.

More weeks.

I'm starting to show. I stare at myself in the mirror, rubbing my stomach, feeling the bump. It's weird. There's a life growing inside of me right now.

The doctor tells me it's a girl.

You have a daughter, Jonathan, and you don't even know. I feel the fluttering as she moves around, and my heart is soaring. I'm still scared, *so scared,* but when I feel her, this overwhelming sense of love flows through me, and I smile.

I'm smiling again.

It's like I've finally figured out the point of it all, the purpose of our story—it's *her.*

More months.

426

The world is thawing. Spring comes.

I'm six months along and sitting on the porch, in one of the rocking chairs, bundled up to ward off the chill, when you pop up. The black town car slowly pulls up to the curb in front of the house, and *there you are.* My mother has to stop my father from storming out of the house.

You look like yourself from afar, but as you approach, I see the eyes are all wrong. It's early, the sun barely in the sky, and you're still awake from last night. You linger somewhere in the gray area between drunk and hung-over, coherent enough to stand up straight but by no means are you *sober.*

Still as handsome as ever, though. You're wearing a suit and your tie is tugged loose, a glimmer of a teenage rebel I remember.

"Can we talk for a minute?" you ask, stopping near the porch, and I almost laugh at your choice of words, because that's what I asked, too.

I say nothing, staring at you.

"I'm sorry," you say, your voice cracking. "I'm *so* sorry, baby."

Something you'll never know is at that very moment, as you say those words, I forgive you. I don't even know what you're sorry for, but I forgive you for all of it. I don't tell you that, though, because I don't do it for you.

It's for *her.*

I still stare.

You talk some more, going on and on about how wrong you were and how much you miss me and how you haven't had a decent night's sleep, how hard it is not having me to come home to, and all I can think about as I listen to your words is how much growing up you have to do, Jonathan, because every sentence from your lips contains '*I*' or '*My*' or '*Me*', but you can't be the center of the universe anymore.

427

Not *this* universe.

"So it's true?" you ask. "You're pregnant?"

I avert my gaze and nod, because you deserve to know, but I can't find the words I need to tell you anymore.

"I can tell," you say. "You're glowing. You're so beautiful."

I look back at you when you say that.

"Come back to me," you say. "I need another chance, just one more. We can't let it end this way. We're having a baby, and I don't even know... is it a boy? A girl? When are you due? I don't know anything, but I want to. So come with me. *Please.* I'm making money now, and I can take care of you."

If anyone's actually reading this, and I don't know if anyone ever will, this is the moment where I'll lose them, where they'll rant about that *stupid character* messing up the story. And I get it, because so much of me yearns for you to be my happy ending, but I can't apologize for doing what's right.

I shove out of the rocking chair and step off of the porch. Your gaze goes right to my stomach, as do your hands. I don't stop you, though my chest feels like it's caving in. Your eyes are lighting up, and I know—*god, I know*—you'll make a great father, one of the greatest, and you'll love this little girl with every part of your soul.

But that can't happen until you're ready.

"I love you," I whisper, three words you haven't said, as I put my hand on top of yours on my stomach. "More than everything... *except for her.*"

You meet my gaze. "It's a girl?"

I nod, and hesitate, before I kiss you, lingering, letting you have this moment, and if I'm being honest, it's just as much for me.

I need this moment to gather my courage.

And when I do, I pull back and say, "I need you to leave."

You look at me, stunned.

"I need you to go and not come back until you get better," I say. "I'm asking you... no, I'm *begging* you... don't come back here like this again. She's going to need a father, a real one, someone who can love her more than *everything*. There's no place here for an addict. So, please... *leave*, Jonathan."

I go inside, because I can't stand there and look at him, shoving past my father. I sit on the couch. I sit and sit and sit. My father still hangs out *right there*, watching. And an hour later, he says, "He finally left."

It took you an hour.

After you're gone, my mom says, "I'm proud of you. I know that must've been tough."

"I'm surprised the son of a bitch respected her wishes," my dad says. "He never respected mine when I told him to stay away from my daughter."

"Michael," my mom warns. "Now's not the time."

He holds his hands up.

"I'm not surprised he listened," she continues. "He's a good guy."

My dad lets out a loud laugh.

"He is," my mom says. "He's just an addict, and your daughter was his first high. That boy would've run right into traffic if she said she needed him to."

My dad looks at me. "I'll pay you fifty bucks to do it."

"*Michael!*"

"Geez, okay, don't bite my head off, woman," he says, squeezing my shoulder as he says, "I'll throw in some free babysitting, too."

My mom laughs. "You'll be babysitting for free as it is, *Gramps*."

He makes a face, mumbling, "Gonna need a better nickname."

Before my dad can walk away, I ask, "What made you get

429

better?"

He sighs. "You did, kiddo."

"Me?"

"I ruined your birthday," he says. "*Forgot* it was your birthday. Came home wasted, ate your cake before you could, passed out on the couch and pissed myself. Your mother snapped and tried to kill me for it."

"I didn't *try,*" my mom says. "What your father is leaving out is that I kicked him out that morning, but he didn't respect my wishes to stay gone."

"In my defense, I got drunk and forgot I wasn't supposed to be there."

"How is that a *defense?*"

"Guess it's not."

"Anyway, I threatened him so he wouldn't *forget* again."

"I woke up to you pouring liquor on me," he says. "Then you pulled out matches and threatened to light my ass up!"

"Exactly," she says. "I threatened."

I vaguely remember the cake thing, but I don't remember *that.* "So mom scared you sober?"

"Oh, no, as scary as she can be, that wasn't it," he says. "After she put down the matches, I apologized to you. I told you I was sorry, and you said..."

He trails off, so my mom chimes in. "You told him you didn't care about his *sorry* because he wasn't your dad anymore, you decided you didn't want a dad because all they ever did was stuff to be sorry for, so he could go."

"You were only five," he says. "You weren't mad. You were just done."

"*That* did it? But almost being set on fire didn't?"

"Your mother tried to kill me because she loved me and wanted her husband back," he says, ignoring her when she again says she didn't *try*. "You decided you didn't want me anymore. I was like a broken toy that you never liked, so you were okay with your mother tossing it out. I loved you, but I'd never given you a reason to love me. I had to make a change."

"Which Jonathan will do, too," my mom says.

"We'll see," my dad says. "But hey, if he doesn't we never have to see him again, so win-win?"

"I swear, Michael, I should've just struck that match."

They're both joking. It's nice, seeing them happy, knowing they survived everything thrown at them. I can't imagine a life where we aren't a family.

I rub my stomach, feeling those soft nudges as the baby moves around.

Six months turns to seven and then comes eight. I work, eat, and sleep. Wash, rinse, and repeat. Before I know it, summer is upon us. I'm nine months pregnant, those soft nudges full-blown roundhouse kicks.

My water breaks the morning of my due date, right on time, but it still feels too early for me. I'm nowhere near ready. I've got a crib and diapers and all the things she'll need, but I've yet to figure out how to be a mom.

And I'm terrified. I've never been so scared in my life. My mother's beside me, and my father's in the waiting room, and your sister shows up, because she's excited to be an aunt, but you're not here, and I knew you wouldn't be. I told myself that every day. But as the pain tears me apart, and people are yelling at me to *push, push, push*, there's nobody in the world I need more.

I can't do it without you.

431

I can't.

I can't.

I can't.

But then *she's* here, and she's screaming, and I'm crying, and the second they hand her to me, the world tilts again. And that's it. I know for an absolute fact that I will love this beautiful little being for the rest of my life. Until my dying breath, I'll fight to keep her happy, to protect her heart from breaking, because she's the greatest creation that's ever existed, and *we* made her.

She's born at 6:07 in the evening. *Exactly.* Born on the fourth of July. They tell me you came to the hospital the next morning, as the sun was still rising outside. Our little one was in the nursery, and I was sleeping while I had the chance. You went straight to see her, staring through the glass as she slept.

You asked about signing her birth certificate, about putting yourself down as the father, but they told you to go through me. So you came to my room—or so they *tell* me, because I never saw you. The door was open, and you stood in the doorway for a long while, watching me sleep, before you walked away.

You left without holding your daughter.

You left before finding out her name.

So you don't know this, but that girl? That beautiful little one wrapped in pink in the nursery? Her name is *Madison Jacqueline Garfield,* and someday, you're going to know her. Someday, she's going to call you her *daddy.* And when that happens, she's going to steal your heart, and you'll get that chance you asked for. But you need to be ready, Jonathan, because she's here, and she's waiting. Don't make her wait too long before finding your way home.

TWENTY-NINE

KENNEDY

I glance at my watch for the tenth time in the past five minutes, letting out a deep sigh as I shift around in my chair. In three short minutes, it'll be three o'clock.

"He's not coming," Meghan says.

She's sitting to the right of me, an empty seat between us, reserved for a notably absent Jonathan. I've called him a dozen times in the past half hour, but all I get is his generic voicemail. *The person you're calling isn't available.*

I've left a few messages, telling him he better hurry, but I've heard nothing.

"He'll be here," I say. "He promised."

"He *better* come," my father says from his seat to my left. "If the boy knows what's good for him."

There's a scoff from behind me, a familiar voice muttering, "If we're counting on Cunningham using his brain, we're probably going to be disappointed."

I turn around, seeing Mrs. McKleski sitting there, knitting... yes, she's *knitting*. I'm not even sure why she's here. It's an afterschool kindergarten presentation. My gaze scans the small auditorium, surprised by how many people have come to see a handful of little kids do a play about the weather.

Glancing back at Mrs. McKleski, I ask, "What are you doing here?"

"Your father invited me," she says.

I look at my father, who shrugs. "It's my granddaughter's big day. I wanted people to know about it."

"How many people did you invite?"

"Half the town," Mrs. McKleski answers for him.

Shaking my head, I look at the time. *2:59.*

I call Jonathan again. Voicemail.

The teacher comes out along the edge of the stage, in front of the big curtain, the moment the time changes, hitting three o'clock.

Sighing, I hang up without leaving a message, putting my phone away. There's nothing more I can do. I hear the kids moving around behind the curtain, getting into place, and all I can think about is how crushed Maddie's about to be when she realizes he hasn't shown up yet.

The curtain opens, the play starting.

Maddie stands along the back of the stage, wearing her costume—white from head-to-toe, with a fluffy tutu and cutout cardboard snowflakes strapped to her back like wings.

She smiles excitedly, waving at us, but it doesn't take long before she notices the glaringly vacant seat. My father is recording it, and I should tell him to stop, because I'm not sure her first broken heart is something any of us will want to relive, but I can't get those words to form. I can't bring myself to say it.

Can't bring myself to believe it.

Despite everything, I still believe in *him.*

Maddie stands there, no longer smiling, her gaze scanning every face in the auditorium. She's anxious, and every time she looks my way, I see her grow a little sadder. One-by-one, kids step forward to deliver lines. When it's Maddie's turn, she doesn't move.

There's an awkward silence.

The teacher nudges Maddie, whispering something to her. Maddie takes a few steps forward, frowning. Another long pause.

She looks at me.

I want to rip her off the stage and hug her, make this all go away, but instead, I give her a smile, hoping maybe it'll help her.

She smiles back.

Just as she's about to speak, her mouth opening, there's a loud noise at the back of the auditorium, the door bursting open. Maddie looks, her eyes growing wide as she screeches, "Daddy!"

Murmurs flow through the auditorium. People shift around in their seats. Maddie runs right off the stage, heading down the center aisle as fast as her legs can carry her.

I turn, more than a little alarmed that she's running away, and freeze when I see him. *Oh my god.*

Jonathan stands there, head-to-toe in full *Breezeo* costume. He takes a few steps forward, scooping Maddie up. She hugs him, as he carries her back down the aisle, ignoring the looks everyone is casting him. Confusion. Shock. Disbelief. There's some laughter, some excitement, even a bit of annoyance at the interruption. Me? I'm trying not to cry at the moment.

Jonathan deposits Maddie back on the stage before his gaze finds mine. He slips into the chair beside me, whispering, "Sorry I'm late."

"Hey, guys!" Maddie announces, jumping right into her line. "What's got six arms and is like nothing else in the whole world?"

A chorus of kids behind her say, "A snowflake!"

"That's me!" Maddie says. "I'm falling and falling and falling. Where am I going?"

"Down to the ground," the kids say.

She steps away, taking her place in the back, the play continuing like the disruption hadn't happened. Maddie no longer pays attention to the play, staring at her father, fidgeting, grinning, like she's just waiting for it to be over.

The teacher nudges her. She has to give the last line of the play. Maddie steps forward, and I see it as she blanks. She forgot her line. A second passes, and then another, before she shrugs.

"I gots a line here but I dunno," she says. "So I'm improvising like my daddy says."

People around us laugh.

Jonathan shakes his head.

The kids are supposed to line up and bow as the crowd

cheers, but they have to do it without Maddie, because she's running off the stage again. Jonathan stands up, catching her as she jumps off the side, not even bothering to use the steps this time.

My father stops recording then, shaking his head. "Never a dull moment with that kid."

"I knew you'd come, Daddy!" Maddie says when he sets her on her feet. "Did I do good acting?"

"The best," he says. "I'm sorry I missed the beginning."

"It's okay." She shrugs. "You didn't need to see them other people, anyway."

The play officially comes to an end as kids stream off of the stage, meeting their families out in the audience. It's chaos then, unsurprisingly, as people swarm Jonathan.

My father takes Maddie's hand, pulling her away from the center of it. "You did great, kiddo. I'm proud of you."

"Did you record it?" she asks.

"Of course!"

"Can I watch?" she asks, jumping around. "I wanna see!"

He hands his phone to her, so she can see the video, as he steers her toward the exit. Meghan and I are right behind. Jonathan lingers for a moment longer before following, signing a few autographs along the way, before breaking from the crowd once we're outside.

"Cunningham," my father says. "Glad to see you."

"You, too, sir," he says. "Glad to be here."

It's all so cordial. It's so much not *them*.

But I have to wonder, as they shake hands and my father bids us goodbye before leaving, if maybe I'm wrong about that. Maybe it's them *now*, the doting grandfather and the dad that's trying to be better, no longer adversaries in a political-turned-personal nightmare.

Their stories changed, too.

We head to the parking lot. Parked in front of the blue Porsche, not even in a proper spot, is a raggedy old station wagon, a familiar guy sitting on the hood. *Jack*.

"Did you make it?" Jack asks, munching on a small bag of potato chips.

"Just in time," Jonathan says, smoothing Maddie's hair. "She was about to deliver her lines when I ran in."

"Good deal," Jack says, eyeing Maddie. "So you're the kid, huh? Heard a lot about you."

"Who are you?" she asks, eyeing him back.

"Name's Jack," he says, holding his bag of chips out to her, offering one. "Chip?"

She stares at the bag for a second before glancing at Jonathan and whisper-shouting, "Is he a stranger? 'Cuz then you gotta eat one in case it's poison."

"They're safe," Jonathan says. "Jack's a friend."

Maddie grabs a chip, smiling at him. "Are you best friends?"

Jack makes a face in protest. "I wouldn't go *that* far."

"Excuse me, I'm sorry," Meghan interjects, motioning to her brother. "I hate to break up whatever this is, but why the hell are you wearing *that*? It's weirding me out. Like... it's *weird*."

Jack looks at her in awe, like he's just now noticing her presence. He holds his bag out toward her. "Chip?"

Meghan looks at him, scowling, and I think she might be about to hurt his feelings, but instead she reaches her hand in, plucking out a single chip and popping it in her mouth.

"We wrapped late," Jonathan explains. "Didn't have any time to go to wardrobe. Hell, I didn't even grab my phone from my trailer."

"So that's why you didn't answer when I called," I say. "Thought you were avoiding me."

Jonathan puts his arm around me, pulling me to him. He presses a kiss to the top of my head, whispering, "Never."

"He literally ran off set," Jack says with a laugh. "Weirdest shit I've ever seen, dude wearing tight ass spandex being chased by an angry man in a suit. It was so ridiculous, like a scene ripped straight from one of the stupid Breezeo movies."

"Hey!" Maddie says, narrowing her eyes at him. "Don't say

that! Breezeo's not stupid!"

"You tell him," Jonathan says, nudging her.

"My bad," Jack says, holding out the bag again, like a peace offering. "More chips?"

Maddie doesn't hesitate, snatching an entire handful out, so many that some fall to the ground. Jack looks at her with shock before glancing in the bag, holding it upside down. *Empty.*

"You don't deserve none," she tells him. "*Only* if you like Breezeo can you have some."

"Ah, that's foul," he says. "Does it count that I love the comic books?"

She considers that before handing him a single, broken chip.

He eats it, as Meghan stares at him, a peculiar look on her face. "So, Jack, how is it you know my brother? You weren't, like, his coke dealer, were you?"

Jack's eyes widen as he looks at her. "Your *brother*?"

"That's my Aunt Meghan," Maddie tells him, finishing the rest the chips.

"Meghan Cunningham," Meghan says, holding her hand out as she introduces herself. "My brother doesn't claim our family, so I'm not surprised he hasn't mentioned me."

Jack takes her hand. "Oh, he's mentioned you. He just failed to tell me you were so goddamn beautiful."

Meghan blinks at him, surprised, her cheeks turning pink when he kisses the back of her hand. Oh my god, she's *blushing.*

"Well, uh, thank you," she says, pulling her hand away.

"And I wasn't his dealer," Jack says. "Although, whoever was is probably filthy rich by now, so I sort of *wish* I was. But no, I help keep the jackass sober, which really is a thankless job."

"I thank you all the time," Jonathan says.

Jack waves him off. "Whatever, dude."

"So, you're a sober coach," Meghan says.

"More like an intern," he tells her. "I don't get paid for it. Should, though. I mean, have you ever had to *deal* with the guy?"

Jonathan laughs. "You know I'm right here, right?"

438

"Impossible not to see you," Jack says. "What, with you dressed like it's Comic-Con."

Meghan laughs, like she finds that hilarious. "Well, this has been a blast, but I should get going. Maddie, my cinnamon-strudel banana-bread, you were brilliant. Thanks for inviting me. I'll see you guys later." She turns, looking at Jack. "It was a pleasure. Hopefully, I'll see you around."

"You can count on it," Jack says as she starts to walk away. He watches for a moment before turning to Jonathan, raising an eyebrow as he nods toward Meghan. "Might *that* be my reward?"

"Don't even think about it," Jonathan says.

"Not gonna think about it," Jack says, hopping off the hood of the car. "I'm just gonna go for it."

"Good luck," I say, while Jonathan grumbles, glaring at Jack as he jogs to catch up to Meghan.

"What's he doing?" Maddie asks, glancing at me.

"I think he's going to ask your Aunt Meghan out."

Her eyes widen. "Like on a date?"

"Yep," I say.

"Oh, tell her she's pretty!" Maddie yells, jumping around. "And bring flowers! Right, Daddy?"

"Right," Jonathan says, although he doesn't look as excited about the idea as Maddie does.

"Why don't we leave them to it and head home?" I suggest.

"Home," Jonathan says. "Sounds nice."

✿ ✿ ✿

The fresh blue notebook lays on the coffee table, the gel pen on top of it, the ink almost depleted because I've used it so much.

Jonathan pauses in front of it in the living room. "I see you got my gift."

"Of course," I say, slipping my arms around him from behind, resting my head against his back. "Thank you."

"You're welcome," he says, pulling me around into a hug.

He holds me, and I feel like I'm melting in his arms, the warmth swallowing me up. I could get used to it.

Get used to having him around.

"How long are you here for?" I ask, dreading his possible answer that being here is temporary. He brought nothing with him—no clothes, not even his phone. For all I know, he's just passing through.

"I told you before I left," he says. "I'm here for as long as I'm wanted."

"That's not a real answer, Jonathan."

"Why isn't it?"

"Because I've wanted you since I was seventeen years old. Saying that is like promising forever. I need a *real* answer."

He's quiet for a moment, resting his head on top of mine before he asks, "What's wrong with forever?"

"Nothing," I say, "as long as you mean it."

"Would you believe me if I promised it?"

"Yes," I whisper. "That's why I need you not to."

He sighs, loosening his hold a bit to look at me. His eyes scan my face as a slight smile touches his lips. "I might've destroyed my career today."

I blink at him. "What?"

"It's a long story," he says, "but I just can't keep doing it."

"But that's your dream."

"Dreams change," he says. "The way I was living... I was miserable. I want my life back, and I'm *taking* it back, because I've wasted too much time. I'll never give up on acting. It's who I am. But it's not *all* I am. I'm a father, and I want to be the man you thought I'd be. I'd be so much happier doing community theater, if it came to that, as long as I got to come home to you, than I ever was being *Johnny Cunning* without you. So if you want forever, goddamn it, I'll be there."

My heart, it hammers hard in my chest, viciously battering my ribcage. I want to say so much, but I don't even know where to start. Guilt. Fear. Excitement. A whole swarm of butterflies flutter in my stomach. "Forever."

He nods, whispering, "I promise."

"*Ta-da!*" Maddie's excited yell shatters the moment as she runs into the room, dressed in her Breezeo costume. We've been home ten minutes and she's already abandoned the snowflake getup. "Look, Daddy! We're the same!"

Jonathan laughs. "We are."

"Come on," she says, grabbing his hand and tugging on it, yanking him away from me. "We can play, 'cuz you're home now!"

Jonathan shoots me a conflicted look.

"Go on." I wave him away. "Go have your fun without me."

He manages to sneak a quick kiss before Maddie drags him to her bedroom. They play for hours, stopping only to grab sandwiches for dinner.

Darkness has fallen by the time Jonathan resurfaces, cornering me in the kitchen. He wraps his arms around me from behind and kisses my neck. I hum as tingles flow down my spine. "You done playing Breezeo now?"

"I'm just getting started," he says, turning me around so I'm facing him. "Maddie's asleep, so I think it's *your* turn to have a little fun. I remember promising once that I'd do whatever I could for you to someday see me in this costume."

My face grows warm. "You remember that?"

"Of course," he says. "It's the whole reason I auditioned."

"You told me your manager talked you out of that."

"He did, but I said fuck it. He told me I had no shot in hell, but you believed in me, so I went for it, and look at me now."

I can hardly bring myself to look at him. It's impossible to wrap my mind around. It's like my wildest fantasy is converging with reality and my brain can't handle it. *How is this real?* I run my hands along his broad chest, feeling the slick material. "Do you get to keep this?"

"Not supposed to," he says. "They might even call the police because I took it."

"Hmm, then we probably ought to make good use of it while we can, huh?"

"Probably ought to," he agrees.

I squeal when he grabs ahold of me, lifting me up. Wrapping my legs around his waist, I cling to him as he staggers to the bedroom. He almost drops me twice, the material so slick I nearly lose my hold, and I laugh when we fall onto the bed, him landing right on top of me.

He kisses me, mouth eagerly exploring as he strips me out of my clothes, hands touching and caressing every inch of my body. His fingers, they explore, making me a writhing mess with just a few strokes.

"You're going to have to unzip the suit," he says. "I can't do it myself."

"Hmm, so what you're saying is if I refuse, you'll have no choice but to keep it on?"

"That's exactly what I'm saying."

"So why would I help you?"

"Because I can't fuck you with the suit on," he says, "and I've got a funny feeling you *really* want to be fucked right now."

Those words set my body on fire, tingles engulfing every inch of my skin. I reach behind him, tugging on the zipper, pulling it down as far as I can get it.

He strips out of it, and I watch him, trying not to laugh. It takes him damn near ten minutes of struggling before he climbs back into bed.

"Kind of killed the mood, huh?" he asks with a laugh. "Destroyed over a decade's worth of fantasies in just a few minutes."

"That takes some skill," I say. "But maybe, if you're good to me, I'll forgive you."

"I can do that," he murmurs against my lips, on top of me, *inside* of me, ever so slowly pushing in. He makes love to me, giving me all of him, in no rush for it to be over.

All night long, again and again, he brings me to the edge,

leaving me a sticky, trembling mess. Daylight is already trying to peak through, the sky outside starting to lighten. I lay here, staring at the ceiling. My muscles no longer care to work.

Jonathan's still at it, going strong, his lips trailing along my stomach, going lower and lower and lower, as he strokes my inner thigh, the light touch making parts of me tingle. I don't know how he does it. Just when I think I'm done, when I think I can't take anymore. "*Oh god.*"

His mouth is on me, his face buried between my thighs. I grasp his hair, shifting my hips, unable to stay still. A minute, maybe two, before he's got me seeing stars. I squeeze my eyes shut, crying out as pleasure flows through me in waves.

Once I relax again, breathing heavily, he kisses along my inner thigh before biting down gently. Laughing, I swat him away as I clamp my thighs closed. I don't even have the energy to put up a real fight.

"You're definitely forgiven," I whisper. "That was… *wow.*"

Laughing, he collapses onto the bed. "Thank god, because I'm exhausted."

"So am I," I say. "I don't even think I can make it to the shower."

"Me, either. Hell, I don't even have any clothes I can put on. Can't call Jack to make him get my stuff since I don't have my phone."

"Hmm, well, I know one way you might get ahold of him," I say, grabbing my phone from the bedside stand. "I'll call your sister."

Before I can even try to make the call, Jonathan snatches the phone from my hand and tosses it behind him, throwing it right on the floor. "I don't even want to *think* about him being somewhere with my sister at this hour. I'd rather stay naked."

I laugh, snuggling against him, pressing a light kiss to his chest. "I love you, Jonathan."

"I love you, too." He wraps his arms around me before whispering, "You're the queen, baby."

EPILOGUE

ONE YEAR LATER

Click. Click. Click.

The incessant flash of bulbs was bright and blinding as camera shudders went off in rapid succession, taking dozens of photographs every few seconds, immortalizing the moment. Hundreds—maybe thousands—of fans lined the metal barricades along the street in front of the famed Hollywood theater. People camped out for days, desperate to be a part of it, desperate to be there for the Breezeo red carpet.

Thump. Thump. Thump.

Jonathan's erratic heartbeat thumped and echoed in his ears. He had done enough events over the years that this should've been a breeze, but he found himself nervous. Not for himself, no... for *her.* The little girl who clung tightly to his hand, wearing a pretty pink dress her mother had picked out. It was her first time in Hollywood, first time being involved in that part of his life.

He didn't want her to be overwhelmed.

"Johnny! Johnny! Over here!" People shouted from all around them, trying to get his attention. "This way! Turn to the left! On your right! Johnny, wait! Stop right there! Look up!"

They stopped to pose for more pictures after walking a few feet, and Jonathan bent down to her level, giving her a smile as the cameras continued to flash.

"Are you okay?" he whispered.

She nodded, grinning, her blue eyes twinkling under the lights. "I'm being a snowflake again, so I can't hear nobody."

"Good girl," he said. "Just keep smiling."

Jonathan leaned over, kissing her cheek, as a chorus of *oohs* and *ahhs* surrounded them. She'd stolen the spotlight the moment they exited the limo, capturing everybody's attention, this beautiful little girl with stars in her eyes.

Click. Click. Click.

They continued to walk along the carpet, posing, before the handlers steered them toward the media outlets. Interviews. This was the part of it that he hated most—being forced to answer questions, some of them uncomfortable.

"Ladies and Gentlemen, the man you've been waiting for, the star of the night—Johnny Cunning!" The petite blonde reporter smiled dazzlingly as he stepped up on the circular platform to join her for a live stream. "How are you doing tonight, Johnny?"

"Wonderful," he said. "Happy to be here."

"Well, I must say—you look truly amazing," the reporter declared. "You have a glow about you, and, my word, might it have something to do with this precious little girl with you?"

"Without a doubt," he said. "I'm the luckiest man in the world tonight."

Questions. So many questions.

He answered everything he could.

"Now before you go, you know we have to ask," the reporter says. "It was announced this morning that the Breezeo comics were being re-launched. Any chance we'll see you slip back into the suit for another movie?"

He smiled. "Right now, I'm just trying to enjoy my family, but I'm certainly not going to rule anything out."

Over and over, the questions flowed—some personal, but most not. He moved from reporter to reporter, a dozen of them total.

Tap. Tap. Tap.

Jonathan looked down as Madison tapped his leg to get his attention after they'd cleared the media section. Next, he would sign autographs for the fans, and then they'd head inside the theater to watch *Ghosted*. "Daddy, look, it's Maryanne."

He turned, looking the direction his daughter was facing, seeing Serena Markson posing with her date—Hollywood's new 'it' guy, Gerard Jackson. Clifford Caldwell lurked near them, watching. Jonathan had officially severed ties with the man a few weeks earlier, the moment his contract gave him an opening, and he'd signed with someone else—someone who understood that his family took priority.

Jonathan turned away, signing those autographs, chatting and letting them snap a few quick photos, before leading Madison along the carpet to the theater entrance.

Clack. Clack. Clack.

Madison's dress shoes clattered along the marble floor as they approached a group gathered in the lobby, the sound announcing their arrival. His team of people, all of them new—new management, new PR, even a new lawyer. He kept his agent, and he still had Jack, but everything else required a clean slate. Too much had been tainted by Clifford Caldwell.

The man had once tried to taint the woman he loved, too. Jonathan learned that while reading a long-ago story scribbled in an old spiral notebook. He read every word, no matter how painful. Everything he hadn't known... he knew it all now.

Kennedy stood amongst the group, wearing a simple black dress. The diamond on her left ring finger shimmered under the theater lights as she absently tinkered with it.

She was nervous... too nervous to walk the red carpet.

It made her sick to the stomach when she thought about it.

Jonathan had sold his mansion in LA and built a house in Bennett Landing, down the road from the Landing Inn, making them McKleski's neighbors. He'd proposed on a whim, although he'd had the ring for a while, and to his surprise, she'd said yes without even needing to think about it. He worried for a moment that they might be moving too fast, but he realized it didn't matter.

He'd lost too much time as it was.

He wasn't going to waste another second.

Tick. Tick. Tick.

"Can we talk for a minute?" Kennedy asked when he slid into the crowd beside her. People steadily streamed into the theater. They needed to find their seats soon.

"Of course," he said, wrapping his arm around her waist to pull her to him, holding up his free hand to tell his new manager to wait when the man nearly interrupted them. "What's wrong?"

"Nothing's wrong," she said, smiling, a glow on her flushed cheeks. And before she could even open her mouth again, before she could say the words, he already knew, but it still didn't fail to shock him to the core when she whispered, *"I'm pregnant."*

ACKNOWLEDGMENTS

Twenty years ago, I posted my very first fan-fiction online—an *NSYNC & *Tales From the Crypt* crossover horror story. I was fourteen at the time. Two years before that, I wrote a Greek mythology play based on the East Coast/West Coast rap feud between Biggie and Tupac. Since then, I've written countless stories spanning many fandoms, some of which nobody will ever read, but I wrote them because I wanted to, because something had inspired me. So first and foremost, I need to acknowledge the fandoms, the source material, and my fellow fangirls/fanboys. Without these communities, without these people and these characters and these books and bands and movies and shows, I don't know who I'd be today. I'd certainly not be a writer if it weren't for them (notably *Twilight*, for making me believe in myself enough to make the leap into original fiction). To my fellow con-goers, those who have slept on sidewalks to get into panels and who have camped out for days to see red carpets. I'll never forget the nights spent online analyzing grainy photos covered in red circles like we're private investigators.

To my friends, and family, and to everyone who helped me along the way with his book—you know who you are. I love you and owe you so much for your help and your support. To the readers and bloggers and book lovers—so much gratitude. Thank you for taking a chance on my words. To Kimberly Brower and her team—thank you for believing in me!

Esther Cristofori, also known as "wickedalbion", drew the *Breezeo* art for this book. She's extremely talented, and her fan art stole my heart the moment I saw it. I'm extremely honored she was willing to bring my *Breezeo* to life. Give her a look!

http://wickedalbion.tumblr.com
https://www.instagram.com/wickedalbion/
https://twitter.com/wickedalbion